S0-DZB-667

Cassie's Fortune

LINDA SHERTZER

JOVE BOOKS, NEW YORK

If you purchased this book without a cover, you should be aware that this book is stolen property. It was reported as "unsold and destroyed" to the publisher and neither the author nor the publisher has received any payment for this "stripped book."

This is a work of fiction. Names, characters, places, and incidents are either the product of the author's imagination or are used fictitiously, and any resemblance to actual persons, living or dead, business establishments, events, or locales is entirely coincidental.

MAGICAL LOVE is a trademark of Penguin Putnam Inc.

CASSIE'S FORTUNE

A Jove Book / published by arrangement with
the author

PRINTING HISTORY
Jove edition / June 2000

All rights reserved.
Copyright © 2000 by Linda Shertzer.
This book may not be reproduced in whole or in part,
by mimeograph or any other means, without permission.
For information address: The Berkley Publishing Group,
a division of Penguin Putnam Inc.,
375 Hudson Street, New York, New York 10014.

The Penguin Putnam Inc. World Wide Web site address is
http://www.penguinputnam.com

ISBN: 0-515-12837-6

A JOVE BOOK®
Jove Books are published by The Berkley Publishing Group,
a division of Penguin Putnam Inc.,
375 Hudson Street, New York, New York 10014.
JOVE and the "J" design
are trademarks belonging to Penguin Putnam Inc.

PRINTED IN THE UNITED STATES OF AMERICA

10 9 8 7 6 5 4 3 2 1

To the Members of the Band,
Donna, Kevin, Trish, Lynda, & Alicia,
for restoring my faith

One

LYMAN'S GAP, PENNSYLVANIA—1859

"You must lose something you can't afford to lose, trust someone you have no reason to trust, and love someone with no hope of him ever loving you in return," the frail old woman intoned.

Cassie Bowen stopped in the doorway between the foyer and the parlor of her aunt's home. She hadn't seen Aunt Flora in three years. What sort of greeting was that? It sounded more like a prediction. Or a curse! She gave her aunt a strained smile, and tried not to let her bewilderment show.

"It's good to see you again, too, Aunt Flora," she replied.

"I warned you she was a little touched in the head," the man behind Cassie whispered. She shivered as his breath warmed the back of her neck. Something about Brent Conway had been making her tingle ever since he'd met her at the train station.

She had to admit that he had warned her, during the bumpy wagon ride over the fifteen miles of rough mountain road from Pittsburgh to Lyman's Gap, that the townspeople considered her aunt slightly crazy. That was nothing new. Family talk said Aunt Flora had acted fairly normally until Great-Aunt Charlotte died. After that she had turned downright eccentric.

Cassie had no doubt Mr. Conway had tried to be tactful, but the message was the same nonetheless, and it had disturbed her. What family thought was one thing. What strangers gossiped about was an entirely different matter.

Her sense of family pride was strong, but her common sense was stronger. The duration of the trip had not been the occasion to defend her aunt.

Now she was safely delivered to her destination. She didn't have to worry about offending Mr. Conway and being deposited, with all her bags, alone by the side of the road in the wilderness, and ending up as dinner for a passing bear.

She tried to sound as haughty as possible as she murmured through tightened lips, "I'll thank you not to talk about my aunt that way."

Mr. Conway chuckled. "I'll bring in the rest of your bags."

"Speak up, Cassie, dear." Aunt Flora blinked her rheumy blue eyes. "I fear I'm going a bit deaf."

"I was . . . thanking Mr. Conway for . . . bringing in my things."

"Mr. Conway is such a help to me."

Cassie wondered if her aunt knew what Mr. Conway and the rest of her neighbors really thought of her. Well, *she* certainly wasn't about to hurt her aunt's feelings by telling her.

"He's always doing considerate things for me, such as picking you up at the train station," Aunt Flora continued. A wan smile creased her wrinkled face, and her thin eyebrows turned down in pathetic resignation. "I'm afraid I'm just not strong enough for that grueling journey."

Then she turned a coy smile to Mr. Conway.

"How will I ever be able to repay your many kindnesses to me?"

"Oh, I'm sure I'll think of something, Miss Flora."

He was standing directly behind Cassie, her heavy trunk hoisted onto his broad shoulders. She hadn't heard him come in again.

"Oh, I know what you want, you young rascal. Well, if you

want me to be even more beholden to you, you'll carry my niece's baggage up to her room."

"Which room would that be?"

"Up the stairs to the front right." Aunt Flora raised her thin arm and fluttered her hand in that direction. "Naughty boy. You know very well mine is up the stairs to the front left."

Aunt Flora had seemed such a fragile violet, but when she spoke with Mr. Conway, she fairly bloomed like a fresh rose.

A thought struck Cassie, and not a pleasant one. Why should Mr. Conway know where her aunt's bedroom was? That was the reason, she told herself, for her sudden embarrassment. Or could it actually be the thought that Mr. Conway now knew where *her* bedroom was, too? Preposterous!

As if sensing her niece's consternation, Aunt Flora turned to Cassie and explained, "Mr. Conway and I have an arrangement. He watches my bedroom window to make sure the lamp goes on and off every night, just to make sure I'm still alive."

"How considerate of him," Cassie agreed through a forced smile. "But, Aunt Flora, isn't there someone *else* who could do that instead?"

"No, no. Well, there is Minnie Parker, a nice widowed lady who does the weekly shopping for me and comes in twice a week with her daughter to clean. There's Jerusha Jackson, a fine woman of color who does my laundry, and her husband, Olivier, who takes care of my horses and does other odd jobs around here. But, no. Mr. Conway lives right next door, so I rely on him quite a bit. He never seems to mind."

Cassie could have sworn her aunt actually fluttered her lashes at the man. She never would have imagined her elderly maiden aunt could be such a flirt.

"But come, Cassie, dear. It's been so long since we last saw each other. While Mr. Conway takes care of all that manly business, come sit beside me. You can tell me how you've been, and we'll catch up on all the family gossip."

Aunt Flora reached out both arms to draw Cassie in. In the dimly lit room, the delicate lace at her sleeves and the lace lappets dangling from either side of her cap drifted about her face like an ethereal mist.

The yellow light of the setting sun and the soft glow of the candles gave the polished oak furniture and the brown and ivory damask upholstery a golden cast. Aunt Flora's translucent skin transformed to a waxen pallor. The pearl bracelets at her wrists rattled softly together, like grating bones. It was almost as if she were a corpse or a ghost already.

Cassie hesitated.

"Go on in. She won't bite," Mr. Conway urged. "Not you, anyway, seeing as you're kin."

As he moved toward the stairs, he nudged her in the rear with her own suitcase. Cassie jumped.

"Pardon. Sorry." The words were an apology, but behind her back she heard him chuckle. That was no accident!

How dare he touch her like that! she thought with indignation. How dare he insinuate her dear aunt might do anything to harm her. Boldly she rushed toward her aunt.

The old woman patted the seat beside her. Her thin fingers, poking through her fingerless gloves, scratched against the fabric like the pale claws of a little bird. Cassie bent forward and placed a kiss on her aunt's wrinkled cheek.

The sweet fragrance of beeswax mingled with the scent of lavender. Her aunt was soft and warm and very comforting, just as Cassie had remembered her all these years. How foolish she'd been to be afraid. She sat down close beside her.

Aunt Flora leaned toward her and gave a little giggle. "I can't help baiting him," she whispered behind her hand. "He's such a wicked scoundrel!"

"Mr. Conway? He was pleasant to me on the drive here."

"And well he needs to be. So few people in town like him."

Cassie was surprised. "Why not?"

"Oh, some of the less discerning ladies think he's awfully handsome."

Cassie felt a twinge of guilt for falling into the category of a less discerning lady. She'd noticed how his pale blue eyes twinkled with obvious affection when he'd told her about the folks in Lyman's Gap. He must be strong, too. He didn't seem to have any difficulty lifting her heavy trunk or carrying it up the stairs.

On the other hand, if he was as frank and forthright about everything else as he'd been in expressing his opinion of her aunt, many people just might regard him as rude and abrasive.

"But he's not like his father, nothing like his father at all," Aunt Flora lamented. "People in town respected that man—educated, well read, knew his politics. He worked hard to establish the *Argus*, our town's small but reputable newspaper."

"Like the fellow in Greek mythology with one hundred eyes watching out for everything. How apt."

"When that rascal Brent inherited it, he took all those eyes and turned them toward every bit of dirt and gossip in the town, the state, the whole nation. Why, even toward doings in territories that aren't part of this country yet. He turned his father's fine newspaper into a sordid, sensationalist rag. Edgar Conway would turn in his grave if he knew. Of course, Brent's also making a lot more money than his father ever dreamed of, but, well, some folks set store by integrity."

Cassie glanced nervously toward the doorway. What if Mr. Conway overheard the unflattering things Aunt Flora was saying about him? Considering what he'd said about her, it would serve him right, she decided.

She had no trouble summoning Mr. Conway's image clearly to her recollection. There hadn't been anything in particular about his buggy or his bay horse to indicate a man of wealth. There hadn't been anything about his brown corduroy jacket or his brown-and-red plaid woolen trousers to indicate a gentleman of fashion, with his finger on the pulse of the nation. Obviously there was more to the man than met the eye.

Cassie wouldn't want anyone to think she was interested in him or anything he did, but perhaps there wouldn't be any harm in asking her aunt a little more about him—especially since they were going to be neighbors.

"You say Mr. Conway has no integrity?"

"Most folks around here would describe him as ruthless."

"Fetching me from the train station and single-handedly hauling my baggage upstairs aren't exactly the acts of a ruthless man," Cassie noted. "Making sure you're still alive each evening isn't, either."

Aunt Flora gave her a knowing wink. "Oh, he's a likable schemer. He'd do anything to make sure I stay alive long enough—anything to flatter and cajole me into selling him that piece of land a couple of miles outside of town. The young charlatan tells me it's worthless, but I know he thinks the railroad is going to build a line into Lyman's Gap and come through there."

She gave an indelicate snort of disdain.

"He thinks I won't sell because I know about the railroad, too, and I'm holding out for more money. But the railroad won't be coming through there, and I have other plans for that land." She pointed a gnarled finger at Cassie. "You will, too."

"Plans?" Cassie repeated, but her question went unanswered.

"I'll be looking out for you tonight, Miss Flora," Mr. Conway called from the doorway.

"Thank you, dear boy," Aunt Flora replied sweetly.

"Shall I keep an eye out for you, too, Miss Cassie?" He cast her a devilish grin.

Cassie certainly didn't want to consent to his offer, especially if he was as unscrupulous as her aunt implied. On the other hand, she certainly didn't want to alienate him on the remote chance that she *might* need him.

"Thank you, but I don't think that will be necessary, Mr. Conway," she replied politely.

He touched his fingertips to his temple. "Then I'll bid you lovely ladies each a very good evening and pleasant dreams."

Cassie heard the glass panels rattle in the polished wood as the front door closed.

"Don't hesitate to get him to help you if you need anything."

Cassie looked at her aunt with surprise. "I thought you said he didn't have an ounce of integrity."

"Other folks say that. He'll help you if he thinks he'll derive some benefit from it. You don't have to avoid him if you can get something you need from him, either."

Aunt Flora was certainly pragmatic, Cassie decided. She wondered if people in town would describe her aunt as ruthless, too.

"I doubt I'll be needing Mr. Conway."

"You never know. Especially once . . . once you own that land. Just remember the black ooze and don't let it go!"

"What on earth are you talking about?"

In the past three years, had her eccentric aunt truly gone completely crazy? How would she care for her properly? How could she keep the neighbors from finding out?

Aunt Flora took Cassie's hand and rested her thin, palsied hand on top of it. "I'm so delighted you've come to spend this remaining time with me. I always did like you better than Robert. It's a shame, too, because you really deserve better than this."

"I don't mind living here with you, Aunt Flora."

"I guess you would think it is good living here. That house in Philadelphia isn't big enough to hold Letitia and *anybody else* peacefully."

"It wasn't *that* horrible, and Ralphie and little Marguerite are adorable," Cassie offered in defense of her niece and nephew.

"They're spoiled brats," Aunt Flora stated with a sour twist of her lips. "If they're representatives of it, I truly fear for the coming generation." She shook her head. "I tried to warn your brother not to marry that carping, pretentious, ambitious . . . Ah, but that's the whole trouble. No one ever believes a word I say."

"Oh, but *I* believe you, Aunt Flora."

"No, you don't. Nobody does. The rest of you didn't expect your father to be killed suddenly five years ago, either. You'd think they'd all have learned by now, but no." Aunt Flora's voice cracked, more with sorrow and regret than from old age. "Even my own brother wouldn't listen to me when I told him not to travel on that ship."

Cassie closed her eyes with remembered pain. To her dying day she would recall her father's name listed among the 150 casualties of that nautical disaster. What was it that "the rest of them" didn't know about it that Aunt Flora claimed she did?

"I don't think anyone expected the steamship *Arctic* would be hit by that French vessel off the coast of Newfoundland."

"*I* did!" Aunt Flora clutched at the cushion in a gesture that spoke utter frustration and impotence. "But nobody ever listens to me." Her voice dropped to a whisper but lost none of its intensity or pain. *"Nobody!"*

She sat very still for a few moments, making an obvious effort to compose herself. She dabbed at her eyes with her lace handkerchief.

Then more calmly, she continued. "Poor Cassie. You thought you were coming here to take care of me in my dotage, and to escape Letitia in the bargain. Now you must know the *real* reason you're here. I fear, once you hear the whole story, you won't regard it as a much better fate."

Cassie waited. She had to admit Aunt Flora did possess a talent for dramatic pauses.

"I've been frugal with what I inherited, Cassie. I've also made some profitable investments over the years. I'm sure the family has made some comments about them."

Cassie recalled family stories of how everyone thought Aunt Flora was foolish for pulling all her investments out of the cotton market—until prices plummeted in the '30s. Everyone laughed at her in '47 when she bought all that land upstream from Mr. Sutter's mill—until they'd found gold in the river, and Aunt Flora grew wealthier still. They'd laughed their hardest ten years ago when she'd uprooted from Philadelphia for this small, remote town.

"Oh, I know they do," Aunt Flora stated. "I know a lot more than they'd ever give me credit for. You don't have to maintain a discreet silence around me."

Cassie squirmed in her seat.

"I own this house and everything in it." Aunt Flora glanced

around the ornately cluttered room. "There are the outbuildings, a little over two acres of grounds, and two horses and the buggy, too. I own a couple of hundred acres outside of town, some stocks and bonds in some pretty reputable companies, and lots of very pretty jewelry. There's a tidy sum tucked away in the local bank, not to mention the money under the mattress in my bedroom and some in a little leather bag at the bottom of the flour bin in the pantry," Aunt Flora enumerated. "You can't always trust banks, you know."

Aunt Flora took a deep breath and announced, "I'm bequeathing my entire fortune to you."

"To me?" Cassie's hand flew to her heart beating wildly with astonishment. "My gracious! Thank you. I . . . I'd expected a token—perhaps a piece of jewelry or two. But—"

"You thought Robert would inherit it all, and that Letitia would commandeer all the really valuable jewelry."

"Well, yes."

"Well, no. I inherited from my aunt, and she from her aunt, and she from hers."

"Sort of like an old family custom?" Cassie offered.

"Custom. Curse. Something like that."

Aunt Flora shrugged, as if the whole matter were unimportant. Then she fixed Cassie with a penetrating gaze. Cassie watched with growing worry the unfathomable depths of sadness so evident in her aunt's eyes.

"Have you ever noticed how, in each generation of us Bowens, there is a son and a daughter—no more and certainly no less?"

"I had sort of remarked on that once while looking through the family Bible," Cassie admitted reluctantly. "There was Father and you."

"And I never married."

"There was Grandpa Bowen and Great-Aunt Charlotte."

"Who never married."

"There are Robert and myself."

"You're not married."

"Not yet," Cassie hurried to add, even though she had no

immediate prospects. She wasn't exactly sure in which direction her aunt was taking this conversation, but she had a nasty suspicion she wasn't going to like how it eventually came to pertain to her.

"I had a Grandpa Bowen, too, and a Great-Aunt Hester, who never married. Great-grandpa Bowen had a sister, Great-Great-Aunt Prudence, who never married."

"What a strange coincidence." She had to say that, rather than acknowledge what she suspected.

"Coincidence, my eye! Don't you see a pattern developing here, Cassie?"

"I think so."

"Good. I need to show you what else—probably the most important thing—you'll be inheriting."

Aunt Flora rose unsteadily and slowly made her way to an ornate japanned cabinet in the far corner of the room. The cabinet door creaked as she opened it. She reached inside and pulled out a large bag made of red Moroccan leather.

"What is it?"

Aunt Flora set the bag on the table. Slowly, almost reverently, she unfastened the brass clasp and opened the bag.

Cassie breathed a sigh of relief when the odor of rotting flesh didn't spew forth. In fact, she decided after she'd cautiously drawn a tentative breath, the interior of the bag smelled like roses.

"Sebastian likes roses," Aunt Flora explained.

"Sebastian? Who—?"

"Cassie, I'd like to introduce you to Sebastian." With a regal flourish of swinging pearls and fluttering lace, Aunt Flora drew a large crystal ball from the bag and set it on the table directly in front of Cassie.

Cassie stared at a perfectly clear, perfectly round crystal ball about the same size as a human head. It was nestled in a dark, ancient, wooden ring about four inches high, slightly wider at the bottom, and inlaid with gold, turquoise, carnelians, and lapis lazuli, to form designs that looked like Egyptian hieroglyphs.

Fascinated, she peered into the depths of the sphere. A tiny flaw appeared. It grew wider, then broader and deeper. It became a small sphere, about the size of a human eye. It opened. Cassie could have sworn it winked! She pulled back abruptly, cowering against the cushions of the sofa.

"Oh, don't be afraid of him, dear. He won't hurt you."

"He . . . it . . . won't hurt . . . winked!" Cassie could barely think, much less speak coherently. She stared at it, and the ball turned perfectly clear once again.

Aunt Flora laughed. "Sebastian is the other part of the Bowen family curse."

"Is that what you call that thing?" Cassie demanded, nodding toward it.

"It's not a thing, dear. It's Sebastian. I call him that because that's what his name is."

"He told you that?"

"Well, in a manner of speaking, yes."

Cassie was still having trouble merely breathing and focusing. She was going to have an even more difficult time reasoning out what her eccentric aunt was telling her.

"The time has come for me to explain it all, Cassie. I'm genuinely fond of you, so it's difficult for me to have to pass the responsibility of this curse on to you."

"Curse?"

Aunt Flora was silent for a moment. Cassie could only stare at the crystal ball.

"Sebastian is a crystal ball," Aunt Flora explained.

"I . . . I see that."

"Ah, good. I'm glad you're coming around. I was so afraid I'd have to climb all the way upstairs to get my vinaigrette to snap you out of it."

"I . . . I'm fine. I'll be . . . fine."

"Of course you will. I managed. All of us Bowen women, in spite of everything, have always managed." Aunt Flora smiled with compassion. "The family legend has it that many centuries ago, far away in England, a feeble old gypsy woman came to the Bowens's vast estates. After she told their fortunes they refused to pay her; drove her from their castle barefoot, into a raging snowstorm without her crystal ball; and threatened to have her tortured and burnt alive as a witch if she ever dared darken their doorway again."

Cassie wondered if this was the original family legend the way it had been passed down to Aunt Flora, or if her aunt was adding her own inimitable flair for the melodramatic to the tale.

"Before she left, the gypsy cursed them all. Since they had kept Sebastian, she cursed them with his presence forever—and more."

"I'd say Sebastian himself was quite enough."

"In each generation, a brother and sister are born. The man who bears the name marries and has a son so that the family will never die out and thus perpetuate the curse, and a daughter on whom the curse will eventually fall. This luckless girl, instead of the joys of a home and family of her own, has Sebastian. No one—*no one*" Aunt Flora repeated solemnly as she pointed a bony finger under Cassie's nose—"but a female of the direct line can *ever* know of Sebastian's existence. In times of trouble or uncertainty, gaze into his depths, and he will show you the future. Believe him. Do as he shows you because he will *always* show you the truth."

"But—"

"No matter how unpalatable that truth may be, Sebastian will *always* show you the truth."

"But—"

"How do you think I made all my money?" Aunt Flora demanded, hands on hips, as if that argument alone would be enough to convince Cassie. "But—and this is the *real* curse—*no one*, not *one living soul*, will ever believe a word of your predictions."

"But—"

"You see, the curse has not yet passed from me to you, because even you don't believe a word I say about this."

"How can I? Anyone in her right mind would think this was completely preposterous."

"But you will believe me, Cassie. You will—and soon."

"So, I'm doomed to this life?"

"As were we all—Aunt Charlotte and Aunt Hester, Aunt Prudence and Aunt Elizabeth, Aunt Matilda and Aunt Rosamunde. Just as I am doomed to spend what's left of my life as a lonely old maid, and doomed to pass the curse along to you, my hapless niece."

At the ripe old age of five-and-twenty, Cassie had somewhat resigned herself to remaining unwed. Yet, deep inside, she kept alive the hope that someday, a man would love her. But now?

"Is there nothing . . . ?"

Aunt Flora's ashen face seemed to grow even paler.

"There is a chance to break the curse—a chance that in four hundred years has never once come to pass."

"What is it?" Cassie demanded eagerly. Perhaps the others had failed. But she was a sensible woman, well-read, educated in the best private school her father could afford. She was modern and scientific, not steeped in unreasonable fears and quaint superstitions, like people in the past. Surely she, of them all, ought to stand the best chance of breaking this curse.

"Someone must actually believe you."

"It's that simple?"

"It's never that simple. The very nature of the curse assures that no one will ever believe your predictions."

"But surely—"

"And—"

"I should have known there was more," Cassie mumbled in resignation.

"That's the part another person must fulfill. For *your* part, you must lose something you can't afford to lose, trust someone you have no reason to trust, and love someone with no hope of him ever loving you in return."

"This sounds familiar, Aunt Flora."

"I'm glad that—even if you don't believe me—you at least remember what I've told you. You'll be glad you remembered it later." Aunt Flora held out the crystal ball, balancing on its ancient stand. "Now, I want you to take Sebastian."

"What? No! Not now. I . . . he . . . it still belongs to you." She tried to shove it away, back into the bag where it belonged.

"Well, yes, for a little while longer. But I think you two need to get better acquainted."

Aunt Flora pushed Sebastian back into Cassie's hands so that she had to take him or drop him on the floor. However preposterous she thought her aunt's tale, Sebastian and his stand were obviously extremely old and no doubt extremely valuable. She could hardly let him drop and shatter because of her squeamishness.

"Take Sebastian up to your room, set him on your night table, and get to know each other."

Cassie still held the ball out at arm's length. "Can't I at least put him back in his case?"

"Don't be silly. How else will you get to really know him if you can't see him?"

Cassie's arms grew weary holding the weight of the crystal ball out in front of her. On the other hand, she certainly didn't feel comfortable cradling the darned thing to her bosom like a long-lost child. It was part of a curse on her and her entire family for generations. She thought she'd seen the blasted thing wink. She didn't want to get to know this . . . this Sebastian thing. She didn't want to be in the same room, much less be alone with it.

Cassie started awake. The room was dark and silent. What had awakened her? Could it be she was so overwrought from her journey? Perhaps she had eaten too much of the rich food she wasn't used to at dinner. Maybe it was the bed. She simply wasn't accustomed to sleeping in one this large.

Maybe the noises were to blame. She strained to hear what had awakened her. The sounds in this small country town were very different from those in a bustling city like Philadelphia. She was used to pigeons cooing and vendors hawking their wares and wagons rumbling over cobblestones; not *whoo*ing owls and *moo*ing cows and *chirp*ing crickets. She heard the little clock on the mantel chime three.

A shaft of moonlight shone through the window onto Sebastian. No, it was just a crystal ball, an inanimate object, she told herself. It had no right to a name.

Even if it did have a bizarre name and an even more bizarre story attached to it, the clear crystal was incredibly fascinating, she had to admit.

Suddenly Sebastian captured the moon's glow and encapsulated it into fragments of a picture.

Preposterous! Even as she stared at Sebastian, transfixed in the darkness, Cassie couldn't believe she saw a picture forming inside. It wasn't like a painting on the outside, or even the inside, of the glass. It didn't have the translucent quality of an ambrotype, photographed on glass. Little figures formed and moved *inside* the solid ball.

Even more incredibly, one of the images was herself. Her long, loose hair flowed down her back, over her shoulders, and across her breasts. Goodness gracious! She was naked—and she was not alone!

A naked man held her in his strong arms. She ran her fingers with wild abandon through his tousled, dark brown hair. Her fingertips traced the corded muscles across his shoulders and down the valley of his back. Her palm passed over a small, flat mole on his left hip. She pressed her hands against his smooth buttocks, pulling him to her until she could feel his manhood arching insistently against her stomach.

No man had ever cupped her breasts in his strong, calloused hands, or pressed kisses with his burning lips against her fevered skin. She couldn't even call to mind any man of her acquaintance that she would *want* to have hold her in such a way.

The two figures circled within the crystal ball in a rapturous dance. She saw her own back, and his hands urgently caressing the swell of her hips. The man lifted his head from where he had nestled his kisses at the base of her throat. At last she could see his face.

She and Brent Conway were crushed together in that passionate, naked embrace!

She recalled her aunt's words with a sobering jolt. Sebastian would *always* show her the truth.

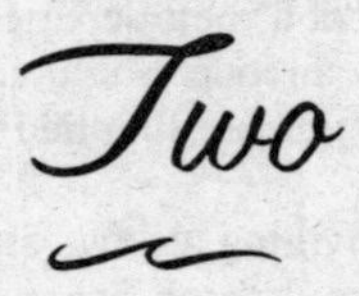

Ever after, Cassie would remember that night and time—three o'clock, the dead of night, the very night Aunt Flora died. How uncanny, how fitting that Sebastian should have chosen that exact moment and that precise manner to show her that the family curse had indeed fallen upon her.

Still, she thought wryly, he could have gotten her attention with a much less sensational, scintillating vision. Why couldn't he have warned her about her aunt's death? Considering everything that had happened in the past three days, at least Sebastian could have shown her something that would have helped her to cope with this unpleasant experience and all these new, well-meaning people. But all Sebastian had shown her had been visions of Brent Conway—and certainly not in any manner that was the least bit helpful!

Night after night, Cassie had felt racked with guilt, lying in her bed in the moonlight, watching with prurient fascination as Sebastian played out each tantalizing scene between Brent and her—when she ought to have been praying or doing something else worthwhile.

Now Aunt Flora was truly gone, buried this morning in the small graveyard behind the church. Cassie sat in the middle of the sofa in the parlor in what was now her house. Her aunt's friends milled about, chatting amongst themselves and eating. From time to time small groups of her aunt's neighbors would introduce themselves and sit beside her. They offered her their deepest condolences, and then departed.

Cassie didn't know anyone. She'd never remember them all. Sebastian could have at least supplied her with some names to go with these faces.

"Have you had anything to eat yet, Miss Bowen?" Brent Conway's voice broke through her musing.

Brent she already knew—and, thanks to Sebastian, far too well! So well, in fact, that she couldn't refer to him as anything but "Brent," at least in her thoughts.

Taken unaware by his innocuous question, she had to think a moment before answering. "Yes. Yes, I have, thank you. Mrs. Parker brought me some of her chicken salad and a glass of lemonade."

"Did you *eat* it?"

"Of course I did." Was the curse taking effect so quickly? Did he already not believe a word she said?

He picked up the half-full plate on the low table in front of her. "Then I guess this must not be yours." Nevertheless, he offered it to her.

"Oh."

She grinned sheepishly, but still couldn't summon the courage to look him in the eye. She'd seen her pallid reflection in the mirror as she dressed to confront the trials of each morning, and as she undressed before she collapsed wearily into bed each night. In spite of her inordinate pallor from the shock and strain she'd been blushing profusely every time Brent came around. She could feel her face warming again even now. Darn Sebastian for showing her such unsettling things about this man. Darn this man for making her remember them so vividly! Darn her for wanting to remember them at all!

She took the plate Brent offered and tried to eat, but the food stuck in her dry throat. She reached for her glass of lemonade, but Brent already held it out for her. She took it eagerly.

"Thank you."

"I looked out for Miss Flora. I suppose I can help you from time to time, too," he told her with a broad grin.

"Yes, you've been extremely helpful to me."

"As much as you hate to admit it?"

"Of course not," Cassie protested. "I'm sincerely grateful for everything you've done for my aunt and me."

On the other hand, Aunt Flora had warned her Brent was a charlatan of the first degree, who would do anything to flatter and cajole her into selling the property. She hadn't believed Aunt Flora at the time, but the truth of her aunt's words stood before her offering lemonade and sympathy. Brent *was* a scoundrel who could easily transfer his flattering attentions from her aunt to her.

Even so, after all his help, she could hardly be rude. She would simply exercise a healthy caution around him.

"Please sit down, Mr. Conway." Cassie indicated the cushion beside her. She could only hope he wouldn't sit too close. What would she do if he actually touched her? Probably drop the plate of chicken salad upside down in her lap.

"Only if you continue eating."

She managed a glance up at him. He stood there, legs astride, his arms crossed over his chest.

Did he have to be so tall as he loomed over her? Did his white shirt collar have to contrast so well with his sun-browned neck and face? Did his black woolen coat—obviously cut much more fashionably out of a much better grade of material than his brown one—have to stretch quite so nicely over his broad shoulders? Did his black trousers have to stretch so enticingly over . . .

Goodness gracious, Cassie! she scolded herself and stabbed her fork at a piece of chicken. She dared not put it in her mouth, chew, and swallow until she was certain she could do it without choking.

In an effort to distract him, she asked, "Are you going to stand over me like a stern schoolmaster until I do?"

"If I have to. I'm a patient man."

Brent rocked back and forth on his heels. He'd waited for Aunt Flora to sell that property and now was prepared to work on her. He certainly was patient, she reasoned. Stubborn, too.

Why waste time trying to out-wait him? she figured. She ate the forkful. Then he sat down. Thank goodness he maintained an appropriate distance between them.

"I don't know what I would have done, who I could have turned to," Cassie told him. "I hadn't met the minister yet. I didn't know who in town would make the coffin."

"All the ladies came here as quickly as they could to help you. Reverend Markham came by, as soon as he heard, to offer his condolences. I just beat them all to it because I'm your nearest neighbor. Everyone in town liked your aunt very much."

"I thought you said everyone in town thought she was crazy?"

"That doesn't mean we all didn't love and respect her. She was kind. She wasn't stingy or selfish. Not quite three years ago, she lent Abel Warner money to start his store when the banks wouldn't. When that no-good sot that Becky Galloway called a husband up and left her and their five kids without a cent, Miss Flora lent her the money to establish herself as a seamstress so they wouldn't all starve."

"I didn't know that."

"Well, *she* never would have said a word about it."

No, she wouldn't, Cassie mused.

"When Jerusha and Olivier Jackson moved up here from New Orleans, she was the first one to hire them. After that, everybody else set aside their caution. Some of them even followed her example and hired Olivier to do odd jobs or Jerusha to do the laundry."

"Did you?"

Brent chuckled. "Does that sound like something I'd do?"

Silently and sadly, Cassie had to admit, according to what Aunt Flora had told her, it did not sound like something Brent would do. Not one bit.

"When Miss Flora was a little younger and able to get

around better, I understand she spent a lot of her time working on what she considered worthy causes—although if she'd lived to be a hundred, she'd never have been able to convince me women ought to vote."

His derisive chuckle turned into a small sound of resignation. Very slowly, and with what seemed to Cassie like genuine regret, he said, "She will be greatly missed."

From Brent's glowing account, Cassie saw there'd been a lot more to Aunt Flora than pearls, lace, and a cursed crystal ball. She was an example of wealth worthy of emulation.

Tears welled in Cassie's eyes—but she couldn't let Brent see her cry and find a point of weakness. He was ruthless. Aunt Flora had told her so.

She cleared her throat in an effort to chase her tears. "My goodness, Mr. Conway, maybe you should have delivered the eulogy this morning."

He shook his head and laughed heartily, but Cassie thought she detected the slightest tinge of bitterness.

"Not me. Reverend Markham was much more appropriate. If I were the spokesman, everybody would have figured your poor aunt was surely doomed to hell."

Considering Aunt Flora's account of what the townspeople generally thought of him, Brent was probably right. Amazed that he could joke about it, Cassie suppressed a grin.

More in keeping with the somber occasion, she replied softly, "I only wish I'd been able to spend more time with her. There's so much I never got to say, and so much she didn't get to tell me."

"I don't suppose she might have mentioned how she wanted her property distributed?"

That was probably the broadest hint Cassie had ever heard. She turned and stared at him with a mixture of indignation and disbelief.

"Well, at least you waited until my aunt was buried. For a patient man, you don't waste much time, do you, Mr. Conway?"

He grinned at her. His blue eyes were wide with what she

was sure was a carefully studied innocence. Innocence was the *last* characteristic she'd have attributed to this man.

"Sorry. I might be patient, but in the newspaper business, a man learns to come right to the point."

"Well, you certainly did that."

Cassie reluctantly returned his smile. She'd rather bite her own tongue than admit that the slightly crooked grin of this charming rascal was the least bit contagious.

"It's really no secret. Sooner or later everyone in town is going to know anyway. Aunt Flora left everything to me."

Brent's eyebrows rose with surprise, but his eyes maintained a cool, calm—Cassie was almost tempted to describe it as calculating—expression.

This time she couldn't help smiling. "You're not as shocked as my brother's going to be when he finds out."

"I guess not. I also should've figured Miss Flora had another reason for asking you to come here."

Cassie shrugged evasively.

"Miss Flora was a faithful churchgoer. Did she tell you of any bequest for some mission or charity or—"

"No. There might be something in her will, but—"

"Not even instructions on what to keep and which property to sell?"

"If there is, I'm sure it's Miss Bowen's business and none of yours, Brent," the gentleman standing in front of them interjected.

Cassie looked up quickly. The man was as tall as Brent, but not as broad-shouldered. She seriously doubted whether he could have single-handedly carried her trunk up the stairs as Brent had. He was probably much better at carrying around legal briefs.

"Miss Bowen, I'm August Harvey, your late aunt's attorney," he said as he made a deep bow. "I introduced myself to you earlier, but I suppose you were too distraught—"

"No. I remember you very well, Mr. Harvey. I'm sorry if I gave you the impression that I wouldn't. Please, sit down."

"I couldn't help overhearing your conversation," he said as

he sat down beside her. "I assume, then, that your aunt told you of the provisions of her Last Will and Testament before she passed away."

"Briefly."

"Yes, I'm sure you two had many other, much more pleasant matters for ladies to discuss. There are certain business and financial matters that need a more serious review, however, I understand your father passed away some time ago."

"Yes. Five years ago." *What does that have to do with anything?* she wondered. "I lived with my brother and his family until Aunt Flora invited me to stay here with her."

"Will your brother be visiting Lyman's Gap anytime soon?"

"I don't expect him to. Even if I had sent him a telegraph, he never would have arrived in time to attend the funeral. What would be the point of him visiting now?"

"I assumed, you being as yet without a husband, that he'd be taking care of your money and property for you. Certainly you have no experience in such matters."

"I hadn't really considered the matter." She'd been too busy with the funeral and with watching what Sebastian showed her. Obviously Sebastian had been the source of Aunt Flora's advice. She'd assumed he'd be hers, too.

"Then please consider this. I shall correspond with him, and between us we'll determine what's best for you and your investments. Will you be staying in town long, Miss Bowen?"

"Yes, I shall."

I shall remain here, as Aunt Flora had, for the rest of my life. All alone, too, Cassie thought sadly. *Until I, too, must pass this horrible curse on to poor little Marguerite, and she on to Ralphie's daughter, who would pass it to her niece.*

Her head suddenly felt very light, her thoughts strangely remote. She felt gripped by her own mortality, and yet uncannily propelled into the future, knowing for a certainty that someday awkward, tongue-tied Ralphie would indeed grow to be a man, marry, and father a son and a daughter.

Her heart felt extraordinarily heavy when she realized that smiling, golden-haired Marguerite would have only Sebastian—

and all the property, money, and jewelry. Small compensation for a life spent alone. That thought, and its certainty for her, gave Cassie a fearful chill.

"You certainly don't intend to live all alone in a house this big," Brent said.

"It wasn't too big for my aunt."

"But your aunt had friends who frequently came to call," Brent protested. "You're new in town. You know very few people here, none you could call friends."

"Do you think I'm incapable of making new friends, Mr. Conway?" she snapped.

"Miss Bowen, I can readily understand your reluctance to sell everything your beloved aunt left you so soon after her passing," Brent said gently.

Oh, he was a conniving scoundrel, Cassie thought, to effect such a strategic change of tactics when confronted with her obvious irritation at his first foray.

"You might first consider selling that property outside of town, however," Brent suggested. "It's pretty remote. There aren't any roads there yet, just an old hunting trail that probably dates back to the Indians. Nobody could build anything there. Goodness, nobody even wants to picnic or stroll through there for all the black grease that gets all over their shoes. Pretty worthless place, if you ask me."

"If the place is so worthless, why do you want to buy it?" she countered.

Brent frowned and pressed his lips tightly together. "You could take that money, invest it wisely, and move back to Philadelphia where you'll be among family and friends," he suggested. "Later, you can decide what to do about selling this house and its contents."

In spite of her annoyance with him, Cassie had to admit he made a valid point. Her only remaining family, and the few friends of hers Letitia had tolerated, lived in Philadelphia. How could she live here all alone?

On the other hand, how would she transport all these fine things to Philadelphia? She certainly couldn't get rid of the beautiful, exotic, and incredibly diverse furniture pieces and ornaments Aunt Flora had accumulated over the years.

She was positively enthralled with the Bluthner piano and would dearly love to take it back with her. She hadn't played a decent piano since her mother passed away almost ten years ago, and, in spite of Cassie's tearful protests, her brother had sold their mother's cherished Broadwood piano to make room for Letitia's enormous new davenport.

Where would Letitia allow her to keep these wonderful things? *If* she allowed her to keep them at all? Cassie frowned with concern. How could she prevent clumsy Ralphie and boisterous Marguerite from breaking everything to bits?

Cassie was very quiet as she thought for a moment. All the guests had left. She could hear the ticking of the clock in the foyer echoing loudly through the big, almost empty house. Mrs. Parker remained, supervising Jerusha, who was clattering dishes as she bustled back and forth between the dining room and the kitchen.

Brent and Mr. Harvey waited silently on either side of her. In spite of what appeared to be their concern for her welfare, she couldn't help regarding them as two vultures, ready to pounce on and divide up her corpse when she wasn't even dead yet.

Brent was pretty clear about what he wanted. What was Mr. Harvey after?

"As your dear departed aunt's attorney and trusted advisor, if I may so flatter myself—"

"I've never known you not to, August," Brent interjected with a deep chuckle.

Mr. Harvey threw Brent a scathing glance. His lips tightened, and he gave a sort of mumbled growl. Did Mr. Harvey regard Brent as a rival for her attention? Preposterous! They barely knew her. Their obvious animosity must stem from much further back.

Mr. Harvey cleared his throat, turned very slowly and deliberately from Brent to Cassie, and continued. "In the absence of your father and brother, I should hope to remain your advisor as well, Miss Bowen. You may determine for yourself my complete competence and trustworthiness."

"If my aunt trusted you, I'm sure I shall, too, Mr. Harvey."

"Then, at present I would counsel you not to make any hasty decisions."

"Everything has happened so quickly, I can hardly decide what to wear or what to have for breakfast each morning, much less decide on matters of importance." She gave a weak, self-effacing laugh.

"Excuse me, Miss Bowen," Mrs. Parker bustled forward, her hand outstretched to take the empty plate. "There's still some of Marilyn Vandergraft's potato salad left. That's the kind with the hard-cooked eggs that your aunt used to like so much. Not Dorie Klinger's with the bacon and vinegar in it." She puckered her lips. "Let me get you some."

"No more, thank you."

Mrs. Parker clucked her tongue and shook her head. "You've got to eat to keep up your strength."

"I appreciate your concern, but your delicious chicken salad filled me up."

Cassie was grateful she was lifting the last bit on the plate to her mouth as she spoke. She could hardly lie to the kind lady who had single-handedly organized each of the ladies in town to donate a dish to feed her aunt's friends who called after the funeral. She was also grateful to her for interrupting Brent and Mr. Harvey's vigil over her.

"Your aunt was very fond of my cooking. Miss Bowen, I realize this is hardly the time to be bringing up this matter, but, well . . . Tomorrow is Thursday, my usual day for coming here and, well, I wonder if you'll still need me."

Before Cassie could reply, Brent broke in. "I see no reason why a healthy young woman like Miss Bowen would need as much help as a frail, elderly lady. She can probably cook and do her own shopping. Why, I'd be surprised if she needed you at all."

Cassie watched Mrs. Parker's eyes grow wide with worry. "Well, it's still an awfully big house for just one—"

"Nonsense. It wasn't too big for Miss Flora."

Cassie blinked in disbelief, dumbstruck by Brent's words. Hadn't she just used that same argument against him? The man *was* unscrupulous!

"Still," Mrs. Parker babbled, "Miss Bowen can hardly have had experience running a household—"

"Perhaps you're right. You'd still come the same days for Miss Bowen as you did for Miss Flora—Mondays and Thursdays, wasn't it?"

"Certainly, if that's convenient."

Brent turned to Cassie. "Is that convenient, Miss Bowen?"

Cassie was too overwhelmed to do anything but nod.

He turned back to Mrs. Parker. "You'll continue to do the same work for the same pay."

"Certainly." Mrs. Parker nodded. "That's fair enough."

Cassie watched Mrs. Parker breathe a deep sigh of relief and quickly turn to her other tasks.

Cassie could feel her face flush again, but this time in genuine anger. She turned to Brent and whispered sternly, "What brass. What unmitigated gall. How dare you be so overbearing. How dare you interfere—!"

"You don't know when Mrs. Parker came in for your aunt, what work she did, or how long she stayed, do you?" he countered calmly.

"No," she was forced to admit.

"Well, *I* do."

"That's because you've been watching the old lady and everything she owned like a hawk for the past two years," Mr. Harvey muttered loudly.

Brent snorted. "You don't know what your aunt paid Mrs. Parker, but I'll bet she was just about ready to play on your grief and her years of loyal service to ask you to raise her wages."

"How can you say that about her?" Cassie was growing increasingly angry with Brent and his unfounded suspicions.

"Because I've had experience in this kind of situation. Experience I'm sure you've never had."

"You're starting to believe the hogwash you print in your own newspaper, Brent," Mr. Harvey accused with a derisive laugh. "Not everyone is as underhanded as you."

"My aunt trusted Mrs. Parker," Cassie said. "I see no reason why I shouldn't."

Brent might have had years of experience with countless different kinds of people, but Aunt Flora had had Sebastian, and Sebastian had always shown her the truth.

"I never said you shouldn't trust her. I just don't think you need to be raising her pay."

"What I pay my hired help doesn't concern you in the least. It doesn't concern you if I clean my own house, hire someone to do it, or let the whole thing get buried under a thick layer of dust. Neither should where I live or what I choose to sell or keep concern you. Aunt Flora left all this to *me*!"

Suddenly Cassie realized that for the first time in her life, she didn't have to answer to anyone—not her father, her brother and his domineering wife, her aunt's attorney, or this meddling neighbor.

"No! I won't be selling this place," she stated with a sudden certainty she'd never felt about anything before.

She drew in a deep breath. She knew that once she started explaining, she wasn't going to stop. If she stopped, she might run out of nerve. She couldn't let that happen.

"You don't understand, either of you. For the past five years, I've lived with my brother and his wife. Robert's a pleasant man, but Letitia never missed an opportunity to point out to me that I live with them on their charity, at her sufferance, and that the least I could do was make myself useful taking care of my niece and nephew. I have no intention of returning to live with them. Until now, I've never had a home I could truly call my own. Except for a small allowance, I've never even had any money of my own."

She spread her arms out wide, as if to encompass the entire contents of the parlor, the house and grounds, and everything that was now hers—right out to that supposedly worthless property.

"Suddenly I have everything I ever could have dreamed of—a home, money, beautiful things that are truly mine. Investments, savings for my old age—and something neither of you could ever understand or appreciate the way I do now. I have my *independence!*"

She clasped her hands together and settled them in her lap. She hoped this gesture indicated to both of them that she was more serious about this than about anything else in her life.

"So, gentlemen, please forgive me if at this moment—and for many days, perhaps even weeks or years to come—I'm not prepared to relinquish it so readily."

She straightened her back and lifted her chin proudly.

"So you intend to wait," Mr. Harvey said slowly.

"Exactly."

"What are you waiting for?" Brent demanded. "Some sort of a sign?"

Cassie almost told him yes. Then she closed her mouth and just shrugged. He would never know how close he'd come to the truth.

"You and your aunt had a lot more in common than I figured," Brent said with a humorless chuckle. He rose. "Good afternoon, Miss Bowen. And remember, no matter how much you may not want to, please, for your late aunt's sake, don't hesitate to call on me."

Cassie realized she was frowning as she watched him move into the foyer. As he turned toward the front door, she felt incredibly sorry he had gone.

"I never could understand why your aunt tolerated that man," Mr. Harvey said. "In fact, she actually seemed to like him."

"Did you get that impression?" Cassie asked. Considering Brent and Mr. Harvey's mutual animosity, and their conflicting views on what she ought to do with her inheritance, she was extremely interested in anything her aunt's attorney had to say about her neighbor.

"It was a shame the way he'd been taking advantage of her affection for him to badger that poor old dear into selling him that property. I, of course, always managed to talk her out of it."

"Oh, did you really?"

She tried to sound ingenuous. As taken with him as Mr. Harvey appeared to be with himself, she had no doubt he believed he'd impressed her immeasurably. Actually she'd put more credence in her aunt's faith in Sebastian than in any influence Mr. Harvey might have had.

"By the way, Mr. Harvey, do you know anything more about Aunt Flora's plans for that property?"

Mr. Harvey frowned and released a labored breath. "I don't mean to speak ill of the dead, Miss Bowen, especially since your late aunt was probably my best client. But she did have more than her fair share of eccentric moments. She told me once that there was an oily black ooze under these hills. She always claimed she'd get around to digging for it someday as soon as she figured out how. At the time I just dismissed it as another of those bizarre things she'd say from time to time."

"I understand she did that fairly often."

"I'm sure we're all aware of tar pits on the surface in California and out in Araby. A bit farther north here in Pennsylvania, folks have been dipping up oil seepage for decades." Mr. Harvey chuckled. "Did you ever try that rock oil medicine—what's it called—Kier's Petroleum?"

"I can't say as I have."

"I'm not certain I want to use as medicine something that can also be used to light my lamps and lubricate machinery."

"I don't think I would, either," Cassie had to agree.

"Still, there's been a lot of talk about finding a more profitable way to obtain more of that oil. Several men have tried. I never was convinced a woman—even one as shrewd as your aunt—would know how when the problem has baffled men of science and industry. Are you?"

"I never gave it much thought until now." Both her aunt and Sebastian had been strangely reticent on this matter. If only Sebastian would start making some serious, credible predictions!

"Well, of course not. Why would you worry your pretty little head about such things? Until you're more familiar with Mr. Conway and his ways, however, I'd suggest you exhibit the same caution your late aunt did regarding him."

"I intend to."

"Ah, that's wise on your part." He nodded his approval.

At first Mr. Harvey was all smiles and jocularity. Then he tried to assume the air of a stern authoritarian. Cassie didn't feel either role suited him. Neither of them sat well with her, either.

"I'm sure many well-meaning people will try to tell an attractive young lady away from home—and not under the guidance and supervision of an older, wiser man—to do many things that could ultimately prove quite harmful to her and her estate."

"I promise you, I'll only take the advice of an older, wiser. . . ."

Cassie let her voice trail off, hoping Mr. Harvey would assume she was agreeing with him. In spite of his name, she couldn't be sure Sebastian was a man—or even really a person. But he definitely had a personality.

Aunt Flora had claimed Sebastian was very wise, although Cassie believed he could have made better choices regarding his visions.

She was pretty sure Sebastian was far older than the ages of the entire population of the town all put together.

So technically she wasn't lying. Anyway, she wasn't Sebastian. She didn't always have to tell the truth.

"Before I do anything, I'll certainly think about what you've told me." *And weigh it very carefully against what Sebastian shows me*, she silently added.

For a moment Cassie doubted her own powers of reason. She'd actually taken the word of an inanimate object over the advice of a sensible, serious, well-educated human being.

Maybe having Sebastian in the first place was what drove Aunt Flora insane.

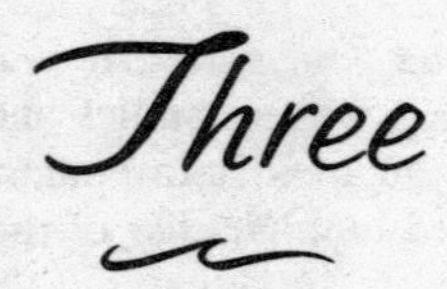

Brent closed his front door and glanced across the wide expanse of green lawn toward Miss Flora's house. His house was equally as big, but the grounds were virtually bare except for clover and grass, and the house itself was practically empty compared to hers.

He didn't share Miss Flora's penchant for collecting gaudy, useless knickknacks, and wouldn't have bought any of those foolish, foreign fandangles and folderols if he did have the money to waste.

Every spare penny went into building his business. Someday he'd own a big newspaper in a big city—shucks, why stop there? In *several* big cities!

But he would like to have something in that house someday besides a bed, a chest of drawers, a sofa, and a kitchen table and two chairs. Why bother now, when no one in town liked him enough to come visit him? Maybe someday his wife would take great pleasure in furnishing the house with beautiful, expensive things. Evaline McAlister would have been the type to spend his money on expensive knickknacks and foreign folderols. Was Cassie Bowen?

Dangerous speculation, my boy. Move on, he warned himself.

He glanced up to the window he'd checked every evening before retiring and every morning upon rising for the past two years. Miss Flora had seemed to enjoy the harmless flirtation between them. He knew every woman, regardless of her age, but especially when the wrinkles and gray hair appeared, enjoyed being treated as if she was still special to someone.

She'd always regarded his watchfulness as a joke, suspecting he was up to something. With his reputation, he could hardly blame her. She'd never know he'd been sincerely concerned about her—a frail, elderly woman living in that big house, all alone, with all those steep stairs.

Mrs. Parker only came around twice a week. Jerusha Jackson only came with the laundry once a week, and Olivier only cared for the horses and the grounds, and rarely went into the house at all. Why, if Miss Flora had fallen and broken a leg or a hip, she might have lain there for days, maybe even died, before someone found her.

He'd enjoyed the spry old lady's witty banter. He'd even enjoyed her affectionate baiting. Yes, he was going to miss her. He grimaced and suppressed a sigh. It was time to get back to work.

Well, if that wasn't a stroke of good luck or good timing, Brent silently congratulated himself. He couldn't help but grin. Down the front steps that very minute came pretty Miss Cassie Bowen. If he hurried, he could meet her where his front walk met the dirt lane that folks in town generously referred to as Elm Street, without looking as if he'd hurried to meet her. He wasn't that eager to get to the newspaper office this morning anyway.

She'd seemed so shy, until she discovered she'd inherited everything. It was just as he'd always suspected, even with the ones that seemed sweet and pretty. Lots of money made a lot of difference in the way people acted, and having lots of money made a lot of difference in how people treated you.

If she was refusing to sell that property in the hope of getting him to pay more for it, well, he was wise to her. He could wait.

Her head was bent down while she fidgeted with something in her purse. He enjoyed watching her dark green skirt sway over her hips, from side to side, in rhythm with her walk. The skirt's waistband gathered closely around her tiny waist.

He could only see a little bit of the pale, ivory skin of her cheeks. He wondered if her skin was as smooth to the touch as it looked. How would it feel to pull out her hairpins, loosen her braids, and run his fingers through her lengths of auburn hair? How would it feel to unfasten her clothing, and run his hands over her smooth, pale body?

Whoa! Don't go asking for trouble, he warned himself again.

Her voice could take on a hard edge when she was angry. He chuckled when he recalled how she'd suddenly turned when it came to protecting her inheritance and her so-called independence. Mostly she sounded soft and feminine. He wondered what it would sound like to have her whisper his name . . . in the dark . . . sighing heavily.

Now that really is enough, Brent Howard Conway! he scolded himself. *Control yourself before you talk to that pretty lady in front of you.*

He thought she'd look up before she ran into him. He figured he'd have time to get out of her way. He'd figured wrong.

She walked right into him. As her body collided with his, he held out both arms to encircle her and prevent her from falling backward into the dirt. She stared up at him, her bright blue eyes wide with shock. Her lips were so close, he could have easily bent to place a kiss on their rosy softness. He tightened his embrace, savoring her suppleness in spite of the corset, savoring the fragrance of lavender from her bodice.

She melted in his embrace, molding the tender curves of her body against his bone and sinew. From the reflections in her eyes, he could see a thousand thoughts wildly running through her mind. For the life of him, he couldn't figure out what a one of them was.

"Well, good morning, Miss Bowen."

Suddenly she pulled back. She reached up to right her bonnet, set askew by the collision. She reached down, brushing away the wrinkles in her skirt with more force than necessary.

"Good morning, Mr. Conway. I didn't expect to find you standing in the middle of the road."

"Oh, I was just admiring my house and comparing it to yours." He gestured back and forth between the two buildings. "They're very similar in size. Do you live there all alone?"

"Yes."

"My, my, and without even a housekeeper."

He slanted his eyes to watch her. She grinned slyly at him.

"I will confess, I cheat a little." He returned her smile.

"How so?"

"I get Jerusha Jackson to do my laundry for me."

"As my aunt did?"

"Well, not exactly. I don't have any petticoats."

Cassie laughed. The faintest blush colored her ivory cheeks. Brent longed to reach up and touch her smooth skin.

"I thought you said you hadn't hired the Jacksons."

"No. I just asked you if it sounded like something I'd do. Obviously, to you, it didn't."

"I'm sorry I underestimated you."

"Well, all will be forgiven if you admire my house."

She laughed again. He enjoyed hearing her happy.

"I had the house built two years ago. I couldn't wait to move out of the dilapidated old shack I grew up in."

"I believe my aunt was a bit more keen on gardening than you seem to be, if you don't mind my saying so."

"Oh, her garden's been growing for a good ten years, but Olivier's worked it into the shape it is today. You missed the daffodils in March and the lilacs this April. It's not time yet for the roses. They get fairly out of hand, climbing up the trellises on the sides of the house and spilling over the porch rails." He gestured toward the greenery spreading over Miss Flora's house. Then he flipped his hand toward his own. "Me? I can't even get a few straggling petunias to grow. Maybe I ought to talk to Olivier about looking after my garden, too. That man does have a way with horses and growing things."

"You do have that big oak tree in your backyard," she pointed out.

"That's probably been there since the pilgrims landed. It gives good shade on a hot summer's day, so I'm not about to chop it down."

"Those little maple trees in the front on either side of the walk ought to look fairly nice, too, when they get bigger."

"Oh, they just sprang up there, and I haven't had the heart—or the time—to cut them down."

"I see. Maybe you really ought to talk to Olivier." She glanced at the watch hung on a chain at her waist. "Oh, dear. I really must be on my way."

She turned and started to head down Elm Street. Brent fell in step beside her.

"So, what do you intend to do with yourself today, Miss Bowen?"

"Count my money," she replied impishly. "Try on all my jewelry."

"My, my. You've got a busy day planned for yourself all alone."

"Yes. Alone. I mean no offense, Mr. Conway, but I don't think any of Aunt Flora's jewelry would look particularly attractive on you."

"Nothing that would go with brown corduroy?" he asked, tugging at the lapel of his jacket.

"Not a thing."

"I didn't think so. Anyway, I was just trying to be neighborly."

"Yes, you've been very neighborly. Perhaps someday I'll be able to return the favor. But there's an appropriate time for neighborliness, and now the time has come for some equally appropriate privacy."

"So you're going to the lawyer's office, eh?"

Cassie stopped and stared at him. Did Brent happen to have his own family's version of Sebastian hidden somewhere in that big house of his? Was his oracle showing him the same sort of scintillating visions Sebastian was showing her?

"What makes you think I'm going to see Mr. Harvey?" Her voice cracked.

She hoped Brent wouldn't assume she was nervous about going to see the attorney and needed his help and support. It would be worse yet if he knew that thoughts of him were the real reason her throat felt tight and her voice sounded husky.

Brent's gaze swept up and down her body, taking in everything from the tops of her slightly scuffed shoes to the white muslin lining of her bonnet. She wished she'd worn a larger, deeper bonnet to shield her from his scrutiny. She wished she'd worn thicker hose and a more stiffly boned corset. She wished she'd carried her walking parasol, the one with the long, steel finial, so she could poke it at him to make him keep his distance. How could this man, with one simple glance, seem to strip her bare?

She felt herself growing warm with the very thought that Brent might think about her in the same way that she'd been thinking about him. No, he was doing nothing of the sort. She wouldn't allow herself to think the man had any kind of interest in her besides the obvious desire to persuade her to sell him her property. She wouldn't be so foolish to succumb to the temptations Sebastian warned her about.

Although, she had to admit, lately Sebastian had been behaving himself much better—at least where Brent was concerned. Most of the images he showed her still made little or no sense.

Last night he'd shown her fifteen squirming newborn piglets and a dirty, disheveled urchin tripping up the church steps and breaking his arm. She'd also seen two very tiny but perfectly healthy, newborn baby girls surrounded by six husky brothers.

She had to admit, as odd and disjointed as the visions were, they were mostly cheerful—and definitely improving in moral quality. Perhaps Sebastian had just been testing her before. At last, these were visions of things she could believe could actually occur.

"You're all dressed up this morning," Brent commented. "You're not dressed to go traveling—I've seen that outfit, and you do look mighty fine in it."

"How kind of you to notice," she replied coolly as she kept walking.

"It's not Sunday, so you're not dressed for church," he continued.

Was there no stopping this persistent man?

"It's a little too soon for a very proper lady such as yourself to leave off mourning to go visiting or to tea parties, and it's a little early in the day for that, anyway. So, the only appropriate place I can figure for you to be going is to see Mr. Harvey."

Cassie smiled in spite of herself. "You're quite observant."

"But am I right?"

"Apparently your experience gathering news serves you well in other areas, too."

"So, I am right."

"Yes, you are," she admitted reluctantly.

"You don't sound too happy. Is it because I figured out where you were going, or that you're not too happy about going there?"

"This is not exactly the same as attending an Independence Day parade and picnic."

"Having second thoughts about going alone?"

"No," she responded flatly.

"About this foolish notion of female independence?"

"No," she responded more sharply.

"Would you like me to go with you, just to make sure Mr. Harvey doesn't try to—?"

"Not at all. Thank you, Mr. Conway," she stated sternly. "I can manage this on my own."

"I promise not to say a word—"

"As you did yesterday with Mrs. Parker?"

"Look, Miss Bowen, I'm right sorry about that."

He spread his arms out in front of him, palms up, in a

gesture that bespoke abject penitence. Cassie wasn't fooled for a minute.

"I guess my protective instincts got carried away. But I'm not such a rascal as some folks around here might lead you to believe, and I do know how to handle my money."

"That doesn't mean I'm going to let you handle mine."

"I didn't make my money on wild, bizarre speculations like Miss Flora did, you know. I saw what people wanted, and I gave it to them."

"And you make them pay handsomely for the privilege?"

"Can I help it if people are willing to pay more for bad news than for good?"

"And the worse, the better?"

"Look, I know a lot better than a stranger like you does what most people around here think of me." His voice took on a hard edge.

Aunt Flora hadn't mentioned that Mr. Conway had a quick temper. Perhaps she'd made a mistake in goading him.

"People respected my father—an upstanding, God-fearing man, pillar of the community and all that sort of thing. Well, what good did it do him?"

Brent kicked at a stray pebble on the sidewalk.

"People don't pay you a plugged dollar for your respectability. People only saw what they wanted to see in my father, and he only saw what he wanted to see in them. They never acknowledged the fact that we were as poor as church mice."

"There's no shame in being poor."

He released a bitter laugh. "That's easy for you to say, isn't it?"

"I'm not just mouthing platitudes. Aunt Flora, not my father, had the money in my family. I'm so new at this, I'm still working on being well-to-do. I haven't yet begun to be able to consider myself *rich*."

Brent silently studied her very closely for a moment. She didn't feel as if he were stripping her down to bare skin this time. This time she felt as if he were trying to pry into the very depths of her soul. What was he trying to discover? Whether she was telling the truth?

"My father made a little money," Brent told her. "He was just never any good at holding on to it for very long. I promised myself that when I grew up I'd never be poor again. I'd never let my children suffer the humiliations I did—going to school in trousers that had patches on patches; having only a head of cabbage and boiled potatoes for dinner and considering ourselves darned lucky if we had a little bacon grease or a blob of rancid butter to flavor it. And—"

Brent shoved his hands deep into his trouser pockets as he continued to saunter along beside her. They turned along the dirt road the townspeople referred to as Main Street. The heels of their shoes thunked on the smooth boards laid side by side that made up the sidewalk to lift pedestrians above the ruts and mud puddles.

"And?" she prompted.

"Well, just . . . never mind all that."

"Surely it couldn't have been that bad. I mean, rancid butter? Have you been listening to too many of Aunt Flora's melodramatic tales?"

"Well, maybe not *completely* rancid," he confessed. "And we did have a scrap of opossum or raccoon to sort of round out the meal."

"I see. Well, at least you should be thankful you didn't have to wear an older sister's hand-me-down skirt to school."

He stopped and stared at her. She grinned at him. He laughed and resumed walking. She caught up to him this time.

"My sister is younger than I. Thanks for shaking me off that limb of self-pity."

"Goodness, what are neighbors for?"

"What do you say to a truce, Miss Bowen?"

"I didn't realize we'd declared war, Mr. Conway."

"An agreement then. Like your aunt and I had."

"What sort of agreement? I won't have you looking in my bedroom window or nagging me about selling my land."

"You drive a hard bargain. Well . . . I promise not to badger you about selling that property."

Should she trust him? Wasn't this the very type of situation with Mr. Conway that Mr. Harvey had warned her about?

Well, Sebastian hadn't warned her. As a matter of fact, that lascivious crystal ball seemed to be all in favor of her getting to know Brent better.

Cautiously Cassie asked, "What do I have to do for you in return?"

Before Brent could answer, a lanky fellow in a red-checked shirt and trousers, torn at both knees, waved frantically to him from across the street. "Hey, Brent! Brent! C'mere!"

Cassie couldn't recall seeing the man at her aunt's funeral. Whoever the fellow was, he was obviously one of the people in town who didn't dislike Brent. "Who's that?"

"Woodbury Tucker. Folks call him Woody."

"I see."

"He's usually pretty quiet."

"He's doing everything but cartwheels in the middle of the street to get your attention."

"It must be something mighty important. Come on then," Brent said, offering her his arm as he turned to cross the street. "I guess we ought to see what he's raising all this fuss about."

"But—"

"Mr. Harvey will be sitting there in his office, checking the clock, shuffling and sorting papers, and tying them up with red tape to keep them in order, waiting for you—all the livelong afternoon."

"Being late would be rude."

"Remember, *you're* his best client now. He put up with a lot of guff from Miss Flora for several years. I think he'll forgive you for being a few minutes late." When Cassie still hesitated, he reminded her, "Weren't you trying to be independent from him, too?"

She had to admit Brent was right.

He was still holding his arm out to her. Taking his arm would be nowhere near as unsettling as colliding with him had been. The warm hardness of his body next to hers had brought back all too clearly the recollection of the visions she'd seen in Sebastian.

Thank goodness Sebastian didn't have the power to make her actually *feel* what those images were experiencing. Her own far too vivid imagination was doing that for her well enough. Touching Brent reminded her all too forcefully of the growing desire she felt to be near him like that in reality.

Reluctantly Cassie placed her hand in the crook of Brent's elbow. His arm was solid and muscular. Goodness, he probably could have picked her up and carried her across the street.

No, don't think of that, she scolded herself. *Don't think of anything that will remind you of Brent holding you in his arms.*

"Woody's a decent fellow," Brent was telling her.

Apparently her touch wasn't unsettling to him. Well, of course it wouldn't be. *He* didn't have Sebastian inciting him.

"Not too bright, but good-hearted and a darn good farmer, and inordinately proud of his livestock."

"What does he raise?"

"Pigs."

The wind changed, and Cassie realized she would have been able to guess anyway.

"Brent! It's time! Y'gotta see this!" Woody was yelling excitedly. "Mehetabel's poppin' out piglets!"

"Great!" Brent responded, clapping Woody heartily on the shoulder. The odor of pigs increased in proportion to the amount of brown dust that rose from Woody's clothing.

Cassie made a mental note not to take *that* hand if Brent offered to assist her in recrossing the street.

She followed Brent and Woody down a side road. It was actually more like a dirt path that got narrower, muddier, and more rutted as they traveled down it. They walked around to the back of a ramshackle red barn. The path ended. They walked over the grass to a smaller, whitewashed lean-to surrounded by a rickety fence.

About a dozen men were leaning against the weathered rails. A dozen boys were perched upon the rails, lounging against the posts, or scampering around in the field and jumping over the small creek nearby.

She heard some of the boys shouting. "No fair!"

"Is, too!" others retorted.

She turned to watch two boys pull a third, dripping wet, from the creek. They turned on another group of boys, singling out the tallest one.

"You cheated, Lem. Wally woulda made that jump if'n you hadn'ta pushed him. You're nothin' but a big, fat, dirty cheater, Lemuel Hopkins! That's what you are!"

"Yeah, yer sister eats snots, and likes it, too!" the ragged, redheaded, freckle-faced boy shouted back. "Yep, she finds it mighty tasty! Yum, yum, slurp!"

"Aw, she just likes yer maw's cookin'!"

"Sez who?" The red-haired boy called Lem clenched his fists at his side and stalked the other boy.

"Hey, you kids. Lay off over there, the lot of ya, or I'll tell yer ol' man!" one of the men yelled. "Then your hides're in for a tannin'!" The warring groups of boys scattered in several directions.

Brent chuckled as he led Cassie onward. She sniffed. Yes, indeed. This was the pigsty. Of that she could have no doubt.

On a bed of surprisingly clean straw lay Mehetabel. It had to be her—all round and pink. In the straw squirmed several much smaller but equally as round and pink piglets.

"How many?" Brent asked.

"Two so far, but she ain't done yet," Woody answered.

"Wooo! Wooo! Make that three!" someone else corrected excitedly.

"We're taking bets if you want in," another man added.

Cassie peered at the face hidden beneath the straw hat. That looked like Mr. Calvin Andrews from the bank. He and his wife had called for the funeral. He certainly looked different today.

"I'm fer eight," Woody fairly crowed. "Ya see how big she is. No less than eight."

"Naw. That's mostly that cornmeal mush you've been feeding her," Mr. Andrews said. "Six. That's my wager." He tossed two bits into a battered, upturned hat held by one of the boys.

Woody tossed in his coins.

"Five." Another coin went into the hat.

"Six and a runt." Some more coins went into the hat.

The boy sat there jingling the growing pot.

"You in, Brent?"

"Sure, count me in. I never could resist a good bet. Nine, that's what I say. Nine." Brent dug into his pocket, pulled out two bits, and tossed it into the hat.

"Fifteen," Cassie said quietly.

Brent turned to her. "What's that?"

"I said fifteen. None dead. No runts. Fifteen."

"What do you know about pigs?" Brent asked her quietly.

"Properly prepared, they make excellent ham, bacon, sausages, and chops."

"In other words, nothing."

"Nothing," Cassie admitted. "I was born and raised in Philadelphia."

"City girl through and through, huh?"

She nodded.

He twisted around so that his back was to the men. "Look, don't wager like this," he whispered. "It's a man's amusement, anyway."

"Did Aunt Flora ever wager?"

"As a matter of fact, yes. It . . . Well, I really hate to admit this, but she was positively addicted to horse races and silly little wagers like this. She always seemed to win, too, but—"

"Fifteen," Cassie repeated insistently.

"Look, you're not your aunt. She was an older woman. She could get away with this sort of thing. But you. You're different."

"How so?" she pressed him.

"You're younger."

"We've established that."

"You're sweet and innocent and need to worry about maintaining your reputation. Especially you, especially in this town," he warned.

"Fiddlesticks!"

What difference would this little wager make on her reputation? What business was it of Brent's, anyway?

"Fifteen." She grinned at him defiantly. Those visions were starting to make sense at last. She'd trust Sebastian.

"Naw, never fifteen," Mr. Andrews said, shaking his head.

"Not even Mehetabel," Woody said, shaking his head, too.

"Mehetabel ain't got enough teats fer fifteen."

"How do you know, Mike? You ever rooted down there and counted 'em?"

"No, and it's pretty dang evident she ain't, either." Mike jerked his head in Cassie's direction.

Cassie felt a hot flush rising from beneath her collar. Well, she reasoned, it was a pigpen, quite the appropriate place for such earthy allusions.

"No, we can't take your wager, Miss Bowen," Brent said.

"You remember what I told you, Brent Conway. Fifteen." She was half-tempted to shake a finger under his nose—but that was too much like something her aunt would have done. She didn't think it would be wise to remind everyone how much she resembled crazy Aunt Flora.

"City women." One of the men hooted.

The rest laughed. Cassie thought she heard some of them murmuring something about "Miss Flora's niece." They laughed harder.

She saw the corners of Brent's mouth twitching. He was trying awfully hard not to laugh at her. But she knew very well that once she left, and he was alone with the rest of the men, he'd laugh at her prediction just as hard as any of these country yokels.

Aunt Flora had been right. No one would ever believe a word of even the most insignificant prediction. How had she gotten herself into this fix when her aunt had warned her? How was she going to get out of it? How soon before these men forgot about her silliness?

Embarrassed by her own boldness, she turned away. She marched down the narrow dirt path until she arrived back at Main Street. She smoothed her skirt, patted at her hair under her bonnet, and proceeded to Mr. Harvey's office. He might be condescending, but at least he was polite about it. At least he didn't laugh at her.

Cassie left Mr. Harvey's office more astonished than when she'd entered. She couldn't begin to comprehend the extent of the wealth in bonds and stocks in various successful companies, or the amount of capital in the bank—not even after Mr. Harvey had patiently explained it to her several times.

She'd been pleasantly surprised to find several hundred dollars in paper script in a linen bag under Aunt Flora's mattress, and several thousand in gold coins in the leather bag at the bottom of the flour bin.

She wondered if Aunt Flora had any more caches around the house that she hadn't remembered to tell Cassie about. She made a mental note to check all the drawers when she got home.

Home. What a wonderful word. Especially when it referred to a home of her very own.

She'd been delighted beyond words at the exquisite beauty of the jewelry Aunt Flora had managed to accumulate—not only lustrous pearls but rose-cut diamonds, rectangular emeralds, pale sea-blue aquamarines, and garnets so dark they appeared a bloodied purple.

How could she keep from squandering all her money? How could she be sure to invest it properly to increase the wealth? Had Aunt Flora been some sort of financial wizard? Well, *she* certainly wasn't.

Or had Aunt Flora done it with Sebastian's help? But could Cassie really trust Sebastian? Her momentary confidence in the pig prediction rapidly fled. What if Sebastian decided to show some awfully odd, improbable things that got her ridiculed or, worse yet, impoverished her? She refused to crawl back, empty-handed, to a gloating Letitia.

For a very brief moment, Cassie was tempted to hand it all over to Mr. Harvey, or Robert, or even Brent. Then her pride reared up again. She'd do it, just as her aunt had. With Sebastian's help, she'd do it.

Outside the door to Mr. Harvey's office, Cassie noticed the same group of boys playing a game of tag that involved the church steps. They thundered up the steps and banged on the red church door as their base. Eventually Reverend Markham, who'd obviously been trying to work inside, tired of them and came out and chased them away. Two minutes later, they were back again, thundering up the steps and banging on the door.

Cassie watched and held her breath. Any moment now, she fully expected one of those boys to go sprawling up the steps and break his arm. Hadn't Sebastian showed her that very scene? But nothing like that happened.

Mr. Andrews came up to her, smiling sheepishly. He extended the battered hatful of coins. "It's for you, Miss Bowen."

"What's this? Why me?" She didn't dare accept it.

"You were right about Mehetabel and the piglets, you know."

"Yes, I know." *Oh, don't sound so smug,* she silently scolded herself. *You, too, doubted Sebastian.*

"Mehetabel had fifteen of them, none dead, no runts—just like you said. Fifteen fat, sassy little piglets all squirming around in the sty in back of Woody's barn." He laughed. "Why, he's as proud and happy as if he was the papa."

Cassie laughed, too. Woody couldn't actually *be* the papa, but he sure smelled like it.

"What a lucky guess!"

"I suppose so."

"Just like your aunt was—Lord rest her soul—plumb brimming over with good luck."

"Oh, I don't know if you could call it that," Cassie replied modestly.

"So we figured since you were right, you ought to get the pot."

Cassie blinked with surprise. "But I didn't wager anything."

"Well, yes, but you did win. And, well . . . we feel sort of . . . bad about laughing at a lady and all." He held the hat out to her.

She certainly wasn't about to touch it—no matter how much money it contained.

"I can't take that money, Mr. Andrews. I'll tell you what. I understand Mrs. Andrews is quite active in the missionary work of the church."

"Oh, that she is. Why, she claims she'd send me to China to convert the heathens if she could find a box big enough, and if I didn't act like such a heathen myself most of the time." He chuckled, clearly unashamed.

"Why don't you give it to her then, for the mission?"

Mr. Andrews stopped laughing and twisted his lips into an awful grimace. He reached up and rubbed the back of his neck.

"Well, you see, the missus doesn't hold with gambling, Miss Bowen. Nor swearing, nor drinking, nor dancing. As a matter of fact, she'd be downright perturbed if she knew I'd been wagering on Woody's pigs. She'd never take money gained in such brazen sinfulness and base debauchery for the good work of the church."

If Mrs. Andrews thought betting on how many pigs were in a litter was brazen sinfulness and base debauchery, Cassie marveled that Mr. Andrews didn't volunteer to go to China just to get away from her. She wondered what Mrs. Andrews's reaction would be to Sebastian.

"Well, since it's technically my money," Cassie told him, "but I never really put any money in the hat, then I wasn't actually gambling, was I?"

"I guess not."

"So, Mrs. Andrews could certainly accept a donation for the church from *me*."

Mr. Andrews's eyes brightened. "Say, that's a great idea. Miss Bowen, I've got to tip my hat to you. You're just about as shrewd as your dear departed aunt." He took off down the street at a brisk stride.

"Oh, thank *you*, Mr. Andrews," Cassie replied. How could he know she was actually thanking him for taking away that smelly hat?

How could he have understood that she hadn't really been taking a chance when guessing the number of piglets? Sebastian had been quite clear about the exact number.

Cassie drew her brows together as she walked steadily along, staring at the planks of the sidewalk, as if their smooth, worn evenness would help her concentrate on the undoubtedly bumpy path ahead of her. If Sebastian had been right about the piglets, and Aunt Flora had claimed he was right about *everything*, that meant the images he showed her of herself and Brent would eventually come true.

In spite of the warm spring sunshine beaming down on her, Cassie shivered. She wasn't really cold. She was definitely nervous. She wouldn't dare admit that part of the cause of the tingle running through her body was a strange anticipation, brought on by merely thinking that someday Brent would hold her in his passionate, naked embrace.

"Your aunt always used to sit right up front there," Mrs. Andrews told Cassie. She extended her arm to indicate the very first pew on the left.

Cassie stood in the tiny vestibule of the small church and peered into its hazy, candlelit recesses. The morning sun slanted through the shining, tinted windows. It was all so beautiful, and yet nothing was the right color. She tugged her handkerchief so tightly that she was afraid, any moment now, she'd hear the fine Irish lace and linen rip.

"Oh, no," Cassie protested. "I couldn't possibly sit all the way up there."

"Why not? Your aunt paid for that front pew until July. She did every year since she moved here. She probably would have done it next year, too, if she hadn't been called home." Mrs. Andrews paused, then slyly insinuated, "She'd probably expect you to do the same next year, too. You might as well use it now."

Still, Cassie hung back. She could hear people behind her arriving for Sunday morning service, lining up, waiting to sit down. After all, they, too, had paid good money for those seats—except *she* was in the way.

It was bad enough, after the piglet fiasco, that she seemed to have taken her aunt's place as the town crank. She simply wasn't ready to move into any other place her aunt might have occupied in the community.

"The only other folks who can afford—or want—a front pew are the McAlisters," Mrs. Andrews whispered. "But they're traveling in Europe now."

Not only would she be sitting in front of everyone—she'd be the only one there. Cassie knew she was definitely not ready to claim any social position in the town.

"I'm not used to sitting so close—"

"Nonsense."

"I have to sit in the back. I think I'm allergic to—"

"Oh, pish-tosh. No one's allergic to lilies of the valley." Mrs. Andrews dismissed her protest with a wave of her hand.

"I tripped on the rug in the upstairs hallway yesterday. I guess I'm not familiar with the layout of the house yet, and . . . my ankle still aches a bit. I don't think I can walk all the way up the aisle."

Mrs. Andrews stared at her. The entire church wasn't more than forty feet long and twenty-four feet wide. Well, all right, Cassie had to admit with a sly giggle behind her gloved hand, that one was a pretty lame excuse.

"I have a bit of an upset stomach and believe it would be best to sit near the door so I can leave quickly if I have to . . . so as not to disturb the sermon."

"Well, perhaps that would be a good idea," Mrs. Andrews at last conceded. Then she turned to greet the people behind Cassie.

Cassie breathed a sigh of relief to be shed of the insistent woman.

She sat in the last pew in the very back. Even though she kept her head down and her gaze glued to the tiny print in the hymnal she was thumbing through, she could feel the eyes of everyone in the church boring into her. Maybe they'd think she was praying and, in truth, she was—that she wouldn't make a fool of herself in front of all these people.

Perhaps she should have taken the seat Mrs. Andrews had shown her instead of making all that fuss in the vestibule and drawing undue attention to herself.

The polished wood smelled of wax and dust sifting down from the cobwebbed rafters. The hymnal had a faintly musty scent from sitting unused every day but Sunday. The lady at the pump organ pressed out a high, reedy tune, punctuated by deep, resonant chords. She frowned ominously at the boy pushing and tugging on the pump handle. He applied himself more vigorously, and the volume increased.

Cassie had been nervous coming alone to a strange church in a strange town for the first time. Little by little, the peaceful atmosphere of the sanctuary calmed and comforted her.

Suddenly a low whisper surged through the congregation like the first uneasy stirring of the leaves before an approaching thunderstorm. Cassie looked up from under her brows. The ladies were fidgeting, trying to turn around in their seats without being too obvious about it. The gentlemen just plain turned around and stared. Cassie didn't dare turn around, no matter how much her curiosity prickled her.

"What is it?" the lady in front of Cassie demanded of her husband, seated beside her.

"The devil's come to church," he mumbled.

The lady fanned herself more rapidly. "No, no. Do tell."

"Brent Conway."

"Hush, hush!" she commanded, slapping her husband's shoulder with her fan. "Here he comes! Oh, wouldn't you know he'd have to sit near us. Suppose someone thinks we actually *consort* with him?"

Cassie turned around just in time to face Brent, standing in the aisle beside her. Clutching the brim, he rolled his hat around in his hands. He looked exceptionally nervous, Cassie decided, highly unusual for a man with Mr. Conway's brazen nerves. Maybe he was waiting for God to strike him with lightning.

"Good morning, Mrs. Green, Mr. Green." Brent nodded to

the couple seated in the pew. They nodded politely in response, and quickly turned to a minute examination of their hymnals.

Then he had the unmitigated gall to sit down right beside Cassie. Oh, she knew she should have listened to Mrs. Andrews. Brent never would have tracked her down if she'd sat at the front of the church. But that darn Sebastian hadn't warned her. As a matter of fact, from the gossip she'd heard from her aunt and others, Brent never went to church—not even on Easter or Christmas.

"Good morning to you, too, Miss Bowen," Brent said. "I'm surprised to find you sitting back here with the rest of us sinners who haven't paid enough to be close to God."

"I might have to leave quickly."

Brent nodded. "Too tired to walk that far up the aisle?"

"Not too tired," she corrected. "Perhaps when I know more people in town, I'll feel better about walking the full length of the aisle in view of everyone, and taking Aunt Flora's place. Right now, I prefer blissful anonymity—or anything as close to it as I can get."

"Well, aside from that, how are you this fine spring Sunday?"

"I'm fairly well, thank you. And yourself?"

"Fine. You're looking mighty pretty this morning."

"How kind of you to say so, Mr. Conway."

Cassie could see Mrs. Green trying to lean back unobtrusively so she could better hear what Brent was saying. She was also pretty sure Mrs. Green wouldn't hesitate to notify people that Miss Bowen was "consorting" with the disreputable Brent Conway.

"That necklace looks right fine with that blue dress."

"Thank you for noticing, Mr. Conway."

Mrs. Green leaned back so far her hat almost fell off her head right into Cassie's lap. She—and every other woman there—were probably just dying to turn around and see what Cassie had appropriated from her late aunt's extensive jewelry box. What in the world was Brent up to?

Cassie lifted her head proudly. The small gold cross, hung from a delicate gold chain, was very appropriate for a young, unmarried lady to wear to church—even if it was studded with tiny pearls and small sapphires. She had every right to wear it.

Even if it wasn't and she didn't, Cassie was beginning to think she'd enjoy being considered a little eccentric—not as much as Aunt Flora had been—but enough to let her get away with doing what she wanted to. Oh, if only she *really* had the nerve to do so!

Brent leaned nearer and whispered, "And with your beautiful blue eyes."

Mrs. Green rustled the pages of her hymnal as if frantically searching for that elusive first hymn of the day.

"I don't think it's proper to say such things in church, Mr. Conway."

"Where else do you think would be a good place to be thankful for one of God's loveliest creations?"

"Mr. Conway, please!" she protested. Oh, the man was a scoundrel of the highest—or lowest—degree!

"My goodness," Brent remarked in a more normal tone of voice. He lounged back against the pew, stretching his legs out in front of him. "If I had known you were coming to church this morning, we could have strolled down Elm Street together. Now, wouldn't that have been pleasant?"

"I suppose so."

"Walking to church with me wouldn't completely ruin your reputation, would it?" he asked. "After all, we're neighbors who happen to be heading in the same direction for the same worthwhile purpose."

"I was under the impression you were . . . not particularly regular in your church attendance," she said as tactfully as she could.

"That's true. On the other hand, folks are always talking about the influence a good woman can have on a man."

Cassie released a deep breath. "You flatter me too much, Mr. Conway."

"Perhaps we could walk home together," he suggested.

That shouldn't cause any alarm, she figured. After all, it wasn't as if they were locked in a torrid embrace in public, or blatantly going into one of their houses *together*, or anything like that to make the neighbors talk. They'd talk enough anyway, Cassie thought with a mental grimace.

"Perhaps you wouldn't mind if I invited myself in for a cup of coffee afterward," Brent suggested.

Mrs. Green fairly broke her neck trying to twist around.

"I don't think so. I . . . I usually spend my Sunday afternoons at home. Quietly. Alone. Reading. Sermons."

Oh, what a liar! If she'd been planning on doing anything this afternoon it was playing that wonderful piano. But she had to say something—anything—to convince Mrs. Green she wasn't some sort of loose woman come to town to be the ruination of all their menfolk.

Cassie was saved by the soaring chords of the introduction to the first hymn. She concentrated on Reverend Markham's scripture readings, the hymns, and the choir's anthem. She refused to look at Brent at all during the sermon. Reverend Markham droned on and on.

"Ooh! Ooh!" A loud cry went up from the middle of the church. A thin-faced lady with streaks of gray at her temples struggled to her feet, supported by a very tall, very worried-looking man. "Oh, no! It can't be time yet."

"It's all right, sweet thing," the man comforted her. "You've been through this many times before and did right fine."

"But it's been so long."

"Naw, you're an old hand at this. You've always done fine before," her husband murmured encouragement as he pushed his way ahead of her, past everyone else seated in the pew and out into the aisle.

The rest of the congregation whispered amongst themselves. Cassie could hear the excitement in their voices, and also a large degree of concern.

"Who are they?" Cassie whispered to Brent.

"George and Gertrude Wilcox."

"I don't think I met them."

"He might've shown up at Miss Flora's funeral, but not his wife. She's in the family way."

"I can see that."

Now that the couple stood in the middle of the aisle, it was easy to see Mrs. Wilcox's skirt tucked up under her swollen bosom, covering her rounded abdomen. With her fingers spread over her bulging stomach, she continued to moan, and leaned heavily against her husband.

"Oh my," Mrs. Green, shaking her head, lamented to Mr. Green. "It's not time yet. Too soon, too soon. She never went this soon with all the others."

Cassie turned a questioning look to Brent, who merely shrugged.

"Don't look at me," he protested. "I don't know anything about babies."

"But you must know something about Mr. and Mrs. Wilcox."

"She's not due for another month," Mrs. Green continued without turning around, but loud enough for Cassie to figure the information was for her benefit. "How sad if something should go wrong. She was so counting on delivering a girl this time."

"She's been counting on having a girl for the past six times," Mr. Green grumbled.

Cassie hadn't really made any connection until she watched Mr. and Mrs. Wilcox hurrying from the church, followed by what looked like a moving staircase of six strapping sons, each one the spitting image of their father.

"She has six sons?" Cassie began to smile. But when she looked around, she felt like a grinning simpleton. Everyone else was frowning with concern. But then, none of them had Sebastian.

"For a while there, it was sort of a tradition in Lyman's Gap. Mrs. Wilcox had a boy about every eighteen months,"

Brent said. "Then she wasn't in the family way for . . . oh, must be five years. Now, there's this last one."

"There are some who say she's far too old to be bearing another baby safely," Mrs. Green added, as if irritated at being excluded even momentarily from the gossip. "Doc Carver being among them. She's too old, and the baby's too big. But what's a woman to do?" She sighed. "She always did so have her heart set on having a daughter, and what does she get? Six husky sons right in a row. Not that there's anything wrong with that, mind you," she quickly added, then left Cassie speculating, trailing off, "but . . ."

"Does anyone else in town have six sons?" Cassie asked.

"Yes," Brent said.

The smile faded slightly from Cassie's face. Sebastian hadn't exactly shown her the Wilcoxes specifically.

"The Dumonts have six sons and three daughters," he continued. "The McIntyres have six sons and—"

"But no one else has only six sons, no daughters?"

"Not to my recollection."

Cassie leaned back against the pew and breathed a sigh of relief. At last she could allow herself a complete smile.

"What are you so happy about?" Brent demanded. "I mean, I'm not exactly an expert on the subject of babies, never having had any myself, but I do believe this is a mighty trying time for a woman, even when she's already had six boys and considering this one's early—"

"She'll be fine," Cassie assured him as she picked up the hymnal, ready for Reverend Markham to resume the service. "She and her two little girls will be just fine."

"Two girls?" Brent stared at her.

Mrs. Green dropped her hymnal.

"Don't look at me like I'm crazy," Cassie scolded him.

"Don't say things that make me look at you like you're crazy," Brent scolded right back. He leaned a bit closer and warned in a lower tone, "Don't say things that'll make the neighbors look at you like you're crazy."

"Like they did my aunt?"

Brent grimaced.

"I was right about the pigs," she reminded him.

"Luck. Sheer luck."

"I'm right about this, too."

"Pigs and humans are two different things."

Cassie turned to him and grinned with supreme self-confidence. "Would you care to make a small wager on this, Mr. Conway?"

"What? Here in church?"

"Don't pretend to be shocked for my sake. I think I'm beginning to know you better than that."

Brent shook his head. "Nope. I won't bet against you on this."

Cassie felt a chill. She tried to swallow, but her throat closed up on her. "Do . . . do you believe me, then?" she demanded hoarsely.

"Shucks no. But, well . . ."

"Is it because I'm a proper lady?"

"No, but . . . I mean, yes, but . . . Well, I can't bet against you when you're sure to lose."

"Oh." Cassie tried not to sound too disappointed. She shrugged. "Suit yourself."

She turned to face the front of the church, where Reverend Markham had reestablished order after all the excitement, and was leading a prayer commending Mrs. Wilcox and the new baby into God's merciful care.

"Twin girls," Cassie repeated to Brent, nodding her head with assurance. "You wait and see."

Mrs. Green snickered behind her hand.

Sebastian had always shown her pictures of the nighttime—twinkling stars, silver clouds sailing across a luminous moon, shining down on Brent and her. She'd always assumed that was because Sebastian only showed her things happening at night.

Even the images of the piglets, the baby girls, and the others had been singular figures without a noticeable, or even identifiable, background.

But this time, in spite of the midnight hour, the sun shone brightly in the crystal ball. Crowds of grimy, busy workmen milled to and fro. She didn't recognize anyone. A tall, tapering square, wooden tower loomed high over a field of greasy, trampled grass, casting a dark shadow over low, wooden buildings and a huge pile of barrels. Inside, a steam engine puffed and pounded a heavy drill through a metal tube, deep into the earth. The darkness seemed to pull her down with the drill into the ground—deeper and deeper.

How could it be possible for her to see into the bowels of the earth? Deeper and deeper until she found the hidden well—until she found the oily black ooze—petroleum, in great abundance, under that land outside of town.

That's what Aunt Flora had been babbling about. What those men farther north had been trying to do and failed. Now she knew why, and what to do so as *not* to fail.

She knew for certain now that Sebastian was showing her the truth. He would always show her the truth. She knew now that it was also very important that she do what he showed her. She must tap the thick liquid from the earth with a wooden tower and a steel drill like that.

Brent slowed down as he passed Abel Warner's general store. Ordinarily on Monday morning, all the ladies in town who couldn't afford to send their laundry out to Jerusha—and that was most of them—would be bending over their washboards, doing their own. But there they were instead, bustling around inside the store, chattering with each other.

No doubt, they were discussing the birth of the Wilcoxes' twin girls last night. Nothing else that exciting had happened in Lyman's Gap since the British and the Indians tore through on their way to Fort Pitt during the Revolution.

He almost walked on by. He usually just bought what he needed and left. Abel didn't like him hanging around much, not after the disagreement they'd had three years ago. Darn shame since they'd once been such close friends. Even more of a shame that money should have been the cause of all their problems.

Besides, no man in his right mind would venture into that bastion of feminine domesticity today.

Then he perked up. He'd recognize that auburn hair anywhere.

Cassie was leaning over the counter, deep in discussion with Abel. Brent doubted she was asking him whether to buy cinnamon or nutmeg. What in the world was so important that she'd have to discuss it so intently, and with him, of all people? He pushed open the door and felt practically slammed in the face by a thick wall of feminine chatter.

"Gertrude Wilcox couldn't be happier. Finally, not one, but two girls," Mrs. Andrews said.

"They're so awfully small, though," Mrs. Green fretted.

"Doc Carver says they're healthy enough."

"But they were born almost a month early."

"Doc Carver says they're healthy as can be," Mrs. Andrews insisted.

"So what's she going to name them?"

"Henrietta and Harriet."

Mrs. Green paused and stared at her friend for a moment, then pleaded, "Oh, Irma, tell me you are joking, please."

Mrs. Andrews shook her head.

"I cannot believe she'd do that. Doesn't she realize they'll end up being called Henry and Harry? Especially with six older brothers to contend with."

"Apparently not."

"After six boys, you'd think Gertrude would be delighted to finally be able to choose two real *girls'* names—something all feminine and flowery, like Rose and Lily . . . or Violet and Iris . . . or Daisy and Petunia . . . or even Pansy and Buttercup!"

"It just goes to show, Susannah," Mrs. Andrews pronounced, pressing her lips together with disapproval, "there's no accounting for taste."

Brent was trying to pass among the ladies as quickly and unobtrusively as he could. Getting trapped with all these women ooh-ing and ah-ing over babies was the last thing he wanted, especially when what he really wanted was to be near Cassie.

But there he was, stuck behind Mrs. Green and Mrs. Andrews, two of the worst gossips a body could encounter. There was no way around them or through them, and he wasn't about to try climbing over them.

Then Mrs. Green's whispered gossip and snide laugh caught his attention. "You did hear that Flora Bowen's niece claimed she knew it was going to be twins all along, didn't you?"

Mrs. Andrews sniffed. "Well, they say insanity runs in that family."

"Imagine claiming to know something like that when she just arrived here and doesn't know those people from Adam or Eve." Mrs. Green snickered.

"As far as twins are concerned, well, anyone could see how fertile Gertrude is."

"I thought she was awfully big this time to be having only one."

"Anyone could have told you, after six sons, the odds were in her favor to have a girl sooner or later."

"Why, Mrs. Andrews, I thought you didn't hold with gambling," Brent said.

Mrs. Andrews puffed herself up like a rattler ready to strike him dead for daring to question her moral integrity. "I most certainly do *not*!" she declared haughtily.

Brent took advantage of their surprise and indignation to slip sideways between the ladies.

"I never thought for a moment you did, ma'am."

He nodded to each and moved quickly on, smiling and nodding to the ladies he passed as he made his way to the counter and Cassie. In spite of the wary frown Abel cast him, he sidled up beside her.

"Well, you're certainly up early to do your shopping, Miss Bowen," Brent stated boldly. "Guess you just couldn't wait to spend some of that money."

Cassie turned very slowly from Abel to him. Her bright blue eyes seemed to flash sparks of opalescent fire.

"How very contradictory you are, Mr. Conway. The other day you seemed to be encouraging me *not* to wait to sell things. Now you seem to think I *should* wait to buy things. What you can't seem to understand is that I'm not taking any of your advice regarding my finances." She smiled at him very sweetly, then turned back to Abel. "How long do you think until I can get it all delivered?"

"Usually takes about a month or two for something that big," Abel responded, scratching the back of his head.

Abel was only thirty, the same age as Brent. But while Abel still had all his hair in back, the hairline in front was receding rapidly. Trying not to look too obvious about it, Brent ran his hand across his forehead, just checking to make sure his hair was all still there where he'd last seen it in the shaving mirror earlier that morning.

"That long?" She sounded truly dismayed. Then she seemed to cheer up again. "Then I guess I'd better get started."

"Are you sure you wouldn't like to hire somebody who already owns all this expensive equipment to do your digging?"

"No. It's very important that it all belongs to me. There are certain minor changes I'll have to make in the design."

"Do you know how to do that, Miss Bowen?" Abel was clearly aghast. Brent was pretty darned surprised himself. Of all the unusual things about Cassie, he didn't think studying mechanics or engineering was among them.

Instead of answering his question, Cassie said, "I'd hate to have something happen to someone else's machinery."

Abel scratched the back of his head again. "What could go wrong?"

"Just please order all the equipment on my list, Mr. Warner. I'll have Mr. Harvey write a draft for the correct amount immediately."

Brent frowned, straining to read upside down the long list Abel held down on the table in front of him. Darn, if he would just move his index finger a little more to the right, he could see the whole thing instead of only the first two or three letters of each item.

"I'll send the order as soon as I get the draft. But, well . . . Miss Bowen, honestly now, are you sure a lady such as yourself knows how to work all those mechanical contraptions? Even if you do, you're a lady. You're just not strong enough."

"I'll learn to do it. Or I'll hire someone else who can."

"Whatever you say, miss," Abel responded.

Brent chuckled. "Yes, indeed. Stubborn. Independent. You're becoming more and more like your aunt the longer you live in that house."

"Thank you, Mr. Conway. How very kind of you to say so."

She turned back to Abel. Not only was she stubborn and independent, the woman had a single-mindedness of purpose that was hidden very well by that softly curved body.

"Say, Brent, I'll thank you not to be annoying my customers," Abel said.

"I've got every right to speak politely to Miss Bowen, Abel," Brent protested. "I live right next door to her."

"I don't care if you live next door to the Queen of England, the King of France, and the Czar of all the Russias. I won't have you bothering cash-paying customers in my store."

Brent watched Cassie turn from him to Abel and back again as they spoke. She was intelligent. She couldn't have missed the animosity August Harvey had shown him at Miss Flora's funeral. She certainly couldn't miss the fact that Abel evidently didn't care a hill of beans for him, either.

"Yeah, Abel. I know what great store you set by your cash."

He backed away from the counter a step or two. He hadn't finished conversing with Cassie yet, but it was pretty obvious Abel was done with him.

"Thank you for taking care of this for me, Mr. Warner," Cassie said. "It's going to be a pleasure doing business with you."

Abel nodded. "Whatever you say, Miss Bowen. I'll place that order for the drilling equipment right away."

"Drilling equipment?" Brent looked at her with surprise. "That house has a perfectly good well system already. Why in the world are you ordering equipment to dig a well?"

"It's a business venture," she told him.

"Are you going into the well-digging business yourself, or do you intend to try to make money selling pure, mountain spring water?" he asked with a chuckle.

"It's a business venture," she repeated.

"If you'll forgive me for saying so, this is probably just about as crazy as some of those stunts Miss Flora used to pull."

"It's not a stunt, Mr. Conway. It's business."

Her delicate brows drew down into a frown over her bright blue eyes. Her full lips compressed tightly, until they practically disappeared.

What would she do if he grabbed her up in his arms and pressed a firm kiss full on those stubbornly tense lips? Cassie would surely slap his face. Abel would throw him out of his store for sure. Boy, that would certainly give all these women something to gossip about.

But he'd feel a whole lot better.

"Digging wells is an interesting business for a lady to want to go into," Brent commented.

"You'd never believe *how* interesting," Cassie muttered, half to him and half to herself, as she turned away from the counter.

What else could she say? Brent would never believe her if she told him the truth. Nobody else would, either. At least Mr. Warner had taken her unusual order without too much fuss. She'd insist Mr. Harvey write the bank draft without giving her any arguments, either—just as Aunt Flora probably would have. After all, it was her money now, wasn't it?

Oh, why should she even think it mattered if Brent believed her or not?

Cassie tried to make her way toward the door, through the group of chattering women. As she smiled, nodded, and mumbled "excuse me" trying to get out of the crowded store, she heard Mrs. Andrews making a few grim predictions of her own.

"Mark my words, no good will come of it," the lady declared. "No one can set herself up as some sort of false prophet without calling down all sorts of justly deserved retribution on her head. She's riding for a fall, that she is. All that playing at making predictions—work of the devil, if you ask me."

"But, haven't her predictions been right?" Brent interjected.

"Making predictions is never right. There are just some things man isn't meant to know," Mrs. Andrews replied with a firm nod.

Cassie didn't even bother to excuse herself as she elbowed her way through the crowd to confront Mrs. Andrews face-to-face.

"I beg to differ with you on that issue, Mrs. Andrews," she declared as loudly as she could in order to be heard above the surrounding chatter.

Cassie had been raised to be polite. She knew she was naturally timid. She was beginning to suspect that, in some cases, she was downright subservient. But now she couldn't help but confront Mrs. Andrews.

She didn't need Sebastian to show her. All on her own, she had a bad feeling in the pit of her stomach that she was going to regret this. But the honor of her aunt, of her family—her own honor—was at stake.

She wasn't about to let Brent bully his way through this for her, either. No matter how much he tried to assume the role of her self-appointed guardian, she couldn't allow him to think he had any sort of influence in her life.

"If one agrees that there are some things man wasn't meant to know," Cassie proposed, "then one must also logically agree that there are some things that man—and woman—*were* meant to know. Isn't that correct?"

Cassie sent up a silent prayer of thanks for ancient Professor Crispin Fortesque, instructor of mathematics, geometry, and logic at Mrs. Harmander's Academy for Young Ladies in Philadelphia. Professor Fortesque had maintained that ladies in a new and growing country ought to study truly useful subjects in addition to merely ornamental activities such as painting, needlework, and dancing.

"Yes. No," Mrs. Andrews quickly amended. "There's a difference. I wouldn't expect someone like you to understand."

"I might. Please explain it to me. What sort of difference?"

"Well . . . ," Mrs. Andrews intoned slowly, long and drawn-out, as if she needed time to gather her thoughts but didn't want to say nothing, as if silence would only accentuate her ignorance. "God shows us what he wants us to know."

"I'll agree to that."

Mrs. Andrews raised her eyebrows. Obviously the lady was shocked to find Cassie was not among the completely unregenerate heathens that showed up at her church from time to time just to test her patience.

"And God doesn't tell us what he doesn't want us to know."

"I certainly won't argue with you there, either."

Mrs. Andrews's eyebrows rose even higher.

Cassie wasn't sure Sebastian's visions came from God, considering the tempting and decidedly earthy nature of some of the things she'd seen. On the other hand, Reverend Markham had preached last Sunday that the Lord worked in mysterious ways.

"But what sorts of things are we supposed to know and not know?" Cassie persisted.

She spared a brief glance at Brent. He stood leaning against a shelf, resting his crossed arms over his broad chest. He was grinning at her, eyebrows raised expectantly, as if he were silently goading her on. Oh, why would she even care if Brent supported her on this doomed foray?

"Well . . . well, I don't know what we're not supposed to know, because I'm not supposed to know it, so I don't," Mrs. Andrews stated. "But I do know what I am supposed to know about."

"Such as, perhaps, the United States?" Cassie offered. "The entire Western Hemisphere?"

"What do you mean? Of course I know about the United States—*and* the Western Hemo . . . Hema . . . the Western part."

"Did George Washington know?"

"Of course he knew. He was our first president. Oh, now you're just being silly for the sake of argument."

"Did King George the First know? Did Queen Elizabeth?" Cassie gave silent thanks also for corpulent Professor Alvin Godwin, instructor of history at Mrs. Harmander's Academy, who had maintained that in order for a young country to know where it was headed, its people needed to know the history and traditions they'd come from. "Did Richard the Lion-Hearted know? Or Alfred the Great?"

"Of course not! Now you really are being ridiculous." Mrs. Andrews's eyebrows rose higher. She lifted her chin and looked down her nose at Cassie. "Those people died long before. How could they possibly know?"

"Do you suppose God didn't want those illustrious rulers to know that someday there'd be our wonderful, free, and democratic nation?"

"What are you trying to prove with your silly examples?" Mrs. Andrews countered. She clutched her purse more tightly under her bosom, as if everything she cherished was contained therein, and she wasn't about to let anyone steal it from her.

"Well, nobody knew anything about North or South America until after fourteen ninety-two, did they?"

"No," Mrs. Andrews slowly agreed.

"But all this was here nonetheless, wasn't it?" When Mrs. Andrews didn't respond, Cassie added, "I mean, it wasn't as if an entire half of the earth—people, plants and animals, and gigantic, ancient temples of stone—materialized out of nowhere, was it?"

It took an irate Mrs. Andrews a long time to answer. "Well, I suppose not."

"What about the United States?" Cassie pressed her advantage. "The United States of America didn't exist until seventeen seventy-six, did it?"

"No," Mrs. Andrews answered more quietly, as if some of the wind had gone out of her sails.

"So, wouldn't you logically suppose there are some things we don't know about until the time is right for us to find out about it, or for it to come to pass?"

"Well, you may think that if it pleases you to be wrong."

Mrs. Andrews snorted and turned away muttering, "Work of the devil, if you ask me."

"You may think I'm wrong until the time is right for you to discover otherwise," Cassie called after her opponent's retreating figure.

Cassie was appalled at her own behavior! What in the world was happening to her? Was it the confidence that having a lot of money brought? Was it the assurance that Sebastian showed her what was going to happen, and that he always showed her the truth? Was it the fact that Brent had been quietly supporting her, even at a distance? Whatever it was, however appalling her behavior, she was beginning to feel good about it.

She held her head high, a triumphant smile on her face. The other ladies all backed up, making a path for her as she headed out of Abel Warner's store. She had to get out of there quickly, before all her newfound confidence drained away.

As she passed Brent, she saw the strange look on his face. Why should he look at her strangely now when he'd been supporting her all along? Or had he?

He looked shocked that she'd confronted Mrs. Andrews like that. She didn't blame him. She was pretty surprised herself.

He looked at her with worshipful admiration, as if she'd just done something that he, and most of the people in Lyman's Gap, had been wanting to do for some time now, and had never been able to summon up the nerve.

He also looked astounded that she should have the intellect to reason Mrs. Andrews out of her self-satisfied complacency. She was more than slightly perturbed about that. Did he think she should stay home and bake cookies instead of reading and using the brain God gave her?

She knew Brent followed her out of the store. She was grateful for the way he'd initially tried to defend her, even if she knew he thought she was crazy, too. But she'd said enough. She didn't feel like talking anymore, not to him, not to anyone.

Obviously Brent had other ideas. "Well, you certainly gave Mrs. Andrews a stern dressing-down back there. One she's been needing for a long time." He chuckled as he followed her up the sidewalk.

Cassie remained silent.

"You know, you've changed a lot from the first day I met you," he told her. "Maybe those silly ideas of yours about feminine independence are really taking effect."

Cassie could find nothing to say.

"I think you inherited a certain measure of Miss Flora's intrepid nature," he continued, obviously undaunted by her pensive silence. "Even though you may have hidden it very well all this time."

She still made no response.

"I wonder if you've inherited her shrewdness and uncanny second sight about doing business, too. Her eyes had a certain wary watchfulness though. Maybe you could even call it a certain world-weariness."

He spoke as if he were actually thinking out loud.

"But you know, it's strange. No matter how outlandish Miss Flora's schemes sounded, in the end they always seemed to work out to her advantage."

He gave a little chuckle.

"You know, there are moments when I see you becoming as bold and independent as Miss Flora. Except you don't have that weariness in your eyes yet."

Not yet, Cassie thought morosely. But how much longer, how many more visions from Sebastian would it take?

"Yes indeed, I suppose you could do worse than to turn out like her."

Cassie stopped abruptly in the middle of the sidewalk and turned to face Brent. Her head felt so heavy with hurt and worry that she couldn't help but draw her eyebrows down into a frown.

"I know people talked about my aunt that way, Mr. Conway. But did people talk *to* my aunt that way?"

"No, of course not." He seemed surprised that she should even ask. "People showed Miss Flora respect for her age and tolerance for her . . . for her . . . advanced age."

"Don't you mean tolerance for her deteriorating mental faculties?"

Brent glanced uneasily up and down the street and kicked at the dust on the sidewalk. He didn't answer her.

"That's what I thought," Cassie remarked. She turned to head home. "At least your silence is honest."

"Wait, Miss Bowen. You see, Miss Flora lived in Lyman's Gap for almost ten years," he explained as he caught up to her. "People were used to her. Give them a little time, and they'll get used to your . . . eccentricities, too."

"So, if I live here long enough, they won't mind that I'm crazy? Oh, that's encouraging," Cassie muttered as she plodded along.

"Crazy. Crazy. Crazy lady," the ragged, red-haired boy chanted as he followed after her in the middle of the road. "Crazy lady livin' in the crazy ol' lady's house."

She recognized Lemuel Hopkins, red-haired and freckle-faced, the big, fat, dirty cheater from the creek-jumping contest.

Lem pranced and gamboled about in the middle of the street, zigzagging, advancing and retreating. He crossed his eyes and let his tongue waggle out of his mouth. He twirled his fingers around in little circles at his temples.

It was easy to see why the other boys didn't like him. At this point, Cassie wasn't too fond of him herself.

"Sayin' crazy things. Doin' crazy things. Watch out they don't lock you up in a madhouse, crazy lady."

"Hey, kid, you can't talk to a lady that way!" Brent commanded. "Go on. Get out of here!"

"You can't make me." He poked out his tongue. "My pa's bigger'n you, and he'll whup you good."

"More than likely your pa'll switch you good."

"Ha! My ol' man don't care. He think's she's crazy, too."

Cassie hadn't met Lem's pa, but she doubted Lem had seen Brent hauling around heavy objects, as he had her trunk when she'd first arrived. She was grateful for his strength, even though at this moment she didn't need any protection from physical harm. At least, she didn't think she did. Wouldn't Sebastian have warned her?

She was even grateful, for once, that Brent tried to take the situation in hand. She supposed, in spite of any wealth or longed-for freedom, sometimes even an independent lady needed a gentleman to assist her.

Cassie kept walking away from the wretched urchin, hoping that pretty soon he'd tire of his shenanigans here and go find some flies to pluck the wings off, a nice barn to set on fire, or some other activity in keeping with his vile, detestable personality.

But Lem kept following her, taunting her.

"Hey, be a little more respectful of a lady," Brent growled.

"Can't respect no crazy lady." Lem skittered back and forth, complete with accompanying gestures, chanting, "Crazy lady. Crazy lady. Talkin' crazy, crazy lady."

Then Cassie remembered where else she'd seen Lem before—in Sebastian, running up the church steps and breaking his arm. Now she understood why no one had been hurt at their game the other day.

She supposed she'd been correct about the time having to be right for some things to transpire. She also supposed that some people simply had to learn the hard way.

She stopped, stared Lem straight in the eye, and pointed an unwavering finger at him, exactly the way she'd seen Aunt Flora do. Lem lurched to a stop in the middle of his prancing and took two steps backward.

"If I were you," Cassie said very slowly, in the deepest, most haunting whisper she could summon, "I'd be very, very careful about who I addressed in such a rude manner. If I were you, I'd be especially careful not to be so disrespectful that I'd go running up the church steps anymore." She turned to walk away.

Things were extremely quiet for about thirty seconds.

"You can't scare me!" Lem challenged, even more loudly than before. "You're just a crazy lady who don't know beans. Crazy lady!"

He started skipping about in ever-widening circles. He switched to running back and forth in the street. Then he headed for the church.

"No! Stop!" Cassie cried. She reached out, as if she could grab the boy and snatch him back from imminent danger. "Stop! I didn't mean it!"

"Crazy lady, I ain't afraid of you at all!"

Cassie couldn't watch. She'd already seen it once before, and it wasn't pleasant. She didn't want to have to watch it again. Still, the sounds accompanied her memory.

The *thunk* as the scuffed toe of Lem's shoe caught under the tread of the bottom step of the church. The scrape as he sprawled headfirst up the stairs. His left elbow landed with a sickening *crunch*.

"Ow!" Lem set up a howl that brought the ladies flooding out of Warner's General Store and Reverend Markham peeking out of the door of his church.

"Someone go get Doc Carver," Mrs. Green ordered.

"Owowow!" Lem wailed, good and loud—and almost convincingly. But Cassie watched him as his eyes darted about through squinted lids to see who came to sympathize with him.

"Hush up, son," Reverend Markham advised, kneeling at the boy's side. "It isn't as if you haven't been warned about running up and down those steps. Now you're just going to have to bear with patience and long-suffering what you've been begging for all along."

Cassie had to admire Reverend Markham for never missing an opportunity to deliver a well-timed sermon. Obviously Lem had miscalculated the level of sympathy of this group.

Still concerned, Cassie tried to mingle with the crowd, lingering inconspicuously at the back.

At last Doc Carver arrived. He set his black bag down in the grass beside the church steps and knelt to the other side of the boy.

"Well, what have we here?" Doc bent over, examining Lem's crooked arm with skilled fingers.

"She did it!" Lem exclaimed, pointing with his good hand at Cassie. "Ow!"

"I see." Doc glanced back at her.

Cassie could imagine the villagers grabbing torches, chanting "Burn the witch!" and setting up a funeral pyre for her in the town square. Could she count on Brent to protect her from all of them?

"Hmm," Doc mumbled. "So, that little lady hit you and knocked down a big, strong fellow like you, eh?"

"Well, no. Ow!"

"Oh, I see. She pushed you so hard you flew clear across the road from Warner's store to land on the church steps and broke that arm, eh?"

" 'Course not! Ow!"

"Didn't think so." Doc rummaged through his bag.

Cassie breathed a sigh of relief.

"But she did it anyhow. Ow!" Lem insisted.

"That so?" Doc gave the boy a dose of paregoric. He looked up and scanned the crowd. "Can I get someone here to give me a hand carrying this poor, beleaguered fellow to my office?"

"I can walk!" Lem insisted. "I ain't no baby, and I don't need no help from nobody."

He struggled to rise while holding his injured arm with the other. He teetered and plopped back down on his bottom on the step.

"C'mon, tough guy." In spite of the boy's increasingly feeble protests, Brent scooped him up gently and carried him to Doc Carver's office.

After all the commotion had settled down, Cassie plodded along the side of the road. Silently she studied the dirt and pebbles she was about to tread on. Walking around this way was getting to be a habit—one she'd just as soon break.

She could feel Brent's gaze occasionally resting upon her as he walked beside her. She was glad that he didn't insist on making idle chatter, but she was grateful for his presence nonetheless.

She couldn't bear the thought of having company or being in a crowd. Neither could she bear the thought of being completely alone. There were so many problems clamoring to be pondered, so many unsettling occurrences intruding into what had once been her normal, harmless, and usually pleasant, day-to-day thoughts—until she'd arrived here. She didn't want to be troubled by any of them.

Well, she consoled herself, Brent certainly had the ability to distract her. On the other hand, he also presented her with an entire set of problems all his own.

As they neared the front walk of his house, Cassie slowed. She didn't want to be too bold and ask him to stay with her. It was bad enough he thought she was a crazy lady. She didn't want him to think she was a woman of loose morals, too.

"Thank you for walking me this far, Mr. Conway."

"I'll walk with you the rest of the way, too," he offered.

"I wouldn't want to impose." Could he tell how halfhearted her protest was? she wondered. "I mean, it isn't as if we'd been on an outing together and you're responsible for escorting me safely home."

Brent chuckled. "It's not as if there are wild Indians or ravenous wolves prowling around in the woods anymore, either, ready to slaughter you before you travel the additional distance to your house. But I'd still feel better if you let me accompany you—at least to your front steps."

Considering the way Brent had been intruding into her life, Cassie wasn't surprised that he'd volunteered so readily and so insistently. For once she was glad of it. They continued on to her front walk.

"I'm sorry I haven't been much for conversation."

"Between Lem and Mrs. Andrews, I figured you might have run out of things to say to me."

"I feel so bad about what happened to that boy."

Brent lifted his hand, as if to place it on her shoulder in a comforting gesture, but he stopped and let his hand drop to his side. They'd climbed the short flight of steps and now stood on the brink of the privacy of her own front door. Oh, for once she wished he'd be bold enough to invite himself in.

"For a long time now, those kids have been making a game out of running up and down the front steps of the church, and annoying the bejeepers out of Reverend Markham. Every one of them was begging to get hurt sooner or later."

She knew he was trying to console her. But mere words weren't the same as if he'd touched her shoulder or held her hand—merely in a comforting gesture, of course. She appreciated his effort nonetheless.

"Just between you and me, it might as well have been Lem as anybody else. That kid has always been mean to the others. I'm surprised they haven't all ganged up on him and whaled the living tar out of him by now."

"He's mighty sassy to the grown-ups, too," Cassie remarked.

"I never figured the little vermin would pester you. But, well, it appears to me as if somebody else was out to get him, too." He raised his eyes heavenward. "Yes, indeed, if you ask me, the rotten kid got exactly what he deserved."

"I suppose so."

"Golly, even Reverend Markham seemed to think so, and who's going to argue with him?"

"I really didn't cause it to happen, did I? I mean, I was only trying to warn him."

"You? Cause it?" He rubbed his hand over his mouth in a feeble effort to hide his laugh. "Oh, now, pretty lady, if you think that, you're getting to be as eccentric as your aunt was."

"Do you think that's it?" Believing what one saw—goodness, just *seeing things*—in a crystal ball would certainly be considered eccentric in some segments of society, and considerably worse in others. "It's just being eccentric? That's all?"

"Of course. What else could it be?"

Cassie didn't dare answer that question.

"You had a long, tiring trip for a lady traveling all alone. It was a terrible shock when Miss Flora passed away almost immediately after your arrival. Frankly, I was surprised you didn't faint right away or take to your bed with the vapors."

She was glad to hear someone agreeing that she'd been through—and was still going through—a very trying time.

"It's annoying enough to have a kid as mean as Lem pester you." He pressed his lips together and shook his head. "And that Irma Andrews, she's always been such a conceited, self-righteous, pretentious—"

"I *hated* to have to do that," Cassie confessed. "I don't like to make enemies. I hate to argue."

"You certainly fooled me."

"I'm no good at it."

He rubbed his chin with mock pensiveness. "Hmm. Fooled me there, too."

"In my entire life, I've never raised my voice in anger to another human being, not even to my brother on the few occasions when we argued as children. But I shouted at her in public, in front of so many people."

She shook her head in dismay. She could feel the tears brimming on the edges of her eyelashes. Any moment now the first drop would fall. Once the tears began, she knew she wouldn't be able to stop them. "I was brought up to respect my elders."

"Irma Andrews isn't that much older than you. At least, that's what she claims," he added with a chuckle. "She's just all wrinkled from holding her face pinched up for so long."

Brent screwed his face in imitation. The best Cassie could manage was a tiny laugh. That small laugh was enough to open a chink in the damn that had been holding back all her tightly repressed emotions. All the wrong ones came flooding out.

The memory of the boy's taunting and the woman's cruel accusation that she, her beloved aunt, and all her female ancestors had been doing the work of the devil, was the last straw.

Tears spilled out and she didn't bother to hold them back. She longed to rest her weary head on Brent's strong shoulder and find some comfort there.

"I hate to cry in front of strangers," she mumbled.

"I'm not a stranger." Brent wrapped his arms around her and held her gently to him.

His tenderness touched her. He was strong and solid. For the first time since she'd left Philadelphia, she felt safe.

"We're neighbors. I hope we're friends, Cassie."

She had spent so much time in his presence. Sebastian had shown her such intimate visions of them together. Cassie had to admit she really couldn't consider Brent a stranger any longer.

Through her sobs, she tried to explain. "You see, I think I understand how it works now, although that doesn't seem to make it any easier."

"How what works?"

"I can't tell you."

She sniffed loudly. How could he ever understand unless he witnessed it himself? She doubted he would see in Sebastian what she saw. After all, *he* wasn't the one who was cursed. It didn't matter. She couldn't allow anyone to see Sebastian anyway.

"Ordinary conversation doesn't seem to be a problem. No one denounced me for a brazen liar when I told them I came from Philadelphia. Everyone believes me if I tell them my dress is blue, or if I say I'd like to have peas and carrots with my dinner."

"What in thunderation are you talking about?"

"I can't tell you," she repeated, still sobbing.

He didn't ask again.

"Nobody believes a word of what I predict. They ridicule me. They call me crazy. Then, after those things really happen, everyone admires my foresight. Everyone thinks how clever or how lucky I am. The only trouble is, they still remember that I'm crazy Flora Bowen's niece and suspect I'm crazy, too. They never take a word I say seriously—and they never will."

The front of Brent's jacket was soaked with her tears. Pieces of lint stuck to her nose and lashes. She pulled away from him and rubbed her face with the back of her hand, but it didn't seem to help. She fumbled around in her purse for her elusive handkerchief.

Brent readily pulled his big white square from his pocket and handed it to her.

"You don't think what I do is the work of the devil, do you?" She wiped away her tears with the handkerchief. She held it to her nose, lingering to breathe in more of the scent of him—bay rum and tobacco. Soothing, comforting scents.

"You? Not you. You're—" He drew in a deep gulp of air, and let out on a breath, "You're an angel. The most beautiful woman I've ever laid eyes on."

She wasn't crying anymore, but he drew her closer to him in the shelter of the porch.

"Gracious! We're right out in view of the neighbors," she protested feebly. Nevertheless, she didn't pull away from him.

"I'm your only neighbor," Brent pointed out to her.

"Someone could come walking by."

"Since this dirt road that people generously refer to as Elm Street stops at the end of your property, there's very little chance that anyone will actually come this way."

"Still—"

"Not to mention that your front porch is fairly secluded under the overhanging branches of the rosebushes."

She knew she ought to offer a further modest, maidenly resistance. But after watching the images of Brent and herself in Sebastian for so long, she'd been able to imagine what it felt like to be held by him. She'd been so busy crying, she'd almost missed the wonderful sensation in reality. She wanted to pay attention this time. She needed to savor every moment of his tender strength.

He smelled good. Soap and coffee. He felt good on the outside, like a well-worn, comfortable, cuddly jacket she wanted to wrap herself in. He felt good all the way through. Strong and muscular.

She nestled her cheek into the fabric of his lapel. She felt his chest moving up and down with his rhythmic breathing. She heard his strong heart pounding in his chest. She closed her eyes and relished the feel of his arms around her.

"The very first time I saw you at the train station," he murmured into her hair, "standing there on the platform with what little baggage you had piled beside you, looking all lost and bewildered, I thought you were the most beautiful woman I'd ever seen."

He reached up and tucked his crooked finger under her chin. His hand was warm. His touch was tender and caring. He lifted her face to his.

"You were so shy when I first met you. As I recall, I did most of the talking. You just made a few brief, polite responses and never ventured a comment of your own the entire trip to Lyman's Gap."

"There really wasn't much to tell you. My life was very uneventful—until I arrived here."

His callused fingers brushed roughly against the side of her face, arousing her heightened sensitivity. Her throat constricted. She opened her mouth to draw in a gasping breath.

With his thumb, he brushed away one last, lingering tear that dampened her cheek. "Your eyes are so blue, like the sky on a summer day. Your cheeks are so soft."

His hand returned to support her chin. Slowly he lowered his lips to hers. It was just a brief, gentle kiss. He pulled back almost immediately. Cassie felt as if her lips and soul had been seared by the quickest spark of lightning.

Until now, her life had been so cold. He engendered warmth, heat, passion—all those things she'd never felt in her life, or in her heart. She wanted—needed—more of him. So much more.

She gazed up at him. She couldn't ask. She had her pride. She had her self-respect. But, oh, she wanted him!

As if he read through her eyes the desire in her heart, Brent brought his lips down upon hers again. This time he pulled her close against him and pressed her lips with heated passion. He kissed her cheeks and trailed warming kisses down her neck.

Her breasts tingled with the feel of him so close. She

reached her arms up, entwining her fingers in his dark hair, and pulled him closer to her. She closed her eyes and drank in the warm, masculine smell of him. She savored the press of his hard body against hers.

She smiled through his kisses. She felt as if she were swirling around with joy. The visions Sebastian had shown her were coming true.

No, they weren't. She and Brent were fully dressed. They weren't in a bedroom. They were on her front porch in full view of anyone passing by—regardless of the rosebushes.

She needed to touch his bare skin, in more places than just his cheeks and rugged jaw. She needed him to caress not only her chin and throat, but the entire length of her body. She wanted to feel every inch of him, and she wanted him to know every secret part of her.

It *would* happen. She was sure of it now. There was so much more of this to come.

Was she ready for any of it? No more than she'd been ready for her aunt's death, or Sebastian's visions, or all the other incredible things that had happened to her since then.

She barely knew Brent Conway. What she knew of him by reputation wasn't very savory. Yet what she knew of him from personal experience she found caring and tender. He was a man driven by ambition, but not entirely ruthless—not at all the scoundrel people made him out to be. There were times when he irritated her. But there were other times when he'd protected and defended her. He couldn't be all bad.

She knew that events unfolded as they must. But if she could she had to make things proceed a little more slowly. She simply wasn't ready for all this to happen so soon.

"Brent, no." Cassie pulled away from his embrace. "Wait."

"Oh, Cassie." He held her tightly, continued to kiss her passionately.

She pushed away more forcefully. He unlocked his arms immediately, freeing her. He stepped back a pace or two, his arms still extended, as if he were trying to assure her he wouldn't hold her to him if she needed to be free.

"Oh, Cassie. Miss Bowen," he quickly corrected.

He tugged at the collar of his shirt and reached up to wipe beads of perspiration from his forehead. Cassie could feel her own hair, trapped in tiny ringlets stuck to the back of her neck. She longed for a breeze to cool her fevered emotions and she longed to hold Brent once again to her aching breasts.

He spoke so rapidly, Cassie could hardly still her own spinning head and twirling thoughts enough to make sense of his words.

"I didn't mean to get carried away like that."

He tugged his jacket back into place and straightened his skewed lapels.

"Well, actually, yes, I did. I know what Miss Flora . . . what other people have told you about me. I'm not like that. Not really. Not to you. I meant no disrespect. I'd never want to hurt you. But . . ."

He turned his back to her, tugged at his belt and the top of his trousers, then faced her again. He took a deep breath. His speech slowed to normal. The fire remained in his eyes.

"I've been wanting to do that since I first laid eyes on you. But I didn't mean to insult you. I don't want you, of all people, to think I'm a scoundrel. I won't do that again—unless you want me to."

He strode quickly down the front steps. He was already halfway across the lawn, heading toward his own house, before Cassie could regain her voice enough to whisper, "I do want you, Brent. Oh, I do."

In the darkness, Cassie sat on the edge of her bed. She gazed into Sebastian—smiling, waiting for the vivid visions of pleasure she knew were sure to come. Visions of Brent and her that didn't seem so far-fetched now that they had begun to come true. She was looking forward to it all.

Slowly the moonlight swirled inside the crystal, arching up and around, breaking into rainbow sparkles that turned into parts of images, that coalesced into complete pictures.

Brent. Naked, virile, ready. Yes. She waited for more.

Herself. Naked, pliant, willing. Yes. She longed for more.

The images of Brent and her faded.

"No, wait. Bring them back," she pleaded, reaching out, yet afraid to touch Sebastian while images still formed inside him.

The figure of a tall, gaunt man took shape inside Sebastian.

"Who in the world is he?" Cassie demanded with surprise and just a little indignation. "What is *he* doing in my private world?"

She leaned closer to Sebastian, the better to see what he was showing her. Maybe if she picked him up and shook him, he'd return to the first, far more pleasing image.

The man wore a black suit and a tall, stovepipe hat. His rugged face, with its prominent chin and cheekbones, looked as if it had been chiseled out of the side of a mountain, and not with too refined a tool, either. He had enormous ears, a broad forehead, and a large mole to the right side of his nose.

Cassie, studying the image, frowned. For some unaccountable reason, she felt he'd look better if he grew a beard. Merely a matter of taste, she supposed. Not a big, bushy one complete with mustache. Just a little something around his rugged jaw and chin.

But his dark eyes were what struck her most. Never before had she seen eyes filled with such compassion—or such sorrow. Who was he? Where did he come from? What could make such a man so grief-stricken?

What an extraordinary man to lead this country! Cassie blinked and frowned harder at Sebastian. There was no doubt in her mind. Sebastian showed her with complete certainty that this man was going to be president of the United States at a time when the country needed him most.

Then Sebastian proceeded to show her exactly why.

Cassie awoke the next morning, still wiping the tears from her eyes. She was amazed that she'd been able to sleep at all, except from sheer emotional exhaustion.

Sebastian sat on her night table, where she'd left him. Trembling, she slid away from him, across the pillow still damp from her tears, across the sheets rumpled by her desperate tossing and turning.

Slowly and deliberately, she got out of the big bed on the other side. She didn't care what anyone had ever told her about not getting out on the wrong side of the bed. Whatever else happened to her today, or for the rest of her life, couldn't possibly be as bad as what she'd seen last night. Whatever bad mood she might wind up in paled in comparison to the wretched anguish she now felt.

She didn't want to be anywhere near Sebastian and risk having him show her more heartbreaking visions.

Shaking, she made her way to the mirror to confront her white-faced reflection. Red-rimmed, bloodshot, dark-circled eyes stared back at her. Her nose was pink, her upper lip swollen from crying through the night.

With the distance across the room serving as a safe barrier, Cassie turned and confronted Sebastian.

"You cruel, horrible, monstrous thing," she accused in a hoarse whisper. "I ought to lock you in your bag and never open it again. I'd like to weight you with rocks, throw you in the river, and hope you sink to the bottom, never to be retrieved in a million years, so you could never hurt anybody ever again. But I don't even want to touch you."

With the back of her hand, she wiped away tears she still couldn't control.

"I hate you. I hate the pictures you show me. I ought to throw you in the trash," she threatened. "Except when they're good, your visions are so compelling. Are you the thing in the curse that I can't afford to lose, just as Aunt Flora predicted? How can I lose you and still keep the curse? I'm so confused."

She hung her head in her hands.

"How dare you show me such terrible things! Terrible is too mild a word for it. All those men—bleeding, maimed, starving, dying, unburied. Women and children, too. So sick, so hungry. Beautiful brick and white cities in ruins and ashes. The dead, men and horses, lying bloated and unburied all around. The land runs with blood and reeks of death."

Cassie paced back and forth across her bedroom carpet, still maintaining a safe distance from the disturbing crystal ball.

"Oh, you were such a clever scoundrel at first, luring me in with tantalizing visions of Brent and me in situations I could hardly resist. You tricked me. I see now why you're a curse. You played away my initial misgivings with cute, funny images of fat, squirming piglets, and happy images of long-awaited twin girls. I didn't even feel too bad when that ornery Lem broke his arm. After all, Doc Carver said it wasn't a serious break and, after a while, it would be as good as new."

She swung angrily and faced Sebastian, still sitting serenely on her night stand, as if he hadn't heard a word she'd said, or didn't care. Emboldened by his lack of response, and exhausted from a sleepless night, she plopped down on the edge of her bed and glared at him.

"I don't know why Aunt Flora seemed so fond of you, you wretched, overrated piece of rock. I hate you! I hate you!"

She felt the urge to drum her heels against the side of the bed and beat her fists against the mattress, but that seemed so incredibly childish. She felt as if she'd been forced to grow ancient and wise overnight, and yet she still felt so ignorant and powerless. She sat motionless and glared at Sebastian.

"Why am I wasting my breath telling you this when you probably already know it all anyway?"

Sebastian did nothing.

"Why did you pick *me* as the victim of your miserable visions? I'll bet you never showed Aunt Flora anything that horrible, did you? That's why she could be so cheerful handing you over to me. I'll bet you never showed Great-Aunt Charlotte, or Great-Great-Aunt Prudence, or—"

Light glowed and swirled within Sebastian.

"No! I won't let you put me through that again!"

Cassie raised her hands to cover her eyes. She couldn't bear to see any more. Her hands stopped halfway, resting on her cheeks instead. She was spellbound—compelled to watch what Sebastian showed her. She was powerless to turn away.

The images flowed. Soldiers in red coats, in coats of blue and buckskin; bewigged cavaliers and crop-haired Puritans; knights in shining armor on caparisoned chargers passed before her eyes. Battered, bloody, starving, dying. Women and children, too. Cities of wood and great stone castles reduced to ruins and ashes. The lands ran red with blood and reeked of death.

"That's not the future," Cassie protested, but weakly. She poked at the images inside the crystal ball. "I know. I studied all those things with Professor Godwin."

Then, in a whisper, as realization dawned on her, she continued, "But it was the future when you showed it to Great-Aunt Hester and Great-Great-Aunt Rosamunde. When you showed it to each of them in turn, wasn't it?"

The scenes in Sebastian changed. Burnt out lands grew green. New buildings arose. Men and women made love. Babies were born. Marvels appeared from the ashes.

Gradually Cassie felt her initial anger ebbing. It was replaced with a deepening sense of humility and a sepulchral chill.

She'd agreed with Mrs. Andrews that there were some things mankind was simply not supposed to know. She'd also maintained that some things had to wait for their proper time to be made known.

She'd been so smugly self-satisfied. It was easy to think how wonderful it was to know things before other people did. It was rather gratifying, in an arrogant sort of way, to know that what you said was right, especially when everyone else was wrong. And if other people didn't believe you? Well, then, the devil take them!

But last night's long, terrifying vision had been extremely humbling. Was it some sort of punishment for her pride?

She realized she had no control over Sebastian or over the images he showed her. All she did was open her mouth once too often and arrogantly say things that had no right to be said.

Wagering on piglets or horse races was one thing. She had to be very careful with what she did with her visions. She had never even considered, until now, that the future shown to her was almost a sacred trust. She had never considered that, even though people would find them out eventually, there were some things it was better *not* to know.

The fact that she knew them filled her with an indescribable sadness. She had also seen some good times to come, as well. Love, peace, and prosperity. Somehow she had to find the balance to enable her to live in the world between the two.

Aunt Flora's words echoed in her memory. "All of us Bowen women, in spite of everything, have always managed." Like all the women of the Bowen family who had suffered under this curse, she, too, would manage.

Straightening her shoulders with family pride and lifting her chin with determination, Cassie faced the crystal ball.

"And someday," she foretold, all on her own, "someone will finally believe what I predict. I'll lose something I can't afford to lose, I'll trust someone I have no reason to trust, and I'll love someone with no hope of him ever loving me in return."

She pointed her finger at Sebastian, just as Aunt Flora had done to her and as she had done to Lem, to make sure they were really paying attention.

"Someday, so that no Bowen woman will ever have to suffer like this ever again, I'll stop this ancient curse," she vowed to Sebastian. "Even if it breaks my heart."

Cassie had always placed Sebastian in his red leather bag and locked him in the cabinet. She didn't want to take the chance that Mrs. Parker or Jerusha might come by with laundry or something from the grocer's while she was out and discover Sebastian.

After what he'd shown her, she didn't want to touch him ever again. But she couldn't allow her hurt to jeopardize everything. She had to put Sebastian away.

At first she'd felt the urge to dump him unceremoniously into his bag and toss him in the cabinet. But, in the end, she'd placed him in it with all the respect she figured he was due.

"Maybe it's not easy on you, either, Sebastian," Cassie said as she carried him down the stairs, "being a crystal ball and *having* to show people such horrible sights. Maybe you don't have any control over what you show people any more than I have any control over what I see. I really ought to be more sympathetic to you. After all, I've only had you for a week or so. You've been doing this for—goodness!—four hundred years. Maybe it's not easy on you, either."

Cassie closed and locked the cabinet.

"Even if you don't give a tinker's damn about me—or any of us, I figure it's probably not a good idea to antagonize the family curse."

She patted the door, her way of politely saying so long to Sebastian until the evening.

She didn't want to leave the house. She wanted to pull the covers over her head and stay in bed all day. She didn't want to have to see or talk to anyone. She also knew that if she remained indoors, the only things that would continually come to mind were memories of Sebastian's horrible visions.

If she went out, if she kept busy, maybe she could keep her memories at bay.

She was all too aware of how haggard and disheveled she looked. She'd managed to bathe and arrange her hair. If only cucumbers were in season, she wished, but instead she dabbed cool water on her eyes and hoped that would take away the redness and swelling.

She'd even worn her brightest, yellow-and-white-striped dress with the green trim, and her straw bonnet with the fabric daisies sprinkled across the top and a bright yellow satin ribbon tied under her chin in a feeble attempt to cheer herself.

As she stepped out onto her porch, Brent called to her from across the yard.

"Good morning, my lovely neighbor."

She looked through the tangled branches of the climbing roses, trying to find him. She was surprised to see him in front of his own house, on his knees, waving a trowel overhead.

How in the world had he spotted her through the roses? He must have been waiting, watching for her. She felt a momentary wave of anxiety. The last thing she needed was to have him see her looking like this.

She was tempted to duck back into the house and lock the door behind her. If she was quick enough, maybe he'd think he was having hallucinations from working out in the hot sun too long.

But it was only the end of May, and rather cool even for this time of year. On the other hand, she was used to hot, humid Philadelphia weather. Certainly the weather in the mountains ought to seem cooler.

Yet she wanted to see Brent. His cheerfulness and tenderness were the very comfort she needed. She descended the porch steps and made her way across the lawn toward him.

"Good morning," Brent called again. "Did you decide to sleep in, you slugabed? Or did you take the extra time to make yourself look so lovely this morning? If so, it was certainly time well spent."

"I slept a little later than usual. I miss the city noises. I . . . I guess I'm still not used to the country."

"Can't abide those noisy owls and crickets, eh?"

Yes, yes. Blame it on the owls and crickets, she figured. At least *that* was a believable excuse. How could she explain to him that her crystal ball had kept her awake all night?

She came and stood over him.

"I was beginning to worry about you," Brent said. "I was thinking maybe I ought to make arrangements to check on you as I did for your aunt."

"You promised you wouldn't come peeking in my windows."

"Did I?"

"I recall I warned you not to."

"But I don't recall agreeing to anything specific."

Cassie thought a moment. By golly, he was right.

"Perhaps now would be a good time to change the subject. What are you doing here?" she asked, gazing at the plot of dirt with more interest than any mere plot of dirt had ever before inspired.

He pointed to the farthest of the freshly dug rectangles along the front wall of the house. "Well, I've got daisies over there, petunias there, marigolds there." Working his way closer, he finally pointed to the ground at his knees. "And something blue right here."

"Something blue?"

"I forget what it said on the seed packet."

"Forget-me-nots?" she suggested.

"Probably. But I forget." He chuckled. "It doesn't matter anyway. I've always liked surprises, don't you?"

"It depends on the surprise," she replied cautiously.

"Personally, I'd be real surprised if any of these actually sprout, much less bloom."

Cassie laughed just a little, a lot more than she felt like laughing. How could she not respond when Brent looked up at her like that? Almost like a little boy, eagerly seeking his favorite teacher's approval. On the other hand, Cassie decided as she stood there watching him, there wasn't anything about Brent that didn't boldly announce his total adult masculinity.

She was tempted to reach down, cradle his head under her breasts, and feel the warmth of his face against her stomach.

"What an ambitious garden."

"Oh, that's just in front of the house," he continued enthusiastically. "Out back, I've put in pole beans and a row of squash, some pumpkins, some lettuce, and radishes. *Anybody* can get radishes to grow—at least, that's what I've been told, and I'm counting on it."

"My goodness. To have gotten this much done, you must have been up at the crack of dawn."

"Not quite."

"Well, you've certainly been very busy."

"Yes. I figured I'd give myself one more try at killing off something green this summer before I give up entirely and hand the whole thing over to Olivier next year."

Was the yellow-and-white-striped dress she'd donned finally starting to do its job? Was it being outdoors in the bright sunshine instead of being cooped up indoors with Sebastian and his gloomy predictions?

Cassie suspected it was more likely to be Brent, with his stale jokes and unflagging optimism, that was making her feel so much better already. Memories of last night's horrible visions were blowing away like cobwebs in the attic caught in a freshening breeze when someone threw open a window.

The sun bathed his dark brown hair, bringing out golden highlights. His pale blue eyes, shining up at her as the corners of his eyes creased with laughter, also made her feel much better.

Never mind the fact that his shirt collar lay open, revealing the tanned, corded muscles of his throat and short wisps of hair trailing up from his chest. Never mind that he'd rolled up his shirtsleeves, revealing hairy, muscular forearms. That was enough to distract her from her morbid thoughts. Longing to see more in reality of what she'd already seen quite clearly in Sebastian was almost enough to make her forgive that horrible piece of crystal for what he'd shown her last night.

Brent laid aside his trowel and rose to his feet. He stripped off his work gloves and tossed them down to land atop the trowel. He brushed the dirt and grass from the knees of his trousers. It was pretty apparent he wasn't aware of the streak of rich brown earth smeared along his left cheek and across the bridge of his nose.

"That might help your trousers, but it's not doing a bit of good for your face," Cassie told him.

"What about my face?" Brent peered cross-eyed down at his nose. "It's served me quite well up to now. Protected me from wind, rain, and cold. Made it easier for people to recognize me. Kept my eyeballs from popping out of their sockets when I sneezed, and the bugs out of my teeth."

"No, no. It's not your face. It's the dirt coating it."

He looked so ridiculous, and at the same time so incredibly appealing. In spite of herself, Cassie giggled.

Brent brushed his hand across his face, spreading the smudge wider, and even adding a little more dirt as he went along.

"Now it's worse. Why did you even bother to wear gloves?" Cassie scolded. "You've got more dirt *in* them than *on* them."

"I guess I'm just the kind of fellow who really believes in throwing himself into his work."

"It appears to me more as if you've thrown your work onto yourself. Here, let me help."

Cassie dug her handkerchief out of her purse. She stepped closer to Brent. Tentatively she reached up and dabbed at the smudge on his cheek.

"This little handkerchief is not helping one bit," she lamented. "I'm going to have to drench you with a couple of buckets of hot, sudsy water to get you clean."

"That sounds like fun."

"I don't know why I'm doing this."

"Well, don't stop. It feels mighty good from my perspective."

Cassie could feel her face warming. Touching him had also made her insides quiver. Several other parts of her were growing warm as well.

"On the chance that none of this gardening works out," Brent said as she flicked the handkerchief across his nose, "if I'm starving in the dead of winter, can I come beg a crust of bread at your doorstep? I promise to come to the back door so as not to embarrass you in front of the neighbors."

Cassie tried not to grin as she threw him a playfully disdainful glance. "Yes, Mr. Conway, I'll deign to toss you a crust of bread. But I warn you, it'll be stale."

"Anything from your hand, my lady, will seem as nectar and ambrosia."

"Oh, you *are* the silver-tongued devil my aunt warned me about."

Before she could move her hand away, he had wrapped his large, warm hand around her fingers, trapping her hand on his cheek. He pressed her hand closer, so that her palm could feel the smooth warmth of him.

His eyes seemed to gleam a deeper blue as his gaze fixed on her. He took a step closer.

"I'll hold you to that promise about coming to the back door, too," she warned. She wanted to sound playful, but she could barely raise her voice above a whisper.

"I'll hold you to that promise of a crust of bread. Maybe something more, if I ask very politely."

"Slowly," she murmured, so softly that she feared he hadn't heard her.

"I'll ask very slowly and very politely."

"No." She slipped her hand from his. "Not 'no.' Just slowly, Brent. I know you want me. I . . . I want you, too. You know I do. But really, we barely know each other. We've got to take our time. You've got to give me time. Please. Give me time to think."

Brent tried to smile at her. Wasn't that what Evaline had

asked for? Time to think. Where was she now? he wondered, but he really didn't want to know. Cassie wasn't like Evaline. Not at all. She never could be.

"I'll give you all the time you need, Cassie," he answered.

He released her hand and backed up several paces.

"I'll tell you what," he declared in a much more cheerful tone of voice. "You look so pretty today, as if you've planned something special. I have a sneaking suspicion you're going to see that blasted lawyer again, however, and there's nothing special about him at all."

"Yes. I was so distracted by everything that happened yesterday, I forgot to tell Mr. Harvey to write a draft to pay for my drilling equipment."

Brent clenched his jaw and tried not to roll his eyes with incredulous disgust. She was so sweet, he didn't want to hurt her feelings. Maybe she'd think his grimace was directed at August, not at her.

She was also awfully stubborn once she got hold of an idea. What was in this woman's head to make her want to go digging up the ground for strange things? Why couldn't she just stay home, bake pies, do needlepoint, love her husband, and make babies?

No, no. Brent's fists clenched and relaxed at his side. *Don't rush her. Don't ridicule. Don't condescend,* he warned himself. *Don't let her suspect you think she's as crazy as her aunt or you've lost her. Then what will you do with the rest of your life? Then how lonely will you be?*

So instead Brent laughed and said, "Considering the way August likes to drone on, that ought to give me plenty of time to clean up after my gardening adventure. After he's bored you enough and you can make your escape, why don't you stop by the *Argus* office and I'll show you my newspaper."

"You sound very proud of it."

"I am. Come see it," he invited. "You'll see it's not the sordid rag some people make it out to be, and I'm not the unmitigated scoundrel they make me out to be."

Cassie nodded. "I'll be there."

• • •

"Two thousand dollars?" Mr. Harvey bellowed.

He leaned forward across his large mahogany desk and stared at her, wide-eyed. Cassie felt as if the dark paneled walls were closing in on her, and the plush, maroon velvet draperies were smothering her.

Then, more slowly, but just as incredulously, he repeated, "Two thousand dollars. What could you possibly want to buy that costs that much? You haven't had the money long enough to be able to think of something worth two thousand dollars that you'd want to buy."

Cassie sat, clenching her cotton gloves and trying not to cringe farther back into the large, leather chair. Mr. Harvey probably would have preferred to see her cowering, with her head down. She tried to keep her chin held high so she could look him straight in the eye.

"It doesn't matter what I want to buy," she asserted boldly. "It's my money. I want to spend some of it. I have every right to spend some of it."

"I have no objection to you spending any of it. I just would have expected you to be spending it in smaller quantities."

"I truly, seriously need that much in one sum, Mr. Harvey."

Slowly and rhythmically, he tapped his fingertip on the top of the desk. "In all deference to the good common sense you must have, Miss Bowen, and out of the great respect I bear for the memory of your late aunt—whose trusted advisor I was for many years, if I may remind you—I must insist you tell me why you need *that much* money all at once?"

"It's a business venture," she explained, trying very hard to keep her voice from quaking in the face of Mr. Harvey's obvious irritation. Confronting this formidable man was a good bit different from confronting crotchety, opinionated, and ultimately powerless Mrs. Andrews. "I am purchasing a small steam engine and some drilling equipment and—"

"That's what I was afraid of."

Mr. Harvey picked up a small pile of papers on his desk.

He held them out to her, but not close enough for her to actually take them and study them.

"Look, Miss Bowen, since we last spoke about that rather unusual idea of your aunt's, I've done some checking into the matter—obviously something you have not."

"Indeed I have, Mr. Harvey. Long before you did. I've got my resources, too."

"I doubt they're as reliable as mine."

Well, *he* might not think so. "Do yours always tell you the absolute truth, Mr. Harvey?"

He laid the pile of papers on his desk and glared at her over the top of them.

"Men have been extracting rock oil from surface pools in this country for many years, but never in sufficient quantities to make it profitable. Why, even now this Seneca Oil Company of Connecticut is looking into drilling a little farther to the north, around Titusville. But these are reputable businessmen who formed a reliable company, and they're still running short of money and investors from time to time. How can you expect to fund this venture entirely with your aunt's money? You'll bankrupt yourself."

"And you'll have lost your best client," she interjected.

Mr. Harvey pressed his lips together and was silent for a moment.

"Miss Bowen, none of these men have succeeded yet—and they're successful businessmen and scientists from the foremost educational institutions. They've done chemical studies of the rock oil and geological surveys of the terrain. Have you—or your reputedly reliable sources—done any of that?"

"No, not exactly."

"Don't you see what a waste this is of your time *and* money?"

He paused, as if waiting for his words to sink in. Was he expecting her to suddenly jump up, declare she'd seen the error of her ways as if she were at a Methodist camp meeting, and beg his forgiveness for her stubbornness? He'd have an awfully long wait, Cassie decided.

"Miss Bowen, why don't you just go home and bake some cookies? Or go back to Philadelphia and spend your inheritance on silk gowns, French perfume, and a trip to Europe? Why don't you try to find yourself an even wealthier—even a titled—husband, like any normal, wealthy, unmarried lady would?"

"Because." She couldn't tell him it was because her crystal ball had told her to do this. "Because I've been given some reliable advice and—"

"By whom?"

Cassie refrained from answering.

"Not that blasted Brent Conway!" Mr. Harvey thundered.

"No."

He huffed with relief. "Well, I'm certainly glad to hear that. It shows you've at least retained a modicum of the common sense you were probably born with." He shuffled some papers on his desk as if that would make him look busier and more important.

"However—"

"Now, I suggest you be a sensible little lady and put this entire silly venture—"

"I will *not* put it out of my pretty little head, Mr. Harvey," she snapped. "It is *not* a silly venture."

She leaned forward in her chair, tapping her fingertip on the top of his desk just as he had, rhythmically but much faster. If he wanted to indicate to her how angry he was with her foolishness, she could certainly go him one better, showing him how angry she was with his foolish belief that he had any power over her.

"It's *my* money, and I will buy what I wish with it. Your job, as my attorney, is to write the bank draft for me."

"My job as your attorney is also to advise you not to—and even prevent you, if need be, from doing something foolish that you'll only regret later."

She shook her head. "This is not foolish. I will not regret doing this. It's just going to take some time to show results and profits."

After all, she knew things happened when they were supposed to. Mr. Harvey didn't have the certainty that Sebastian gave.

"Now, please be so good as to write me the draft . . . and spare me the sermon."

"I will *not*!" He rose, slamming his fist emphatically on his desk.

Cassie rose, too. She didn't think she was up to duplicating his gesture. If he expected her to be frightened by his pounding, if he expected her to burst into tears and immediately comply with his commands—well, he certainly had another think coming. She'd been through far worse last night than his petty ranting.

Very calmly she raised her chin so she could glare at him haughtily. "If you will not, I'll find someone who will."

"I repeat, most emphatically, I will *not*."

"Then, Mr. Harvey, as of this moment you may consider yourself no longer on my retainer."

"What?"

He slammed both hands, palms down, on his desk. Loose papers fluttered out on the gust and drifted down to the floor. He looked up at her, not with an expression of injured masculine pride and frustrated business acumen. He looked more as if she had just dropped an anvil on his toe.

"You can't!"

"Yes. I can." Her eyebrows shot up with surprise. "As a matter of fact, I believe I just did. Or were you so absorbed in your own self-importance that you weren't paying attention?"

"But . . . but I've been your aunt's advisor for years."

"You *were* my aunt's advisor," she stressed. "And I'm certain you always did precisely what she requested."

"Of course. But she always listened to my advice."

"And then I'm sure she went ahead and did exactly what she'd intended to do all along and made you comply."

Mr. Harvey grimaced but said nothing. Obviously Cassie had guessed right.

"Then do not believe for one second, Mr. Harvey, that just because I'm not as old as my aunt was, and don't have her vast range of experience, that I don't know exactly what I want. Or that I'm any less determined to get it—any way I can."

She headed toward the door.

"Miss Bowen, I counseled you once not to make any hasty decisions. Why don't you go home, make yourself a nice, soothing pot of tea, and calmly reconsider this move? Then I'm sure you'll see your mistake—"

She turned and stared at him steadily.

"There *is* no mistake," she corrected. "I've made up my mind, Mr. Harvey. There's nothing you can do or say to dissuade me. I also suggest you go home and calmly reconsider *your* mistake in trying to treat an educated, intelligent, grown woman like an obtuse child."

As she seized the knob, Cassie looked at the window in the door. The name August Harvey, Esq., was painted in large, black letters on the frosted glass, but it read backward. She felt as if it suited him, all backward thinking, at least as far as she was concerned. She opened the door.

"Then you'll have to suffer the consequences of your actions," he warned her.

"I am prepared for that—far better than you think I am. If you can't give me what I need, I'll find someone else who can. If I can't find someone else, I'll do it myself."

"You can try, Miss Bowen," Mr. Harvey said. His voice sounded as if he was endeavoring to regain some of his former self-importance.

He settled himself into his enormous, brown leather chair. He leaned back and crossed his arms over his chest.

"There's no one else in this town—not Mr. Andrews at the bank, not even Mr. McAlister at the mine—who knows as much about investing as I do."

"You weren't born knowing all that. If you could learn it, so can I." Cassie wished she truly felt as confident of her abilities as she sounded.

He laughed. "Just as you intend to learn how to use all that complicated mechanical equipment?" He laughed again. It seemed to Cassie as if he was actually forcing himself to laugh that hard.

"Yes, indeed. Sit there and laugh all you want, Mr. Harvey—and watch me!"

Seven

Just to show Mr. Harvey how very serious she was, Cassie closed the door behind her with a sharp slam that made the pane of glass rattle.

She had to keep walking steadily and with purpose. Mr. Harvey could still see her, silhouetted against the glass. She couldn't allow her footsteps to waiver, or he'd think she regretted her actions, and he'd won.

She strode straight across his outer office, her heels clicking loudly on the hardwood floor.

The nib of the clerk's pen scratched frantically against the paper. The little weasel was trying desperately to pretend he hadn't been listening to a single word of what had been said—or rather, shouted—in that inner office, Cassie surmised.

"Good afternoon to you, too, Mr. Cramer," she said very pointedly.

He started. Before he could recover and rise to see her out, she had also closed the outer door firmly behind her.

With the thickness of the stout oaken door safely between her and Mr. Harvey and his lackey, Cassie at last drew in a deep breath and leaned her back against the solid door for support.

What in the world had she done? Her temples were throbbing. She felt as if she wanted to cry all over again. This was turning out to be one of the worst days in one of the worst weeks of her entire life.

Even when her parents had died, she'd had Aunt Flora, her brother, and neighbors and friends to comfort and support her. This time, she felt so incredibly alone, so completely abandoned.

Sebastian hadn't shown her to dismiss Mr. Harvey. How incredibly foolish she was to have fired the man her aunt had trusted for so many years!

Panic seized her. She'd made a big mistake. She grabbed the doorknob, ready to twist it, walk back in, and apologize profusely.

Reason struggled for control. She couldn't go back in immediately, she decided. She'd appear too weak, just the sort of image of frail, fallible womanhood that she'd bet Mr. Harvey relished. She refused to give him that satisfaction.

She'd wait—a few hours, a day or two, a week or so. Make it appear as if she'd taken the time to reconsider her actions in the light of dispassionate reason. Then she'd return, apologize prettily, flutter her eyelashes at him, and all would be forgiven. Mr. Harvey was the sort of man who could be influenced by such behavior.

But was she the kind of woman who worked that way to get what she wanted?

No, she decided. She never had been. She never would be. She wanted to be independent. That meant being free to make her own mistakes and to learn from them.

If she went crawling back, she'd never again be able to convince him to do what she wanted. She'd probably never be able to summon up the nerve to dismiss him again. By the time he died, she'd be so used to being cowed by anyone who presumed authority over her that she'd listen to whichever young whippersnapper took his place. It would be as bad as being back in Philadelphia, under Letitia's oppressive thumb.

Cassie released the doorknob. She'd compose a formal letter

of dismissal to Mr. Harvey as soon as she got home, she decided. She'd get Mr. Andrews from the bank to write her the draft so Mr. Warner could order her drilling equipment as soon as possible. Time was growing short for what she had to do.

She headed for the *Argus* and Brent.

She didn't care what anyone else said about him. She trusted Brent.

"You did come."

Brushing his ink-stained hands on his leather work apron, Brent rushed across the room to greet her.

"I told you I would. Did you think I wasn't a woman of my word?"

"No. I'll always believe you, Cassie."

No, you won't, Cassie silently replied. *It's part of the curse, don't you know? But eventually I'll learn to live with it,* she decided. *I hope you will.*

"Did you have a nice time with Mr. Harvey?" he asked, sarcasm dripping from his voice.

"No." She was reluctant to continue, but he'd find out soon enough anyway. "As a matter of fact, I dismissed him as my attorney."

A loud laugh exploded from him. "You didn't!"

"Yes. But—"

"Oh, I'd love to have seen the look on his face."

"It wasn't pretty," Cassie stated blandly.

"August has *never* been pretty—even if he thinks he is. What did he say?"

"He shouted a bit."

"You sound a little hoarse, too."

She raised her hand to the base of her throat. "I guess you could say I did my fair share of shouting, too," she admitted.

"You? Shouted? At August Harvey?"

She nodded. Brent laughed all the harder.

"I'm so sorry I wasn't there to witness that."

"It's not funny, Brent."

She hoped the tone of her voice would convince him of the

gravity of the situation. The way he continued to chuckle, she didn't think she was succeeding.

"I told you I've never raised my voice in anger all these years. Now, in a few days' time, I've had more arguments—*loud* arguments—with more people than I'd have believed possible. Why am I suddenly so contentious? Does having a lot of money make people mean? Is there something in the water around here?"

She couldn't tell him she suspected the real source of her problem was Sebastian and the visions he showed her.

At last Brent managed to control his laughter. He pressed his hands to his stomach and groaned. "Oh, my aching sides."

"Serves you right."

Then his expression turned serious.

"I think perhaps it may be because, for the first time in your life, you're experiencing what you claimed you wanted so desperately: your independence. I think you're discovering that sometimes one has to fight for one's independence."

Cassie grimaced. "I knew that."

Hadn't Professor Alvin Godwin told her that when they'd studied the American War for Independence? She just never figured it would apply to her so personally.

"I have a slight problem, Brent. I think I'll still need some advice from time to time. Some assistance with investments. I'd really rather not ask Mr. Andrews at the bank. Although he's a pleasant enough fellow, and probably very competent, I'd rather avoid any possible intrusion from Mrs. Andrews."

"I understand." His eyes, still watery from laughter, were now intently studying her with genuine interest. "A wise move."

"Mr. Harvey mentioned someone named Mr. McAlister from the mine. Mrs. Andrews mentioned him in passing, too, as renting the front pew in church. He must be rather rich."

Brent was still smiling, but the spark had faded from his eyes. She'd never met this Mr. McAlister. Obviously Brent had. What more did he know about him than that he was good with money? What did he know about McAlister that would cause such apparent dislike?

"Mr. McAlister *owns* the mine."

"Oh. I see. I've never met him, and his pew at church was empty."

"He and his family have been abroad for a while. But frankly I don't think he'd condescend to offer *anyone* any advice. Certainly not for free."

"I understand. I also understand that—well, not to be too inquisitive, but—you've built the *Argus* into a profitable newspaper."

"After a lot of hard work and long hours. And just barely profitable, I must modestly add."

"You told me once you were good at handling money."

Brent nodded and stroked his chin. "As I recall at the time you also told me you weren't about to let me manage yours."

"As you can see, circumstances have changed. I don't know those other men. But I do know you, Brent. I trust you."

"You do?"

"Will you help me?"

She looked toward him with pleading in her eyes. She was above weeping and whining to get what she wanted. She certainly was above batting her eyelashes at him to get him to do as she wanted. Would he take her seriously? Certainly no one else had.

"Will you give me some advice from time to time, when I ask?"

"Of course."

He'd answered so readily. Her tense shoulders relaxed with relief. Then a nagging suspicion snagged her. What would he expect in return?

"Not too much advice," she warned him.

"Of course not."

"And only advice about the things I tell you I need advice about—financial matters, for instance. *Not* personal matters."

"Of course not. I'll be better than any of those other fellows ever could be."

"But just from time to time," she stressed.

"I know. You want to be independent."

"Don't say 'independent' as if it gives you a bad taste in your mouth."

"Sorry. I'll behave myself better the next time you come asking for my advice."

"I certainly expect you to." She hoped he took good notice of the playful gleam in her eyes.

"I also hope you don't find it necessary to argue with me for your independence." The playful gleam in his blue eyes mirrored her own.

"So do I." As much as he irritated her at times, she honestly couldn't imagine herself shouting in anger at Brent—at least not anymore. Still, she had a task to pursue and she needed to make sure he got it done, too. Quickly she blurted out, "So I'd appreciate it if you'd see that Mr. Warner got that bank draft for two thousand dollars so he can order that equipment for me."

He hesitated. "Um, Cassie, I'm not sure I'm going to like handling that much of someone else's money."

"You promised you wouldn't give me an argument," she reminded him.

He grimaced. "That I did. Sorry." He rubbed the back of his neck. "Well then, I guess I'd better get to it."

"As soon as possible," she reminded him.

"As soon as I can possibly get around to it," he amended.

Cassie breathed a sigh of relief. "Ah, now that that's taken care of, I can truly enjoy my tour of your wonderful newspaper office."

She glanced around the large room. "So this is the Argus. My, it certainly is . . . interesting." She had no idea what she was looking at.

A long counter separated a narrow aisle for customers from the actual work area. Light streamed in behind her from the large, paned window opening onto the street. The two side walls were lined alternately with tall, uncurtained windows to admit as much light as possible, and several desks with slanted tops filled with numerous little cubbyholes.

"Let me show you." Brent held out his hand to her.

She placed her hand in his palm and allowed him to lead her to the area behind the counter. Underneath, on the other side, were other larger cubbyholes filled with papers.

"It's not just a newspaper," he explained. "We do all sorts of printing here. Some of this is work we've done that's waiting to be picked up—handbills, pamphlets, notices, and such that people hire us to do. Some of these things are pieces we've already done. We keep a few copies so folks can see examples of the things we do."

He pointed to the various composing desks and at a thin, dark-haired man who sat atop a tall stool at one of them. He was busily choosing small metal cubes of type from the tiny cubicles and setting them into rows with the aid of a narrow, metal rule.

"This is Sam Wells." Then he gestured toward a younger, fair-haired fellow who was rolling ink over a block of type. "This is Dave Watson."

The men nodded. Sam made a token gesture to rise.

"Good afternoon, gentlemen." Cassie held her hands out, as if that could keep him from standing and spilling out the case on his lap. What a catastrophe that would be.

"These hold different styles and sizes of typeface. Italic. Humanist. Slab Serif. I'm always trying to find new ones. Got to keep the customers interested, you know."

"Yes, of course."

He showed her another metal cabinet. This, and everything else, seemed coated with a slick oil and a fine dusting of black ink.

"After this, I'm afraid my dress will never be the same."

"What a shame, too, since you look so lovely in it," Brent replied.

The warmth in his gaze caused Cassie's pulse to quicken. One corner of his mouth turned upward in the start of a grin. Then he turned back to the cabinet.

"This contains the engraving plates for pictures. It attracts more customers to have illustrations—even though I can't provide them with as many as *Harper's* does."

"I'm sure the *Argus* is fine just the way you print it."

"That doesn't mean I can't hope to improve it. I wish somebody'd figure out a way to print actual pictures from daguerreotypes, instead of relying on sketches that can sometimes be pretty inaccurate."

She nodded. "Oh, they will. Someday," she added quickly. "I'm sure someday . . . somebody is bound to figure out a way. Somehow."

She gave herself a little mental kick. Hadn't she already warned herself to watch what she said about all the marvelous things to come that Sebastian showed her? Did she have to be so very careful even on the little things?

She pointed to a door in the blank, rear wall. "What's through there?"

"Oh, you don't want to go back there," Brent said. "That's where we do the actual printing. Much too noisy. You'd go deaf with all the noise from the presses. And dirty. That pretty little dress wouldn't stand a chance back there. But I've got plans."

"What sort of plans?"

How odd that Sebastian hadn't even hinted to her of anything regarding the success or failure of Brent's beloved newspaper. Maybe because she'd never asked him to show her. Then again, she hadn't asked to see images of war and destruction, either.

"I'd like to buy a bigger building. Put the presses in there, add steam power, hire more men. Buy another paper in another town. You know, expand. A few weeks ago, I was looking into buying a newspaper in Harper's Ferry—"

"Oh, no. You don't want to go there," she said quickly. A little too quickly.

He gave her a puzzled, almost worried look. "It's a nice little town," he protested. "If you like climbing hills."

My gracious! She really hadn't learned when to keep silent, had she? Maybe she never would.

"I . . . I understand they have a lot of floods there. You really wouldn't want to see your presses go floating down the river, would you?"

He reached up and rubbed the back of his neck. "No, I guess not."

Cassie had a nagging feeling that Brent wasn't really paying attention to a word she said—at least, not about his business.

Trying to change the subject, she glanced frantically around the room. She spotted a wooden desk. It was larger than the one Mr. Harvey used, but it was plain, sturdy oak, not fancy mahogany. It didn't have the fancy feet, carved decorations, and ornate brass locks and handles. On the other hand, it did have a lot more work piled on top than Mr. Harvey's had. Or maybe Mr. Harvey just had a more efficient filing system.

"Is this your desk?"

"It's mine." She could hear the pride in his voice.

My goodness, he's probably even proud of the dust in the corners of this place.

She strolled over to the desk. "You must be incredibly busy here."

"I try to be," he said, coming up to stand behind her. "If I'm not busy, it means I have no work to do, and that means I'm not making any money."

"I see." Could he hear the disappointment in her voice? Did he know she was disappointed to hear from his own lips what other people had said about him? That all he cared about was making money, any way he could.

"And that means I can't pay my employees—or my bills," he added.

When she'd heard him speak before about making money, it had always been to build a nicer home, or to invest it in his newspaper. Now the way he spoke made her believe his primary concern was to pay his workers. That was certainly a different purpose than what others had accused him of.

She didn't want to appear too nosy and go lifting papers on

his desk, reading things she had no business reading. She'd already had her fill of seeing things she didn't think she had any business seeing.

But she couldn't help glancing at the papers scattered over his desk. After all, if the things contained there were truly secrets, he ought to have kept them locked away in a drawer. It was a newspaper office, where people printed things that were meant to be shown all over town.

She noticed old newspapers from other cities. She lifted the edge of one.

"Keeping track of what the competition is doing?" she asked.

"Of course. Sometimes editors take foreign, odd, interesting, or pertinent articles from one paper and reprint them in their own papers. I do in the *Argus*."

One paper in particular caught her eye. She couldn't help picking it up.

"Who is this?" She extended the paper and pointed to a small illustration of several men in individual, oval frames.

"Who? Him? Let's see." Peering intently at the small print beneath the illustration, he read, "Abraham Lincoln."

"I can see that. Who *is* he?"

"Well, he was a congressman from Illinois a couple of years ago. Only lasted one term, I understand. Can't be much of a politician."

"Why do you have this?" She tried not to sound too concerned.

"My sister and her family live in Illinois now. They send me issues of their newspaper from time to time. I'd meant to file it but, as you can see, I'm pretty busy with other things. My brother-in-law is pretty interested in politics."

"Does he support this Mr. Lincoln?"

"Shucks, no!" Brent laughed. "My brother-in-law is a genuine, devoted, dyed-in-the-wool Democrat. He wouldn't vote for that fellow even if he was a candidate for anything."

"He's not a candidate?"

"Not that I'm aware of. He's a lawyer with one of the railroads, I think. I understand he travels about, public speaking in Illinois, Indiana, Ohio. But there are a lot of other men better qualified, better suited than he."

"No, there are not."

Brent stared at her. "Oh, really. Maybe you ought to talk to my brother-in-law. So what's this fellow supposed to be qualified for?"

"President."

"Of what? The local dog and pony circus?" He laughed.

"Of the United States."

"Yes. Certainly. And I'll be King of England someday."

"Well, Your Majesty," Mrs. Andrews called loudly from her side of the counter, "would you please be so kind as to give me the handbills we ordered? Or have you been too busy polishing your crown to get them done?"

Cassie jumped. For a moment she considered making a dash for the door in the back so she could hide there. She would take her chances with the dirt and noise rather than face Mrs. Andrews again. After the way this day was turning out, she didn't need to finish it off with any more contention.

"Your handbills? Certainly they're done, Mrs. Andrews." Brent hurried to the counter. He bent over and searched the cubbyholes. "I couldn't disappoint one of my best customers. Here we are."

He pulled out a stack of elaborately printed handbills.

Mrs. Andrews scrutinized them minutely. "Yes, yes. They'll do. I'll post one in Warner's store, one outside the church, one at the blacksmith's."

Then she turned to Cassie and pushed a handbill into her hand.

"You *are* coming to the Lyman's Gap Volunteer Firemen's Association's Annual Fish Fry and Charity Auction, aren't you, Miss Bowen?" Mrs. Andrews demanded, as if it were a summons, not a question.

"When is it?" Cassie glanced over the elaborately printed page.

"Next Wednesday evening, in the town hall. It's an annual

affair that your aunt never missed. As a matter of fact, she often declared we ought to make it a semiannual affair, and I, for one, agree with her."

"Is that all they serve? Fried fish?"

"Of course not. There'll be potato salad, and some of the German immigrants are bound to donate some coleslaw and some of that sauerkraut concoction of theirs." She ticked the menu off on her fingers. "Pickle and corn relishes. Pickled red beets. Apple butter. Jerusha and Olivier said they'd make us something from New Orleans—bennies—something like that. Of course, the fish are fresh from Lake Erie."

"Well, frankly, I'm not as fond of fried fish as my aunt was, but—"

"I'm certain you'll still want to make a generous donation. After all, one never knows when one will need the prompt and efficient services of the Volunteer Fire Brigade, does one?"

"I do."

She'd pay for that, she knew! She should've learned her lesson about being so smug. But it was Mrs. Andrews, and Cassie just couldn't resist baiting her. If she could forgive Sebastian for showing her those horrible sights, couldn't he forgive this one little slip of hubris?

"Well . . . well, I certainly hope you're better at predicting that sort of catastrophe than you are at choosing political candidates. Oh, yes, indeed, I overheard what you were saying when I came in."

"I wasn't trying to keep secrets, Mrs. Andrews."

"Abraham what's-his-name? Lincoln? Never heard of him." Mrs. Andrews snickered. "President?" She chuckled. "Of course!" She guffawed.

Cassie pressed her lips together and remained silent. This was one prediction she knew she wasn't in any hurry to see proven true.

Mrs. Andrews reached into her purse and pulled out a handkerchief. "Oh, my gracious," she said with a gasp as she dabbed at her watering eyes. "I haven't had that good a laugh since Margaret Finkle tripped and fell into a mud puddle last Easter. Oh, dear."

Cassie didn't see anything that incredibly funny in what she'd said. If the rest of them could see what she'd seen, they wouldn't think it was so blasted funny, either. Even without an audience, Mrs. Andrews was obviously making the most of any opportunity to humiliate her.

Mrs. Andrews released one last little snicker, then turned and called through the open doorway. "Harold. Oh, Harold. Come in and help me with these handbills."

A lanky adolescent sauntered through the door. Cassie held her breath and watched him as he drew nearer. He wore a pair of brown woolen trousers and a green and beige plaid shirt. Nothing out of the ordinary.

Cassie remembered his face all too well—except when last she saw it it had been topped with a blue forage cap, and a blue woolen uniform had buttoned tightly up to his chin.

"Hello, Harold," Brent greeted him.

"Hello, Mr. Conway." Harold nodded.

"Miss Bowen, I'd like you to meet my nephew, Harold Andrews," Mrs. Andrews said.

To Cassie it sounded as if Mrs. Andrews was speaking from a thousand miles away, through a hollow tube that made everything echo in her ears—the shots, the explosions, the screams.

"Harold is my husband's older brother's son. He's visiting from—"

Cassie felt as if she were watching him through the wrong end of a telescope. Instead of bringing the faraway nearer, she felt as if everything that was near to her had been transported far away, and she was watching it all in her head while her body was still trapped in the present.

As if in a trance, she extended a trembling hand to the boy. "It's an honor to have met such a hero."

"Not me, ma'am." Harold grinned and blushed. "Oh, well, once I did get Taffy Puckett's kitten out of that tree but—"

"No, not that. But, yes. Yes, you are. You will be," she said very solemnly. "I will remember you. We will all remember you."

"Me? Gosh, what for?"

Cassie's tears had been welling so close to the surface all day. Her argument with Mr. Harvey and her cheerful banter with Brent had kept them at bay. Now she could contain them no longer.

"You'll save all the men in your unit," she recited automatically, as if she had no control over her speech whatsoever. "But . . . oh, how heroic of you to sacrifice yourself."

"No, no. Not me, ma'am," Harold stammered and turned a deeper red.

"What are you talking about?" Mrs. Andrews demanded irately.

Mrs. Andrews interposed herself between Cassie and Harold so that Cassie had to release his hand. Her telescoping vision returned to normal. Her frayed nerves did not.

"Yes, you. Oh, excuse me," she whispered, and bolted from the building.

"Cassie!" Brent called after her.

"Oh, *now* what in heaven's name is wrong with that girl?" Mrs. Andrews demanded testily. "I swear, she is so strange."

"I thought you didn't hold with swearing, Mrs. Andrews," Brent said.

She *harrumph*ed and turned to her nephew. "Harold," she commanded, "don't you pay one bit of attention to a word that crazy woman says."

"No, ma'am. Not at all," Harold responded dutifully. "I've heard what you and the other ladies have said about those Bowen women."

On the other hand, Brent noticed the boy did continue to watch Cassie with undeniable interest as she fled up the street.

"Oh, Harold," Mrs. Andrews said bitterly, "this one's far worse than her aunt ever was!"

Eight

"Those handbills are free for the Volunteer Firemen's Association, Mrs. Andrews," Brent called over his shoulder as he sprinted out of the newspaper office after Cassie. "Compliments of the Argus and Conway Printing Company."

He'd already made arrangements with Foster Englehard, this year's captain of the volunteers, to accept a nominal fee. But, at this moment, he'd rather take care of Cassie than contend with Mrs. Andrews. How could that blasted woman haggle about an already agreed-upon price?

Brent caught up with Cassie where the wooden sidewalk ended. Huffing and out of breath, he drew up beside her.

"Lord Almighty, Cassie! If you hadn't slowed down, I never would've caught you. I wouldn't have believed a little thing like you could run so fast."

"Nobody believes me anyway, no matter what," she snapped.

Tears were still running down her cheeks as she turned up the dirt road toward her own home. Her white-knuckled fingers bunched up fistfuls of her skirt, hiking it off the ground. She kicked up a cloud of dust behind her.

He followed her, nursing a stitch in his side and trying to catch his breath.

She bustled up the front porch steps. Brent figured, this time, she must really be upset. Usually she stepped so quietly. Now he could hear her footsteps practically thundering on the wooden treads.

She swung open the front door, then ducked quickly behind it. She tried to close the door, but Brent caught it with his hand. He should have known better—he was already familiar with doors, but he should have known Cassie better—and used his foot.

"Ow! Don't slam my hand in there." He pulled his hand back and sucked on his bruised knuckles and pinched fingers. "I need it to write editorials."

"Go buy a typewriter," she grumbled, trying again to close the door.

"A *what*? What the dickens is that?"

In spite of her unusual command, at least he had the presence of mind this time to stick his foot in the door. The wood closed painlessly on his tough boot sole. What the hell *was* a "typewriter"? Where had she come up with that word?

"Never mind. Don't go sticking your hand in places it doesn't belong, trying to stop me."

"Cassie, we need to talk about this." Slowly he pushed the door a little wider.

She released her grasp and didn't resist when he came inside. She retreated to the parlor and sat on the sofa. She folded her hands in her lap, looking as if she were a student who had just misbehaved and was waiting for a birching from the headmaster.

Brent figured the way she'd been acting, it was more likely that *he* was going to end up the one who felt as if he'd been switched.

Cautiously he entered the parlor. He sat on the sofa, too, but at the other end, away from her. He watched her in silence, waiting. When she didn't speak, he figured he might as well ask.

"Cassie, are you going to offer some sort of explanation for your increasingly bizarre behavior?"

"No. I don't know how to explain it."

"Try. Please."

"I did once. You didn't believe a word I said."

"Why don't you try again?"

She shook her head. "Because the same thing will only happen all over again.

"Look, Cassie. Somebody has to say something. It might as well be me."

He truly wanted to help this distraught, confused young woman. Wasn't he always the one championing the underdog? Favoring the dark horse? And getting into trouble for doing so, he reminded himself. Considering all the troubles Cassie had caused in the few days she'd been here, his problems couldn't get much worse.

"Cassie," he said softly. "Even though we haven't known each other very long, you know I was a friend of Miss Flora's. I'd like to think you consider me more than just a neighbor who's always butting into your business. I'd like to think you, too, consider me a friend."

"I . . . I do, Brent."

"So I'd like to understand why you're saying and doing these strange things."

"It's hard to explain," she warned him.

"Try."

"It's *very* hard to explain," she emphasized.

"Let's see. You fired Mr. Harvey because—" He waited for a reply.

The very mention of her argument with Mr. Harvey brought back her frown.

"He refused to let me spend a little money—my *own* money, mind you—on that drilling equipment I ordered."

Brent grimaced. This wasn't the best example to start with.

"Well, now, I think you already know how I feel about that, Cassie. But, by golly, it's your money. You ought to be able to do what you want with it."

"That's what I said."

"How much is a little?"

"Only two thousand dollars."

Brent blinked and tried not to shout at her.

Stay calm, he ordered himself. Shouting wouldn't help the situation. Getting upset wouldn't make her feel like confiding in you. Then how would he be able to help her? How would he be able to convince her to stop her silly predictions?

"Only two thousand dollars," he repeated. "Look, Cassie." He scooted across the sofa cushion a little closer to her. He was relieved when she didn't get up and run away.

"You can think what you please. You even have the right to *say* what you please, even though people are going to think you're a little—"

"Eccentric?"

"Well, yes."

"I'm getting used to it." She sighed with resignation.

"But if you keep saying and doing things like that, they're going to think you're downright crazy!"

"I guess they can think what they like about me."

He placed his hand atop the two she held clenched so tightly in her lap. That was a friendly, consoling gesture, wasn't it? he demanded of himself and assured himself, all at the same time. Nothing more.

"Listen, Cassie. I don't have to warn you about this. You can pretty well figure August will use this incident, and any others he can dig up, as opportunities to contact your brother and his wife and have you declared incurably insane—or at best incompetent."

Her head shot up, and she watched him, worry in her eyes. Beneath his hand, he could feel her fingers clenching.

"I'm *not* insane," she insisted.

"I don't think that will matter much to them. Between the three of them, they'll carve up your inheritance and leave you chained up in an insane asylum. Do you know what they do to people in those places?"

"No."

A lady like Cassie shouldn't know. Many of his readers had complained when he'd printed articles in the *Argus*, exposing the horrendous treatment of inmates in those places. He'd been trying to incense them to take some sort of action to improve those conditions. If he was going to make any impression on Cassie whatsoever, he'd have to be very blunt.

"If you're lucky, you'll get fed on a regular basis, although what and how much they're serving is anyone's guess. They'll come and throw cold water on you every once in a while just to neaten you up. Or beat you, just to straighten out your thinking. Put you on display. Naked."

It was the thought of Cassie naked that did it. The sun glittering through the windows turned her hair to bronze.

He reached up and brushed a loose auburn curl back into place. He couldn't resist tracing the in-and-out lines of her plaited hair as it swept back into a loose knot at the nape of her neck. He couldn't resist brushing his finger down the side of her face once again, and running his finger along the line of her soft chin.

"I can't bear the thought of those morbidly curious people gawking at you like an animal on display. God only knows what else they'd do to a beautiful woman like you in a horrible place like that."

She was silent.

"I hope you're sitting here, so quiet, really considering the things I've been telling you so you don't end up in a place like that."

"I am."

From the tone of her voice, he could believe she truly was thinking about what he'd said.

"I hope you're not going to give Mr. Harvey any more reasons to try to have you committed."

"I'll try."

"I hope you're going to resolve to try to behave yourself in the future."

"I really will try."

From the tone of her voice, he was beginning to doubt that,

even if she tried very hard, she wasn't going to succeed. He might as well be completely honest with her.

"On the other hand, from what I know of you, I highly doubt it."

"I'm sorry."

From the tone of her voice, he knew she really was sorry. He also could tell she couldn't help being what she was, any more than he could not be driven by his ambitions.

He watched her press her pink lips tightly together. Oh, lips like that weren't made to suffer for her having to think so hard about what she was going to do. Lips like that were made for tender kissing.

He laid his arm lightly on her shoulder. He was trying to be casual, friendly. If only memories of Cassie in his embrace wouldn't keep intruding when he was trying to talk to her like a Dutch uncle.

"Cassie, sometimes I wonder how Miss Flora managed all those years, being so eccentric, without someone to watch out for her."

He felt her slim shoulders rise and fall with a weary sigh.

"She managed. I'll manage. We've all managed."

"All?" he repeated. "How many crazy women are there in your family?"

"Every one of us."

Cassie laid her head on his shoulder, almost as if everything she thought she knew had suddenly grown too heavy for her weary head, and she had to rest it somewhere. He was glad she felt comfortable with him.

"She did have you to check on her every evening," she said.

"Yes, she did. But that was just to make sure she was still alive."

She gave a little laugh. Brent thought it was good to hear her laugh again.

"Maybe I should check in with you every evening to make sure I haven't said or done something during the day that would land me in an insane asylum," she suggested.

Thoughts of Cassie coming to him every evening quickly

diverged from what someone might envision as an ordinary report—sort of like a soldier checking in with his commanding officer. He had a more vivid image of slipping into a soft, comfortable bed beside her every evening.

Down, Brent, he commanded himself. *Stick to what you need to say to her for her own good.* But the tantalizing image persisted.

"Sometimes I wonder why Miss Flora never married," he said.

"I suppose she had her reasons."

"I mean, she was too young to have had a beau and lose him in the Second War for Independence."

"She never mentioned anyone."

"Did she lose one in the war with Mexico?"

"Honestly, I can never recall anyone in the family even mentioning that Aunt Flora had a beau—ever. Did she ever mention anyone to you?"

"I tried to ask her once," he admitted, "but you know your aunt. She always evaded me. Slippery as an eel, she was."

"And silent as a clam? The way you prefer women to act." Cassie laughed.

Brent could feel her shoulders moving up and down against his arm and her head moving gently against his shoulder. He liked the way she felt, nestled in his arm.

He chuckled. "Well, not completely silent. Your aunt was *never* silent. But she wasn't real forthcoming with that sort of information."

"I'm not surprised."

Somehow Brent got the impression she really wasn't, either. What was it with these Bowen women?

The sun was going down. Her hair had turned to a fiery gold. Her eyes glowed a lustrous blue. She was close enough to kiss again. His arms ached to pull her closer. His loins ached to cradle her in his arms, carry her upstairs—front right bedroom—and love her as she deserved.

"According to your aunt, you're twenty-five."

Cassie turned to face him. There was a flash of blue fire in her eyes.

"Well, goodness. She might not like to talk about herself much, but she was mighty free with information about me, wasn't she?"

"Are you angry? I only asked her before I fetched you from the train station to make sure I didn't get the wrong Cassie Bowen."

"No. I'm just joking."

"I'm glad to hear that you still can." He raised his hand to touch her cheek. "I'm glad to see you can still joke and smile and laugh and—"

"Almost act normal?" she supplied.

"Are you joking again?"

She didn't answer right away.

"I just want to make sure, so I don't do anything—well, anything more—to make you angry with me, Cassie."

She laughed. "No. I don't think you've done anything lately that would make me angry with you."

"It was a shame your aunt spent her life alone, without someone to watch out for her."

"Oh, I think she did well enough on her own."

"How will you do, Cassie?" He tucked his finger under her soft chin and lifted her face to his. "How will you fare without someone to watch out for you?"

"I. . . ."

"You don't sound too confident."

She remained silent. Her gaze searched his eyes. What was she hoping to find there? he wondered. Was he imagining things? Or could he believe she wanted him to hold her and care for her? Shelter her from harm? Protect her from the mean people in the world who wouldn't be so tolerant of her little eccentricities?

"Sometimes I wonder why you're not married yet, Cassie."

He felt her shoulders rise and fall again with the same noncommittal shrug.

"I suppose I haven't met a man I truly loved, who truly loved me."

He wanted to tell her, but it was too soon and he didn't have the proper words. He hoped his actions alone would tell her.

Slowly his lips descended on hers. He could feel her pressing toward him. Warm. Eager. Irresistible.

She wrapped her arms about his neck, returning his caresses as willingly and eagerly as he. Her breath was warm and sweet as she welcomed his kisses.

He reached up and unfastened the pins from her hair. The auburn cascade tumbled down her shoulders and back.

"You're so lovely. The first time I saw you, I wanted you."

"At the train station?" She laughed. "With me looking all sooty and disheveled from travel?"

"Oh, yes."

He kissed her cheek, and trailed his tongue across her chin. She giggled and licked her tongue across his chin. He trickled small kisses down her throat.

"It's probably not ladylike to admit this," she whispered, "but I've felt . . . excited about you ever since I saw you. Even when Aunt Flora told me—"

"What a scoundrel I was?"

"Oh, yes. And I'm so glad."

His lips, pressed against her flesh, could feel her pulse pounding excitedly in her throat. He kissed her again, reaching up to unfasten just the top button of her dress. She drew in a small gasp.

"I'll stop if you—"

"No. That *would* make you a scoundrel."

He unfastened the second button, trailing his hand over her softly rounded breast as he wrapped his other hand about her waist. He enjoyed the feel of the pliant curves of her body against his hot hands.

With fumbling fingers, Cassie fidgeted with the top button of his shirt. It was pretty evident she'd never unfastened a man's clothes before. He smiled. He really hadn't expected otherwise.

Leaning back slightly, Brent slipped out of his jacket, tossed it over the back of the sofa, and bent to her again. She reclined against the cushions, waiting for him.

Two buttons, three unfastened.

"I don't want to frighten you, Cassie."

"You don't frighten me, Brent. You . . . you excite me. Tempt me. Tantalize me. That's not frightening."

The hell with the rest of the buttons. He tore open his shirt. He heard a popped button hit the floor somewhere to the left.

The cool air made the muscles of his chest and stomach contract. Oh, if he wasn't already in enough pain, wanting her so badly, not having her. Now he ached with the need for her from his loins clear up to his throat.

She reached up, smoothing her warm palms over his body, scratching her fingertips through the hair on his chest, brushing his tiny nipples to erection. As if he wasn't ready enough.

He reached down to the middle of her bodice. Three buttons. Four unfastened the bodice of her dress. He drew aside the halves of fabric, revealing her opalescent breasts—pale white, blue-veined, rosy-tipped—emerging from the top of her corset, pulsing with the pounding of her heart.

He tucked one finger inside her chemise, into the cleavage between her breasts. She was even warmer there. His head spun, thinking of the warm places of her body.

He flipped out the ends of the narrow ribbon that held the gathers of her chemise. He pulled one end. The bow untied. Gradually he loosened the folds of fabric, revealing more of her softly rounded breasts.

He cupped his hand over one breast. His fingers contacted warm, soft flesh. His palms felt cool muslin and rigid stays. Damn these corsets.

"I would love to love you, Cassie," he told her.

"So would I, Brent."

"I want to touch your soft skin, feel your warmth."

"Hold me. Touch me."

"Not here. Not on the sofa."

"Yes, here."

"Not now."

"Yes, now."

"Do you really want me, Cassie?"

"Yes, I do, Brent. I really do."

He couldn't take her through the seamless crotch of her pantaloons. It seemed so tawdry, so common, to cheapen her that way. She deserved time and consideration, and all the attention he could lavish on her beautiful body.

He fumbled aside the folds of her skirt and her petticoat, trying to push them out of the way. His arms tightened and his fingers ached as his hands encountered the soft muslin of her pantaloons.

His swollen manhood pressed against the restraints of his trousers. He smoothed his hands up and down her thighs. He tucked his finger into the drawstring of her pantaloons, searching for the narrow ribbon's ends.

"I had imagined this happening in a different place," he told her. "A different time. Different circumstances."

"I am quite content." She smiled at him trustingly.

She kissed the tip of her finger, then placed it against his lips. Her soft fingertips traced tiny trails across his brow, down his cheeks, around his chin.

"I don't want you to think badly of me." He supported himself on one forearm as his fingers gently tugged at the drawstring.

"I never could," she replied.

"I really care about you, Cassie," he whispered in her ear. "I care what happens to you."

"I know." Her voice was breathless, husky—just as he'd imagined it would sound when they were alone together, naked, in the dim twilight.

"Is that another prediction?" he murmured.

"Do you believe me?"

"Yes."

She sighed. "Then I suppose it's not a prediction."

"I care very deeply for you, Cassie." He had more than just a tiny suspicion that he was actually in love with her. Then why couldn't he just come out and tell her? Did she really need to be told? Couldn't she tell?

As urgently as he wanted her, needed her, he had to go slowly, for her sake.

"I don't want you to ever look back upon this moment with any hurt feelings, any injured pride."

"I won't."

"I don't want you to have any regrets about what once was, what might have been, what never would be."

"I have no regrets." She grinned. "Not yet, at least."

He drew her more tightly to him, the better to show her how much he really loved her. What else could he say to let her know? What did a person do when he feared that someone he cared about very much was absolutely nuts?

"I don't want you to ever be hurt, not by me, not by anything any unfeeling oaf says about your silly predictions."

"What?" She lay there, very, very still. Her gaze bored into him. "Wait a minute!"

"I mean—"

"They only seem silly because you're too pigheaded to believe them."

He felt her muscles tighten. Her hands clamped down on his at her waist. Her blue eyes lost their dreamy look, and grew suddenly sharper.

"What does that have to do with anything, anyway?" she demanded, pushing his hands away.

She struggled to push him off her. Tangling his legs in her skirt, he tumbled over and off the sofa, hitting the floor with his bottom. She sat up and pulled the halves of her bodice tightly together.

"I'm only asking you to do what your aunt did. If you must make predictions in public, limit them to unimportant things."

"Like horse racing? Or pigs? So it's all right to talk about the little things?"

Brent grimaced. He'd really loved that old lady. She'd almost been like another grandmother to him. But from the posthumous influence she was having on Cassie, he was almost beginning to hate her.

"Cassie, I'll tell you. You can make all the wagers you want on pigs or horse races or how many flies will land on a piece of manure," he desperately bartered. "I won't say a single word about wagering not being a ladylike pastime, or about me not believing your predictions."

"Will you believe any of them?"

Brent thought he detected a gleam of hope in her eyes. But he couldn't tell her yes. He couldn't lie to her.

"Probably not," he admitted. Quickly he went on. "It doesn't matter whether I believe them or not. It doesn't matter whether *anyone* believes them."

"Yes, it does," she insisted. Crossing her arms, she sat there staring at the floor like a petulant child.

The tender moment had vanished. He had no idea how he'd ever re-create it. Not now, anyway. He stood and tried to tuck his shirt back into his trousers without doing himself damage. He'd be heading home soon, to a quick dowsing with cold water from the pump.

"Why do you talk like you do? Especially in front of Mrs. Andrews. You know she doesn't like you anyway." He roamed around to the other side of the sofa to retrieve his discarded jacket.

"Don't you think I know that?"

"She's not going to miss any opportunity to spread nasty tales about you all over town. She's made enough out of the twins and the pigs."

Cassie looked at him, angry and worried at the same time.

"Oh, yes," Brent continued. "She managed to wheedle information out of poor Mr. Andrews about all of us wagering on the pigs. Now he's sleeping on the sofa. Don't you see where these predictions of yours are getting you and everyone who associates with you?"

"I'm very sorry about Mr. Andrews, but *that*, at least, wasn't my fault."

"It might not have been, except for everyone chattering about how you predicted the right number."

"It's *my* lucky guess. It's *their* fault if they want to gamble and can't keep *their* mouths shut," she insisted.

"Don't you see? After today, Mrs. Andrews has two new tales to spread around about you. Can you imagine what will happen when August hears about this? Why do you have to give them more ammunition to use against you?"

"Oh, don't even use such words around me." Cassie clapped her hands over her ears.

Brent wasn't about to let the matter go. She hadn't listened to a word he'd said. If she was so determined to continue her course of self-destruction, he was equally determined to stop her.

"You tell us a nobody like this Lincoln fellow is going to be president. Then you have to go claiming Mrs. Andrews's nephew—of all people, *her* nephew—is going to become some kind of hero, saving his unit—which is all well and good. But to claim he'll do it by sacrificing himself. Why, you talk as if there's going to be some kind of war and he's going to die."

"There is," she said quietly. She also sounded very, very sad. "And he is. And so will many others."

He sat on the sofa where he'd originally sat. He'd never felt so far away from her.

"Well," he said resignedly, "there's always some kind of fighting going on with the Mexicans or the Indians or—say, it's not the British coming back to get whipped a third time, is it?"

"No, not that." She shook her head. "And don't make light of it, Brent. This is like nothing we've ever seen."

"Who are we fighting?"

She swallowed with great difficulty. Her voice was cracked and hoarse. "Each other."

Brent felt an icy chill of foreboding. He shook it off. "No, no. You talk as if you really believe this is going to happen."

"I do. I have to."

"You've got to stop this, Cassie. I'm only telling you this for your own good."

"It's awfully hard to control yourself when you've seen so much death and destruction all around. I know. I've seen it."

Her eyes held the same far-off glaze he'd seen when she'd first met Harold Andrews. Dazed. Troubled. Confused. Yet very much aware of everything that was transpiring.

"How can you be so sure? Did you read about it somewhere?"

"No."

"You know, at a party once in Charleston, I saw an old slave telling all the ladies' fortunes with cowrie shells she claimed her great-grandma had managed to bring over all the way from Africa. You don't have any shells, do you?"

"Just the ones Aunt Flora collected, over there in that case." She pointed to the far corner of the parlor, to a tall, glass case. "Right there with the stones, the stuffed owl, and the stuffed baby alligator all the way from the swamps in Florida."

"I saw a gypsy at a circus once telling fortunes by reading palms. Is that it?"

"No."

"You know, the ancient Romans used to tell the future by reading sheep livers."

"No. Now *you're* being silly."

"A friend of my aunt's claimed her grandmother could tell fortunes by reading tea leaves. Is that how you do it?"

"No. Please don't ask me again. And *don't* ridicule me."

"I'm not making fun of you, Cassie."

"I think you'd better go."

He caressed her cheek, and trailed his fingers down her neck and shoulder, down her arm to take her hand. Lifting her hand, he kissed it.

"I'll be back tomorrow," he promised. "I know sometimes doing what's right isn't always easy."

"That's what I keep trying to tell you."

• • •

Cassie rearranged her clothes. Even after she'd washed her face and brushed her hair again, she would have preferred to retire to bed for the rest of the day. But it was only late afternoon, and she had an entire evening ahead of her.

Even playing the piano didn't hold as much fascination for her when compared to holding Brent in her arms, or being held by him.

Cassie heard a knocking on the back door. When she opened it, Jerusha stood there with a basket of clean laundry.

"Goodness, Jerusha." She tugged at her clothing, even though she'd already made sure everything was back in place. Guilty conscience, she scolded herself. "I'd forgotten it was your day to bring the laundry."

"Then it's a good thing I remembered for you, isn't it?"

"Thank you. I'm sorry if I'm causing you more trouble than my aunt did."

"Oh, you're no trouble, miss. Neither was your aunt. She sort of had a way of staying out of real trouble."

"But everyone thought she was crazy," Cassie blurted out. Then, realizing the incredible tactlessness of what she'd said, she clapped her hands over her mouth.

Jerusha laughed as she set the laundry basket on the floor. "A body can be crazy and not cause any trouble. Miss Flora just learned the difference between what was important and what wasn't. And she learned how to keep her mouth shut about it."

Cassie stared at Jerusha as the woman headed for the back door.

Cassie knew she loved Brent, even if he didn't believe her, even if he thought she was insane. She knew he loved her, even if he hadn't told her in those precise words. Why else would he worry about what people thought of her?

She'd never expected to come all the way out here from Philadelphia and find a man she could truly love. But then, in Philadelphia, she'd never had Sebastian.

She rolled over in bed and gazed at Sebastian, resting on

her night table, in the soft, rose-pink and lemon-yellow light of dawn. The crickets quieted from their nightly serenade. The breeze picked up. A robin began to sing.

The lights began to swirl inside the crystal ball again. Silently she dared Sebastian to make anything horrible out of the beautiful light that surrounded them. Images began to take shape.

Brent. Fully clothed, although she couldn't clearly discern exactly what he was wearing. He looked as handsome and virile as ever.

"Well, that's certainly different from the other images," she told Sebastian. Considering the problem she'd just encountered, she began to worry more.

Herself. Also fully clothed, even though she couldn't figure out exactly which outfit of hers that was. She was seated across from Brent at a table with a bright red-and-white checkered cloth over it. At least they were still together. Maybe she'd been worrying too much.

Abel Warner. Abel? No. What was *he* doing there?

Cassie's eyes grew wide with surprise and terror as Sebastian showed Abel, springing to his feet from his chair at a dinner table. Grabbing his throat. Trying to cough, trying to breathe. Turning red and purple. His eyes growing wider, more rounded, bloodshot. The veins in his neck and at his temples bulging until she feared they would burst.

He was dying before her very eyes, and there wasn't a thing she could do about it!

“What do I do for him?” Cassie cried.

She bolted upright in her bed. All pleasant thoughts of Brent fled as she watched Abel choking, sinking to the floor. His pregnant wife and two little girls gathered around him in his dying agonies.

Wait a minute. Brent had been in this vision, too. Where was he now? Why wasn’t he doing something to help?

Cassie recalled Brent and Abel didn’t seem to like each other, but Brent was hardly the sort of man who would stand there and let another man—even one he didn’t like—die in cold blood without lifting a hand to aid him. Wasn’t he?

“What can I do for him?” Cassie repeated, hoping a new image would form, one that would show her exactly how to save Abel’s life.

But the image in Sebastian faded away.

“Nothing?” she asked.

No other image formed to take its place.

“Nothing? Damn you!”

In frustration, she seized the blank crystal ball with both hands and shook it. She was sorely tempted to smash it against the wall, if she could have thrown the heavy thing.

"Don't show me Abel dying if you can't show me how to help him, too!" she scolded.

Just like the coming war, she realized with a horrifying chill, there wasn't anything she or anyone else could do about it. She hadn't been able to do anything to prevent Lem from breaking his arm. In fact, she still wasn't convinced she hadn't caused the accident by mentioning it in the first place.

"There has to be *something* I can do!" she beseeched Sebastian for an answer, but he remained blank. "If I can't save his life, maybe someone else can."

She replaced Sebastian in his stand, hoping he'd take the hint and show her a hero. Sebastian remained blank.

"How can I warn Abel when I promised Brent I'd try to keep quiet about these kinds of things in public? Thunderation! I can't even tell Brent without having him worry about me being insane. How can I tell anyone when no one—not even Brent—ever believes a word I say?"

"Morning, Abel," Brent called cheerily as he entered the general store.

"Morning, Brent," Abel responded curtly. He didn't even bother to glance up from the list he was tallying. He licked the tip of his pencil and jotted down a column of figures. "I understand you're supposed to be taking care of a bank draft for Miss Bowen so I can finally send off that big order for all that drilling equipment."

"Well, I've been pretty busy at the newspaper, and I haven't quite gotten around to it yet," Brent confessed.

He wasn't going to, either, he'd decided, unless she really insisted on it. Maybe, if he waited long enough, Cassie would do like Miss Flora sometimes did. She'd finally get tired of one harebrained scheme and move on to something else. He hoped next time it would be something harmless, like collecting ancient Egyptian mummies, and certainly something nowhere near as expensive.

"Well, try to find time for it, won't you? She's promised me a fee for handling the order for her."

"I'll try."

Abel shrugged and returned to his work. "So what can I do for you today?"

"Looks like I've run out of coffee again."

Abel put down his pencil and looked up from his list. "Want me to grind it for you, or do you want to grind it yourself?"

"Grind it for me, please. I don't have that much time anymore."

"I noticed."

"Shucks, I'm not awake enough in the morning to do anything but brew it and drink it. Sometimes after I'm done with it, it's not all that drinkable, anyway."

Brent chuckled. He'd hoped Abel would laugh, too—or at least glance up at him. Without saying another word, Abel dipped a scoop into the bin of coffee beans, poured the measure into his grinder, and started cranking.

The store filled with a metallic grinding sound, and the aroma of the roasted beans, blending with the pervasive scent of cinnamon. When he was finished, Abel poured the dark brown powder into a brown paper bag and folded down the top.

"Of course, if I had a devoted wife like you do, she'd have it all ground for me," Brent ventured.

"Yep."

"It would taste a lot better, too."

"Probably."

"If I had a good wife like you do, I wouldn't have run out of coffee in the first place."

"Probably not."

"Sure would be nice to have a sweet little wife, waking me up with a fresh brewed cup of coffee, like you have."

"Sure would. Anything else you need while you're here?"

"Sugar."

Without saying a word, Abel retrieved a small cone wrapped in blue paper.

Brent glanced around the empty store. He'd chosen the right time to come in. Everyone had heard of their old disagreement and were probably still amazed that their grudge had lasted this long. No one in town could help but notice the dirty looks Abel still tossed his way.

Abel's dirty looks didn't help Brent's reputation in town any, either. On the other hand, having witnesses usually kept Abel at least civil to him.

"Nowhere near as crowded in here today," Brent noted. He didn't think Abel really gave a damn about anything he said, but he just couldn't bear the deafening silence.

Abel grunted. He picked up the pencil and returned to his ciphering.

Brent chuckled. "Not like it was a couple of days ago, with all those excited ladies cackling about those twins."

"Yep."

"Why, a body would've thought this was a henhouse instead of a general store."

"Yep."

Apparently Abel wasn't in a jocular mood. Maybe he'd try a little more serious subject. "I heard Lem's arm's going to be all right."

"Yep."

Try again. Aha! He hit on a subject that had to be a winner.

"Say, your wife ought to be just about ready to deliver that new baby by now," Brent ventured.

That should be the one subject safe enough for both of them to discuss without a disagreement, and one that Abel was bound to show enough interest in to respond to him with more than grunts and "yep."

Abel nodded. "About two more months."

"So, how many kids does that make for you two now?"

"Shucks, Brent." He slammed his pencil down on the counter. "You see us going to church every—well, no. I guess *you* don't. We've got two girls, Lucy and Edith."

"How old are they now?"

"Six and four."

"Well, I hope it's a boy this time."

"Thanks. Me, too." Abel picked up his pencil and returned to studying his list.

"What do you think you'll name him?"

"Carson."

"For your pa?"

"Yep." Abel licked the tip of his pencil again and continued totting up figures.

"And just in case it's another girl?" Brent prompted.

"Grace." Abel kept writing.

"After Sally's mother?"

"Yep."

"Pretty name." Since it didn't appear as if Abel was going to look him in the eye, Brent decided to glance around the store again. "Looks as if things are going fairly well for you here."

"Not as if it would interest you, but I'm doing fine. Just fine."

"I am interested, Abel."

"That's great now." He wrote with such ferocity that the tip of his pencil broke. He slammed it down on the counter. "You weren't too all-fired interested three years ago."

"Three years ago I was in no position to help anyone."

"Too busy helping yourself." Abel reached into his back pocket, pulled out a penknife, and began whittling a new point to his pencil.

"My father had just died. I'd inherited an expiring newspaper and a pile of debts clean up to the roof. What was I supposed to do? Sell everything and starve so you could build your store?"

"We could've gone into this store together, as partners, just like we always talked about."

"No, just like *you* always talked about. You knew I always wanted to follow in my father's footsteps in the newspaper business."

"You were doing it, too. You had a newspaper of your own that was running fine. Excuse me if I wanted something more for myself than merely to work in a general store like my father did. I wanted to own one. You could've expanded into part ownership with me."

"And let the newspaper stumble along as it always had? I wanted to make something of the *Argus*, something to be proud of."

"If you were really following in his footsteps, you wouldn't have turned the *Argus* into some kind of scandal sheet. Yeah, your pa would be real proud of that."

"*I'm* proud of it. It's making more money than—"

"Aw, hell, Brent. There isn't any sense in wasting my breath telling you this. It's all water under the bridge now, anyway. But you still could've lent me a little money. Then I wouldn't have had to go to strangers."

"Miss Flora wasn't a stranger."

"But *we* were friends, Brent," Abel stressed. "Even afterward, after you started making money hand over fist, building a big, fancy new house, buying fancy new clothes, you couldn't throw me a bone."

"You were doing well by then. I still had to put everything back into the business."

"Or put everything into impressing . . . certain people."

"I *needed* a new suit of clothes. For Pete's sake, Abel, I hadn't had anything new to wear since we were confirmed. I'd been wearing my father's old clothes because my own trousers came halfway up to my knees, and dang, they cut in the crotch, if you get a fellow's meaning. I couldn't go meeting some of the people I had to meet looking as if I'd just fallen off the hay wagon."

Brent hated to get started on this subject. It was too painful. He envied Abel his home and family, and the man who had been his friend needed to know it.

"At the time, I also thought I'd be needing a house big enough for a family, but—"

"Well, that big mansion of yours just might come in handy again after all." Abel gave a low chuckle that Brent didn't like the sound of, not at all.

"What do you mean?" Brent asked, eyeing Abel cautiously.

What was the man up to? What did he know that Brent didn't?

"You've got some letters." Abel tilted his head toward the corner of his store he'd outfitted as a post office.

A counter with a wrought-iron grill atop it was all that officially separated the area of the post office from that of the general store. But Abel always made a very firm distinction between his personal job as proprietor of his own shop and his official position as postmaster of Lyman's Gap.

Brent figured Abel had every right to take great pride in his general store. He took even greater pride in the fact that he was postmaster. Not that it entailed any weighty responsibilities, but it was important as far as folks in Lyman's Gap were concerned.

Abel pushed his black sleeve protectors farther up over his elbows and grabbed his visor. He sorted through the little slots of mail and handed Brent two letters.

"Yep, you just might be glad you built that big house after all." Abel nodded to the two letters. "Especially if one of them is from who I suspect it's from."

Brent looked down at the letters. The top one was plain, inexpensive white paper. The address was penned in what looked like the backward slanting, slightly awkward handwriting of his sister, Alma, out in Illinois. Two sooty finger smudges marred the lower left-hand corner. Too small to be the postman's, Brent noticed. What had his nephew been into?

He stared at the other letter. High quality, watermarked stationery, he noted. In the warmth of his hand, the slight trace of expensive perfume wafted up from the letter. The address was in an elegant, practiced script.

Evaline McAlister.

Brent felt his throat tighten and heard his heart pounding in his ears. He was too young to have a stroke like his father, wasn't he?

"Guess her pa's finally relented about her at least writing to you, huh?" Abel asked with a snide chuckle.

Brent shrugged. Stay calm, he told himself.

"No. It's probably just the announcement of her wedding to

some fat, cigar-puffing, railroad-owning rich man in New York, or a bloody British duke, or some frog-and-snail-eating French count."

He jammed the letter into his pocket, crumpling the fine stationery. He didn't want Abel to think it meant that much to him. It didn't. He would read it later, in private.

He tapped the other letter against his hand.

"This one's from Alma." He tore it open.

After allowing him a few minutes to read it in silence, Abel asked, "How are they all doing?"

Brent guessed Abel must have figured it was safe to ask about his sister and her family without showing any real interest in him personally.

Brent chuckled. "Hey, I'm an uncle again."

"You dang fool. I always knew you'd be the uncle. Do you have a new niece or nephew?" Abel demanded with a genuinely lighthearted laugh.

For just a moment, Brent could almost believe their old friendship might be resurrected, even after all this time.

"Another nephew," Brent announced proudly. "Stephen Douglas McCaffrey. He'll keep James Buchanan McCaffrey company."

"Golly, can't tell your brother-in-law's political leanings, can you?" Abel joked.

Brent took heart at Abel's humor. "He's a staunch Democrat. And it's a good name—President Buchanan's Pennsylvania born and bred. Still, I can't imagine what Alma and Walter would name a girl if they ever have one."

"I think your sister might have something to say in that case. How is she?"

Brent glanced down at the letter, but he'd already practically memorized it.

"Alma's doing fine, too. She says Walter's been going to a lot of political rallies, speeches, debates, and things."

"Sally's not too happy when I have to keep the store open late. How's that sit with Alma?"

"She likes it. She says it keeps him out of her hair. I can't say as I blame her."

The bells attached to the top of the rear door jangled. Brent turned. That was unusual. No one ever came in the back door.

Without even looking to see who was there, Abel called, "Come on in, Mrs. Jackson."

Jerusha's coffee and cream face appeared, framed in the storeroom doorway. She'd wrapped a white kerchief around her hair. Her wicker basket, with a red-checked cloth thrown over it, hung from her arm.

"Morning, Mr. Warner." Her voice dripped of Spanish moss and bayou. Her eyes, like bright chips of obsidian, darted around the store, then settled on Brent. "Morning, Mr. Conway. I thought no one else was here. I'll just do my shopping and be gone."

"You know I don't mind you shopping while I'm here, Mrs. Jackson," Brent said as he refolded his sister's letter and slipped it into his inside breast pocket. Not the same pocket he'd put Evaline's letter in. For some reason he couldn't quite name, he felt he needed to keep the two separated.

"Take your time, Jerusha," Abel told her.

"Thanks, Mr. Warner. You're the only store nearby and you don't seem to mind doing business with Olivier and me. Not like some places we've been."

"It's a pleasure doing business with you. You and Olivier always pay your bill on time. That'll endear you to any shopkeeper."

"I know some folks around here still aren't too used to shopping with folks of color. I wouldn't want to cause you any trouble."

"You're no trouble, Mrs. Jackson." Abel shrugged. "Maybe someday they'll get used to it."

She sniffed. "I'll never live that long."

"That's their loss. Although someday I'd like to see you come through that front door," Abel said.

She laughed. "Someday I'd like to see me and Olivier own our own store."

• • •

Brent slammed his front door closed. He tore off his jacket and tossed it onto the sofa, the only piece of furniture in his parlor. Tarnation! He hadn't even bothered with a rug or a lamp.

He propped the letter from Alma on the mantle, against the daguerreotype of Walter and her, taken on their wedding day five years ago. She looked so young, so thin, so happy, standing beside Walter seated in that ornate chair, one hand holding her bouquet, the other resting on his shoulder.

He wondered how married life and two children had changed her. She'd probably put on a little weight. Maybe she didn't giggle as much as she used to. He'd noticed those changes with some of the other young matrons in town he'd grown up with. Bearing children had a way of taking the silliness out of most women.

He just hoped Alma hadn't changed as their mother had—thin, gray, and wrinkled before her time. Of course, Walter made enough to support them all, and if Brent knew his brother-in-law, the man didn't go throwing it all away, as Edgar Conway had, on dubious charities and lost causes, and any tramp with a plausible tale of woe.

"I wish I had a newer picture of you and your children," he told the daguerreotype. "I'm getting tired of looking at old Walter's pasty face, having his bug-eyes staring out at me all the time. It's about time I looked at something prettier."

He chuckled.

"Of course, I could hang a nice, big painting of Mehetabel and her piglets over the mantel, and it would look prettier than Walter."

He moved over to look at the daguerrotype of his parents, taken shortly before his mother had died. Even though his parents had never lived in the house Brent had built, images of them somehow made the big place seem less empty, made him feel a little less lonesome as night closed in.

He rested his knuckles on his hips and rocked back and forth on his heels, admiring the pictures of his family.

"Someday I'm going to take a little time away from the newspaper," Brent promised the image of Alma. "I think Sam and Dave can handle things at the *Argus* for two or three weeks without mixing up the type too much. I'll come out there and spend a little time with you. Wrestle with my nephews when they get old enough. Spoil a niece if I ever have one. Buy them a puppy to track mud through the house, howl all night, chew Walter's slippers, and generally pester the living daylights out of him."

He shook his head.

"Somehow I just can't picture staid old Walter, in his fancy suit, chasing after a lop-eared hound."

Brent studied the images of his mother and father.

"Ma and Pa would've been proud of how well Walter's doing with the railroad," Brent told the unblinking image of his sister. "They'd have been delighted with their two grandsons, too, although you know Ma wouldn't have stopped nagging you until you'd given her that granddaughter. I suppose you two won't stop at only two though."

His lips twisted into a wry grimace.

"Of course, with the salary Walter's making, you won't have any trouble supporting a large family. Shucks, he might even hire you a maid. So I guess it really doesn't matter how many children you have. None of them will have to wear hand-me-downs, will they? Or go to school in patched trousers. Or have to pretend they're overjoyed to be the recipients of the proceeds of the Firemen's Charity Auction. No dinners of bacon grease and boiled potatoes for you all. No, siree. Steaks and asparagus. Oysters and celery. Capons and artichokes. And fancy bottled ketchup. Maybe even some of that imported Worcestershire sauce."

He chuckled to himself.

"I just hope it doesn't take you six boys to finally get that girl, the way it did Gertrude Wilcox. Maybe I ought to ask Cassie what she thinks about that."

He smiled when he thought of Cassie, all flustered and uncertain when she made those crazy predictions, but so very sure of the predictions themselves. She'd been correct on a couple of them. Shucks, pretty near all of them. He stroked his chin. He couldn't recollect anyone else ever having that much good luck—except Miss Flora. Then he laughed.

"It wouldn't do any good to ask Cassie. Her guesses aren't any better or any worse than anyone else's. You'd like her, Alma. Sweet and pretty. Maybe a little too outspoken for Walter's tastes. I'm sure he wouldn't like her politics. I wonder if Walter's ever been to any of this Lincoln fellow's speeches."

He paced back and forth in front of the fireplace.

"What do you think, Alma? Would Ma and Pa have been as proud of me as they would've been of Walter?" he wondered aloud. "Ma went to her grave lamenting that, with all my vain ambitions, I'd end up a wealthy, lonely old curmudgeon without a friend in the world, except the ones I could buy, and when I died, I'd go straight to hell. Most folks in town would tend to agree with her."

Brent plopped down on the sofa, leaned back, and crossed one leg over the other. He studied the pictures of his parents.

"Never mind that I've made a paying operation out of that consarn newspaper. Never mind that I've got more money saved in the bank right now than Pa ever saw in his entire life. I've done business with men Pa'd only read about."

He thumped his fist on the back of the sofa.

"I've even got a few friends, but none that Ma would ever deem worthy. Maybe they don't have all their teeth and don't know how to read too well. But they're decent, caring human beings who work hard and are careful with their money so they don't have to feed their children rancid butter. Their kids actually know what meat tastes like, not something that was found along the side of a road. Their kids don't have the wind and snow biting their butts through threadbare clothes when they go to school, either. Bah!"

He threw up his hands in frustration.

When his hand landed, it touched his jacket. The jacket lay there across the back of the sofa, like Pandora's box, a constant reminder of the mysteries it still contained. Evaline was still a mystery to him, too.

"If this doesn't beat all. Evaline writes me once to say she's having a great time in London, doesn't write to me for another six months, and now this."

He studied the envelope with narrowed eyes.

"What's she up to?" he asked the image of his sister.

She didn't answer.

"Only one way to find out, you cotton-brained sot," he scolded himself.

"Boy, I'm talking to myself and to pictures of folks who are either dead or living halfway across the country. I must be going crazy. It must be contagious, from living next door to Miss Flora for so long."

Or from kissing Cassie, he told himself. A grin widened across his lips. For just a moment, his heart felt lighter again. If she was the source of the contagion, let him die a pest-ridden, happy man.

Then the thought made him stop for a moment to reconsider.

When he was growing up, all he ever wanted was to have enough money so the other kids in school wouldn't make fun of him, his raggedy clothes, and cheese sandwich lunches.

When he grew older, his goals changed slightly. All he wanted was to have enough money to marry beautiful Evaline McAlister. He wanted to be able to give her the same kind of life her wealthy father, with his coal mines and all his investments, could.

Brent waited until he had a thriving business and other investments. He waited until he had money in the bank and a big house. Then he proposed marriage.

Evaline—all coy and ladylike—had blushed behind her fan, declared his proposal was totally unexpected—even though they'd been keeping company for over six months—and asked for time to consider. She'd told him he'd have to respect all the social proprieties and speak to her father first.

Brent had expected as much from a well-bred young lady. He'd summoned up his courage and approached the formidable old man to ask for his daughter's hand in marriage.

Mr. Horace T. McAlister—his cigar smoke blowing in Brent's face, his jowls jiggling, and his paunch bouncing with ridicule—had just laughed. Not a word, not a no, certainly not a yes, not even a "never darken my door again." Horace T. McAlister had simply packed up his obedient wife and dutiful daughter for a yearlong European tour.

Evaline had left without so much as a farewell.

Brent liked to believe their hasty departure was her father's fault. She'd sent him a brief letter from Europe, telling of the wonderful sights they'd seen. She'd even dared mention that she missed him—obviously a letter her father had not perused before allowing it to be sent off. Of course, she'd also sent more letters to Reverend Markham, Miss Flora, Mrs. Andrews, Mrs. Green, and even Sally Warner.

What had Evaline sent him now? Was she in Venice or Paris? Was she married? Did she still love him? Had she ever?

Pulling that letter out of his pocket was like reaching into a snake hole. He didn't know exactly what he was going to get—a diamond, a handful of dirt, or a painful, poisonous bite.

He pulled out the letter and smoothed it flat. A United States postage stamp. She was back in this country, that much closer to him.

He broke the seal and unfolded the letter. To fill the emptiness of the house, and stave off the encroaching loneliness, he read aloud to himself. " 'My dearest Brent.' "

He blinked. This one had certainly gotten past her father!

" 'I have missed you terribly,' " he continued reading aloud. " 'We are currently staying in New York with friends. We will be returning to Lyman's Gap soon, but not soon enough. I cannot wait to see you again and renew old acquaintances. Your most affectionate friend, Evaline.' "

Renew old acquaintances? Most affectionate friend? A year ago, those words would have sent his heart soaring.

But things had changed. He'd held Cassie Bowen in his arms and kissed her. When he lay in bed at night, visions of Cassie lying beside him ran through his head. Cassie, naked in his arms, her long auburn hair streaming down her smooth back and slender waist, her skin the pale color of perfect ivory. His hands caressing her rounded buttocks and softly curved breasts, like two luminous pearls in his hands. Her hands running lightly, tormentingly over his body until he felt he would explode.

He wanted Cassie, not some distant reminder of his juvenile affections, suddenly returned to "renew old acquaintances." Although the folks in town couldn't have helped but notice them keeping company, at least he'd had the good sense not to have made his true feelings and intentions toward Evaline public. Thank goodness.

How could he explain Cassie to Evaline now? Or Evaline to Cassie? If he tried to explain Evaline to Cassie, would Cassie make some misguided claim that she'd known about it all along?

Evaline had been the most elegantly beautiful woman he'd ever seen in his life. But Cassie was by far the most interesting—and that made her more beautiful than anything else.

"Excuse me, but you've got a problem here, Mr. Conway."

Brent jumped up from the sofa as if that imaginary snake in his jacket pocket had just shouted in his ear. How could that snake be talking to him? Unless it was the same snake from the Garden of Eden. In that case, he didn't need any legless reptile telling him he was in trouble all the way up to his ears. He knew that already.

"Excuse me, Mr. Conway. I didn't mean to startle you." Jerusha stood in the doorway.

Brent drew a deep breath in relief. He smiled. "I'm sorry, Jerusha. I didn't hear you come in. Have . . . have you been waiting there long?" How much had she overheard?

"You know I wouldn't ordinarily come barging in where I got no right to be."

"I know that, Jerusha."

"But I knocked and knocked and still didn't get no answer. I called your name a couple of times before I went wandering through the house, but I still didn't get no answer, and I was starting to worry about you. So I came looking."

"Thanks. That's very kind of you. I was just . . . lost in thought."

"I'd have just come in the back door and stayed in the kitchen, but I saw a mouse when I was coming through and thought I ought to let you know. You might want to think about getting yourself a good cat."

"I might do that."

"I hear Mrs. Norton's cat had kittens that ought to be ready to leave their mama in a week or so."

"I'll look into it," Brent promised.

"Of course," she said, glancing around, "pardon me for saying so, but there's not too much here a mouse could damage."

"No, there's not."

"I got your clean laundry here." She held out the wicker basket piled with clean, pressed, and neatly folded clothing and linen. She looked around, frowning. "Where do you want me to put it?"

Did she think he was so lost in thought that he wouldn't even have noticed something as big as the laundry basket?

"Thank you, Jerusha. You can set it down there on the floor."

"I suppose just about anywhere on this floor will do."

"Yes, thanks."

"Aren't too many things I could set it on, are there?"

"I'm afraid not."

"If you don't mind my asking, Mr. Conway, what happened to all your furniture?"

"I never had any," he confessed.

"Hush, Mr. Conway, that's no way for a gentleman to talk," Jerusha scolded.

"It's true. I don't have any."

"That still don't mean you got to admit it."

Brent just stared at her, puzzled.

"You got to tell folks you had it sent out to be 'repaired'," she drawled. "It *sounds* better."

"I understand."

"It's all in how you present yourself, Mr. Conway. You ought to know that by now."

He reached into his pocket for Jerusha's payment. "Well, I trust you won't go telling anyone—"

Jerusha nodded sagely, accepting the proffered coins. "Of course, you can trust me, Mr. Conway. I've seen this sort of thing before on some of those big plantations in Louisiana when a cotton or a sugar crop failed. All the furniture moved into the front company rooms, and upstairs them fine folks was sleeping on corn-husk mattress ticks on the floor. Folks keeping up appearances was all it always amounted to."

"No, no, it's not that," Brent protested. "It's not what you think. I have the money. I just don't have any furniture."

When she didn't ask why, he continued.

"When I tore down that miserable old shack I lived in as a boy, that my parents had the nerve to call a house, I got rid of all that rickety, broken-down furniture, too. Most of it made good kindling. I never got around to buying anything except what I absolutely needed. You see, I was waiting for—"

"You don't have to explain anything to me, Mr. Conway." She waved her hand in front of her. "I know how to keep my secrets—and other folks', too." She turned and headed for the back door. "I'll be by next week."

"You . . . you can go out the front door, Jerusha. I don't mind if—"

"No, thank you, Mr. Conway," Jerusha replied firmly. "I always go out the door I came in. It's an old . . . habit of mine."

Ten

"Miss Bowen, I would consider it a singular honor if you would allow me the pleasure of escorting you this evening to the Lyman's Gap Volunteer Firemen's Association's Annual Fish Fry and Charity Auction."

Brent doffed his hat and swept it across his extended foot in an exaggerated bow. Cassie had to smile at him, standing there grinning in her doorway.

"My, don't you look extremely gallant," Cassie exclaimed.

The light of the setting sun cast golden highlights in his dark hair. He was dressed in a fine suit of dark blue broadcloth. He looked hopeful and repentant, and at the same time supremely confident that his irresistible personal charms would induce her to forgive him. It was awfully hard for Cassie to say no.

Still, she'd exerted herself to the utmost the past few days. Sebastian had tried her patience with persistent images she didn't understand but nonetheless believed. She just didn't feel like being sociable this evening.

"Oh, no. Thank you for your kind invitation, but I couldn't possibly."

The smile fell from his face. "You still haven't forgiven me?"

"No, no." She shook her head.

"I realize you believe I sounded thoughtless and unfeeling. Maybe even rude."

"No, no."

"I only talked that way because I care about you, Cassie." His gaze grew soft, but the look was still intense. "I worry because I haven't seen you out of this house in days."

"You've been watching me?" She cocked her head and stared at him.

"Well, it's sort of easy to keep on eye on your house while I've been doing so much gardening. Not to mention I worry about you," he repeated.

How could she not forgive him? "That's sweet of you, Brent, but—"

"I'm going—and you have to come with me."

She shook her head. "No. It's out of the question."

"I've gone every year since I was five years old. I've never once missed the Fish Fry. I don't intend to miss it this year, either."

"Then you may go this year, too. But you'll be going alone."

"Each year, I've gone with my parents or with Miss Flora. Don't make me go alone this year. *You* wouldn't want to have to go alone, would you?"

"*I* want to stay at home."

"But, if you *were* going, you'd want some company, wouldn't you? It's no fun eating alone."

"I suppose you're right."

"I can't think of anyone else in the world I'd rather go with than you."

"Now I think you're exaggerating," she accused.

"Not one bit."

The gleam in his eyes inspired almost as much assurance as the glow that came from Sebastian's ever-truthful visions. Brent in real life made her feel much more wonderful than

Sebastian ever could. But could she trust Brent as she did Sebastian?

"I don't suppose people would gossip if two neighbors, who happen to be heading in the same direction for the same event, were to be strolling along together. Do you?" Brent asked.

"Of course, they won't gossip. Especially since the two neighbors will *not* be you and I."

"But you *must* go, you know."

"Mrs. Andrews will be there," Cassie wailed out the truth of her reluctance.

"So will Mr. Harvey."

"Oh, no." She groaned.

"All the more reason to go," he insisted.

"Why must you be so persistent about this?"

"Because you need to show them you're as sound of mind as you are of body."

Brent's gaze swept her figure. She'd donned a pink-and-white-flowered calico dress with little shell buttons she'd had for two or three years. Since she hadn't figured on leaving the house and ordinarily wouldn't have figured on receiving callers, either, she hadn't even bothered with a corset today. But then, she ought to have counted on Brent to come around interfering.

"I won't be sound of body," she still protested. "You know I hate fish."

"You're not going to lose your dinner as long as you don't eat any fish. Just eat the fried potatoes and corn relish—and dessert. You can't forget dessert."

"You don't understand. It's not just the taste of fish. It's not just the awful smell of fish. It's the very thought of fish that makes me ill."

She figured that pretty much summed up her dislike of fish. Still Brent stood on her porch, long legs astride, his arms crossed over his broad chest. She tried to keep her chin low, looking up at him from under her lashes, very pathetic and appealing—helpless in the face of the memory of boatloads of abominably reeking fish.

"What do you have against fish? What did they ever do to you?"

Obviously Brent was not sympathetic to her plight.

"It's not what they did to me. It's what I had to do to them." Already she could feel her lips curl with distaste and her stomach begin to churn.

Brent eyed her warily. Was he still afraid that this time she'd claim that something was not only making her say strange things, but also it was making her do strange things to fish? Clearly Brent deserved a further explanation.

"My father loved to fish."

"Yes . . . ?" Brent looked at her expectantly. He'd obviously surmised there was more to this story. He was waiting for it.

"He had rods and reels, lures and creels, flies and nets, even a special lucky fishing hat. Why, he practically had a standing reservation at his favorite secret spot at the old fishing hole."

"I'd call that love," Brent agreed.

"He was good at it, too. Or lucky."

"That's good."

"No." She shook her head. "It was very good for him and made him very happy. We ate well very cheaply, which made my mother happy. But after he'd bring home his catch, my mother and I would have to clean it—every last scaly, smelly, glassy-eyed one of them."

"That made you very unhappy."

"I'd try to claim friends had invited me on an outing. That excuse worked every day but Thursday. We could only afford a servant from time to time, and God forbid Letitia should soil her lily-white hands scaling and gutting fish. So usually it was just my mother and me, every Thursday afternoon—scraping and cutting, scraping and cutting. Up to our elbows in fish guts! Even after Mama died and Papa kept up his hobby, Letitia maintained I had 'experience' and she didn't, and insisted I ought to continue. If I never see another fish again in my life, it will be too soon."

"Do you realize that if you don't go, Mrs. Andrews will expect a donation at least five times the price of the dinner?"

"Is that what Aunt Flora usually gave?"

"No. She ate the fish."

Cassie placed one hand on her hip, cocked her head, and grinned at him. "You know, Brent, I'm discovering that's probably one of the nicer aspects of being wealthy. I can actually *pay* not to have to do something I find unpleasant."

Brent placed his hand on his hip, cocked his head, and grinned at her in perfect imitation. "You know, Cassie, that's probably one of the stranger aspects of being wealthy."

He dropped his mocking stance and regarded her in a more normal, masculine demeanor.

"You can pay people to do things for you that you don't want to do yourself. You can even pay some people to say nice things about you, even if they don't really believe it about you, and even if you don't really deserve the compliments. But you can't buy people's good opinion of you. At least, not from people whose good opinion you'd value."

He was right, but instead of admitting it to him, Cassie just twisted her lips. "I still don't see any need for me to actually go there."

"Let me put it this way. You won't get Irma Andrews and August Harvey to leave you alone unless you can prove to them and to the rest of the town that they're wrong about you. That you can conduct yourself properly out there in the world with normal folks."

"You mean sane folks, and not make a blasted fool of myself?"

"I did not say that. I wasn't even thinking it."

Cassie pressed her lips together, considering. At last she said, "I won't actually have to *eat* any fish?"

"Not a morsel."

"We can get a seat near the door in case I have to make a hasty exit?"

"Of course."

"You'll stay with me and make sure I don't say anything stupid?"

"Oh, Cassie." He reached out to take her hand. "Don't you

know by now? It doesn't matter if you say something stupid, or if you say things that make Isaac Newton and Leonardo da Vinci look like babbling simpletons. Don't you know I don't want to leave your side for a minute?"

She didn't reply to that question. If she told him what she was really thinking, that she wanted him with her every waking—and sleeping—moment, they'd never make it to the Fish Fry. She'd grab his hand, pull him inside the house, and securely lock the door behind them. Then let the townspeople gossip!

"I realized after you left last week. You were right," she admitted. "I do have to learn when to keep quiet, and to behave myself in public. Especially in front of Mrs. Andrews and Mr. Harvey."

"Especially in front of *everyone*," Brent corrected. "You never know when someone will even accidentally let slip something you've said."

"I know. I know all these things, but it's just so difficult. I wanted my independence and now I'm more restricted than ever."

Brent took her hand. Her fingers rested lightly in his palm while his thumb moved slowly across the back of her hand.

"Don't think about that now. Come with me and have a good time."

She still stood there. Lips pressed together, she was still trying to decide if the benefits to her reputation of going to the celebrated Fish Fry outweighed the disadvantages of vomiting in public.

"I'll bet you haven't really enjoyed yourself in a long, long time."

"Well," she grumbled with mock irritation, "I *was* pretty much enjoying myself with you the other day—before you practically accused me of being a raving maniac."

Brent dropped her hand and stood in front of her, appearing very commanding.

"All right, Cassie. I know I promised you I wouldn't interfere in your private life. I know I promised to give you advice only when and if you asked for it. But the time has come for me to drop all polite pretenses and take charge."

She looked up at him and blinked. "Well, I'm not surprised."

"You are coming with me to eat potato salad, applesauce, and gingerbread." He glared down at her. "Don't give me any arguments."

"I wasn't going to."

"Oh, right," he quipped sarcastically.

"I was just about to agree with you."

"Well then, not that you don't look very lovely in that, but go on upstairs and change into something much, much fancier."

"Fancier?" She looked down at her dress. She'd figured all along she'd have to don her corset. But to put on something really fancy? "I didn't bring anything really fancy with me. And I'm still in mourning."

"Just wear less jewelry," he suggested.

"That's the biggest disappointment!" she protested. "You know, someday I'm going back to Philadelphia to pay a visit to Robert and Letitia and I'm going to wear every blasted piece of jewelry Aunt Flora left me."

"From what you've told me about your sister-in-law, that ought to outright make her turn green and keel over dead from sheer envy."

"I'm not a greedy woman. I'd settle for her turning green with envy."

"But you've got to wear something really special tonight, Cassie. Aside from the Independence Day Picnic, this is the most important annual event in Lyman's Gap. The only other event that came close to it was . . ." He reached up to rub the back of his neck, as if that could help him think better. "Oh, golly, I guess it was my own sister's wedding four years ago."

"I see. In that case, if you don't mind waiting here on the porch, I'll change into the fanciest dress I have, as quickly as I can."

His eyebrows drooped with disappointment. "Wait on the

porch? Don't you need any help, you know, fastening or unfastening? Tying, buttoning? Unbuttoning?" He raised an eyebrow and grinned at her.

"I think I can manage very well by myself this time, thank you."

"Good thing, too," he agreed, pulling down the sleeves of his jacket. "Or we'd never get to the Fish Fry."

"Wait here." She threw him a playful glance as she closed the front door.

She donned her dark purple satin gown—the fanciest thing she owned. She'd only worn it once, to Ophelia Langenfelder's Christmas party last year. The neckline was a good bit lower than she was accustomed to, and a little lower off the shoulders, but she had a fine lace shawl with which to cover herself if the evening grew too chilly—or she lost her nerve.

She'd seen Robert and Letitia dressed to go out one evening. Robert had looked so handsome in evening wear. Letitia's rose satin and lace gown had been unbelievably beautiful. She wondered how far Robert had gone into debt to buy it for her.

Anyway, this wasn't Philadelphia. Cassie figured this gown was about as fancy as they'd get in Lyman's Gap.

The only jewelry she wore was a single strand of Aunt Flora's pearls and a pair of small pearl drop earrings. She figured that ought to be perfectly acceptable.

"Is this suitable attire for the Lyman's Gap Volunteer Firemen's Association's Annual Fish Fry and Charity Auction?" she asked as she emerged from the house. She held her skirt full out to her sides as she twirled around on the front porch.

Brent pushed himself from the porch rail where he'd been leaning, and emitted a low whistle. Cassie grinned.

"No, it's not suitable," he pronounced, shaking his head forlornly. "Not suitable at all."

Before the grin could fade from Cassie's face, he came to stand close beside her, encircling her waist with his hands. His warm breath brushed against her cheek, stirring small tendrils of hair that escaped from the braid wrapped around her head, and stirring tremulous feelings within her breast.

"Why, pray tell, is this lovely gown not suitable?" she demanded.

"I can't decide if it's a waste of fabric," he whispered, "covering up all the lovely parts of things I've seen. Things I can't wait to see more of. All the beautiful, delicate parts of you I want to hold close to me."

He pulled her closer, pressing his firm body against hers.

"Or if it's a shameless scandal, letting other men see even a tiny bit of those beautiful parts I want to keep all for myself."

He tucked his finger into the top of her bodice, and pretended to pull it out so he could peek down it. She slapped at this hand.

"Stop! If I let you do that, we'll never arrive at the Fish Fry on time."

"The devil take the fish." He nibbled gently at her earlobe.

"If you swallow my aunt's pearls, I'll—"

"You'll wear another pair," he finished for her.

He silenced all other conversation with a passionate kiss under her ear. It made chills run up her neck. She giggled and pulled her shoulder up, pressing him closer to her.

She closed her eyes and let his warmth and passion surge over her. She wanted him. Now. Slowly, as if prolonging the exquisite torture it was for her to be parted from him, she pulled away.

"Slowly, Brent. Slowly," she whispered breathlessly. "I want you, too. You know I do, but I can't . . . I need to think you respect me, and believe at least a little of what I say."

"I'm trying, Cassie," he whispered earnestly. "It's just so darn hard to believe some of the stuff you come up with. But I do respect you, and . . ." His voice grew louder, more jovial. "And there is no way I'm going to risk spoiling this evening the way I did last time by talking about anything else."

Cassie supposed, considering she'd inherited a very strange family curse, that was the best she could expect.

She placed her hands atop his and slowly pushed them away from her waist.

"If we don't leave, we'll never get to the Fish Fry," she repeated.

Before Brent could open his mouth with his expected retort, Cassie placed a hushing finger to his lips.

"If we don't leave now, there won't be any fish left for me to get sick over. Won't that disappoint all those people—and we know who they are—who would just delight in seeing me ill?"

"I feel it only fair to warn you that you might live to regret this evening's meal anyway," he told her as they proceeded down the porch steps.

"How's that?"

"Were you aware that the men are doing the cooking?"

Cassie paused and placed her hand to her breast with mock horror. "The men?"

"Woody and Marvin Ellis used to do the cooking."

"Woody? Oh, God!" Cassie halted completely in the middle of the walk. "We're not eating Mehetabel or her babies, are we?"

"Of course not."

"Who is this Marvin Ellis?"

"He ran a hardware store in town until he died about a year and a half ago."

"Goodness! I hope he didn't die of food poisoning."

"Well then, at least you don't have to worry about his cooking anymore."

"You're horrible."

"He was eighty-two years old."

"That doesn't make the joke any better."

"We weren't sure Woody could handle the job by himself. Then someone discovered that Olivier is one of the best fish friers north of the Mason-Dixon Line."

The school in Lyman's Gap served many other functions—a hall for school spelling bees and commencement day exercises, a place for town meetings and patriotic celebrations, a fellowship hall for church functions, a reception hall for winter weddings when it was too cold to eat outside or not all the guests would fit in the bride's father's barn, and, most important of all, a dining hall for the Volunteer Fireman's Association's Annual Fish Fry and Charity Auction.

Judging from the crowd gathered around the door, it seemed to Cassie as if the entire town had turned out.

All the chairs and desks had been cleared away. The teacher's large desk had been pushed to the rear. The flag flew proudly beside a print of a painting of George Washington hanging on the back wall. Colorful bunting draped from the ceiling.

"The only thing missing is a brass band," Cassie whispered to Brent.

"We had one once."

"Here? In Lyman's Gap?" The town didn't seem large enough.

"Orville Webster was our tuba player, but—"

"Don't tell me he died, too!"

"No, he moved out to Chicago, and we haven't been able to find a replacement yet."

Cassie sighed with relief. As they drew closer, she looked around at all the people "It looks as if everyone in town came."

"They did."

"Everyone is so dressed up."

"I told you most people would be in their absolute, better-than-Sunday-best best." Brent nodded to several of the families. "Now aren't you glad you listened to me?"

"Yes. I just wish you'd listen to me half as well," she mumbled.

"Mrs. Green looks very elegant in that blue satin."

"Yes, she does. Mrs. Vandergraft and Mrs. Klinger look as if they're competing for who can wear the widest ruffle at the bottom of their skirt."

"It's a good thing the fireplaces aren't lit this time of year. If they got within three feet of them, they'd burst into flames."

"I'm glad I chose my purple gown."

Brent wasn't watching her. Cassie felt a pang of jealousy

until she followed his line of sight and realized who he was looking at.

"Now, I must admit, Cassie, in all modesty, I think I'm a fair judge of feminine pulchritude."

"Probably."

"On the other hand, while I appreciate the total picture of a beautiful woman, I'm not a real . . . what you might call connoisseur of fashion."

"Probably not."

"But I do think Mrs. Andrews has outdone herself tonight."

Mrs. Andrews wore a gold-colored velvet gown, with two tall peacock feathers stuck in her hair.

"Mr. Conway, you are without a doubt a man of refined taste and impeccable discernment. I'll bet you five dollars she faints from the heat before the night is over."

"Me? Bet against you? Not a chance!" Brent laughed so heartily, Cassie couldn't be offended.

"Miss Bowen, Mr. Conway. Will you be dining together this evening?" Chester Farnsworth greeted them at the door with exaggerated politeness. The adolescent's warm brown eyes danced merrily above his freckled nose and rosy, round cheeks.

"Yes, thank you, my good man," Brent responded with equally jocular haughtiness.

Did the hint of pride Cassie detected in Brent's voice come from being seen with her? She hoped so. He looked so handsome tonight, she was proud to be seen with him.

"We'd prefer a table near the door—or at least an open window," Brent added, giving Cassie a wink.

"Miss Bowen, Mr. Conway, come right this way, please." The lanky youth led them to a table by an open window at the far end of the hall.

"You make a great maitre d', Chester," Brent told him with a chuckle.

"It's a far cry from pushing a plow through a cornfield," Chester said as he led them across the polished wooden floor of the hall. "But unfortunately just about as exciting."

"Well, if it's excitement you want, young man," Brent told him, "you'll have to be planning to travel out west."

"I just might do that someday, Mr. Conway," Chester told him. He stroked his fuzzy chin. "Grow a real beard. Learn to shoot a gun real well."

After the boy had left, Cassie leaned forward and murmured to Brent, "He will, too."

Brent pointed a finger at her. "Now, stop that!" he scolded in a whisper that traveled no farther than the edge of the table.

Cassie sat back and studied the empty plate in front of her. "I'm sorry, Brent. I know I promised, but you see how hard it is. Are you going to get up and leave me all alone?"

She peeked up at him from under her lashes. Oh, she'd sworn never to try that foolishness to get her way. Somehow with Brent she sort of liked it. She had a feeling he did, too.

He grinned at her. His eyes glowed with warmth and caring. He began to move his hand across the table to take hers, then stopped. Apparently he'd changed his mind. Was it because he didn't want to compromise her reputation or he didn't want to be too closely connected with the crazy lady?

"Are you sure you don't mind being seen with me, Cassie?" he asked. "After all, I am supposed to be a pretty disreputable character."

"That's all right," she responded with a laugh. "I'm supposed to be crazy."

"Personally I think we make a terrific pair."

"I believe anyone who contributes to a volunteer firemen's fund can't be all bad."

"Yes, but I still think anyone who abhors fish and still comes to a fish fry has got to be a little crazy."

Cassie tried to laugh, but the excitement and confusion of coming here was starting to wear off. She was startled to notice more things than Brent, and which lady was wearing what. Was her memory getting better, or were Sebastian's visions growing so horrifying that they were getting harder to forget?

The red and white tablecloth suddenly stood out clearly in her memory.

She knew with macabre certainty everything that was going to happen in this hall this evening. She knew Mrs. Green would compliment Mrs. Vandergraft on her delicious potato salad, even though Cassie also knew, even without Sebastian's assistance, that Mrs. Green detested Mrs. Vandergraft's potato salad.

She knew Harold Andrews would drop a tray of dirty dishes.

She knew Abel Warner was going to choke to death, right before the eyes of his horrified wife and terrified young daughters.

Where was he?

Cassie nervously scanned the large room. Abel was nowhere in sight.

Could he be working in the kitchen with Woody and Olivier?

Could he have been here earlier to dine? Could she have missed the horrible event, and he was already dead, lying in Doc Carver's office until Mortimer Farris could make his coffin? She seriously doubted everyone could or would continue eating heartily and chatting cheerily if a dear friend and neighbor had choked to death before their very eyes.

Most likely, he hadn't arrived yet. She sighed with relief as she realized she still had time. Time for what? To find someone who could help him? Or to wait a little longer for him to die?

She glanced about the room. Once, twice, once again just to make sure she hadn't missed him.

"Cassie. Cassie! Are you all right?" Brent demanded, cutting through her watchful daze.

"I'm fine. Fine," she assured him, all the time continuing to survey the room.

"You can't be fine. You just ordered two plates of fried fish."

"I did not!"

"You most certainly did. As well as fried potatoes, watermelon pickles, corn relish, and sauerkraut."

"Oh, no. I'm going to be so sick tomorrow."

She wanted to cover her eyes in dismay, but her hands only made it to her cheek. After all, if she covered her eyes, how could she keep a lookout for Abel?

"That's all right. I'll eat the fish," Brent volunteered, "even if I do gain twenty pounds from it."

"I'm sorry, Brent. I . . . I'll try to eat some."

"That's all right. I wouldn't want you to choke."

"Don't say that!" She was beginning to panic.

"It won't go to waste. I think we can get Jed Brumwell to eat anything we can't." Brent nodded to a rotund man seated near the door to the kitchen.

Cassie realized she'd been so busy apologizing to Brent and marveling at the size of Jed, that she'd forgotten to keep an eye out for Abel. Frantically her gaze swept the room again.

There was Mr. Harvey, eyeing her coldly. He nodded politely and appeared to turn away. Out of the corner of her eye, Cassie could see him still watching her, like a cat waiting for a mouse he'd cornered to make one tiny misstep. Then he'd pounce.

There Abel was, just coming in the door. Cassie breathed with relief. She hadn't met Sally Warner yet, but she recognized the thin, blond, pregnant woman clinging to Abel's arm.

She recognized the two little girls, too. Their blond curls, the exact shade of Mrs. Warner's, were parted in the middle in a precise line, pulled to either side, and tied up with pink ribbons. One girl was slightly taller than the other, but they were both dressed in identical pink and brown plaid boatneck dresses.

"There's Abel," Brent said. "Have you met his wife?"

Cassie could only shake her head.

"She's very nice."

Cassie nodded as she continued to watch Abel and his family take a seat at a table all the way across the hall from them. How would she ever get to him to warn him in time if he was so far away? Would she look too bizarre if she asked Chester to get them a different table after he'd gone to all the trouble of getting her this one?

"Cassie, you look pale."

Brent took her hand. His thumb moved slowly over the back of her hand and across the skin between her thumb and forefinger. It felt wonderful to have him touch her again. At the same time, it was jarringly distracting. How could her mind pay attention to the very important events that were happening around her when every other part of her body cried out for Brent?

"I'm fine." She pulled her hand away from his caress, and kept watching Abel.

"Is the smell of fish making you sick? I didn't think it was that noticeable this far from the kitchen."

"I just don't like fish."

"Cassie, do you want to go outside for a little fresh air?"

"No, no. I can't leave the room," she insisted.

"Cassie, did I do or say something to make you angry?"

She heard the hurt in his voice. She'd apologize later. Right now, she couldn't explain.

"No."

"Then why won't you look at me?"

"I. . . ." How could she answer him?

"People are going to think you're a little strange if you don't look at your dinner partner."

"They already think I'm strange."

"August will think you're strange."

She had to admit the man had been watching her suspiciously. "I think he's a little strange, too."

"What are you looking at?"

Cassie heard Brent scraping his chair across the floor, moving his seat around the table. He brought his chin nearer to her shoulder so he could see through her line of sight. She tingled at it's nearness, and moved slightly farther away. She could allow herself to be distracted now.

"Why are you staring at Abel and his family?"

"I'm not staring at his family."

"Why are you staring at Abel?"

"I . . . I just remembered he needs that bank draft."

"I . . . I think that'll wait." He sat back in his chair.

"Probably." She still didn't stop watching Abel.

"Cassie, didn't we have a little talk about this sort of unusual and generally unacceptable behavior?"

"No."

"I think we did."

"We did not. You told me not to say anything. I haven't said a word."

Brent released such a breath of disgust that Cassie felt the lace on her sleeves ruffle.

The older Warner girl tugged at her mother's sleeve. Sally Warner leaned over as best she could and allowed the child to whisper in her ear. Cassie watched the little girl point a small, pudgy finger directly at her. Sally looked at her across the room. Cassie smiled and waved. What else could she do? Sally nodded and returned a weak smile.

Sally leaned over as best she could to her other side and whispered something in her husband's ear. Abel looked at her across the room. Cassie smiled and waved. What else could she do? Abel nodded and smiled.

Why shouldn't he? Wasn't she his best customer? Hadn't she spent more in his store in one afternoon than most people spent all year?

Cassie continued to watch him.

"Cassie, what are you doing?" Brent demanded, a sharp edge to his voice. "If you keep this up, people are going to accuse you of chasing after Abel while his poor wife is in a family way—and right under Sally's very nose. Do you want to get *that* kind of reputation?"

His remark piqued her pride. Cassie turned to Brent, frowning. "Is that any better than being labeled insane?"

"Abel? Abel!" Sally's shrill voice cut through the cheerful chatter filling the hall.

"Oh, I knew I shouldn't have taken my eyes off him for an instant!" Cassie wailed as she, and everyone else, focused their attention on Abel.

Abel had risen to his feet. He clutched his throat with both hands. He looked at if he were trying to cough, or speak, or cry for help, but no sound emerged. His face grew red. His eyes bulged.

"Oh, my God!" Sally screamed. "Someone help him!"

Those seated closest to him sprang to their feet. Some people sat, shocked and immobile.

"Help! Oh, help!" Sally pleaded. "Abel, what's wrong?"

Abel only shook his head and clutched his throat.

The little girls clung to each other and cried.

"What's wrong? What's wrong with him?"

"God in heaven! He's choking!"

Still clutching his throat with one hand, Abel hammered on the tabletop with the other fist. Men rushed to stand around him. Ladies crowded around, too, shouting remedies and advice.

Cassie stood as if in a daze and made her way across the hall. Brent grabbed her arm and walked with her. They couldn't get any closer than the far edge of the circle. Cassie could only watch helplessly as the prediction she'd seen in Sebastian came true.

Several men grabbed Abel's arms and lifted them over his head. Abel struggled free from their grasp. His shoulders heaved and shuddered, as if he were trying to cough up something, but nothing came out.

Several other men pounded on his back. Abel pushed them away.

Other men pushed glasses of water at him, urging him to drink. When he tried, the water only came gushing out.

Everyone knew what was wrong. Everyone had a different remedy. None of them worked.

"He can't swallow."

"He can't breathe."

"Something's stuck in his throat."

"Dig in there and see if you can't pull it out."

"Where's Doc Carver?"

"Doc Carver! Go get Doc Carver!" the frantic cry went up.

"By the time he gets here, Abel will be dead," Brent muttered to Cassie. "We've got to do something. What?"

He blustered at his own impotence, and paced wildly back and forth at the edge of the crowd, as close as the townspeople would allow him.

As best she could reckon, Abel hadn't breathed in a long time. He must be growing faint and weak. He fell to the floor, still grasping his throat. The crowd surged forward, pushing Cassie closer.

She turned momentarily from her concerned vigil for Abel to search for Brent. She spotted him at the other end of the hall, near the door. Was he leaving? Now? How could he be so heartless?

Hurt, she turned to watch Abel.

He lay on his side, his knees curled up to his chest. Everyone stepped back, as if they'd given up hope, and only stayed around to be with him to ease his final moments.

"Someone get Reverend Markham." The call was less urgent, more solemn.

Brent had circled back to her.

"You came back."

"Did you think I wouldn't?"

She couldn't tell him she had. Instead, she murmured, "He's going to die unless someone does something."

"What?" Brent demanded. "You're so damn smart about everything else. Tell me. What?"

Cassie shook her head. "I wish I knew." If only that rotten Sebastian had shown her something truly *useful*.

"Somebody's got to do something."

He searched the room. Everyone had a lot of sympathy, but no one had an answer.

"Well, I'm not going to just stand here like a lump and let my best friend die," Brent declared.

He pushed his way through the dazed crowd, shoving everyone—men and ladies—aside, until he stood directly over Abel.

"Abel! Abel! Get up!" he shouted.

"Don't you think he would if he could, you imbecile?" Mr. Green demanded.

"You're not Jesus curing the lame man," Mrs. Andrews scolded. "You can't just tell him to get up and get better."

"Leave him alone, Brent," Mr. Andrews intervened. "Can't you see he's dying? Leave him depart with some dignity. There's nothing you can—"

"There's got to be! Leave me alone." He pushed Mr. Andrews away, too.

"Troublemaker," Mrs. Green murmured in the crowd. "Not an ounce of courtesy in him."

"Been trouble ever since he was a young'un," Mrs. Klinger muttered. "Never learned when to leave decent people alone."

"Probably thinks if he does something good, he'll get paid for it." Mrs. Green snickered.

"Never have known that man to do anything if he didn't think he'd make money on it."

Brent bent over the prostrate form of his friend. "Get up, Abel!" he screamed.

Abel's face was purple. His eyes were red from the broken blood vessels. Resting on his knees and elbows, he turned his face to the floor.

"For the love of God, Brent," Sally pleaded, clinging to his sleeve. "Haven't you hurt him enough already? Leave him die in peace."

He shrugged her off and turned coldly away from her to badger Abel again. "Get up! You can't die. You can't leave Sally here to raise these children alone."

He bent down and seized Abel about the waist and tried to lift him. His grasp wasn't strong enough. Abel fell, too weak to stand on his own.

"You've got to teach Carson to throw a ball, catch fireflies, whistle. You've got to be there to give your daughters away on their wedding day. Get up!"

Brent picked him up again. He shook him in his frustration and rage. Abel fell again.

"I won't let you die, damn it! Not now. Not like this. Not before we've mended our quarrel. I can't have you go to heaven and leave me here in hell, knowing you've never forgiven me. Get up!"

Brent grabbed Abel again around the waist. His encircling arms slipped over Abel's soft stomach, and caught under his rib cage. Holding Abel's back closer to his chest, Brent hauled him up with all his might.

A chunk of fish flew out of Abel's mouth and plopped down on the floor a few feet away.

Abel drew in a great gasp of air. He released it, and drew in another, as if it were the sweetest nectar on earth.

Brent set him down on the floor and collapsed to sit on the floor beside him.

The entire room was silent, except for the welcomed sound of Abel's deep, gasping breaths gradually slowing to normal.

"Papa! Papa! Papa!" His two little girls, their hands and faces shiny from fried fish grease and tears, ran up to Abel, one on either side, and threw their arms around his neck. Four thin little arms were ready to choke him again. They kissed his cheeks again and again, smearing the grease all over his face.

Mrs. Andrews pushed a glass of water into Abel's hand, encouraging him to drink.

At last, Sally placed her hand on Brent's shoulder and whispered, "Thank you."

"Brent, I was fixing to die," Abel rasped. "Why didn't you leave me alone? Why'd you even bother . . . after the way I've treated you all these years?"

"You know me. Once I start something, I just can't leave it. I guess I'm just one stubborn cuss."

Abel weakly clapped Brent on the shoulder. "You're the best dang stubborn cuss I've ever had the good fortune to run across."

"Lucy, Edith, come thank the nice man who saved your papa," Sally told them.

The little girls transferred their hugs and greasy kisses to Brent.

Abel wiped his face with the damp cloth Olivier handed him. He slicked his hands through what was left of his hair. "Boy, if the shock of this doesn't turn me bald overnight, nothing ever will," he said with a hoarse laugh.

"At least your face is back to its normal color," Brent told him optimistically. "Purple just doesn't suit you."

"I bet I'll have dark circles and bloodshot eyes for a few days but . . ." He shrugged.

"It beats all the dickens out of ash-gray as far as I'm concerned."

Woody strolled over and bent down to the floor in front of them.

"Well, salt me down and call me codfish!" Woody declared. Gingerly, between his thumb and forefinger, he held up the chunk of fish and bone that had almost choked Abel. "You saved his life, Brent. I figure that makes you some kinda hero."

"No. Not me."

"Danged if you ain't," Woody insisted.

"He's right," Mr. Andrews agreed. "Brent's a real hero."

Suddenly everyone was hauling Brent to his feet, clapping him heartily on the back, reaching out to tousle his hair in a gesture of goodwill.

Brent had always figured these townsfolk would kill him someday. He just never figured it would be from enthusiastic kindness.

He struggled to get away from the focus of attention of the crowd as much as he'd tried to get through them to help Abel. At last he fought his way back to Cassie's side.

Doc Carver had arrived, probably expecting to have to pronounce someone dead.

Reverend Markham had arrived, probably expecting to have to make funeral service arrangements with the grieving widow.

Woody and Olivier sauntered back to the kitchen.

"They're going to eat?" Cassie asked, watching incredulously as everyone resumed their seats.

"Of course. So am I. We can't let all that fish go to waste."

"But, Abel—"

"Doc Carver's looking after him now. Abel's going to be fine. Anyway, the Fish Fry is the social event of the year," Brent explained. "I guess as long as no one ends up dead, folks are determined to celebrate."

"I guess they might as well."

"I bet everybody chews their food really well after this," Brent said.

"Is that a prediction?" Cassie asked, at last able to laugh after the horrible near-tragedy.

"Shucks, no," Brent said. "You just need some common sense. You don't need a crystal ball to figure that out."

Cassie was very quiet as they made their way back to their table. She tried not to let him see her wide-eyed bewilderment and secret concern.

No, no, she silently assured herself. It was an expression, a mere turn of phrase. That's all. Brent couldn't possibly have been peeking in her bedroom window. He couldn't possibly know.

As Mr. Green passed their table, he slapped Brent on the shoulder.

"We're—why, the whole town's—real proud of you, Brent. I guess we never figured you had it in you," he confessed. "Guess we were wrong."

"Er, thanks, I guess," Brent muttered.

"No, siree," Mr. Green mumbled aloud to himself as he

walked away. "We never would've figured you had it in you to be a hero."

After Mr. Green left, Cassie boldly reached down and took Brent's hand in hers.

"I did," she said.

Brent stood there, staring at her.

"Don't scold me for saying that. It has nothing to do with my silly predictions. It has a lot to do with how I feel about you, Brent."

She looked up into his eyes. Could he see the love and adoration she felt for him gleaming there? She hoped he could. How else could she show him?

He shook his head. "Oh, Cassie, how do you expect me to stay here and eat *now*?"

The sky was a deep indigo blue, not quite black yet. Even the distant stars shone a pale, icy blue. The air was redolent of honeysuckle.

Brent strolled along Elm Street beside Cassie, patting his stomach.

"I ate too much," he groaned.

"We all did," Cassie confessed. "I must admit that's the first time I ever actually enjoyed fish."

"Do you think it was perhaps because, for the first time, you didn't have to clean them?"

"I'd say that had a good deal to do with it. I'd also say it had a good deal to do with Woody and Olivier's cooking."

"I know Woody will never give up pig farming. But I think Olivier and Jerusha ought to give up the idea of owning a modest, nondescript general store, move to a bigger city, and open their own restaurant."

"Jerusha and Olivier want to own a general store?"

"Didn't you know that?"

"No. She never really says much to me. Just takes the dirty laundry, delivers the clean. I thought she was just shy around me because I was new in town or, worse yet, that she resented me for taking my aunt's place."

"Not Jerusha. I don't think she's got a resentful bone in her body. On the other hand, she sure has given me an earful at times." Brent tugged at a pretended aching ear. "Maybe she'll talk more once she gets to know you better."

"I hope so."

"After all, you didn't talk much when you first met me."

He reached up and trailed his finger along her shoulder, toward her neck. She giggled and twitched her shoulder as he slowly drew closer and closer to her ear.

"But look how you can scold me now when I do something you think is wrong."

"I don't mean to scold."

"No?"

"I just need to . . . let people know when they . . . annoy me."

"I see."

He slid his finger across the back of her neck until his arm was draped completely over her shoulder.

"Does that annoy you?"

"No."

Gently he pulled her closer to him until she could snuggle beneath his arm.

"Obviously that doesn't annoy you, either."

"No. Not really."

They had reached her front porch. The sky had turned completely dark. The moon was only a tiny sliver of a crescent. Gray clouds scudding across the sky blotted out the few twinkling stars one by one. The night was even blacker in the shelter of the porch roof.

She could barely see him in the darkness. All she could see was a gleam in his eyes. She could feel him as he placed one hand on her shoulder and turned her to face him.

"I can't seem to annoy you tonight." he said.

One hand remained on her shoulder while the other trailed over the cool, bare skin of her other shoulder, across the shallow ridge of her collarbone, to settle beneath the small hollow at the base of her throat.

"No."

"What *can* I do for you?"

It took all the courage she could summon to tell him. "You excite me, Brent."

His rough knuckles brushed against her skin as he smoothed his hand up her throat, under her chin, and raised her face to his.

"Do I need to tell you how you excite me, Cassie?"

"I know."

"Do you really know, Cassie? Do you know the way you *think* you do, or do you really know how much I want you? The way a man wants the woman he loves?"

His lips descended to cover hers with heated passion. She returned his kisses with the same desire. She raised her arms to encircle his neck, drawing up her breasts to reveal a deeper cleavage.

Brent bent his head to trickle kisses down her cheek and neck, to settle between her breasts. She felt the slick warmth of his tongue as he ran it between her breasts, and the cool relief of the air as it evaporated the heat of his urgent kisses.

She felt her nipples peak in the shiver that ran through her breasts and down to the pit of her stomach. Her nipples puckered, erect and chafing against the soft fabric of the corset. It used to be so comfortable. Now all she could think of was to have Brent take it off her, as quickly as possible.

"Will you open the door, Cassie? Will you let me in?"

"Yes."

She released him to reach for the doorknob. His hand caught hers midway.

"Will you let me in, Cassie?" he repeated.

This time she realized Brent meant more than he was saying.

"Yes." She knew with absolute certainty she meant what she replied.

The door glided open and closed as quietly. In the complete darkness of the house, they held each other again. With his strong arms about her waist, and her own arms raised to embrace his neck, she felt as if they were entwined about each other—as inseparable as a vine grown about the sturdy trunk of an oak.

"I can't believe we're here, alone, together. No townspeople, no problems. No accusations, no protests. I love you, Cassie. I never dared hope you loved me."

"I do, Brent. I do."

He spun her about in his arms until her feet lifted from the floor, and she was supported only by his love. She'd never felt so dependent upon another person, and yet so completely free before in her life.

As he spun her in ever-tightening circles, he headed toward the staircase.

"May I take you upstairs, my love?"

"You may take me anywhere you wish."

With a deep laugh, Brent bent down and quickly snatched her off her feet, into his arms.

She squealed with surprise and delight, and wrapped her arms tightly around his neck. "Don't drop me," she pleaded.

He jostled her just a bit, up and down, back and forth, until she laughed and settled into his cradling arms. He placed his foot on the bottom stair.

"Tell me now if you have reservations."

She shook her head.

"I've got fairly good self-control, but I'll warn you, if you change your mind, it's going to be dang nigh impossible for me to leave you."

She heard the sincerity in his voice.

"I couldn't make you suffer."

"Every moment without you is suffering."

Slowly he climbed the stairs.

"Upstairs front right," Cassie whispered in his ear.

"I know. I've been wishing my house was on the other side and your house was only one story, so it would be easier to peek in your window."

The door stood slightly ajar.

"Before I open this, you must be honest with me. Am I to be blinded when confronted with the forbidden mysteries of what a lady needs to make herself beautiful and enticing to a man?"

Cassie laughed. "It's only my brush and hairpins. A scent bottle. Perhaps a few misplaced stockings. I'm not extraordinarily neat."

He shrugged. "Ah, well, I've been warned."

He pushed the door in with his foot, but hesitated at the threshold. He held her more tightly to him.

"No regrets?" he asked once again.

"Only that I didn't meet you sooner."

"That's mine, too, Cassie," he murmured into her hair as he carried her to the bed and gently sat her on the edge.

He stripped off his jacket with such urgency that he turned the arms inside out. He tossed it across the room. Cassie heard the buttons scraping along the hardwood floor until it came to a stop. He slipped his boots off, then knelt on the bed beside her.

She'd already unfastened the small pearl buttons of the purple satin gown. Brent chuckled when he discovered part of his work was done for him. Slowly he eased off one shoulder, then the other, until the bodice fell open.

As her eyes grew accustomed to the darkness, Cassie could see Brent bent over, puzzling at her corset.

"Tell me how to get you out of this trussed-up thing," he muttered.

She extended a cord to him. He gave it a tug. She felt the untied knot pop against her. The cord purred through the grommets as he unlaced her.

The corset, too, fell away. Cassie's breasts hung, pendulous and aching for him, brushing tantalizingly against the chemise, peaking with longing.

Slowly he felt his way down her thigh, past her knee, until he came to the hem of her chemise. Slowly he lifted the lacy edge over her knees and across her thighs. Gradually he exposed her hips, her waist.

His hands encircled her waist, felt about again, then meandered down her bare thighs.

"What are you looking for?" she asked.

"Where are your pantaloons?"

"I . . . I'm not wearing any."

He laughed.

"Not that I'm not delighted, but why not? What happened to them? Where'd they go?"

"If you'll recall, you were a tad impatient to be gone to the Fish Fry. I didn't want to keep you waiting too long, so—"

"So you're not wearing any," Brent supplied with a low moan. "You haven't been wearing any all night?"

"No."

He groaned and fell backward on the bed.

Cassie felt for him in the darkness. Her searching hands found the sides of his face. She held him tenderly and placed a kiss on his lips.

He groaned again. Tugging and pulling with urgency, he lifted the chemise over her arms and head, and sent it floating to the floor.

His hands reached out to cup her breasts, taut and waiting, as she'd held his face. He placed tender kisses at the tip of each breast. Pressing them closer together, he buried his face between them.

"Let me die here a happy man," he murmured against her.

Cassie tugged at the buttons, on the front of his shirt, and cuffs.

"You've got to let go if we're going to get this shirt off."

"One at a time," he bargained.

"Suit yourself."

Cassie's fingers trembled when she came to the fastening of his trousers.

"I've never—"

Brent groaned again, then moved his hands slowly from her breasts to unfasten his trousers. With two strong kicks, he sent them flying to join the rest of their clothing, piled on the floor in the darkness.

Cassie leaned back against the pillows as Brent climbed into bed beside her.

He cradled her in his arms, placing tender kisses along her neck and arms, down her waist, across her stomach, then up to caress each breast again.

He leaned closer beside her. His manhood pressed, hot and swollen against her thigh. The pit of her stomach and the insides of her legs ached for him.

His finger trailed down her stomach to rest gently against the triangle of curling hair. Gradually he moved his fingers between her legs.

Her legs opened for him.

"I'm doing this right?" she asked.

"You're doing everything exactly right. You're more perfect than I ever could have dreamed of. You're the best thing that ever happened to me in my whole miserable life. I want to be the best thing that ever happened to you."

"Oh, you are, Brent," she let out on a sigh.

He shifted his weight above her. His engorged manhood brushed the top of her thigh, then settled between her legs—hot, moist, throbbing. The tip met her womanhood—moist, hot, waiting.

With tormenting slowness, Brent entered her. Cassie closed her eyes and moved against him, forgetting the searing newness, ignoring everything but how very much she loved him.

With mounting rhythm, he sank into her again and again, rocking her in a primal rhythm, lifting her spirit. Cassie felt her world spinning, higher and higher. She saw dazzling sparkles of light, then a peaceful, serene calm she'd never felt before.

"That was . . . wonderful!" She sighed.

Brent's body, heavy with sweat and exhaustion, pressed against her. He lay so still.

"Brent, are you all right?" she whispered.

"Just . . . savoring. Your sweetness. Your tenderness."

"It was so good. Are we done?"

Brent laughed and slid to her side. "Only for the moment, my love."

• • •

The loud hammering on the front door roused Cassie from sleep.

"Cassie! Cassie!" Mrs. Parker called loudly. "Let me in! Are you all right?"

She'd overslept. Today was Thursday. She'd been so enwrapped in Brent and the wonderful way he made her feel that she'd forgotten today was the day Mrs. Parker came to clean.

Cassie cast off the sheet and bolted from the bed. She was stark naked. She could hardly answer the door like that.

Thank goodness Brent had gone home before dawn, so no passing townspeople could spot him creeping across the lawn from her house to his own and ruin her reputation. How could she have explained his presence to her housekeeper?

She was half tempted to throw on her robe, stick her head out the window, and yell that she'd be right down to let her in—if only she'd stop that infernal banging.

Fishwife. That's what her mother had always called a woman who shouted out of windows. It was bad enough her mother would be appalled at her behavior with Brent. What would she say if her daughter turned into a fishwife?

Oh, bother the corset, the chemise, the petticoat! Cassie threw her dress over her nakedness, and fumbled the buttons together as best she could while running down the stairs.

She paused a moment—she could tolerate a few more poundings on the front door—to push her unruly hair back from her face. She drew in a deep breath.

"Why, good morning, Mrs. Parker," she greeted her brightly as she pulled open the door. "You're early, aren't you?"

Mrs. Parker peeked down at the small watch pinned to her bodice.

"No, indeed. I'm right on time, as usual. Are you well this morning, dear? You don't appear to be very well. Are you sick from eating too much fish last night, like everyone else is?"

"No, I'm feeling . . . fine," Cassie replied. "I overslept."

Mrs. Parker bustled in. "I'll clean the downstairs today, if you don't have anything else you need me to do instead. That was the schedule I usually followed for your aunt."

"That will be fine with me, too, Mrs. Parker."

Cassie certainly wasn't going to tell her to clean the upstairs today when she wasn't exactly sure if Brent had left anything lying around on the floor, or draped conspicuously over the furniture in her bedroom.

"If you don't mind, I'll be upstairs, tidying myself up just a bit more." Cassie headed for the stairs.

"Oh, take your time, my dear. You look as if you could use all the tidying up you can get today."

As soon as Mrs. Parker had disappeared into the kitchen, Cassie lifted her skirt and ran up the stairs. She slammed her bedroom door behind her and leaned against it, as if that additional measure would keep Mrs. Parker out.

The bed was unmade. Her clothing was scattered about the floor but, except for the evidence in her own heart and body, search as she might, she could find no telltale evidence that Brent had ever been there.

As she donned her underthings and fastened her dress, she recalled his love and tenderness. She had given herself to him with no questions, no qualms, no misgivings. She loved him with her entire body, heart, and soul. She would love him for the rest of her life.

She knew it was silly, but she felt bathed in the proverbial rosy glow of love, swathed in her own private little cocoon of bliss. She wanted to hug herself, flop back onto the bed, and bask in the tender memories of their lovemaking.

Suddenly she frowned. Something was very wrong here, and she couldn't quite figure out precisely what. But something was very wrong.

Suddenly she was struck with a sobering and worrisome thought. She knew she loved Brent. She knew he loved her, too, even if he didn't believe her about other things. What was wrong with that?

Everything.

Hadn't Aunt Flora told her? "You must love someone with no hope of him ever loving you in return." She hadn't lost anything she really needed. She'd had a small argument with

Mr. Harvey, but that was no reason not to trust him. No one believed a word she said.

If she loved Brent and he loved her in return, how could the curse be complete? How could she spend her life as a lonely spinster and pass along to her hapless niece the burden of this curse?

Only one way came to mind. She squinted her eyes tight and shook her head, as if that could send the horrible thought flying right out of her ears. The only way she'd spend her life alone would be if Brent should die.

No! Don't think that. Do something else, quick, before you cry. The horrible thought nagged at her.

Was that what had happened to Aunt Flora? Was that why she had never married? Was that why none of the Bowen women had ever married? Had they once loved, truly and deeply, only to have the man they loved taken from them?

Sebastian had shown her, and all the other women, war after war, earthquakes, famines, and floods, in which they would lose the ones they loved.

One thing she knew for certain. Sebastian would always show her the truth, but he didn't always show her the final outcome. Otherwise, how could she have seen Abel sinking to the floor in the last throes of his dying agony, and yet not have seen Brent saving his life? Was a man's demise fixed? Or only to a certain point?

Was it Sebastian's duty to warn them? Or to ensure that the curse was carried on?

Greater minds than hers had pondered this. Oh, she'd go mad if she continued to think about it.

Get dressed, she urged herself. *Go into town and buy something at Warner's. Go downstairs and help Mrs. Parker clean.* Something, anything to think cheery thoughts.

She had to finish getting dressed. She bent to retrieve her shoes from under the bed.

Oh, goodness gracious! There sat Sebastian's leather case, and he was inside. She hadn't had time to replace him in his cabinet. She hadn't wanted to risk having Brent barge in and catch her surreptitiously carrying a head-sized bag. So she'd shoved Sebastian unceremoniously under there last night in her rush to dress for the Fish Fry.

"Oh, Sebastian, I'm so sorry," she crooned to him as if he were a coddled pet she'd inadvertently ignored as she pulled the case out from under the bed. "I hope you forgive me for shoving you under there instead of placing you back in the nice, fancy cabinet where you belong."

Seated on her bed, she removed Sebastian reverently from the case and set him respectfully on her nightstand. If he was only the medium through which these images came, he didn't deserve to be blamed for what they were. If he was an active agent, it wouldn't serve to annoy him.

"I guess you'd like some fresh air and sunshine, too, wouldn't you? After all, you really deserve something nice. I didn't know what to do to help Abel, and even if Brent didn't, and just happened to jar that chunk of fish loose by chance, at least he was able to save his friend's life, and it gave the two of them the opportunity to patch whatever quarrel they once had."

Sebastian just sat there, silent and blank.

"You're not angry with me, are you? I hope you're not going to scold me about what I—what Brent and I—did last night. After all, you're the one who showed me all that in the first place. I love him so much. I never dreamed I could be this happy. I suppose I owe it all to you, actually."

Sunlight gleamed brightly through the crystal. She had to take that as a good sign.

"At least I know you won't go tattling about Brent and me all over town. Nobody else even knows about you. That's a shame, too. More people should know about you because, you know, when you stop showing those horrible pictures of people about to die, you really are a very wonderful crystal ball."

As she held him in her hands, a picture began to form. Cassie emitted a little squeal. She'd never held him while he showed her his images. She'd always been afraid she'd be struck dead by lightning or something from inside the ball.

Well, nothing bad happened so far. Still, she'd feel safer if Sebastian was back on his stand.

As she set him down, the image of a woman, unknown to Cassie, formed inside.

"All right. I know by now you're not my own individual crystal ball. I suppose I'm just sort of your guardian this generation."

She sighed with resignation to the intense feeling of foreboding that began to overshadow her.

"I'm used to you showing me people I don't know. You show me lots and lots of people I don't know—yet. I also know, anytime you show me an individual's face this clearly, there's something particularly important about that person. Now, who is she?" Cassie demanded. "And why does she have to come around spoiling my life?"

The woman's shapely figure continued to take clearer form in the crystal ball. Her bearing was assured and graceful. Her dress was extremely elegant, undoubtedly expensive, and she wore it with unbelievable style. Her accessories were chosen with impeccable taste. She wore jewelry to rival Aunt Flora's collection.

Her clear blue eyes were fringed with long, dark lashes. Her luxurious blond hair was parted precisely in the middle and laid flat to either side, then arranged in fashionable curls at the sides of her winsome face. That was the exact style Cassie wished she could coax her own unruly auburn hair into, instead of having to settle for a mere braid curled into a bun at the nape of her neck.

She was the most beautiful woman Cassie had ever seen. She was everything Cassie might ever have hoped to be.

Cassie hated her on sight.

"I seriously doubt she has anything to do with the coming war," she told Sebastian, as if speaking aloud would help her organize her suspicions as to why this woman was appearing. "Although if Helen of Troy's beauty caused the Trojan War,

I must admit this lady is certainly beautiful enough for men to fight over."

She gave a snide chuckle. "Just between you and me, I can't see her digging in the dirt for anything in that fine dress, with those lily-white hands, and those neatly pared and buffed nails. So I seriously doubt she has anything to do with the petroleum I'm supposed to be digging for if the blasted equipment will ever arrives."

The image remained. Usually Sebastian's visions had been so ephemeral, so fleeting. He must have a very good reason for dwelling on this singular image. Cassie only had to figure out what in tarnation it was.

"The only other image that stayed this long was that Lincoln fellow. Now I believe what you showed me about women voting someday, even if I never live to see it. I even believe the woman you showed me *will* be the president of the United States some day. But I absolutely refuse to believe *this* woman is going to be president."

She pointed at the image in the crystal ball.

"Her hair's not cut short enough. She doesn't have her lips painted red or black paint around her eyes like the other woman will. And especially not in *that* outfit. It doesn't look anything like what the other lady was wearing. It doesn't show her . . . legs. Goodness, even her knees. Don't those people have any shame or modesty in the future?"

Once again, Cassie could have sworn she saw Sebastian wink.

Suddenly, behind the elegant lady, Brent entered the picture. Cassie held her breath and waited to see what he would do.

He stood close, and placed both hands on the woman's shoulders in a possessive gesture. She turned her head, glancing back to him. He bent his head closer to hers.

Cassie's mouth dropped open. She felt as if her eyes were going to pop out of their sockets the way the chunk of fish went flying out of Abel's mouth.

"What does *she* have to do with Brent?" she stammered.

Her heart grew heavier and heavier within her breast, aching more and more. She felt as if a large, sharp spike had been set before her, and her heart—all her happy hopes—were being impaled alive.

She tore her gaze away from Sebastian. She sprang from the bed and headed toward the door. She didn't care if she still hadn't washed her face or dressed completely. She had to get out of this room, away from this disturbing, hurtful vision.

Where would she go? Downstairs and listen to Mrs. Parker's cheery, aimless chatter?

To Mr. Harvey, to be patted on the head and told not to worry her pretty little head about it, or have to listen to him sermonize about how she never should have trusted that man in the first place?

To Reverend Markham, to risk being accused of witchcraft, to be threatened with torture and burning at the stake, just like that poor old gypsy woman who had come to the Bowen estates so many centuries ago, and started this whole darn problem?

To Doc Carver, and risk getting a medical diagnosis of incurable insanity and the recommendation that she be locked away in an asylum for good, so that Robert and Letitia could come in and pirate away everything?

To Brent?

What would she say if she went to Brent? Who is this woman I saw in my crystal ball? What does she have to do with you, and you with her? How will she hurt me? How will *you* hurt me?

How could she ask any questions when she hadn't an inkling who the woman was?

How could she ask any questions and risk giving away the existence of Sebastian?

Cassie started pacing again. From the corner of her eye, she could see the lights in Sebastian flickering again. Thank goodness that horrible vision was gone. But now what would take its place?

"No, no. Don't even bother showing me anything anymore, because I'm not going to look at you. You're still showing me things I don't want to see. Mean, cruel, hard, hurtful things. Things that hurt the entire nation. Things that hurt people I love."

She waved her hand at him but refused to look. She knew how addictive and irresistible Sebastian's visions were. She fought her hardest not to look at him.

"You're not satisfied with that. You need to hurt me, too. Why me? I know it can't be much of a life, spending four hundred years in a leather case. But I am the one who takes care of you, sees that you get put into and taken out of that case on a regular basis. I'm waiting for the roses to bloom to put a couple fresh ones in there because Aunt Flora said you like roses."

Cassie slapped her arms at her sides in frustration.

"Thunderation! I've even polished you when you weren't glowing with pictures. Did anybody else do that for you in four hundred years? Did they?" she demanded.

In an additional effort not to have to look at Sebastian, she paced back and forth across the room.

"You're mean, that's what you are. Just plain, consarn, ornery mean. I was wrong before when I said it must be hard on you, having to show people these horrid visions. Sometimes I think you actually *enjoy* it, you horrible mean thing!"

"Cassie! Cassie!" Mrs. Parker's quavering voice reverberated up the stairwell. "Were you talking to me? You know I can't hear you when you're up there and I'm down here."

Botheration! Cassie cursed to herself. She realized the more hurt and exasperated she grew, the more her voice rose in pitch. She knew tears were falling down her cheeks, and her voice was catching with her sobs. She hadn't realized her voice had also gotten so *loud* with anger that Mrs. Parker could hear it downstairs.

She tried to compose herself enough to speak to Mrs. Parker without revealing she'd been crying.

"Can you hear me?" Mrs. Parker called. "Have you got the door closed?"

Cassie opened the door just a crack so she could call down

the stairs but not risk Mrs. Parker seeing her in her agitated condition.

"It's all right, Mrs. Parker." She tried to make her voice sound calm and cheerful, not hoarse with tears. "I was just . . . just singing a little song to myself."

"It doesn't sound like a particularly happy tune," Mrs. Parker ventured.

"Uh, it's not. I . . . I'm rather partial to sad songs. Really, really mournful Irish ballads."

"Oh, very well." Mrs. Parker probably figured crazy people were always singing little ditties to themselves, and would leave her alone. "But I must say, those are some mighty peculiar lyrics."

Cassie knew she couldn't hide upstairs from Mrs. Parker all day. Sooner or later she'd have to go down for lunch. Mrs. Parker always brought her a big bowl of freshly made chicken salad.

Cassie was beginning to regret complimenting her housekeeper on the chicken salad she'd made for Aunt Flora's funeral. It was still as delicious as ever, but after having it for lunch twice each week, it started to lose some of its novelty.

"I've finished all the work I usually do today," Mrs. Parker told her as they sat across the kitchen table from each other, eating the ubiquitous chicken salad, toasted rolls, and drinking lemonade.

"My, that was quick."

"I also polished some of the silver, which I usually do on Mondays. So actually I'm ahead in my work."

"My aunt was right, Mrs. Parker. You really are a wonderful housekeeper."

"So I hope you don't mind if I leave just a bit earlier than usual." Mrs. Parker peered at her anxiously from above a forkful of chicken salad.

"Certainly not."

Would Brent scold her for allowing Mrs. Parker to take

unfair advantage of her? After all, she didn't know why Mrs. Parker had asked to leave early.

Cassie didn't know exactly what sort of work the woman did for her each day. So, aside from encountering dust balls the size of St. Bernards under the sofa, she wouldn't know if she'd actually done her job or not.

She could be taking her wages and heading for the local tavern to enjoy a good drinking binge until Monday morning. Cassie had to laugh silently at the very thought of the efficient Mrs. Parker doing something so outlandish.

"Mrs. Klinger and I have been hired to go to the McAlister mansion and clean it," Mrs. Parker announced. "Goodness knows, it's going to need it. They've been gone for almost a year, you know."

"I didn't know that."

"Oh, that's right." With her napkin, Mrs. Parker deftly caught an escaping chunk of chicken on her chin. "You haven't been here long enough to know them."

"I've heard of Mr. McAlister," Cassie ventured. "I've never heard mention of the rest of the family."

"Oh, I'd say there are quite a few people who've heard of Horace T. McAlister, what with him owning the local coal mine and a lot of other stuff, too. Mrs. McAlister and Miss McAlister are quite involved in charity work."

"I see. It's a pity they didn't return in time for the Fish Fry."

Mrs. Parker laughed. "Oh, make no mistake. They're not connected with the Volunteer Fireman's Association at all."

"No? It's such a worthwhile cause."

The housekeeper raised her eyebrows, drew her lips into a tight bow, and peered down her nose at Cassie.

"That's far, far beneath them." Her voice took on an elevated tone. "They participate more in things like the Association for the Improvement of the Conditions of the Poor—the *deserving* poor. They make sure those folks work for the charity they receive."

"I see. Where have they been all this time?"

"Traveling around Europe."

"How nice."

"Probably. Frankly I've never had any desire to go there myself. I figure my ancestors came over *here* because they must have had a very good reason to leave *there*. I'm happy here. It's going to take a pretty compelling reason for me to want to go back."

"I understand. While it's a nice city, I have very little reason to return to Philadelphia."

On the other hand, she thought, how very lucky for Mrs. Parker's ancestors to have been able to come to the United States to escape whatever was plaguing them in Europe. *Her* ancestors had brought the darn family curse with them.

"Now, mind you," Mrs. Parker said, leaning over her chicken salad toward Cassie, "I don't know very much about all that high society kind of thing."

"Neither do I."

"But I understand the real social season doesn't end until June, when all the rich men's daughters marry all the dukes and earls they caught with Papa's money. So tell me this. Why should the McAlisters be coming home at the end of May?"

"I'm sure they had some good reason."

Mrs. Parker raised one eyebrow skeptically. "Well, it certainly isn't because their daughter wasn't beautiful enough to catch a duke. It certainly can't be because they ran out of money."

Cassie wasn't qualified to comment on those topics, so she just ate her chicken salad as if it was an entirely new and delightful flavor, instead of the same thing she had had on Monday.

"By the way, where is their mansion?" Cassie asked. "So far, the two biggest houses I've seen in Lyman's Gap are mine and Mr. Conway's."

Mrs. Parker raised her hand and began tracing a map with her fork in the air over the table.

"If you go down that road to the left of the church, and make another left that takes you up this long, winding road that travels almost to the top of the hill. They have a big house that looks down over the whole town."

"I hadn't noticed any mansion on the hillside."

"That's because it's surrounded by trees. They can see out, but you can't see them. I'm certain Mr. McAlister likes it that way."

"I see."

"I'm sure Mr. McAlister gets a big thrill out of looking down on everybody from his home, just the way he does when he's walking around town."

"I see."

Cassie understood Mr. McAlister a lot better all the time. No wonder Brent seemed to dislike him. No wonder Brent had claimed the man wouldn't give her any advice without a price attached.

"I suppose Mrs. McAlister will be expecting someone of suitable social standing in Lyman's Gap to have a welcome home party for them."

"Really?" Cassie was curious, but she was also growing more canny. She had a bad feeling about this proposed party.

"Ordinarily the honor would have been Miss Flora's."

"Oh?" Cassie didn't care if Mrs. Parker heard the depression in her voice. She felt her heart sinking. She had enough problems to cope with without worrying about organizing a party for people she didn't even know.

"Seeing as how your aunt has gone on to her reward, however, and you haven't been living here very long, um . . . Well, *some people* . . . seem to think the honor ought to fall to Irma Andrews."

Cassie's outlook brightened. "Indeed?"

"I mean, seeing as how we don't have a mayor, and Doc Carver's wife died a couple years back, and Irma *is* the wife of the bank president. . . . Well, *some people* think it sort of stands to reason—"

"Mrs. Parker, how very kind of you to keep me abreast of the social hierarchy in town." Cassie tried to keep her voice pleasant. She had no doubts whatsoever that Irma had sent Mrs. Parker here to sound her out.

"*Some people* can be so . . . so perceptive," Cassie continued. "So *some people* ought to be very relieved to hear that I certainly wouldn't want to step on anyone's social toes, especially not Mrs. Andrews's."

"That's very kind and very wise of you, dear."

Cassie merely smiled modestly at the compliment. Mrs. Parker would spread the tale of her magnanimously stepping aside to give Mrs. Andrews a chance to entertain such important people. Cassie wouldn't mind basking in the glow of rumors of her generosity.

She also figured nobody would want to go to a party given by the crazy lady.

Cassie knew she shouldn't go to the *Argus*. She'd seen Brent every evening for the past week. She'd loved him every day and made love with him every night. She really shouldn't interfere with a man when he was trying to work. Especially when he was working as hard as Brent was to make his newspaper a success.

But she needed to be near him. She wanted him to hold her. Even if he couldn't do that in the office, even a mere touch in passing would make her skin tingle, make her ache for more of him. She didn't even need to touch him. Just the nearness of him made her smile, made her heart feel lighter.

She didn't even need to see him. The smell of him was enough to make her legs quiver.

Sometimes he smelled of coffee and strawberry jam. She wondered if his sister had made it, if he had bought it at Abel's store, or if some other lady had given it to him in an attempt to show him what a wonderful wife she would make.

She could almost feel sorry for the unfortunate lady who had lost out to her for Brent's affections. But she worried that he'd expect her to learn to make jam.

Sometimes he smelled of sweat and printer's ink. She enjoyed the hardworking smell of him. He loved his work. She was happy for him.

Sometimes, cuddled up beside her in her bed at night, he smelled of shaving soap and fresh water. Afterward there was a particular fragrance of them joined together in love that only made her want to love him more. There was the scent of him that lingered on her pillow after he had departed into the night—preserving her reputation but not doing much to assuage her loneliness.

She needed to talk to him. But she knew the *Argus* was no place to discuss the mysterious lady. She just needed to see him, to reassure herself of his continuing love.

Perhaps she was being silly. But a little reassurance never hurt anyone, she supposed.

"Oh, no."

She felt her shoulders sag with foreboding when she encountered Lem and his usual following of boisterous boys at the corner of Elm Street and Main. Lem was brandishing his splinted arm in a sling, like some sort of badge of honor. Lined up down the sidewalk all the way to Warner's Store was the rest of the town.

"Hey, whatcha doin' here, crazy lady?" Lem demanded.

Cassie bit her tongue and counted to ten rather than tell him, *I'm here to break your other arm, you little brat*—even though she knew she'd never actually do it, even though he probably deserved it.

She nodded toward the milling crowd. "What's all the fuss about?" she asked.

"You know it all, crazy lady. You figure it out."

"Now's when we need our brass band again," a blond-haired boy told her, tugging at her skirt for attention. "Boy, someday I'm going to learn to play the tuba."

"I'm sure your parents will encourage you," Cassie replied. Encourage him to pick a different instrument, she silently amended.

"Nah, they won't. He's too dumb to learn." Lem swatted at the boy's head with his cap.

"Am not," the boy protested.

Lem gave him a shove into the mud puddled by the sidewalk.

Cassie decided to seek better information farther along the sidewalk. She shook her head as she left Lem. Some people didn't even learn the hard way.

Weaving her way through the crowd, she at last encountered Sally Warner and her two little girls close to the edge of the sidewalk.

"Good morning, Mrs. Warner," Cassie said.

"Oh, good morning, Miss Bowen. Isn't this exciting?" Sally replied.

"I'd probably be excited if I knew what was happening."

"Don't you know? The McAlisters have arrived back in town."

"Mrs. Parker had told me something about cleaning their house to get it ready, but she wasn't sure exactly when."

"They sort of come and go whenever they please," Sally explained. "I guess that's part of the fun of being wealthy." She sighed. "I'll never know, but—"

"Oh, cheer up. I wouldn't be so doubtful," Cassie cautioned. "After all, one never knows, does one?"

"I guess not."

Except that she did, Cassie thought. Was she finally learning to keep her mouth shut about some things? She supposed so, especially when no one was believing a word she said anyway.

"But I have my health and my family," Sally said, placing one hand on her abdomen, and another on top the taller girl's head. "Thank God—and thanks to Brent—I still have my husband."

"Mrs. Warner, you are wealthy indeed."

"Mr. McAlister has this big, fancy carriage," Sally explained. "He even has his very own driver, who's bringing them from the railroad station in Pittsburgh. He's going to drive them right down Main Street, just like a circus parade, only fancier. No one would miss the chance to see that carriage. Or to see what Mrs. McAlister and their daughter, Evaline, are wearing."

Sally giggled behind her hand. "Probably something extraordinarily scandalous from Paris."

"Probably," Cassie replied.

"Oh, here they come. Look, girls, look!"

My goodness, Cassie muttered to herself. How could these people cause such a commotion? *I don't think there's this much fuss when the president goes by.* But she, too, craned her neck to see over the tops of other people's heads, to catch a glimpse of the fantastic carriage and its illustrious occupants.

The horses were perfectly matched bays, each with a white star on their foreheads. She didn't think they could be any more perfectly matched if they were identical twins. Their black leather harness gleamed in the sunlight.

The driver wore a neat black suit. Under his tall black hat, Cassie noticed his reddish hair. She wondered if they'd chosen him specifically to match the horses. He sat as if a ramrod was stuck inside the back of his coat. He tooled the horses through the muddy street, dodging puddles, as Lem and his band of urchins ran after the carriage, waving and shouting.

There was no doubt which one was Mr. McAlister. Rotund. Bewhiskered. Elegantly dressed. Puffing a huge cigar. He doffed his hat, and waved it over his head, graciously accepting all the adulation that he figured was his due.

That must be Mrs. McAlister, seated beside him. Slim. Elegant. Pinch-faced. Oh, yes indeed, Cassie decided. She and Mrs. Andrews must get along famously.

Miss McAlister had to be the young woman riding backward. Slim. Elegant. Timid? Or aloof? She kept her hands folded demurely in her lap and merely nodded to all she passed. Pinch-faced like her mother or beautiful? Cassie almost screamed in frustration. She couldn't tell.

Why wouldn't she turn around? Cassie lamented. She'd like to see the front of that dress. She'd like to see Miss McAlister's face, not just the back of her head.

As the carriage rolled past, and she thought she might at

last get a glimpse, the crowd closed in. By the time she'd shifted herself around, the carriage was positioned so that Mr. McAlister's bulk blocked out anything she might have seen of his daughter's face. By the time she'd shifted herself again, the carriage was so far away, Cassie could make out nothing but a perfectly oval blob of perfect, peaches-and-cream complexion, flanked by blond ringlets.

Cassie stood as if paralyzed, staring after the receding carriage and the young woman in it.

"Wasn't she beautiful?" Sally said breathlessly.

"I'm sure."

"She actually sent me a letter from Paris. I'll keep it always."

"Why not?" Cassie agreed. "It isn't every day one receives a letter from Paris."

"Or from Miss McAlister," Sally gushed.

Brent studied his reflection in the wall mirror. All right, he conceded. He did have another piece of furniture in his bedroom besides his bed—if one counted mirrors as furniture.

He straightened his tie. He made sure the lapels of his best plaid wool jacket laid flat and the collar in back wasn't all bunched up and folded wrong.

He smoothed his hair back neatly with his fingers.

Then he stepped back a pace and studied his reflection again.

"Holy smokes, you'd think I was a debutante getting ready for her first ball," he complained to his reflection. "I sure don't worry about what I look like when I go to work. Shucks, I don't worry this much when I go to see Cassie."

Yes, but Cassie loves you just the way you are, his reflection reminded him. *You still don't know what Horace T. McAlister thinks of you.*

"Except," Brent countered himself, "the last time we spoke, I could pretty well figure he didn't like me. So why has his high and mightiness summoned me to his home this morning?" he demanded of his know-it-all reflection. "Not to his office in town, mind you, or to the big one he has in Pittsburgh. The one he has right in his very own home, where I've never been invited in my whole life. Not even when I was keeping company with Evaline."

His reflection had no reply.

Brent grunted in disgust and then laughed at his own foolishness.

"Maybe I ought to go downstairs and talk to someone more sensible—like the picture of my sister."

He shook his head. If he was talking to pictures and his own reflection, he really was too lonely in this big, empty house. It really was time he got married and filled this house with kids and laughter.

He glanced at his watch, hanging from its chain on his vest.

"Nine o'clock in the morning. Time to go. No one keeps Horace Tiberius McAlister waiting."

Even though he hadn't traveled this way in almost a year, Brent remembered the road to the mansion very well. He recognized the withered butler who opened the door for him.

The interior of the house looked the same, all carved hardwood paneling and marble flooring acting as a backdrop for huge Chinese vases and exquisite paintings. Brent figured McAlister had only bought these things because they were expensive, or because someone else had advised him to. McAlister didn't have the slightest idea about art.

No one else seemed to be at home. He couldn't think of anywhere else in Lyman's Gap that Mrs. McAlister and Evaline could be. On the other hand, in a house this size, it wouldn't be difficult for them to avoid him.

Brent never expected Mr. McAlister to greet him at the door.

"Conway, old man! Good to see you again."

"How are you, Mr. McAlister? Did you—?"

He never expected to receive a hearty pat on the back that nearly broke his shoulder blade. People trying to save Abel's life hadn't hit him that hard.

"Did you . . . and your family have a pleasant trip?"

"Trip? Oh, yes. Pleasant enough."

Brent certainly never expected McAlister to slap one heavy arm over his shoulder and practically drag him into his legendary office. Was the man trying that hard to make sure Evaline didn't see him?

"Damned inedible food there."

From the looks of him, Brent figured the man must have been eating *something* while he was over there.

"Damned Frenchies putting onions and toadstools into everything. Damned Germans putting vinegar and bacon into everything. Damned Italians putting tomatoes and too much garlic into everything. Damned Englishmen not putting anything in any of it—at least that's what it tasted like to me. Might as well have eaten the tablecloth instead, for all the flavor it had."

McAlister released a hearty guffaw.

Brent figured it was a good idea to laugh, too.

"Have a seat." McAlister stationed himself in front of the fireplace and gestured to a large, leather-covered chair to one side. Brent settled himself into one of the most comfortable chairs his bottom and back had ever had the pleasure to encounter.

"Have a cigar, my boy."

McAlister extended a large humidor, opened to display an impressive array of cigars of various shapes, sizes, and shades of brown. Brent took one. McAlister gestured to the cigar cutter on his desk and, while Brent cut the tip of the cigar, he pulled a thin brand from the fireplace to light it.

"You know, some of those nancy-boy Englishmen have taken to smoking these little things they call cigarettes. Supposed to be some kind of heathen Turkish habit they picked up fighting over in the Crimea a couple of years ago."

"I wasn't aware of that." Brent drew in a puff of the fragrant smoke.

"Never catch on here, mark my words. Cigars are a real American man's smoke." McAlister belched out billows of fragrant smoke, like a badly drawing chimney.

Brent nodded. At this point he was still too flabbergasted by McAlister's unbelievable cordiality to disagree with a word the man said. As the room filled with smoke, Brent felt his head getting just about as hazy.

"You're probably wondering why I asked you here tonight, aren't you, Conway?"

Before Brent could respond, McAlister continued. Brent knew he was a man who didn't bother much with what other people had to say when he had an idea of his own he was working on.

"Well, I have a little business proposition for you."

Brent wasn't surprised. The only reason McAlister would have anything to do with him would certainly not be personal. It had to be business. But what kind of business would McAlister have with him? And why with *him*?

Then McAlister announced, "Conway, I've bought a newspaper." He took a long, self-satisfied draw on his cigar.

That bastard! Another newspaper here in this small town, backed up with McAlister's resources. Brent figured he'd be out of business in a month or less.

He felt the bottom falling out of what he had assumed was a sturdy, leather-covered, oaken chair. If the man didn't want him to marry his daughter, all he would've had to do was tell him "no" straight out a year ago, and that would've made an end of it. He didn't have to call him back here just to announce that he planned to ruin him.

"It's a pretty big one, and I hope to be able to make it bigger—out in San Francisco."

Brent couldn't help but release a very audible sigh of relief.

"Trouble is, Brent—may I call you Brent, my boy?"

"Yes . . . yes, sir," Brent stammered. Dang, he hated it when someone took him by surprise at every turn like this.

"Well, the trouble is, Brent, I don't know anything about running a newspaper. All I know is coal mining and how to make a few good investments. A newspaper's different. You know that."

"Yes, sir."

"Now, I've been keeping an eye on how you've taken the *Argus* and turned it from that little nothing newspaper your father ran into a fairly profitable enterprise—and I'm impressed, my boy. Mighty impressed."

"Thank you."

"I figure, if anybody can take that San Francisco newspaper and turn it into something worthwhile, it's you."

"Thank you." Brent could hardly answer what he was thinking, *Of course, I could.*

"And then go and do the same thing with the other newspaper I bought in Sacramento."

"Sacramento?" Brent repeated. Damn, McAlister was throwing surprises at him right and left. It was getting hard to keep track of what all he was offering.

"I want you to take complete editorial charge of both papers. Since it'll require your moving out to California, I'll pay all your traveling expenses," McAlister offered. "There's a very nice house for you, too. I don't think you'll find it too large for your current needs, and suitable for any . . . future needs, if you take my meaning."

"I think I do." Brent had no idea what the man was getting at.

"Of course, any man who runs two newspapers at the same time deserves a commensurate salary."

McAlister dug into his vest pocket, pulled out a slip of paper, and handed it to Brent. Brent unfolded it and blinked when he read the salary penciled there.

"I trust that'll be enough—for a start, of course. There'll be yearly increments, and bonuses, of course."

Brent nodded automatically. "Of course."

"Since you know the business, I'll be giving you free rein as far as all editorial policy goes. And if, while you're out there, you should come across another newspaper you feel could benefit from my—from *our*—expertise, well, I trust you to advise me on its purchase, of course."

"Of course."

Brent was finding it difficult not to smile. This was everything he had ever wanted, everything he'd ever dreamed of since he was a youngster. Complete editorial charge of several reputable newspapers with large circulations in growing cities. A salary that would make old Walter out in Chicago green with envy.

This was all sounding far too good to be true. Brent remembered his mother's words. When something sounds too good to be true, it usually isn't. There was a catch here. Brent had to tread very carefully now so he wouldn't fall into the trap.

"Of course, there's one more thing I'll need you to do before I turn these newspapers entirely over to you."

Aha! He knew it.

"What's that, sir?"

"I want you to make good on your offer to marry my daughter."

Thirteen

"My offer?" Brent repeated. "To marry Evaline?"

"Don't tell me you don't remember." McAlister's voice lost a tinge of its cajoling tone.

"I still remember. Very well. But—"

"Don't tell me it wasn't an *honorable* proposal." McAlister's voice lost a lot of its cajoling tone. "Don't tell me you were just toying with my daughter's affections, boy."

What happened to his calling him Brent? What happened to his affectionate "my boy" and the paternal pat on the shoulder? Even a gruff, businesslike "Conway" would be acceptable. Brent didn't like the threat implied in a simple term like "boy," especially not coming from a man as ruthless as McAlister.

Brent was determined not to be cowed. A year ago he was still feuding with the man who had been his best friend since childhood, and was once again. A year ago he was still struggling with a newspaper that was finally starting to pay. A year ago he hadn't fallen in love with Cassie.

"When you laughed at me, sent me home, and left the next day without another word . . . Well, Mr. McAlister, I sort of took that as a tacit refusal," Brent told him. "I believe any man would."

McAlister took a leisurely puff of his cigar. He casually strolled over to where Brent was seated. The last time he'd done that, McAlister had blown the puff of smoke directly into Brent's face.

This time McAlister sent the smoke curling up to the ceiling. He placed a heavy hand on Brent's shoulder.

"I might've been born to a coal miner, Brent," McAlister explained. "My wife might've been born to a backwoodsman who couldn't sign his own name. But I made my fortune and turned myself into a gentleman and my wife into a fine lady. My Evaline was born the daughter of a gentleman and has been raised to be a fine lady. Wouldn't you agree?"

With McAlister's hammy hand so close to his windpipe, Brent decided disagreeing could be a fatal error. In spite of her unpolished, abrasive father, no one could deny Evaline was always a lady.

"Of course."

"Of course." McAlister removed his hand from Brent's shoulder. "Like any properly reared young lady, my daughter asked you for some time to consider your proposal of marriage."

"A whole year?"

"You couldn't expect her to make a decision that would affect her entire life in a second, could you?" He swung his arm out. "Look what she'd be giving up to live in your little cottage on a dirt road. Look at the type of life she'd be sacrificing to be your wife."

Brent knew his wealth hadn't measured up to McAlister's yet. Maybe it never would. He'd been young and foolish. He'd thought Evaline had loved him and, more foolish still, that love conquered all.

"You certainly wouldn't expect me, as a doting father, to give my darling daughter in marriage and have her settle down to raise a family without taking her on the Grand Tour of Europe. Would you?"

"I suppose not."

"Especially not when you and I both know very well you'd never be able to take her there."

"Well, I don't know about—"

"All I heard from her while we were over there, night and day, day and night, was praise for you. Oh, how wonderful Brent was. How she loved Brent. How she missed Brent."

"How she missed Brent so darn much, she only managed to write to him twice."

"Twice?" McAlister growled. Then he cleared his throat and seemed to purr. "Only twice? No. You know how those foreign countries are. Can't even send a decent letter to civilized people."

"If she's so delighted to marry me, why isn't she here now to greet me?"

"Because she's a proper lady, like I told you. If it's not asking too much, you'll also recall she asked you to speak to me."

"Which I did, all polite and proper—like her little pet monkey on a chain."

"Don't get snide, boy."

"You laughed me out of the room," Brent declared angrily. He was repeating himself, a bad way to argue. But some things stuck in his craw. He had to get rid of them. "She sent me to you to make me look stupid. She was too much of a lady to do it herself."

"Don't *ever* talk like that about my daughter!" McAlister bellowed.

Brent sat there silently, his chin held high. He wouldn't apologize. He wasn't sorry. He was glad he'd gotten that little piece out of his craw. But he still had so much more.

Much to Brent's surprise, McAlister crooned soothingly, "Brent, Brent, it wasn't her fault. You took me by surprise. She's my only daughter, my baby girl. It's difficult for a papa to see his baby grow up, to realize that his daughter has become a young lady with the power to capture men's hearts."

He stood back and placed a pudgy hand over his heart.

"It's sometimes a shock for a papa to realize his baby girl

is now old enough to marry. It all came as such a surprise . . . well, I had to have a little time to discuss it with the wife, time to think about it myself, too."

"A whole year? You three must be slower at thinking things over than Woody Tucker."

"Marriage is not a step to be taken lightly." McAlister's brows drew down in a dark scowl. "My daughter and her future—hell, the future of the estate I worked my whole life to build—deserve a lot more consideration than a herd of pigs."

"I didn't mean it that way."

However he felt about her father, Brent was forced to admit Evaline had never acted in any way other than as a lady, strictly under her father's heavy thumb.

McAlister's frown lifted. He returned to his old, convivial behavior. Brent was still suspicious.

"As her papa, it's my solemn duty to make sure the man she marries is the right man for her. I gave your proposal a lot of consideration."

"And you've finally decided."

"You've got a lot of brass, Brent. I admire that in a man. You've got ambition. I admire that, too, as long as it doesn't interfere with *my* ambition."

"I can't say as I blame you there."

"You show a lot of promise. Just the sort of promise this country needs. I want to make my little girl happy, so I'm allowing you to marry her. And, so you can support her in the manner to which she has become accustomed, I'm offering you those jobs I mentioned. As I see it, that's more than generous."

"I see."

"I might also add, not to be too maudlin, that someday I expect to meet my Maker with a favorable destination planned."

Brent thought McAlister was a singularly optimistic man in that area.

"When I do I'll leave a considerable fortune that neither

Mrs. McAlister nor Evaline is prepared to deal with—except to squander it on silly, feminine furbelows."

Recalling Mrs. McAlister's pinched expression, Brent couldn't believe that woman had ever squandered anything—not even a smile.

"I can't have some ruthless scoundrel come along and cheat them out of it. You know how downright dumb women are when it comes to handling money."

"I think I understand how you think." Brent understood McAlister very well, even though he didn't agree with him. He'd have pitted Miss Flora's business know-how against McAlister's anytime. Although how she'd done it with her wild guesses was still a puzzle to him.

"I need a fellow like you, who knows what it's like to rise from poverty; who knows how to plan and scheme to make his own fortune, his own way in the world; to claw and scrape his way to the top, like a good American businessman."

"And you think I know how to do that?"

"Well, not as well as I do, but I see you're learning."

"I'm flattered." Until then, Brent hadn't realized how pervasive his image as the town scoundrel was. McAlister had taken it too far.

"Of course, as my only son-in-law, you would naturally assume command of my fortune and my vast holdings, not to mention control of Evaline's substantial inheritance."

"I understand."

Brent understood it very well.

He could marry beautiful, elegant Evaline. Move to San Francisco. Run what could turn out to be the two largest newspapers in the state. Possess wealth beyond his wildest dreams. No one would dare make fun of him for being poor again. It was everything he had ever wanted.

He'd have to leave the *Argus*. Shucks, he'd have to leave Lyman's Gap. That meant leaving Cassie, too—beautiful, sensuous, exciting, crazy Cassie. It would mean leaving everything he wanted now.

"Mr. McAlister," Brent began cautiously, rising from his chair, "what if I say no?"

McAlister stared at him, his gaze as cold as ice. "You will *not* say no. You *will* marry Evaline. You will move to San Francisco. You will be editor of my newspapers."

"What if I say no?" Brent stubbornly repeated.

McAlister stood in front of the fireplace, puffing on his cigar until the tip glowed almost as red as the flames behind him. He looked like a rotund demon from hell—the embodiment of pride, gluttony, avarice, envy, and wrath.

Brent waited to hear the man's response to his hypothetical refusal.

At last he removed the cigar from his mouth and announced, "Then I will simply buy *one more* newspaper."

He held up a single, stout finger.

"Right here in Lyman's Gap."

"The *Argus* is not for sale."

McAlister laughed. "Why should I buy that rag? I mean to start my own."

Barely enough happened in Lyman's Gap to support one newspaper. It wasn't big enough for two. Brent knew that, and so did McAlister.

"People here are used to buying the *Argus*," Brent defended.

"For the time being."

"They have for nearly thirty years."

McAlister shook his head. "Wait until they see all the fancy new things I can get—and I've got the money to do it. Hell, I can hire me a Chinaman for a bowl of rice and fish guts a day to sit there and hand color the front page of every damn issue."

"You won't make any money that way."

McAlister's laughter felt like an ice pick hammered into Brent's ears.

"Fool. Don't you know it doesn't matter to me if it makes any money or not? I can afford to keep it running just long enough to force you out of business. Then what will you do? Go back to accepting charity from the firemen's auction? Go to work as a clerk in Abel Warner's store? See if you can get a job mucking out stables with that nigra fellow?"

Brent grit his teeth so tightly together he thought he might crush them all right in his head. He clenched his fist around the cigar, crumbling it to the rug, and searing his hand with the hot ash. He ignored that pain. It was nowhere near as bad as the red-hot anger he felt coursing through him.

At last he regained enough control to speak.

"I'll have to think about this, McAlister."

"What is there to think about? I've made you a clear offer, a damned generous offer. Better than you deserve. I expect an answer."

"You can't expect me to make a decision that will affect my entire life in a second." Brent threw the man's own words back at him.

"You'd better think real fast, boy. I'm not going to wait an entire year."

"You . . . you can't stay?" The pain in Cassie's voice and the disappointment in her eyes hurt Brent, too.

Slowly she unwrapped her arms from around his neck and stepped back a pace. The tips of her fingers still clung to his lapels, as if she couldn't bear to let him go.

How could he bear to let her go? he silently lamented.

Brent hated to see such disappointment in her eyes, but he knew it was better than the hurt he'd see there if she knew the real reason he was cancelling this evening. He was having dinner with the McAlisters. He and Evaline were supposed to "renew old acquaintances."

"I've got a lot of work—"

"I even made dinner myself."

"Fish?"

"No. I think an annual fish fry is about all I'll ever be able to bear."

"Pork chops?"

She shook her head. "After seeing Mehetabel and all her babies, I don't think I'll ever be able to eat pork again."

"Chicken salad?"

She made a little sound of disgust. "Twice a week is enough. Would you settle for a chicken potpie?"

"Sounds delicious."

Brent wanted so badly to wrap his arms around her small waist and draw her to him. He wanted to cover her oval face with heated kisses until the worried expression disappeared. He wanted to strip off his own clothes, strip off Cassie's, and cover her beautiful, creamy body with kisses until she flushed pink with passion.

He wanted to tell McAlister to roll up one of his damned newspapers, and then let him figure out exactly what he could do with it.

In spite of how much, in his misguided youth, he had once desired Evaline—or thought he had—he didn't want her anymore. Not since he'd met Cassie.

He loved Cassie. He wanted to give her everything he'd ever dreamed of, all the things he'd worked so hard for, all the things he had plans for in the future.

The only trouble was, McAlister had placed him in a position where it seemed there was only one way to get everything he had ever wanted. He had to give up Cassie.

There *had* to be another way. Ever since he'd left McAlister's mansion, his brain had been toiling, trying to think of another way. Even now, as part of him wanted to cradle her in his arms, carry her up the stairs, and make warm, passionate love to her, the other part of him was trying to figure out how to keep her and the *Argus*, too; how to not lower himself and his reputation any farther in the eyes of his neighbors; and how to retain for himself some remnant of pride and self-esteem.

There had to be a way to keep Cassie without having McAlister ruin him.

It wouldn't just ruin *him.* What would happen to Sam and Dave and all the other men who worked for him? Would McAlister hire them to work at his newspaper as soon as he'd driven Brent out of business? Brent didn't think so. If he did, would he then fire them when he closed his own newspaper? That was McAlister's style.

Brent wasn't a completely unfeeling scoundrel. How could he refuse McAlister without hurting Evaline's feelings too badly?

If Miss Flora were still alive, he'd have confided his problems to the strangely wise old woman. He smiled at the fond memory of her. She'd have thought about it a day or two and then come up with some incredibly outlandish, unbelievably silly solution that would have actually worked. But she was gone, and he was on his own.

If only he had the time to think, to plan what to do. How long could he stall before McAlister demanded a decision? There *had* to be an alternative.

Until then, he could hardly string Cassie along. It wouldn't be fair. It wouldn't be right.

Sometimes it was so hard to do the right thing.

He stepped back from Cassie, moving blindly backward toward the door. He felt as if that was how he was moving through his life right now—backward, without any kind of guidance.

"I'm sorry I can't stay for dinner. I'm going to have to settle for a cheese sandwich eaten on the run." He hated to lie to her. "There's . . . so much to do. I can't stay."

"Will you come back later tonight?"

"You know, we really ought to be more careful about that. Every night. You know, sooner or later, someone's bound to come by and spot me tiptoeing from my house to yours or back again. Then they'll run tattling to all the world, and your reputation will be ruined."

"But. . . ." Her voice trailed away in a sigh. "Don't you want me anymore, Brent?"

He wrapped his arms around her and held her.

"Oh, my sweet Cassie, of course I want you. I'll always want you. I didn't say never again. Just not tonight."

He wished he knew if he'd eased any of Cassie's pain. It certainly hadn't helped his any.

"I told you once I love you. I'll always love you . . . whatever happens."

She stood with her hands clutched in front of her. She looked like a waif lost in a storm at sea, and he was her only lifeline to shore. And he had just cut her moorings.

"I won't be by tonight. It'll be so late. I'll be dirty. You'll be tired."

"You forget. I have absolutely nothing to do tomorrow. If I want to, I can spend all day in bed, eating sweets and reading novels—and loving you."

"I wish I could, Cassie." That was no lie. "But I really need to do a lot of . . . planning and thinking and work. Probably for a couple of . . . days." Technically, that was no lie, either.

"Are you going to the McAlisters' welcome home party?"

"Probably." Oh, blast! Why did she have to bring that up?

She grinned at him, the way he'd grinned at her the first time he'd teased her. "No one would think it amiss if two neighbors, who just happened to be heading to the same party, would be seen walking together."

"I'm sorry, Cassie," he'd told her. "I have . . . another obligation that evening."

He'd reached the door. Without taking his gaze from Cassie, he opened it farther until he could back out.

Leaving her like this, he truly felt like the scoundrel everyone made him out to be. Sometimes a body had to be cruel to be kind.

"I'll be by for a little while sometime tomorrow—if I can," he promised lamely.

"I'll miss you," she called after him as he pulled the door almost closed. "I'll be here waiting."

He stopped and tried to smile at her through the small crack. He hoped she didn't see the doubt in his eyes. "Will you wait for me, Cassie?"

"I said so, didn't I? Don't you believe me?" She sighed with exasperation.

Brent figured she must get awfully weary of having no one ever believe a word she said. But she said such crazy things.

It was a shame there was nothing he could do about it.

If he could confide his predicament to her, would she, like her aunt, come up with some crazy scheme that would work? If he told her he had to choose between her and his lifelong dreams, what would she say?

Knowing Cassie, she'd be brave and noble and tell him to go fulfil his lifelong dreams. But his dreams had changed. They now included her so inextricably that they meant absolutely nothing without her.

"How long will you wait for me, Cassie?"

"Forever."

"If I really asked you to wait that long, without a word of explanation, would you?"

"I know you don't believe me, Brent. You never do." She gave him a sad little smile. "But I'll wait for you my entire lifetime. I have to."

Cassie walked alone down Elm Street.

This past week had been one of the most miserable weeks in her life. Brent had cancelled several dinners with her, always with some feeble excuse. But she knew where he was going.

Earlier this evening, she'd watched him from her parlor window. Wearing his best suit and looking incredibly handsome, he'd left his house without even sparing a brief glance in her direction. He'd run off into the evening to meet his "other obligation" without another word to her.

He didn't need to say any more. Cassie didn't even need to look into Sebastian. He'd already shown her who the other obligation was, as if she couldn't have guessed.

What could she do? What could she accuse Brent of? He'd said he loved her and asked her to wait. He'd made no other commitment, and she had asked for none.

Once again, as with so many things, Sebastian had shown her the problem, but had neglected to reveal the solution. Would she be able to think of one on her own? Would it come from someone else, as unexpectedly as Brent had saved Abel's life? *Was* there a solution to this predicament?

"Darn you, Sebastian," she muttered to herself as she turned and continued her stroll down Main Street, kicking at imaginary rocks on the sidewalk.

It didn't matter if anyone heard her. People were used to the crazy lady muttering to herself.

"The next time I get cursed, I'm getting a more reliable crystal ball."

Cassie walked alone. No one else in town would accompany the crazy lady.

She passed Warner's Store and, just to be sociable, she stepped inside for a moment.

"My, my, Miss Bowen," Abel said. "You look very lovely tonight. If you don't mind my saying so, aren't you dressed up awful fancy to go shopping?"

Cassie glanced down at her purple satin gown. Then she laughed.

"Oh, it's only the same thing I wore to the Fish Fry. When I left Philadelphia, I had no idea I'd need this many fancy clothes in such a small town."

"We're a group of people who enjoy any reason to celebrate."

Cassie was postponing her final decision on whether this was actually an occasion for celebration.

"This time I decided on an amethyst necklace instead of the pearls, just to make it look a little different," she told Abel as she nervously fingered the necklace.

He nodded. "You look very lovely, Miss Bowen. I wish I could buy my Sally such pretty things."

"Oh, I'll bet you will one day." Some shopkeepers were going to make a lot of money during the coming war. At least Abel was—would be—honest about it. But even with Abel she had to learn to be more circumspect about her predictions.

"Like you bet on the piglets?" Abel asked her with a laugh.

"Not quite the same."

He chuckled. "Well, no offense, but I'll believe it when I see it."

Cassie sighed. That was the only way anyone ever believed her—after it was all over, after it was too late.

"By the way, Miss Bowen, do you still want that drilling equipment or not?"

His question shook her out of her reverie.

"Indeed I do. It should've been delivered by now. I suppose I should've been keeping better track of it than this, but well. . . ." She shrugged. She had to admit, Brent had been a very strong distraction.

Strong. Distracting. Appealing. So sensuous and tender. So incredibly loving and virile. So much more interesting than digging holes in the ground. So incredibly hard to do without.

"Do you know what's causing the delay?"

"I'm still waiting for Brent to give me the bank draft."

She stared at him in shock, then shook her head in disbelief. "Brent never gave you the draft?"

She felt her heart sinking as she realized Brent hadn't believed in her after all. He'd only been humoring her, like all the others. How dare he take charge of her life like that! At least the others had made a hollow gesture of asking her permission. He'd just plain lied to her.

Abel reached up and rubbed the back of his head. "Nope. I don't have it yet. Do you want me to talk to—"

"Oh, no, Mr. Warner." Cassie was sure Abel would notice the venom in her voice. At this point, she didn't care. "I'll be sure to talk to him myself."

Abel shrugged. "Sorry."

"It's not your fault." There was no sense troubling him about the problem. She knew who the source of all her troubles was. She was determined to take her complaint directly to him—as soon as she could find some time to confront him alone.

"Aren't you and Sally going to the party?" she asked.

"No. She claims she's too much in a family way to be seen

in public. She claims she doesn't fit into any of her dresses anymore."

"Oh, but she simply glows."

"She gets tired easily. She likes to prop her feet up when she can."

"You're not going?"

Abel leaned a little farther over the counter and whispered, "I never was too fond of the McAlisters, if you take my meaning."

"I think I do." Even though she'd never met the woman, Cassie herself was not at all fond of Evaline.

"I'm not much on going to parties by myself."

"I understand very well how you feel about that. I'd rather stay home and keep Sally company, and read to the girls to keep them occupied while she rests. You know. The usual things papas do."

"And good husbands," Cassie added with a wistful smile. "Yes. I hope you have a lovely evening." She headed for the door, certain that they would.

"You, too, Miss Bowen."

"Thanks."

She wished she could be as certain for herself. It was going to take a lot more than Abel's cordial wishes for her to enjoy herself at this party.

Site of church functions, site of the annual Fish Fry, and now the school building could add one more item to its long, illustrious list of community activities, Cassie thought as she made her way down Main Street. The site Mrs. Andrews had chosen for the welcome home party for the McAlisters.

"Well, Miss Bowen," Mr. Harvey greeted her with a surprised smile as she entered. "I didn't expect to see you here this evening, alone."

"The invitation I received was very nice."

"But, I mean . . . Well, I hope you have a good time this evening . . . with all the other guests."

"Of course," Cassie replied, with as much politeness, and

also with as much pointed coolness as she could muster. "That's what sane people do, isn't it?"

"You might be in for a surprise or two tonight," he hinted maliciously.

"Oh, I doubt it." Cassie moved along.

She glanced around the gaily decorated room. The desks were gone, even the teacher's big one. She figured if anyone could bully the workmen into moving that enormous desk, it would be Irma Andrews. The patriotic bunting had been taken down. This evening, the print of the portrait of George Washington was surrounded with flowers.

"Evening, Miss Bowen," Mr. Andrews greeted her.

"Everything looks so festive."

"Yep." Mr. Andrews leaned a bit closer to her and muttered, "This darn near took all the festivities right out of my wallet."

"It looks as if all the most prominent citizens are here."

He chuckled. "Around here, that means the folks who have more than one pair of shoes and most of their teeth. The *really* important folks own their own mule."

Cassie laughed and moved on.

"Good evening, Mrs. Klinger. Good evening, Mrs. Norton," Cassie greeted them.

They were standing to the side of the doorway, hands crossed under their bosoms, eyeing the crowd.

"Good evening, Miss Bowen," they replied in unison, as if they'd been rehearsing their eventual encounter with the crazy lady, measuring every word so that nothing would set her off on a tirade.

"Mrs. Norton, I'd like to ask you something," Cassie began.

Mrs. Norton's eyebrows rose with obvious apprehension.

"I understand from Jerusha that your cat had kittens."

"Yes, indeed." Mrs. Norton eyed her warily. "Do you want to guess how many?"

Mrs. Klinger snickered behind her hand.

"Not right now," Cassie replied slowly. "I'm very fond of cats, you know."

She'd need someone besides Sebastian to keep her company

during all the long years of lonely nights that stretched ahead of her.

"Indeed? How do you prefer to prepare them?"

"What? No, no! Goodness gracious, Mrs. Norton, how crazy do you think I am?" How crazy was Mrs. Norton, Cassie wondered, to have turned a simple request for a kitten into a grisly recipe book?

"Oh, not . . . not very."

Well, at least Mrs. Norton was honest.

"I love cats. I used to live with my brother and his wife, who claimed the creatures made her sneeze uncontrollably. She'd never allow me to have one in the house. I'd be delighted to take one, if they're not all spoken for."

"Well, perhaps."

"Thank you, I think. Have you seen Mrs. Parker?" Cassie asked. She was almost ready for them to ask her how she'd cook Mrs. Parker.

Instead, Mrs. Klinger and Mrs. Norton both gave coordinated sniffs of disapproval, and flipped their noses in the air.

"*Minnie* has deigned *not* to honor us with her presence this evening," Mrs. Klinger informed her.

"She's not coming to the party?" Cassie demanded, surprised. "When she came to my house last Monday, it seemed that was all she could talk about. She told me she'd even bought a new gown from Becky Galloway's store."

"We know," they answered together. They turned to each other and nodded knowingly.

"A *red* gown. What does *that* tell you?" Mrs. Norton, her lips pursed and her eyebrows raised, inquired.

Then they sniffed again.

"It figures," Mrs. Klinger said.

"I understand she even dug out that garnet necklace her husband gave her the Christmas before he died."

"Now that *is* significant."

The two nodded together knowingly, sharing the significance only with each other.

"Imagine Minnie getting all gussied up—"

"And foregoing the pleasure of associating with *us* this evening—" Mrs. Norton continued for her.

"Because she preferred the company of Doc Carver," Mrs. Klinger finished.

"Imagine him asking her," Mrs. Norton snickered to Mrs. Klinger.

"She's got to be forty if she's a day."

"Oh, at least."

"He's got to be fifty."

"He hardly looks it."

"What could he possibly see in her?" They conducted their conversation as if Cassie had suddenly disappeared from the face of the earth.

"What could they possibly have in common to talk about?"

"What could she see in him? At his age, he's bound to drop dead soon anyway—of old age or overwork or one of those diseases he treats—and then what will she do?"

"Be a widow again," Mrs. Norton predicted gloomily. "Then she'll have to go back to work, cleaning other people's houses for a living again."

Mrs. Klinger shook her head. "A body can't make any money being a doctor out here in the country."

They gave another coordinated sniff.

"Are you here alone this evening, my dear?" Mrs. Klinger asked, as if she'd just remembered Cassie's existence.

Now it was Mrs. Norton's turn to snicker.

"Yes, I am."

"You usually seem to find it so convenient to have Mr. Conway accompany you everywhere."

"He can be a . . . pleasant companion."

Mrs. Norton snickered again.

"How strange he didn't come with you this evening," Mrs. Klinger commented.

"I believe he has other obligations."

Cassie knew very well what they were, but she wasn't about to admit it to either of these two cackling biddies. Still, they'd lived in Lyman's Gap longer than she had. They didn't need a crystal ball to know what had been going on before she'd arrived, and what was going on now.

Why hadn't someone bothered to warn her? Did they all hate her that much?

"Indeed, Mr. Conway is a very busy man," Mrs. Norton said.

"By the by, have you seen him here tonight?" Mrs. Klinger asked.

She wouldn't let them think she'd come to rely too heavily on Brent. That way, when he left her for Evaline, she could pretend to all the world that he didn't really break her heart that much.

"To tell you the truth, Mrs. Klinger, I haven't even looked for him," she stated boldly.

Mrs. Norton leaned toward Mrs. Klinger and whispered in a voice Cassie couldn't help but hear, "Should we tell her now?"

"Of course not," Mrs. Klinger snapped.

"Tell me what?" Cassie boldly demanded. She hated the snickering behind hands that really wasn't meant to hide a thing.

"If you're supposed to be so good at predicting things—which I highly doubt—you ought to be able to figure this one out by yourself, too," Mrs. Klinger replied.

They nodded knowingly at each other.

"Oh, hush, and look pleasant," Mrs. Norton scolded, slapping at her friend's elbow with her fan. "Try to sound polite. She's coming this way again."

Cassie turned to see who had them so agog.

Evaline McAlister. She should have guessed. Looking at her, Cassie wished she'd stayed home, in bed, with all the lights out, the curtains drawn, and the covers pulled up over her head.

Evaline's golden hair was arranged just as Sebastian had shown her, cascading down from a perfect crown to caress her lily-white, sloping shoulders. Her gown of cream-colored silk floated about her shoulders, rising over perfect cleavage, then billowed out over her wide crinoline, giving her the appearance of a radiant angel on a cloud.

Next to this woman, Cassie felt as fashionable as Mehetabel wallowing in the straw. Sally, great with child, had to be more graceful than Cassie felt at the moment.

Beside the single, small golden chain around her neck, Evaline sported only one other perfect accessory—Brent, guiding her on his left arm.

Brent had never looked so tall and broad-shouldered. He'd never looked more elegantly masculine. Cassie wondered if Evaline had had any say regarding his choice of attire.

Cassie felt she paled into utter insignificance beside the glorious Evaline McAlister. There was no doubt in her mind how he could have chosen Evaline over her. That didn't lessen the hurt.

Cassie stared at him, hoping he'd say hello or smile or do something. Brent greeted Mrs. Klinger, Mrs. Norton, and herself in one sweeping nod. Then, he seemed to find something extremely interesting about his shoes and didn't look up again.

Evaline inclined her head to Mrs. Klinger and to Mrs. Norton, whom she'd obviously already greeted this evening. Then she beamed a brilliant smile at Cassie.

"You must be Miss Bowen."

Evaline was speaking directly to her. Cassie could hardly be impolite. She dragged her gaze away from the rude, cruel, unappreciative Brent.

"I suppose I must. No one else seems to want to be." Cassie couldn't decide if she was trying to be morose or sarcastic.

Apparently Evaline thought she was being funny. She laughed a delicate, tinkling laugh that grated on Cassie's ears and nerves like a shovel on salted ice.

Evaline extended a slim hand in a graceful gesture. Her slender fingers, in their expensive, white kid gloves, barely exerted any pressure on Cassie's hand at all.

Cassie felt as oafish as Woody at a ballet.

"I'm Evaline McAlister."

"So I assumed."

"It's so good to be home again. Thank you so much for coming to this lovely party Mrs. Andrews was kind enough to have for my parents and me. She's a gracious hostess and a dear friend of my mother's."

"I figured."

Compared to the dulcet tones of Evaline's cultured voice, Cassie thought she sounded like a braying jackass kicking an ashcan.

"I understand you recently moved here from Philadelphia."

"Yes."

"Would you by any chance have made the acquaintance of the Charles H. Websters? They have a daughter, Verna, whom I met in London."

"No, I haven't. I didn't go out much in society."

"Oh." With great poise, Evaline deftly changed the subject. "Please do accept my condolences on the recent passing of your aunt."

"Thank you."

"I remember her fondly. My entire family thought quite highly of her."

If so, you're just about the only ones who didn't think she was a raving lunatic, Cassie thought. She decided it was better not to say it, though, and remind everyone that her aunt had been the town's beloved, resident crazy old lady before Cassie arrived and became just the crazy lady.

"She appeared to be in good health when we left. Was she ill long?"

"No. She passed away quite unexpectedly."

"How sad for you. I do hope you're finding the people of Lyman's Gap a blessing in consoling you."

Cassie nodded. "Some of them." She glanced toward Brent again, but he'd now found something extremely interesting about the portrait of George Washington on the far wall and was studying that. He never even spared her a glance.

Evaline tapped his shoulder with her fan. "Brent, do be a dear and get me a lemonade."

Brent nodded again as a sort of general adieu, and left.

"Ladies," Evaline addressed Mrs. Klinger and Mrs. Norton, "please excuse us."

Mrs. Klinger and Mrs. Norton would have nodded their consent until their heads fell off.

"Miss Bowen, do come walk with me."

Cassie was pulled along in her wake like a leaky dingy tied behind a majestic schooner.

Evaline began a graceful, leisurely stroll about the room. Cassie felt she was clumping along beside her as if she'd forgotten someone had taken away the mule and the plough.

"I remember your aunt's extraordinary house very well. She had such interesting, unusual things on display. I know she collected them for many years. I often wonder what else she might have in an attic or a closet that she hadn't gotten around to, or hadn't room to display."

"I haven't found anything else, except what she showed me before she passed away." Cassie figured she wasn't lying.

"I do hope you're not thinking of disposing of any of those wonderful things."

"I must admit, there are moments when I'm tempted." Sebastian and some of his more unpleasant visions immediately came to mind. "But then I reconsider. I don't think I could part with a thing."

"Miss Flora had such a lovely garden. I don't suppose her good influence has worn off on Brent in any way, however."

"Actually, his petunias are sprouting very well." Well, didn't that sound like just about the dumbest thing anyone could ever say? Cassie scolded herself. Things were going from bad to worse. Now she not only had no control over her clumsy feet, but also she had no control over what her mouth was saying without any assistance from her brain.

"Since you are his neighbor, and probably will be for at least a little while longer, I feel you and I ought to get to know each other much better."

Why? Cassie thought. *I already know enough about you to make me sick to my stomach, especially when I recall that vision of you and Brent.*

As much as she wanted to, Cassie didn't say that. As much as she wanted to hate the woman, she had to admit Evaline was being rather pleasant. On the other hand, if Cassie had all the money in the world *and* Brent, she'd be deliriously happy and nice to everyone, too.

Cassie could hardly dump the punch bowl over Evaline's head and declare, "I don't want to know you—ever!"

On the brighter side, if she did, nobody would ever invite her to one of these atrocious social affairs ever again.

On the other hand, that would only add more fuel to the fire Mr. Harvey was trying to roast her over.

"That would be . . . nice," Cassie responded instead.

"In three weeks, my parents are having a very special party at our home," Evaline said. "Of course, you'll be invited."

"Thank you." Another of these affairs, Cassie silently lamented. Maybe now *was* the time to dump the punch bowl over Evaline's head and avoid that one.

"I suppose this really is no secret," Evaline said.

"Especially not if they're planning on sending out invitations," Cassie muttered under her breath.

Had Evaline not heard her, or was she so much of a lady that she was ignoring Cassie's bad manners?

"I suppose it would still be very pleasant to consider you a friend I can confide in."

"That would be . . ."—*Impossible*! Cassie silently screamed—"nice."

Evaline stretched out her pale hand again and placed it on Cassie's arm.

"Could we, just for this evening, pretend we've been bosom friends since childhood. Can I confide in you my happy secret?"

No, no! I don't want to hear your damned secret because I already think I know what it is and I don't like it, not one bit! Cassie bit her tongue and refrained from screaming out her mean and petty thoughts in the middle of the room.

"That would be nice," Cassie managed to croak. She even

managed a smile. Oh, what a hypocrite she was! she scolded herself.

Evaline leaned a little closer and whispered, "At my parents' party in three weeks, Brent and I are going to announce our betrothal."

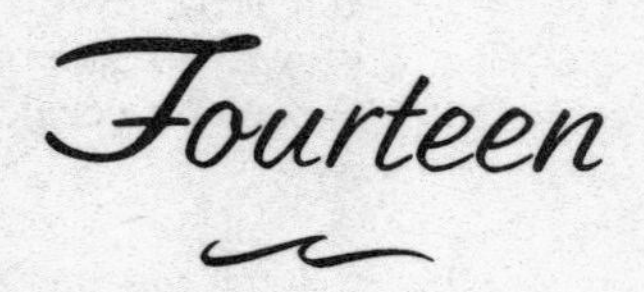

Fourteen

Cassie walked home alone. Peter Markham, Eugene Carmody, and Hiram Sewell asked if they could accompany her, but she knew they only did it because Reverend Markham had asked his son and his friends to do so.

She'd politely refused. She'd noticed Peter eyeing Cecelia Harris all night. Peter should be walking *her* home instead. And Eugene and Hiram should stop sneaking swigs of home brew behind the outhouse.

Anyway, Cassie figured she needed to get used to being alone. She sort of liked being alone sometimes. It gave her time to think.

On the other hand, as she plodded along the dark, dusty road, she realized she was going to have the rest of her life to spend time thinking.

She passed Warner's Store. She'd love to go inside. Talk to Abel and Sally. See what a happy family life could be like—an experience she'd be missing.

No, the doors were closed. The lamps were extinguished. The blinds were drawn down over all the windows and the front doors. It was late, and Sally needed her rest. So did Abel if he was trying to cope with two bouncy little girls.

Right now she didn't think Abel would enjoy hearing her complain about what an unmitigated scoundrel Brent was. She'd rather not depress them with her problems.

On the other hand, maybe Abel would open the store for her briefly, just so she could make a few quick, but extremely urgent purchases. A hatchet. A rope. Some rat poison.

The only trouble was, she couldn't decide who to use them on. Evaline, Brent, or herself.

Cassie plodded on.

Maybe, if she was lucky, Lem was laying in wait for her. He'd push her in the creek as he had that other boy. Without two friends to pull her out, she'd drown.

Maybe, if she was lucky, some hungry mother bear with two ravenous cubs would wander down from the mountains and decide she'd make a delicious midnight snack.

Maybe, if she was very lucky, she'd lose her way on the dark mountain path, end up on the top of the mountain, take one misstep off a cliff, and plummet to her tragic death.

Then all the townspeople would be sorry they'd teased and taunted her. Then Brent would be sorry for the way he'd jilted her.

Or would the townspeople just figure that was what happened to crazy ladies who went wandering off alone at night? Brent would print the story of her unfortunate, but not entirely unexpected, demise in the *Argus*. Maybe her news would even make the front page, and everyone would be sure to buy that issue. The blasted scoundrel would even make money from her death.

They were all so sympathetic to her plight.

Cassie didn't bother to light a lamp when she entered the house. She knew her way by now even in the dark. She closed her bedroom door, threw her shawl over the chair, and sat on the edge of the bed.

What was it Aunt Flora had told her about Sebastian? "In times of trouble or uncertainty, gaze into his depths and he will show you the future."

Well, she certainly was troubled, Cassie decided as she sat

in the darkness. She was, indeed, experiencing a great deal of uncertainty at this point in her life.

Sebastian would always show her the truth. Sebastian might be the only person in this whole town she could actually count on to tell her the truth. She pulled his case from under her bed and reverently lifted him out.

"I'm treating you very nicely," she pointed out to him as she placed him on the table. "I fully expect you to do the same for me. I'm feeling very sad right now. I'd really appreciate some cheery visions—roses, kittens, puppies, snowflakes, Christmas presents. I'd even settle for more piglets. Babies—no, not babies," she quickly amended. "That'll only remind me of what I'll never have."

She gazed into Sebastian with growing hope as lights began to glow inside. Sebastian swirled his rainbows, but showed her nothing specific. Cassie figured that might be his way of showing sympathy, if he had any.

"If you can't show me sunsets and roses, at least show me why Brent did this to me," she pleaded, as if she could conjure up the images. "Show me it's all some sort of mistake. That you're just playing a wicked, devilish, not-so-very-funny-after-all joke on me. Have me wake up in my own bed—with Brent beside me, still in love with me. Let me discover everything that's happened since you showed me Evaline has all been a horrible nightmare. None of this has ever really happened—and never will."

Sebastian chose other images.

The sun shone brightly. Botheration! She wanted to see a dark and stormy night. Something gloomy, to suit her mood.

Workmen were bustling around the same tall, tapering square tower, flanked by lower, rectangular buildings, and piles of stacked barrels, prepared to hold the flow of petroleum.

"Yes, yes." She nodded perfunctorily. "The drill for the petroleum under the ground."

The steam engine driving the drill chugged. The steel drills bit into the rock with a grinding clank. The petroleum, released from its pool underground, rose to the surface.

"Yes, yes. Very interesting," she muttered. "Now get on to something that will help me solve my real problems."

She waited. The engine chugged, the drill clanked, the petroleum flowed.

"Sebastian, I asked for help with Brent," she reminded him a bit peevishly. She waved her hand at the images in the stubborn crystal ball. "Not this greasy stuff."

The sun still shone on the wooden buildings. Cassie heaved a deep sigh.

"Very well then. Show me what you will. I'm just too weary to argue with you tonight."

The field expanded. Newer, larger towers arose. New drills were constructed of designs he'd never shown her before. More barrels of petroleum fed the needs of a growing nation.

"All right. I think I understand what you're trying to tell me. You think this is really important. Tomorrow morning, I'll give Abel the money for the equipment."

Her eyes narrowed, and her lips pressed firm with determination.

"I'll find out why that lying, cheating Brent didn't do as I asked—as we *agreed*. How could I have been so stupid to trust him? Especially when he's been so untrustworthy in more ways than one."

Cassie screamed and threw herself backward on her bed in frustration. "So incredibly perfidious! Traitorous! False! Faithless! Lying! What else?"

She sat up again, as if that would help her to think of more horrible, and more specific, adjectives for Brent.

"That land is incredibly valuable. He'd been urging Aunt Flora to sell it to him for years. He urged me to sell it to him since the first day I inherited it."

Cassie frowned so hard she gave herself a headache. She rose to her feet and began to pace.

"When I refused, and seemed to be taking Mr. Harvey's advice about not selling it, he realized he couldn't get it that way."

She slammed her fist against the wall.

"Ouch!" She rubbed her knuckles. "That was an incredibly stupid thing to do. Why do men do that? Why don't they say ouch when they do that?"

Then, because it felt so good to relieve the anger and tension bottled up inside, she punched the wall again.

"That scoundrel has been playing on my affections until he could talk me into doing just about anything he wanted. And I would have, you know," she told Sebastian. "For Brent, I'd have done almost anything."

She screamed again, but this time, she grabbed her pillow and slapped it against the headboard of her bed. Words came out of her mouth that she'd only heard sailors on the docks using. Fishwife didn't begin to encompass her vocabulary. She directed it all—every scorching, blue word of it—at Brent.

Feathers flew from the tattered pillow ticking. She continued to beat it against the bed.

"He never loved me. Never, ever! He only used my sorrow at the death of Aunt Flora, and my loneliness in a strange town away from my family, and my loneliness from being alone *all my life*. He only used me to try to get that property while, all along, he was planning on marrying beautiful, wealthy Evaline."

At last, out of feathers, out of energy, and out of spleen, Cassie collapsed onto her bed.

She glanced sideways at Sebastian, but he seemed to be stuck in a rut. All he kept showing was the petroleum rigs, constantly working.

Cassie waved a gesture of disgusted dismissal at him.

"Oh, stop already. I got the message."

To her surprise, Sebastian went blank. Without his sparkling, flickering lights, the room was completely dark.

Yes, yes, Cassie decided. This was much more suited to her mood. She stared at the blank, dark ceiling. Tears were trickling out the sides of her eyes, down her temples and into her ears. Her corset pinched. She was very uncomfortable, but that sort of suited her mood, too.

"He never, ever loved me. But, oh . . ." She breathed a deep, sorrowful sigh. "Oh, I loved him. Every gorgeous, muscular inch of him. Was he the man I was supposed to love with no hope of him ever loving me in return? Of course. I've never loved anyone but him. I never shall."

She wiped away her tears with her pillowcase. The way she felt, it was just too darn much trouble to get up and get her handkerchief. It was too darn much trouble to get out of this gown and corset.

Maybe days from now they'd find her dead, emaciated body lying here, and bury her in her finest dress.

"I should have figured it out right from the beginning, when Aunt Flora told me the man only loved money. If only I'd believed her when she first told me about you, Sebastian. Then the curse would have been broken, and I wouldn't have to worry anymore."

She felt her jaws clenching more tightly.

"But what about the rest of the curse? I've lost nothing, except the man I loved more than anything in the world. I guess that's enough to qualify, isn't it?"

She felt her lips drawing tightly together with bitterness.

"I certainly don't trust someone I have no reason to trust because, by golly, I don't trust anyone anymore. Brent just sort of reached into my heart and ripped out all the loving trust I might have treasured there."

She drew in a deep gulp of air and wiped her nose on the empty pillowcase.

"And still, not a soul in this town believes a word I say."

Her chin quivered, and her tears began to fall again. She rolled to her side and pulled her knees to her chest, clutching her empty pillow to her aching breast.

"I wonder if anyone will believe me if I tell them I don't love Brent. That I never loved him. And I don't! Not anymore. I hate him," she rasped in a voice gravely with tears and anger. "I hate him!"

With one last wail, she cried, "And I'll never break this horrible curse."

• • •

The thunderous banging on the front door woke Cassie.

"Oh, for Pete's sake!" she groaned as she rolled to her back.

She rolled her tongue around in her mouth and spit out a feather.

"Is it Monday already? Didn't Mrs. Parker have a good enough time with Doc Carver at the party that she has to come banging on my door at the crack of dawn?"

She pulled open her swollen eyes to nothing but fluffy whiteness and the vague outline of her room beyond.

"Oh, goodness, I cried so much I've gone blind!" she wailed, sitting upright in the bed.

She rubbed at her eyes with the back of her hands. Feathers blew out from her grasp.

With much clearer eyesight, Cassie surveyed her bedroom. There was a small dent in the plaster by the window. Maybe she could hide the damage with new wallpaper, or a nice sampler hung there. Goodness knew, she'd have plenty of time on her hands in the future to stitch a big, complicated one. One with lots of hearts and daggers around the border and a motto that stated: Brent Conway is a big, fat, dirty cheater.

At the rate her luck was going, she'd have enough time to raise the sheep and spin the wool, too.

She looked around the rest of the room. All the furniture was still sitting upright. She couldn't have pitched that much of a conniption fit last night. But her bed, the floor, and herself were covered with feathers. She rubbed her itching cheeks. Feathers peeled off.

At this hour of the morning, who in the world kept banging on her door? Well, fie on them! Anyone who was rude enough to call this early deserved to wait.

Cassie looked down at her crumpled purple gown. Poor Jerusha. She certainly had her work cut out for her making this look presentable again.

Feathers fluttered from the purple satin and clung to her underthings as she dug through her wardrobe for a fresh dress.

As she buttoned the last button at the neckline of her dark

blue serge, the incessant knocking stopped. Cassie held her breath and waited for further sound.

Had her caller given up and gone away? Good. She rushed to the window to watch whoever might be retreating down the walk. No one.

Had someone broken into her house? How had they managed to get in? She hadn't heard any breaking glass. She couldn't remember if she'd locked the doors last night or not. Usually she didn't feel the need to so—in a small town most folks were honest and the creatures from the woods who prowled around upon occasion hadn't learned to work doorknobs yet. Who around here would do such a thing?

Cassie started at the knock on her bedroom door. If it was a burglar, he certainly was unbelievably polite.

"Miss Bowen? Miss Bowen, are you awake?" Jerusha called through the door. "Are you out of bed? Are you presentable?"

"Jerusha, was that *you* pounding like that?" Cassie asked in disbelief. Generally Jerusha, quiet as a shadow, placed the laundry in the kitchen for Mrs. Parker to put away and just as quietly went her way.

"No, miss. I'd never do anything so rude."

"I didn't think you would, but who—"

"I think you're going to want to come down here right soon. You've got callers."

"Callers? Who?"

"Says he's your brother—"

"Oh, no! Oh, my goodness." Cassie fluttered around the room in near panic, stirring up more feathers in her wake. Damn August Harvey! The scoundrel had made good on his threat to go to her brother.

"Your brother's wife's come along, too," Jerusha told her. "Although, if you'll excuse me for saying so, Miss Bowen, it appears to me more like she dragged him all the way."

"Typical," Cassie muttered. More loudly, to be heard through the door, she asked Jerusha, "What are they doing here so early in the morning?"

"Early?" Jerusha repeated with a laugh. "Miss Bowen, it's nearly noon."

She *had* been exhausted last night.

"Miss Bowen, if you don't mind, if you're decent, would you please open this door? It'd make it a whole lot easier explaining this situation to you without risking them two downstairs hearing."

Cassie glanced wildly about the room. It was full of feathers. How could she explain that? Sebastian sat, bold as brass and clear as daylight, in his stand on her night table. She could *never* explain him.

"Just a minute, Jerusha."

She jammed Sebastian into his bag and slid him under her bed. "Sorry," she whispered to him as she patted the bag in parting.

"Now, what were you saying, Jerusha?" Cassie asked as she opened the door.

Jerusha stared at her, her sparkling eyes completely unreadable. "Miss Bowen, what have you been doing to yourself? Do you want them to think you really are crazy?"

Cassie glanced down at her bodice. No, she'd gotten them all buttoned straight. She swung around, trying to see her back, to make sure the hem of her skirt hadn't gotten caught up in the tops of her pantaloons, and she was giving all the world a free show.

"Why are you wearing feathers?" Jerusha glanced up at Cassie's head. "Is this some new hat? Are you fixing to fly anytime soon?"

Cassie's hands flew to her hair. "Oh, my goodness! I can't have them see me like this. They'll claim I'm crazy for sure."

"That's what I've been trying to tell you."

Cassie rushed to her dresser, and began to brush out her hair. All she succeeded in doing was to send more feathers flying, and to goad her unruly hair into more voluminous fluff.

"Here, let me help you with that, Miss Bowen," Jerusha offered. She held out her hand for the brush, which Cassie readily relinquished. "You'll never get out all the feathers in the back."

"Thank you."

"You see, I was delivering your laundry to the back door, like I always do," Jerusha explained as she brushed. "I heard this thunderation on the front door, so I crept through the house and took a peek out a window. Hand me that hairpin, please."

Cassie complied.

"I didn't know who they were or where you were, but I didn't think it was a good idea for them to think this house, with all its wonderful things, was just sitting wide open for the taking. So, I let them in and pretended I was your maid."

"You? My maid."

"Yes," Jerusha replied, as if it went without saying. "Hand me another one of them hairpins, please."

Cassie chuckled and complied. "That was quick thinking. What did you do with them, Jerusha?"

"I invited them to sit in the parlor, like I've seen them do in the fancy houses in New Orleans. I offered them both a glass of cider, too. That's what you'd want me to do, isn't it?"

"No, I'd rather you'd thrown them both out on their ears."

"What?"

"Nothing. Just thinking out loud. Of course, you did the right thing. Thank you, Jerusha."

"There you go, Miss Cassie." Jerusha stepped back.

"Are all the feathers out?" Then Cassie looked into the mirror. "Goodness gracious, Jerusha. What have you done to me?"

"You don't like it? It's all the rage in New Orleans."

"I . . . I . . ." Cassie lifted her hand to her hair, but then stopped, as if fearful of disturbing the elegant creation. "My . . . my hair looks exactly like Evaline's," she murmured.

"Only a much more fascinating color," Jerusha told her. "That pale blond don't add *no* interest to a face."

"How did . . . ?"

"My mama was a hairdresser. Did all the fine white ladies' hair in New Orleans. I just sort of watched her and learned."

"I never would have believed it," Cassie murmured. "Thank you."

Jerusha chuckled. "Now, what jewelry are you going to wear?"

Cassie opened her jewel case. Jerusha gasped with delight as she peered inside.

"You know, Jerusha, I once swore I'd go back and visit Robert and Letitia someday, and wear every piece of jewelry Aunt Flora left me."

"Oh, do it now!" Jerusha urged excitedly. She bounced up and down like a little girl. "Seeing you in all Miss Flora's jewels would be—"

"No, no. Even to spite Letitia, that would be far too much." She peered into the jewel case. "But which one should I wear?"

"Just about anything you have would look beautiful against that dark blue dress. Yes, indeed." Jerusha peeked at her reflection in the mirror, admiring herself. "I'd say just about anything looks beautiful against something dark."

Cassie caught a glimpse of Jerusha primping her own ebony curls in the mirror, and had to smile in agreement.

"Diamonds?" Cassie suggested.

"Too fancy for day."

"Pearls?"

"Too fancy for Lyman's Gap."

"Sapphires?"

"No, same color as the dress."

"Garnets?"

"Different color, but no contrast against that dark fabric."

Cassie and Jerusha stared into the jewel case.

At last, Cassie stood up straight and announced, "Nothing."

"What?" Jerusha's eyes grew round with surprise. "You got all this and you're wearing—"

"Nothing." Cassie closed her jewel case. "I'm not going to wear any jewelry today."

Jerusha shook her head. "I never believed it when the others said you were crazy, Miss Cassie, but I think I'm about to change my mind. You got all that beautiful jewelry and you're not wearing any of it?"

"Robert and Letitia must be two of the greediest persons on earth. She'll be looking for me to show off, wearing my wealth."

"Well, if you got it, what's wrong with that?"

"I don't need to show off, especially not in front of her. I won't give her the satisfaction of knowing what I own. I won't give her the satisfaction of thinking I care what she thinks about me."

Jerusha shrugged. "Suit yourself, Miss Cassie."

"For once in my life, Jerusha, that's exactly what I'm doing."

With her head held high, Cassie proceeded out of her bedroom and down the stairs. In the middle of the stairs, Cassie startled, annoyed. Was Jerusha pinching her shoulder? Why on earth would she do that? She turned to find out. Jerusha, grinning sheepishly, held up one more feather, then tucked it away in her pocket.

"Ah, I'm so glad to see you've made yourselves comfortable," Cassie said as she swept into the parlor.

Robert was shuffling through the books on the shelves to the side of the fireplace. Letitia was inspecting the stuffed alligator in the glass cabinet. Cassie was tempted to sneak up behind her and growl, just to watch her jump.

Those two busybodies had been left down here alone, Cassie worried, to their own devices, for some time while she and Jerusha had been upstairs making her presentable. They looked as if they were taking inventory.

Thank goodness she'd kept Sebastian in her bedroom instead of putting him where Aunt Flora had usually kept him, in the japanned cabinet in the parlor.

What would have happened if they'd discovered him? Hadn't Aunt Flora warned Cassie that only a woman born a Bowen must ever know of its existence? What would happen if someone else saw him?

She glanced around the room. Things were still neatly in their places where she'd left them. The paintings didn't hang askew on the wall. No unique and expensive crystal or porcelain vase was lying smashed on the floor. The usual quiet pervaded the house.

"Where are Ralphie and Marguerite?" she asked. If Robert and Letitia had brought them along, she certainly would have seen or heard them—or their wake of devastation and destruction—by now.

"We left them in Philadelphia," Robert replied. At least he had the good grace to stop pawing through her things and go sit on the sofa.

"With my mother," Letitia added. Slowly she made her way from the stuffed alligator to the piano.

Cassie smiled with relief. All her lovely things were safe for the moment.

"Was that your maid who let us in?" Robert demanded.

Cassie glanced back at Jerusha, who was standing in the doorway to the foyer, her hands folded primly in front of her. She looked every inch the dutiful servant, awaiting further instructions.

"Of course," Cassie answered confidently.

Cassie was surprised to see Jerusha drop a perfect curtsey.

"Didn't waste any time, did you?" Robert demanded. "Hiring a servant."

Cassie gave him a condescending smile. "Aunt Flora already employed Jerusha as the maid and laundress. She also employed Olivier as gardener and coachman, and Mrs. Parker as housekeeper. I merely retained their valuable and indispensable services."

Cassie heard Robert grunt. She could have sworn she heard Letitia growl, "Three?" with disbelief and a large portion of jealousy.

"Miss Cassie, shall I instruct Olivier to take your guests' baggage to their room?" Jerusha asked.

Cassie blinked. Jerusha and Olivier were proud but not arrogant, polite but never servile. It was a bit disconcerting to see her acting so domestic. Cassie was so grateful to her.

"Thank you, Jerusha."

"I'll serve luncheon in half an hour in the dining room."

Cassie blinked again. Where in the world was Jerusha going to get lunch in half an hour? Cassie didn't even have any of Mrs. Parker's leftover chicken salad in the springhouse. Sebastian had shown her some places a person could get food very quickly, but it would take many, many decades instead of just half an hour to get to them.

Well, Jerusha had handled everything so far. She might as well trust her on this, too.

"Thank you, Jerusha."

Jerusha disappeared into the kitchen.

"I wondered if you'd get around to seeing us after we traveled all this way," Letitia grumbled as she settled onto the sofa beside Robert.

"Perhaps I'd have been better prepared if you'd informed me you were coming," Cassie countered.

She grinned to herself with a certain secret satisfaction. Letitia had to be surprised. Cassie had never talked back to her in her life.

Cassie may have felt like an awkward oaf in the presence of Evaline last night. But this morning she felt she could match the grace of a gazelle as she sat in the large winged chair opposite them.

"I didn't think we'd need a special invitation to our own home," Robert grumbled.

"You don't," Cassie replied coolly. "But you do need one to *mine*."

Cassie watched Letitia throw Robert a sharply compelling glance and jab him in the side with her elbow.

"Well now, Cassie," Robert said slowly, "that's not exactly the way we see it."

"I'm sure it isn't. But that's the way it is. Aunt Flora's will was quite clear. She left everything—*everything*—to me."

"That hardly seems fair."

"You inherited everything he had when Papa passed away.

I inherited everything she had when Aunt Flora passed away," Cassie reminded him. "I think it sounds perfectly equitable."

"That may be what Aunt Flora's will said, but sometimes there are certain circumstances that mitigate—"

"You've been talking to August Harvey," Cassie accused.

"Well, he did write to us."

Cassie nodded. She'd expected as much.

"Cassie, my dear," Letitia said, "we know how very shy and retiring you are."

"Indeed?" They certainly would spring out of their seats if she suddenly yelled at them the way she'd shouted at Mrs. Andrews and Mr. Harvey, Cassie thought with a silent laugh. On the other hand, that would only be handing them more evidence on a silver platter that she was stark, staring mad. She knew she must behave herself.

"We know how fond you were of Aunt Flora," Robert added.

"How fond we *all* were," Letitia quickly amended.

"And what a great shock her sudden death must have been to you—"

"To us *all*," Letitia added. "That is why we're able to overlook some of the more eccentric behavior of yours that Mr. Harvey reported to us."

"Considering the equally strange behavior Mr. Harvey reports that Aunt Flora exhibited before her death, however, we . . . we all feel perhaps Aunt Flora was a bit misguided in leaving everything to you."

"Mr. Harvey didn't think so when he drew up the will for her years ago and never bothered to amend it, even in light of her unusual behavior," Cassie countered. "Mr. Harvey didn't think so until I dismissed him."

"We don't feel allowing you complete control of so much money is really a wise move," Letitia said.

"It has nothing to do with you. It's none of your business," Cassie told them bluntly.

"She was Robert's aunt, too," Letitia insisted. "And we . . . he ought to have something."

"Not a cent."

Letitia threw him a scathing glance, and Robert continued, "There was land, stocks, cash—"

"Jewelry," Letitia added.

"Not a cent, not a clump of dirt, not one precious—or even semiprecious—stone," Cassie insisted. She couldn't resist giving a waggish shake of her head at her little pun.

"Your unusual behavior regarding Mr. Harvey is enough to—"

"What unusual behavior?" Cassie demanded coolly. "I had every right to dismiss him as my attorney, just as much as if I chose to buy my dresses and groceries at a different store."

"There was the matter of these pigs—"

Cassie let out a tinkling, ultimately derisive laugh that would have rivaled Evaline or even the bells of St. Mary's for melody.

"A mere wager. A good guess. Sheer luck."

She gave what was, even to herself, a surprisingly graceful, dismissive wave of her hand. For just a moment, she regretted not having worn at least *one* of Aunt Flora's—no, *her*—rings.

That was unimportant now. She didn't have to look wealthy. She acted self-confident, and that was worth more than all the money in the world. She acted sane, and that was worth allowing her to keep all her money and, more importantly, her independence.

"Is it insane to make wagers now?" she asked with feigned ingenuousness. "If it were, I should think they would have to confine the entire country."

"There was an incident involving a young man," Robert continued to enumerate. "You went into some sort of attack of the vapors because you seemed to believe he was going to die in some war."

"Now do you see why we left the children at home?" Letitia demanded.

"Yes, and I'm enormously grateful."

"They're far too young. They need to be sheltered from the

harsh truth that their beloved aunt is . . ." Her voice dropped to a whisper. "Crazy."

Oh, dear, Cassie worried. How was she going to explain her way out of that one? Well, there was one thing that had always sent Robert scurrying, although she doubted it would work on Letitia.

Inconspicuously she held her breath, trying to turn red—the closest thing to a blush she could summon.

"I was a bit . . . overwrought." Behind her hand as if speaking only to Letitia, but loud enough for Robert to hear, she whispered, "Nature's monthly duty, you know."

"Really, Cassie!" Robert protested. "You needn't—"

"Luncheon is served, Miss Cassie," Jerusha announced from the doorway.

"Oh, I am so glad we left the children at home."

"So am I," Cassie said.

"I thought I was glad when yesterday was over," Cassie told Jerusha as the two of them finished tidying up the kitchen after her uninvited guests had retired for the night. "Coping with Robert and Letitia was difficult enough when I was living in their home. It's even worse when I have to put up with them in *my* home."

"If you don't mind my saying so, I find it hard to believe he's your brother," Jerusha commented. "You two had the same mother and the same father?"

"Yes, Jerusha, as odd as that may seem, it's true."

Jerusha laughed.

"I owe you a great debt of gratitude."

" 'Twasn't anything out of the ordinary. I can't speak for Mrs. Parker, but if you need us as long as them folks are here, Olivier and I'll help out."

"Where did you get all that food? And so quickly?"

"Mrs. Andrews."

"Jerusha, I don't mean to sound as if I'm calling you a liar, but Mrs. Andrews is *not* going to be giving me food."

"No, but, you see, it's sort of a tradition around here you

probably haven't been here long enough to know about. After folks have parties that Olivier and I are generally not invited to, folks start to feel guilty."

"No wonder some people were looking at me so strangely when you came to Aunt Flora's funeral."

Jerusha shrugged. "So they send us most of the leftover food. Well, if they don't, it'll just go bad. Olivier gets all stuffy and proud sometimes and doesn't want to take it. But I like it. I don't have to spend as much on food, and we can save up that much more quickly to buy our own store someday."

"I see."

"After that big party last night, Mrs. Andrews gave a lot of that fancy food to Olivier and me. After he took the baggage up, he ran home and got some of it, and ran it back here. He warmed it up while I cleaned the room. I served it while he finished up."

Cassie shook her head. "My goodness, Jerusha, you two conducted that as if you'd been doing it all your lives."

"No, Miss Cassie. Just until we moved here."

"I'm more grateful than I can ever express for what you two did for me today. I'll repay you for this someday."

"I know."

"I certainly would have thought we'd be invited out more," Letitia grumbled as they made their way up the front steps of the church.

"I tried to warn you," Cassie told her. "I'm fairly new in town. I don't know many people. They don't come to my house, and I don't go to theirs."

Cassie's heart gave her a twinge as she recalled the one visitor she used to have. Brent, who'd come into her home and her bed, and into her heart. He'd left her bed. She doubted if he'd be paying very many more visits to her home. She knew, no matter how much she hated him now, the memory of him and his love would never leave her heart.

"Still," Letitia continued to complain, "I never thought that going to church here would be the first time I got out of that weird house."

Cassie paused at the doorway into the sanctuary. She certainly hoped God would forgive her. She still wore no jewelry, just to irk Letitia. But this was one opportunity to really show off. It was almost as if God had given it to her—and it would be such a shame not to take advantage of it.

With very deliberate steps, Cassie made her way to the front pew to the left. She could almost feel the gaze of everyone in church boring into her back as she proceeded up the aisle.

Since she'd arrived here, she'd refrained from sitting in Aunt Flora's pew. It just seemed so ostentatious. But after putting up with Robert and Letitia for the past few days, Cassie felt this morning warranted something a bit different.

"Cassie, Cassie," Letitia whispered as she followed timidly behind her. "Where are you going?"

Without even glancing back, Cassie replied, "Aunt Flora always sat up front."

"Oh, my goodness." Letitia turned to Robert. "*We* never had a front pew."

Cassie let Robert and Letitia into the pew first. Then she stationed herself in the most prominent seat. She wasn't going to allow *anyone*—especially not Robert and Letitia—to mistake who was *really* the important member of this family, at least in Lyman's Gap.

The sunlight gleamed through the colored windows. The candles beamed brightly. The first June roses bloomed on the altar, filling the church with their fragrance. Cassie knew she looked good. She felt good.

And then the devil waltzed into church on the arm of Evaline McAlister.

Mr. and Mrs. McAlister proudly took their places. Cassie allowed herself just a small absolution for her sin of pride. She'd only been trying to impress her annoying sister-in-law. Clearly Mr. McAlister was out to impress the entire town, and he was doing a good job of it, too.

Brent stepped aside to allow Evaline to be seated first. Then he took his place beside her—directly across the aisle from Cassie.

How dare that lying scoundrel set foot in church, Cassie fumed. How dare he sit across from her. She hoped she could duck quickly enough if lightning struck him.

What was worse, in order to watch the minister as he delivered his sermon, she'd have too look directly across Brent.

She hoped he wouldn't lean over and whisper in Evaline's ear the way he'd whispered to her that first Sunday in the back pew. She hoped he wasn't saying sweet things to Evaline that would make her blush the way he'd talked to her. Her heart ached when she figured the scoundrel probably would.

How could she bear to sit there alone, longing to reach out and touch him, when he sat so happily beside Evaline? How could she bear to see him with Evaline without wanting to reach out and smack him in the head with a hymnal?

She could sit quietly, she encouraged herself. She had self-control. She was silently thankful that people usually entered the church one or two at a time, and she'd avoided meeting him coming in.

What would she do when the service was over, and everyone left the church all at once? How long could she still sit there, pretending she was meditating? How long could she struggle with putting the hymnal back in the pew, or fiddle with her purse? How could she avoid coming face-to-face with Brent?

What would she say to him? Evaline had warned her. Their engagement party was only one week away.

The church bells began to ring. Cassie winced. It was time to leave.

"Good morning, Miss Bowen," Evaline said cheerily.

"Good morning," Cassie answered quietly.

All her old insecurities in the face of this beautiful, graceful, and gracious woman came flooding back. Right in front of Letitia, she was going to trip over a huge piece of lint on the aisle carpet and go tumbling to land flat on her face.

"I don't believe I've met your friends."

Oh, that blasted Evaline would have to notice Robert and Letitia, just as Cassie was trying to sneak them out.

"May I introduce my brother, Robert Bowen, and his wife, Letitia. Robert, Letitia, this is Miss Evaline McAlister and her parents, and Mr. Conway." Oh, she hated to include him with their party. "Mr. Conway, I believe you may have heard me speak of my family from time to time."

"Yes, hello. How are you?" Brent extended his hand, and did and said all the polite things a gentleman ought to do—and never once glanced in her direction. "So nice to meet you both."

There. She'd made her polite introductions. *Now* could she go home and bury her head under a pillow?

"How wonderful for you to have them come visit," Evaline said. Cassie hadn't realized Evaline hated her that much. "How long will you be staying?"

"Not long," Cassie answered quickly.

"We're not sure yet," Robert replied.

"It depends on how certain matters work out," Letitia added.

"Our engagment party is still several weeks away, but if you're still in town, I do hope you'll be able to attend," Evaline said. She exerted a little affectionate pressure on Brent's arm.

Cassie wanted to exert a great deal of pressure on Brent's head, with a hammer.

Evaline leaned forward. "We haven't officially announced our engagement yet, but . . ." She gave a coy shrug, as if she just couldn't help being so darn cute.

Cassie started to feel sick to her stomach. She swallowed hard. It wasn't just Evaline who was making her ill. She had to summon up enough nerve to confront Brent about that money.

"Mr. Conway."

At last Brent had to look at her. There was no way even *he* could be so rude as not to.

"Mr. Conway, a certain matter has come to my attention that I need to discuss with you very soon," Cassie said.

Brent eyed her warily. She knew Letitia and Robert were

watching her every move, too. They had to be wondering what her important matter was with another woman's betrothed.

"I don't conduct business on the Sabbath," Brent replied. He nodded and moved to leave.

"The change must be unusual for you," Cassie snapped.

He turned back to her. The muscles of his jaw clenched. His blue eyes clouded with anger.

She wasn't about to be intimidated. "I need to talk to you now, Mr. Conway."

"You have guests." He started walking down the aisle.

"And you have a betrothed, I understand." Head erect, without looking to either side to distract her, Cassie kept pace with him down the aisle and out to the churchyard.

"The betrothal hasn't been announced yet."

"I understand that's only a matter of formality."

"If that's the way you understand it."

"I don't see any other way that I can understand it."

"Then that must be the way it is."

"We're both very busy entertaining, aren't we? Too busy to take care of other pressing business at hand."

Cassie could hear Robert and Letitia gushing over introductions to the McAlisters. If there was only one time in her entire life she was glad for Evaline, it was now, for her ability to distract and entertain her troublesome relatives, not to mention the girl's formidable father.

"I really need to speak to you regarding so many things," Cassie told him. "How odd, I used to see you so often, and now I see you so seldom."

Before Brent could make any sort of lying excuse, Cassie waved her hand in the air and continued.

"I see you've been quite busy. I am perturbed that you've been too busy to send the draft I asked you to send to Abel. I'm particularly surprised because I actually trusted that you'd sent it earlier."

Brent said nothing.

"You will do so Monday morning, won't you?"

"No."

"I beg your pardon."

"No, I will not. It's a silly waste of money. Drilling for petroleum is a foolish scheme that'll never work out. I can't let you—"

"What do you mean, you can't let me? You are my advisor. Who made you my guardian? Who told you you could take the place of my father, or my brother, or . . . or a husband?" she demanded angrily. "Or my own judgement?"

"I told you, I'd try my best to keep you from saying or doing stupid things."

She fixed her gaze on him, as cold and unfeeling, as hard and immobile as he was. "I'd rather spend my life doing and saying stupid things than to be like you, Mr. Conway, doing mean, hurtful things to the people who . . . once loved you."

She turned and walked away.

“That was the last straw!” Cassie declared to Jerusha and Mrs. Parker as she stormed into the kitchen Monday morning.

“What are you talking about?” Mrs. Parker, up to her elbows in bread dough, asked.

“Uh-oh,” Jerusha mumbled over her pan of dishwater.

Cassie threw open the pantry door and headed for the barrel of flour.

“I’ll never trust that man again. Can’t trust him with money. Can’t trust him with . . .” She’d almost said her heart, but that would have given it all away to everyone. “With anything,” she finished.

“Who? Who can’t you trust?” Mrs. Parker demanded, her eyes wide with bewilderment.

“Brent Conway.” She spat out his name as if it were poison.

“Oh, well.” Mrs. Parker resumed her kneading. “We all could’ve told you that a long time ago, dear. I’m surprised your aunt didn’t warn you.”

“She did,” Cassie grumbled. “I wasn’t smart enough to listen.”

“He’s a rascal, that one. Completely disreputable. Untrustworthy," Mrs. Parker continued her damning litany. "Why, he'd do anything for a dollar."

"Unfortunately I'm probably the only one who knows exactly how far he'd go to do anything for a dollar."

Cassie flipped up the top of the barrel and stuck her hand in the flour. Thank goodness Mrs. Parker was baking, and she didn't have too much flour to go through to reach the bottom.

"Oh, be careful, Miss Cassie," Jerusha warned. "Are you sure you know what you're doing?"

"Completely!" she assured her. "It's something I should have done a long time ago."

Cassie pulled out the leather bag full of coins. She gave the bag a jingle. Trails of white flour showered down from the creases.

"There. That ought to be enough."

Flour dusted the front of her dress and powdered her sleeves. Her hair looked prematurely gray. Her face had taken on a ghostly pallor.

"How foolish I was. I wanted to be independent. I wanted to live away from my overbearing family. I wanted to control my own life, my own money. And then I went and did something so incredibly stupid as to entrust it all to a man!"

"Oh, dear," Jerusha lamented, while Mrs. Parker stood there and watched her rant.

"And not just any man. No. Who did I entrust it all to? The very man my own aunt warned me not to trust." She peered at Mrs. Parker. "Do you think a woman could get any more stupid than that?"

"Well, if you ask me, I really don't mind having a man to look out for me," she confessed with a coy little smile that spoke volumes.

That was not the answer Cassie was looking for. Mrs. Parker's usually good judgement was obviously clouded at the moment by her favorable interaction with Doc Carver.

Cassie strode across the kitchen and confronted Jerusha. For all she knew, Jerusha seemed to be a happily married woman.

But Cassie somehow felt Jerusha could take a little more objective perspective on her problem.

"Do *you* think a woman could get any more stupid than I've been?"

"Yes, but she couldn't get much crazier," Jerusha told her bluntly. "Take a good look at yourself in the mirror and you'll see what I mean. It isn't much of an improvement over the feathers."

"Feathers?" Mrs. Parker repeated.

"Make sure you take the back steps upstairs so you don't run into your brother or his wife with you looking like you dove headfirst into the flour barrel, which, come to think of it, you did."

"I can't help where my aunt hid her money."

"You can help running around the house, much less going into town, looking like that, Miss Cassie, and I think you know what I mean. That's just asking for trouble. Please don't do this now. Wait just a little longer."

"I'm *not* crazy," Cassie insisted. "Even if no one else ever believes me. There's only one way to prove it to them all—to Robert and Letitia, to Mrs. Andrews and Mr. Harvey, and especially to the lying, traitorous, Brent Conway. I'll prove to them I'm not crazy. I'll prove to them Aunt Flora wasn't crazy, either. I *will* tap that petroleum."

Cassie tried to brush the flour off the front of her dress as she marched down Main Street. But with floured hands, she only succeeded in making it worse.

As she passed the *Argus*, Brent was just stepping out. He automatically put his arms out in front of her as if to stop her headlong charge down the street. She pulled up and backed away from him as if he held two poisonous snakes, and his embrace would only encourage them to bite her.

"Cassie. Cassie, what happened?"

"Nothing that would interest you," she snapped.

"Why are you rushing—?"

"I'm a busy woman. I have places to go, people to see, and money to spend."

"Looking like that?"

His glance swept her body. Not so very long ago, that look would have sent a shiver, hot and cold at the same time, up and down her spine, making her practically melt with desire for him. Now she felt nothing as his gaze held hers. Nothing, she'd swear it on a stack of Bibles. She felt nothing for him at all. Only an aloof coldness. The longer she stood there feeling cold, and holding herself away from him, the more she hurt.

"Where are you going, Cassie?"

"*You* may refer to me as *Miss Bowen.* All of my *former* business associates do."

"Where are you going?" he repeated.

"None of your business. Now, get out of my way, if you please."

He barred her way along the sidewalk. She tried to sidestep him, but he kept moving in front of her. "Looking like that? What happened? Have you been baking?"

"No. Why?"

"What have you been doing?"

"I've been getting ready to do what you've neglected to do—what I damn well should have done by myself all along."

"It's about that money, isn't it?"

She stopped and slammed her fists onto her hips. The coins in the bag jingled against her side. She glared at him.

"Of course it's about my money. You haven't done anything else to make me angry with you, have you? Oh, no, not you!"

"Cassie, I can explain."

"You can?" She stared at him. "Now you can explain it all to me when you couldn't yesterday. You could barely spare me a civil word yesterday. Did you need time to think up a plausible lie?"

"I'm not lying."

"Then can you please explain to me why you didn't do what I asked? Can you explain to me why you couldn't keep your hands off me, and then you suddenly turn up with a rich, beautiful, witty, intelligent, cultured, refined, graceful fiancée? Can you explain that?"

"Yes, Cassie. I can." Brent glanced around nervously. "But not in the middle of the street."

"No?" She glared at him with feigned surprise. "Well, why not? The state of your reputation never seemed to bother you before. As a matter of fact, I think you rather enjoy that lovable rascal sort of image you cultivated with my aunt just to try to talk her into selling you that property," she accused. "You never cared about her. You never cared about me. You never cared what anybody thought of you."

"Do you really believe that, after everything—?"

"Yes," she stated bluntly.

"I told you before, Cassie, I do care what they think of you."

Cassie paused. She pressed her lips tightly together, as if it could help her think of a better, wittier, more scathing reply, or just prevent her from saying all the dumb things that readily sprang to her tongue.

"That's a good line, Mr. Conway, but it won't work on me anymore. You have a mighty peculiar way of showing how you care about people. As a matter of fact, I'm beginning to believe it's all true what they've said about you all along. You don't care about anything but money."

She waved her hand at him.

"So there. I absolve you of whatever misguided notions you may have had that you needed to oversee my behavior so people wouldn't think badly of me. Now, be so kind as to leave me alone."

Brent didn't budge. "I care about a lot more than money."

"Of course you do. There's business and social position and—"

"I could explain it all, if you'd only wait, if you'd only give me the chance."

"I'm not the one who stopped coming to see you."

They watched each other silently as Cassie felt the seconds drag by. She wanted to slap him and get all her anger out.

Then she could grab hold of him and love him again the way they used to, before Evaline ever came back.

No, it could never be the same.

She roused herself.

"I have more important things to do than stand here with you. If you don't get out of my way immediately, I'll . . . I'll hit you."

Brent reached out and took hold of her hand. Gently, he stroked her knuckles. "I don't think you'll do much damage with these."

His ink-stained, callused fingers, moving slowly along the back of her hand, sent frissons of electricity up her arm, down her spine, and into the pit of her stomach, where it churned, generating a heat of its own. She pulled back her hand quickly.

"I'll bite you. What kind of damage do you think I could do with these?" She bared her gritted teeth at him. For goodness sake, that was even more stupid. What was that man making her do?

Brent slowly lifted his hand to cup her chin. He lifted her face up to his. Her lips relaxed as his face drew closer to hers. How she longed to have him kiss her—if only once again.

Then he raised one eyebrow and grinned at her. She pulled away abruptly, scowling. How could she, for even a second, have allowed him to distract her like that? It only served to reinforce what a scoundrel he was.

"Never mind. I'll cry thief," she tried to threaten once again.

He laughed. "They won't believe you. You're the crazy lady, remember?"

"And you're the town scoundrel. Who will they believe?" Before he could answer, she continued, "Anyway, it doesn't really matter what I scream, as long as I create a scene in the middle of the street. You know I can do it, too. I don't think that will sit particularly well with your charming fiancee and her formidable parents. Now get out of my way."

She didn't mean to touch him. She never wanted to touch him ever again. But as she tried to march past him, her shoulder hit his arm. It was almost as if the scoundrel had deliberately tried to move in front of her.

She ached where she'd hit him, not from the impact, but from the memories he generated. It ached to remember the feel of his arms around her, the feel of his lips on hers, the warmth of him inside her.

"I'm going to Warner's, if you'll excuse me."

She rushed past him, and forced herself to keep walking. She pushed open the door to Abel's store so hard, that instead of giving their usual tinkling sound, the bells jangled jarringly.

She plunked the bag down on the counter in front of Abel. The coins inside, muffled by the leather, jingled against the wooden counter. A cloud of flour puffed up.

"There's enough money in there to pay for it all, Mr. Warner, not to mention a fee for your trouble," she declared. "Order me that equipment immediately. Faster than immediately."

Abel stared at her. "Are you sure?"

She cocked her head and glared at him.

"What have I been raving about this past month? I have to do this. Circumstances have finally gotten to the point that I have absolutely no choice. I have to prove to everyone I'm not crazy. I have to get even with that treacherous Brent."

"Miss Bowen, I know how you feel," Abel said gently. "I used to feel that way, too. I was wrong. I think if you wait a while, think it over, you might discover you're wrong about Brent, too."

Cassie shook her head. "Brent rescued your future, Abel. He's stolen mine."

"Are you feeling poorly again, Miss Cassie?" Jerusha asked as she placed the plate of fried eggs and bacon on the kitchen table in front of Cassie.

Cassie eyed the eggs cautiously, as if they were poised to jump down her throat, grab everything that was in her stomach, and haul it all back up again. She had the horrible feeling that they were actually two huge, yellow eyes, staring back at her, waiting for their chance if she would only open her mouth.

Rather than eat them, Cassie figured she'd talk. "If you were forced to spend every waking minute with Robert and Letitia, wouldn't you be sick, too?"

"Probably. But there's sick and then there's sick."

"What are you talking about? They make me nauseous by their very presence." She shook her head. "Where did I go wrong? I tried so very hard to get away from them. I loved my aunt. I was glad to come here, thinking I'd be able to help her and keep her company. I must admit, knowing I'd be away from Letitia for at least several years was no small inducement."

"At least you can have breakfast in peace," Jerusha comforted her.

"They never slept until noon back in Philadelphia. Ralphie and Marguerite never let them."

Cassie took a stab at an egg with her fork, then changed her mind and pushed it across the plate.

"I feel sorry for Letitia's mother. I wonder if the old woman will still be alive when they get back home—*if* they ever go back home—*if* there's a home left to go back to after Ralphie and Marguerite are done with it."

"I got a bad feeling these two are going to be hard to get rid of, Miss Cassie."

Jerusha had just confirmed her worst suspicions. Cassie hung her head in her hands and moaned.

"You really don't sound too good, Miss Cassie."

"I don't know what's wrong. I don't have a cold. My head feels fine. I'm not sneezing. I just feel slightly sick to my stomach."

"In the mornings only?"

"Yes."

"And real tired all the time?"

"Yes."

Jerusha emitted a long, low hum. "Miss Cassie, you know I think you're a fine lady and a kind, decent person. You know I respect you."

"I'll pay your salary on time, Jerusha," Cassie told her with a little laugh. "Plus a little something more for you and Olivier for all the extra work you've had to do while Robert and Letitia are here. You don't have to flatter me that much."

"I just don't want you to be taking what I'm going to say in the wrong way."

Cassie watched her warily, waiting for what she knew Jerusha was going to say. Sebastian hadn't shown her anything about it, but there were some things a woman knew all by herself, without the need for any crystal ball. She'd suspected it. She didn't know how Jerusha suspected it, too.

"I know before Miss McAlister came back to town you and Mr. Conway were . . . right friendly. If you don't mind my asking, exactly how friendly were you two?"

Cassie could feel the heat rising up her neck and across her cheeks.

"Yep. That's what I thought."

"Jerusha—"

"I got a feeling you're in a family way, Miss Cassie."

"So do I. How did you guess?"

"My mama taught me. It's in the eyes. It's always in the eyes." Jerusha nodded sagely. "So, what are you going to do about it? Are you going to tell Mr. Conway?"

"No."

"Why not?"

"I don't think he'd care."

"Not care about his own baby? Miss Cassie, if you think that, you are seriously underestimating that man. You got to tell him."

"No, I don't. He didn't see his way to tell me about Evaline. It's only fair if I don't quite get around to telling him about the baby."

Jerusha kept washing the dishes.

"You won't tell him, will you?" Cassie asked.

Jerusha shook her head. "Not my secret to tell, Miss Cassie."

"He's too busy with Miss McAlister anyway. She looks so happy. He looks happy. With her money, he'll be able to do all the things he told me he had planned for the *Argus*. Why shouldn't he be happy? Why should I ruin it for him?"

"That's fine talk. What about you? What about that baby? Don't he deserve a papa?"

"Lots of children who deserve to have a papa don't have one for one reason or another. Disease, accidents, the war—all those things take parents from children, and children from parents."

"What do you intend to do when people ask questions?"

"I can sell this house and move somewhere else, far away. Out west maybe, like Chester Farnsworth wants to do. Out west, no one will know me. No one will be able to censure me or the child. I'll tell them I'm a wealthy widow, that my child's father died of some highly respectable disease—like consumption, something very poetic. Or delivering quinine to victims of a yellow fever epidemic—something very heroic. No one will ever know the difference."

"That baby will, sooner or later."

Cassie rose, leaving her breakfast untouched. "Well, we all have to put up with some disappointments in life, don't we?"

Jerusha shook her head and kept wiping the dishes dry.

"But first I have some important work here that I've got to finish," Cassie said.

"What's that?"

"I've got to find that petroleum. I've got a point to prove. For my aunt's sake, I've got to justify her in the eyes of the people of Lyman's Gap. So no one will think of her only as the crazy old lady anymore. She was good to me, and I owe it to her."

Cassie had never felt so sick to her stomach in her entire life, not even that day many summers ago when she and Ophelia Langenfelder had sneaked into Ophelia's older sister's bedroom and ate all the licorice candy hidden under her pillow.

At the same time Cassie's mind had never felt so excited. Long mule teams hauled large, heavy equipment and huge barrels to the oily field outside of town. Rough-dressed, rough-spoken men constructed the tower and the outbuildings, set up the drill and the steam engine that powered it, and set to work. The sun shone brightly, just as in Sebastian's visions.

Even seeing Robert and Mr. Harvey strolling across the field toward her couldn't ruin Cassie's cheerful mood. They joined the other men and boys, lined up along the outside of the rail fence Cassie had ordered built, who'd come to gawk, laugh, and jeer.

"Letitia wouldn't come." Robert was apparently finishing up his explanation to Mr. Harvey, and Cassie only heard the tail end of it. "She claims it takes her longer to clean up after coming out here than it does to walk here and back."

Mr. Harvey glanced down at the soles of his obviously expensive shoes, covered with a black grime of oil and dirt. "I really can't say as I blame her."

"On the other hand, it looks as if those boys enjoy getting all grimy." Robert pointed to several boys playing tag through the trees.

Mr. Harvey smiled, but he was clearly not amused.

"There," Robert said, drawing his attention from the boys by pointing to the tall tower. "Didn't I tell you this was interesting?"

"Interesting, indeed," Mr. Harvey replied. "Most acts of insanity carry a certain 'interest' to them."

"I am not insane, Mr. Harvey," Cassie declared. "Insane would have been me with a shovel trying to dig my way down. But the men I've hired are experts in their fields, engineers and geologists. They'll explain to you quite sanely the actual scientific processes behind all this, if you'd care to listen."

Mr. Harvey made no reply.

"Danged interesting," Robert repeated, as if the interchange between Cassie and Mr. Harvey had never taken place. "Even though it won't work."

"Yeah," Woody said, jabbing Robert in the ribs with his elbow. "How many days do you think it'll take before the whole dang thing comes tumblin' down on her head?"

"I'll give it a week," Mr. Green said.

"No, no. These men are experts. They know what they're doing," Mike argued. "I'll give it two weeks."

"How about you, Calvin?" Mr. Green asked.

Mr. Andrews held up his hands in surrender. "No, no. Count me out. I'm not sleeping on the sofa anymore."

"I'd say the basic structure looks pretty sound," Brent said as he strolled closer to them.

Had a cloud passed over the sun? Cassie wondered. Her world seemed to darken when Brent showed up. He used to be the bright spot in her life. Now, knowing she'd never have him again saddened everything. She wouldn't have believed it if anyone had told her how much she could hate the man she once loved.

"I'll give it a month before they can't drill any deeper, and still haven't hit anything worthwhile, so they'll dismantle the whole thing, go home, and sell this land so the railroad can come through here," Brent predicted.

"Oh, for Pete's sake, Brent," Mr. Harvey complained. "Are you still beating that dead horse?"

"Why not? You're still out here trying to prove Cassie's crazy so you can take charge of her money."

"And you were trying to sweet talk her out of it, until Miss—"

"Which one of us is the bigger scoundrel, August?"

"How dare you accuse me—!"

"Oh, don't get all affronted," Brent said with a dismissive push of his hand. "When you get angry, your nose turns red. It's not a good look for you."

"You're both wrong," Cassie pronounced. "You're *all* wrong. It won't be much longer now. I'll prove Aunt Flora was correct. We can drill for oil instead of waiting for it to ooze up to the surface, and we can drill it in quantities to make it profitable."

Mr. Harvey chuckled.

"And when I do," Cassie continued speaking directly to Mr. Harvey, "I'm going to walk right up to you and smear a big, black blob of rock oil right on your nose."

• • •

"Thank you for going to all the trouble to bring me dinner in bed," Cassie said as Jerusha set the tray on the night table. "I get so tired spending all day out in that field."

The aroma of vegetable barley soup and fresh-baked corn muffins was tantalizing.

"I hope you're wearing your big straw hat."

"I am."

"And drinking lots of water."

"Yes," Cassie replied wearily. She smiled. "Jerusha, you're watching over me like a mother hen."

"Somebody's got to. To tell you the truth, this tray is easier for me than having to set up the dining room. And you look too exhausted to go down there anyway. You just need to rest in bed."

"I'm so glad the Andrews invited Robert and Letitia for dinner, and that they believed my declining the invitation due to illness. I don't think they'd believe me if I told them I was sick of Robert and Letitia."

"They seemed real happy to be going out, eating off of other people for a change," Jerusha observed.

Cassie laughed.

"I'm going home now," Jerusha said as she made her way to the bedroom door. "I'll lock up when I leave."

"It's a shame you can't lock Robert and Letitia out."

After Cassie had eaten her dinner, she relaxed in her bed. It was so good not to have to make polite small talk with Letitia, or to hear her gossip about mutual acquaintances, or to hear her carp about their imagined share of Aunt Flora's estate.

Alone at last after many days, Cassie figured it was finally safe. She reached under her bed and pulled out Sebastian's bag.

"Hi, there," she crooned as she opened the bag and pulled him out. "Do you forgive me for neglecting you for so long? I've still got problems. But I've been busy, and in a way I guess that keeps me as happy as I can expect to be."

She set Sebastian on her night table and waited. Nothing happened.

"You were right about everything. Of course you know it. The field looks exactly the way you showed it to me. I can only hope we can tap the petroleum."

Sebastian remained blank.

"Oh, you really are angry with me for neglecting you, aren't you?" she asked. "Well, I've got a bone to pick with you, too. I think it's a little more serious than having to stay under a bed for a couple of days. Why in the world didn't you warn me I'd get pregnant?" she demanded. "You show me somebody else's pigs, and somebody else's twin girls. Why couldn't you show me my own baby?"

Lights began to twirl inside Sebastian.

"Oh, that woke you up, did it?" She nodded knowingly. "It's about time. Now, show me something important. Something useful." In a small, pleading voice, she asked, "Something happy."

The image formed, stronger and clearer than ever before. Cassie could only stare at the figures of Brent and herself, naked, locked in a passionate, loving embrace.

"Oh, no you don't." She pointed her finger at the image. "You've shown me that before. That's what got me into this fix in the first place. You must show me the future, something new I haven't seen before."

Within the clear, glowing crystal, the image remained.

"No, no, no!" she cried. "You've got it all wrong. That can't possibly be the future. I will *never* be that stupid ever again."

She remembered it too well. It hurt too impossibly bad to see all over again—the things Brent had done to make her feel so incredibly wonderful; the things she had done to Brent that excited her and pleased him; the wonderful loving things they'd done together. It hurt too much to know that he would never again touch her, hold her, caress her like that.

The images in the crystal held her spellbound. She had to watch.

"Now I know," she murmured as she watched. "I have lost

something I cannot afford to lose. I have lost my virginity and—oh!—at what a cost. I have trusted someone I had no reason to trust. Everyone told me Brent was a scoundrel. I realize I let my heart rule my head, to my dismay, but at the time, I truly had no reason to mistrust him. I have loved a man with no hope of him loving me in return."

She frowned at Sebastian.

"Then why are you still showing me these things?" she demanded in a voice barely above a whisper. "I've complied with every one of the preposterous, impossible rules laid down for the unfortunate Bowen women hundreds of years ago. Deliberately or not, I've fulfilled everything I must to break the curse. Why is the curse not broken? Why are you still showing me visions?"

The lights began to swirl around the image of Brent and her.

"The only thing I haven't done is something I can't do anyway. Someone must actually believe me." She sighed. "There's absolutely nothing I can do about that. Even Abel and the men who sold me the equipment and who work the equipment are only doing it because I paid them good money for it. Why didn't you tell me this from the very beginning? There's absolutely nothing I can do—ever—to break this curse."

The image of Brent remained, his golden skin transforming into his usual clothing. Sadly Cassie watched the image of herself fade, as if she were melting away.

"I know I'm no longer a part of Brent's life, Sebastian. I never will be, ever again. You don't have to show me. You don't have to rub salt into an open wound."

Another image began to take shape beside Brent in the crystal.

"Oh, no, Sebastian. Please. I couldn't bear to see Brent and Evaline together again—even if they do have all their clothes on."

The image became clearer.

"August Harvey? Oh, I will *not* believe that about Brent!"

The image of Brent had changed, too. He was angry. He had a gun. Horrified, Cassie watched as Brent shot August Harvey in the chest. Deep red life's blood spread out across his shirt in a widening smear.

Tears of cold horror began to fall down Cassie's cheeks. She swallowed the bile that rose in her throat. Her head and heart ached with the knowledge.

Brent had been able to save his friend's life, but no one could stop the coming war. No one could solve her problems. No one would be able to do anything about this, either.

"If the curse is not broken, and everything you've shown me is always the truth, that means Brent will murder Mr. Harvey in cold blood."

Sixteen

Cassie had heard the scraping earlier that morning, but had assumed it was Mrs. Parker or Jerusha cleaning as usual.

As she descended the staircase, she blinked with surprise.

"What is the sofa doing in the middle of the foyer?" she demanded. She spotted her brother. "Robert, where are you taking Aunt Flora's—no, *my* seascape by Turner?"

Robert stopped. He glanced nervously behind him, then grinned up at her sheepishly. Letitia emerged from the parlor.

"Letitia, why are you carrying around the stuffed alligator?" Cassie demanded.

Letitia didn't answer her.

Cassie knew very well, from the way the woman didn't even look up the stairs at her, that she'd heard her and was ignoring her.

"Just set that down there," she ordered Robert, pointing to a spot by the sofa. She set the alligator on the sofa and returned to the parlor.

What was she going back for? The owl?

Robert glanced quickly at Cassie, then followed Letitia.

Cassie ought to be used to this. They'd ignored her constantly in Philadelphia. But she wouldn't allow that here.

From the middle of the staircase, glaring down at both of them, Cassie repeated in a deep bellow that they couldn't ignore, "What are you doing to my house?"

Emerging from the parlor, Letitia declared, "This place is filthy." She did, indeed, carry the stuffed owl. She patted the back of the owl. "Why, just look at that dust fly."

"I don't see a bit of dust."

"This place is a veritable pile of kindling, just waiting for a spark to set it ablaze," Robert continued.

"And kill us all while we sleep in our beds," Letitia finished.

"This place is *not* filthy. Mrs. Parker is an excellent housekeeper," Cassie corrected them. "Now that I have your undivided attention, shall we try again? Only this time, try to come up with a better excuse. What are you two doing to my house?"

"We had to do this ourselves," Letitia complained. "Honestly, these servants are so insubordinate. They refused to do a lick of work that we asked them to. We need to hire you new ones."

"No. They are my help, not your servants," Cassie corrected. "Now, with or without any help, answer me! What are you doing?"

"Letitia insisted I rearrange the furniture," Robert whined.

"The sunlight is fading the upholstery—"

"And she really would like to get rid of the piano to make room for—"

"Get rid of my piano?" Cassie repeated, her voice as deep and ominous as she could make it. She was not going through that a second time. "*My* piano. You have no right—"

Letitia bustled her way between the sofa and the painting to stand at the foot of the stairs to confront Cassie. "We have every right to make some room in this place to make it clean and comfortable for us."

"We've found a buyer who'll give us a good price—" Robert began.

Cassie took two steps down the stairs. Just enough to keep

herself higher than they were, but enough to let them know she was coming after them.

"You're trying to sell my—"

Suddenly Cassie stopped shouting. She took several deep breaths and waited for her temperature to cool. At last her heart slowed to the point where she could speak without her voice shaking.

She stared at them coldly for a few seconds, just long enough to make them wonder what she was planning. Just long enough to make them believe they might have won this argument and that she was retreating back into the shell they'd badgered her into years ago. As soon as they were lulled into their usual, overbearing complacency, then she'd surprise them both.

"I won't argue with you," she said calmly in a normal tone and volume of voice.

"Good," Letitia said as she proceeded to carry the stuffed owl to the door. "Because, you see, it really is so tiresome and pointless, since—"

"I won't argue with you because there is no question to debate. This is *my* house. Everything in it, every dust mote that rests upon it, every bit of rock and soil that it rests upon, is *mine*. You will not sell one stick of wood, one shard of glass, one piece of lint, not any of this. You will not eat another morsel of my food. You will not remain in this house one day longer."

"You're not serious, Cassie," Robert said with a nervous laugh.

"I'm not laughing. This means I could not possibly be joking."

"But we're family," Letitia protested. "You can't just throw us out."

"Letitia," Cassie said wearily. "All the while I lived with you, you made it quite clear that, family or not, I was there at your sufferance, that I was living there on your charity. Every day, every hour, every opportunity that arose, you made me feel that I was unwelcome in your home. Now it is my turn to tell you that you have long since worn out your welcome here. You will leave tomorrow morning."

"Tomorrow morning? But how?" Letitia stammered. "We don't have train tickets. We have no way to get to a train. We—"

"Olivier will drive you and your baggage into Pittsburgh. Once there, he will give you the money that I will entrust to him for safekeeping—"

"You'll give *him*—?"

"Of course. I trust *him*. Then you both may purchase tickets back to Philadelphia."

"But you can't—"

"If you do not leave, I shall see to it that Olivier throws you and all your baggage out onto my front lawn. You may live there under the trees, if you please. Do not expect me to speak to or acknowledge you when I go in or out of my house. I will not feed you."

Robert gave a loud groan.

"I highly recommend as quite tasty the crackers at Warner's General Store. As for anything else to eat around here, well, there's an annual Fish Fry, but I think you will grow very hungry waiting for it."

Letitia and Robert glared at her, then at each other.

"We can't live in your front yard. We don't even have a tent," Robert complained.

"Then you'd best hope it doesn't rain."

"Oh, won't that look very nice for the neighbors?" Letitia peevishly pointed out to her. "Having your very own kin camped out on your front lawn in destitution while you're living a life of ease and pleasure inside."

"I only have one neighbor, and he's never home anymore," Cassie replied bitterly. "Personally, I don't think he cares what happens to you or anyone else."

"Well, it still won't look very good for anyone who happens to be passing by."

"In case you haven't noticed, this street ends at my property line. There are no passersby. Except maybe for the occasional wolf or bear. But then, they usually only come down from the mountains in the winter, when there's not much game up there. They eat what they can find around here, lying out for them under the trees."

"Bears? Wolves?" Letitia looked around her, as if expecting to see a wolf come bounding out of the kitchen, and a bear come lumbering out of the dining room, intent on dragging her back in there for a marvelous feast.

"I wouldn't worry too much. By the time they come down from the mountains, you'll have long since frozen to death."

Cassie regally descended the stairs, sailing past Letitia with her head held high. She headed for the kitchen, but didn't think she could eat at that moment. Her stomach was churning from nervousness. But she'd never let them know.

"If anyone finds out that you've evicted us from your house, and turned us cruelly out into the world, they'll think you've gone completely insane," Letitia called after her.

"They already think that," Cassie tossed back.

"This will only make them more certain—"

"Excuse me. I'm the one who'll be living in a warm, cozy house," Cassie pointed out to them from the kitchen doorway. "You two will be the ones camped out under the trees, eating acorns. Precisely *who* do you think is going to look more insane?"

Letitia and Robert frowned at each other.

"Before you go"—Cassie waved her hand at the mess in the foyer—"be sure to put this all back where it belongs."

"Jerusha, what if you knew someone was going to do something bad?" Cassie asked as she pushed her uneaten breakfast around on the plate.

Without looking up from her dishpan, Jerusha replied, "I'd try to stop them. You would, too, and you know it, so don't go asking foolish questions you already know the answer to."

"What if—?"

"And I know this concerns you, so don't try to tell me some 'friend' has a problem, either."

"What if the person who was going to do something bad didn't even know yet they were going to do it?"

Jerusha eyed her, one brow raised questioningly. "Well, that's a new one. They don't, but you do?"

"Yes."

Jerusha mumbled a little to herself. "Just how bad is this bad thing?"

"Murder."

Jerusha nodded. "That's bad. Who do you think is going to be murdered?"

"August Harvey."

Jerusha snorted, then grinned at her. "I'd say give the other person a medal and ask him if he can't set his sights on Mr. McAlister next."

Cassie wanted to laugh. Jerusha could afford to make jokes. She didn't know how very real this was.

"Who's supposed to be the fellow who rids us of these problems?"

It was so hard for Cassie to accuse Brent. Jerusha knew they'd been lovers. She knew they'd parted unhappily. She knew Brent was making a separate life for himself that could never include her. Would she think that Cassie was out for revenge in making this unfounded accusation? She hoped, by now, Jerusha knew her better than that.

In a very small voice, Cassie whispered, "Brent Conway."

She'd expected Jerusha to protest Brent's innocence, to call her a liar, or to maintain they ought to throw him in jail before he could do the vile deed.

Instead, Jerusha just kept washing the dishes. "When's this supposed to happen?"

"I don't know. Maybe soon."

"Where's this supposed to happen?"

"Out by my oil field."

"I see." Jerusha paused a moment, as if mulling over the whole problem.

Perhaps there was hope, Cassie thought. Perhaps Jerusha would actually believe a prediction she made. She'd help her break the curse, and together maybe they could stop Brent from doing this horrible deed.

"Well, Miss Cassie," Jerusha said, "if I were you, I'd put this whole outlandish idea straight out of my head."

Cassie's hopes fell, shattered as badly as if they'd been a dish Jerusha might have dropped while washing it. She should have expected as much. How could she be foolish enough to believe she—or anyone—could break a four-hundred-year-old curse?

"I wouldn't let my thoughts dwell on something so morbid and sad, Miss Cassie," Jerusha advised her. "I'd think happy thoughts—like when Robert and Letitia will be leaving."

"This is it, Robert!" Letitia grabbed him by his coatsleeve as the front door slammed shut. "She's gone off inspecting that silly petroleum drill again in that miserable, oily field."

"You know, you really ought to go out there to see it again."

"Once was more than enough."

"It's changed a lot since you first saw it. It really is kind of interesting," Robert said, "even if it never will amount to anything."

"For once, all those groveling, disgustingly loyal servants of hers are out of the house, too. How can she have so many of them?"

Robert shrugged. "She's rich."

"While she thinks we're packing to leave, now is your chance. Mr. Harvey, and the two of you go out to that field and keep an eye on her."

"Again?"

"Don't whine to me. Cassie and Flora are *your* relatives causing me all this trouble. Now, you and Mr. Harvey get out there and gawk with the rest of the yokels at that idiotic tower. Watch Cassie to see if she does anything we can use to prove she's incompetent and have you made her permanent guardian. If she starts heading back home, you run ahead and warn me."

"I can't run." Robert patted his paunch.

"Then give a couple of cents to one of those dirty urchins

who are always running around the fields there. That one with his arm in a sling looks fairly reliable. Have him run and tell me. I have a lot to do here, and the last thing I need is for her to catch me at it."

Letitia shoved him out the door and slammed it shut on his retreating figure. At last she could do, without any interference from anyone, what she'd been dying to do ever since they arrived at this monstrosity of a house out where no civilized people could bear to live.

"Imagine, the nerve of that upstart flibbertigibbet, trying to scare me with stories of bears and wolves. Just because she and that crazy aunt of hers like to keep stuffed owls and alligators around. Poppycock!"

She glared across the room at the contents of the entire glass case.

"Once I take over here, I'm selling the lot of you," she called out in fair warning. "Although who'd want to buy you, I'll never know."

Letitia turned and craned her head back to look up the staircase, toward the bedrooms.

"I'll sell every worthless piece of bric-a-brac in this place, and the house, too. Then I'll move back to Philadelphia in real style."

She stomped up the stairs.

"Now, where did she hide that jewel case?"

She burst into Cassie's tidy bedroom. She headed for the wardrobe and pulled open both doors. Nothing but dresses, skirts, bodices, and crinolines in there. She reached up to feel around the shelf on top. Nothing there but a few hats and shawls. She bent down, pushing the skirts out of the way. Nothing on the bottom but shoes, boots, and slippers.

She headed for the dresser. Nothing on top but her brush and comb, a hand mirror, her hairpin box, and a scent bottle. Letitia lifted the cut glass bottle and pulled out the stopper. She sniffed.

"Not bad."

She splashed some on her throat and wrists.

"Now where?"

Top drawer? She pulled out stockings, garters, and gloves in her search. How disappointing!

Second drawer? She pulled out chemises and drawers.

"I really never wanted to know my sister-in-law that well," she declared as she jammed them back into the drawer and slammed it shut.

Bottom drawer? Scarves and shawls.

Aha! Letitia's hand hit something hard and rectangular under the soft, knitted bulk. She grabbed it and pulled it out. She pushed Cassie's brush and hand mirror out of the way and set the case atop the dresser.

With a wide grin of satisfaction, feeling like a pirate who'd succeeded in his search for buried booty, Letitia flipped open the lid.

A pair of small pearl earrings. A single short strand of pearls with a cut-steel clasp. A garnet necklace. A pair of aquamarine earbobs. A brooch of seed pearls and turquoise.

Letitia screamed with thwarted greed.

"Damn them! They got to them before me. Those blasted servants went through here and stole the valuable things before I could take it all and put the blame on them."

She pushed the jewelry around in the box, searching for a hidden drawer or something.

"Where are the good things?" she demanded. "Where'd she put the good jewelry? I know there was a lot more than these paltry spangles. I know there were sapphires and rubies. I could've sworn the old girl once wore an emerald that would choke a horse. Where is it?"

She dashed over to the night table and pulled open the drawer. A Bible. A handkerchief.

"Nothing! Where could she have hidden them all?"

Letitia dropped to her knees.

"Under the bed. Aha!" Her hand struck something warm and leathery. She felt a handle. She seized it and hauled it out.

"What a beautiful case," Letitia said, admiring the intricately tooled red Moroccan leather. With a feeling of triumph, she exclaimed, "This has got to be it!"

She sat on the floor and wrenched open the two sides of the case. The scent of roses drifted upward. Something glittered inside. Something shiny and tempting. Something *large*.

Letitia reached in.

"What?"

She pulled out the smooth, round object.

"What the hell is this?" She set the ball on the floor in disgust. "A crystal ball? For Pete's sake. What is this? Some sort of carnival, or traveling circus, or gypsy caravan, complete with phony fortune-tellers? I always knew Flora kept weird things, but this is the worst. Why the devil is Cassie keeping it under her bed?"

She drummed her fists on the floor in frustration.

"Where are the rest of the jewels?"

Letitia caught sight of the light in the corner of her eye as the ball began to glow.

She stopped in mid-fit. Her heart had made one immediate, enormous leap into her throat. The light didn't come so much from the late-morning sunlight streaming in the windows, but rather it seemed to come from inside the ball itself.

"What is this thing? What kind of value could this have?" Letitia eyed the crystal ball speculatively. She began to study it with a little more interest. "How much could I get for it if I tried to sell it?"

The lights inside the ball swirled round and round, and eventually moved to form an indistinct image. Fascinated, Letitia bent over so she could peer more closely into the ball. She stared. She could have sworn she saw the image wink invitingly, drawing her in.

Jerusha rushed toward her across the field. "Oh, Miss Cassie, you've got to come home now!"

Cassie grabbed the distraught woman's arm and pulled her to the side, away from the usual crowd. She was having enough trouble with everyone from town coming out every day to jeer at her and her contraptions. She didn't need them believing her help had gone crazy, too.

She especially didn't need to see Brent break off from the crowd perched along the fence and make his way across the field toward her. He'd interfered in enough of her business. He'd ruined her life and her happiness. What more could he want?

"Calm down, Jerusha," Cassie told her. She gently patted the woman's shoulder. "Take a couple of deep breaths."

"No, no!" Jerusha gasped. "Miss Cassie, you've got—"

"Whatever it is, it's waited long enough for you to come out here," Brent said firmly. "It'll wait long enough for you to breathe."

He placed a calming hand on Jerusha's other shoulder and held it there. It seemed to stop her from fidgeting from one foot to the other. When she wasn't bouncing, it seemed easier for her to catch her breath.

"Now, what could be so horrible, Jerusha?" Brent asked.

"Jerusha came out here to fetch me, Mr. Conway," Cassie snapped. "I'll thank you to mind your own business."

"Jerusha's my friend, too," he told her. "I don't want to see her hurt because of any of the crazy things going on in your house."

"What would you know about what goes on in my house anymore?" Cassie countered. "Why would you care? Mind your own business."

Brent glared at her and backed a step or two away from Jerusha. But the irritating man still stood there, watching her and waiting. Cassie could admit he had the right to care about what happened to Jerusha, but he'd relinquished all rights to care about what happened to her.

Jerusha took several more deep gulps of air.

"It's your sister-in-law, Miss Cassie. I don't know what to do for her. I've never heard anything like this in my life."

"Heard? What happened?"

"I can't explain it."

Holding tightly to Jerusha's arm, Cassie hurried with her

across the field. Through the rustling grass, she heard Brent following them.

"What do you want?" she asked as he caught up with them. "Why are you interrupting again?"

"I just thought you might need some help."

"I have Jerusha, thank you."

"Jerusha looks like she's the one who needs help."

"That's why she has me."

"I mean, you might need a man's help," he amended.

"We have Robert and Olivier. I think we'll do fine."

He continued to walk beside her.

"I told you, we're fine," she repeated.

Brent stuck his hands in his pockets and continued to walk beside her. "Oh, I was heading home anyway. I can't help it if we live in the same direction."

As Cassie approached her house, she understood what Jerusha had meant. She, too, could hear Letitia all the way out here.

She wasn't exactly screaming in pain or terror. That was good. She wasn't exactly singing happy little ditties, either. She seemed to alternate between the two.

"I could only hear her," Jerusha explained. "I never figured myself as a cowardly woman, Miss Cassie, but I'm not stupid, either. I'm not about to go in there until I know what's going on."

"I don't blame you."

"I'll go," Brent offered.

"I thought you were going home," Cassie countered.

Brent stood there, watching her. He couldn't possibly care what happened to her anymore, she told herself with great certainty. How could he be bothered with her sister-in-law, a woman he barely knew?

Then why were his eyes so clouded with worry? Why was his glance shifting from one corner of the house to another, as if he were searching for something—or someone.

"Wait here," she told them. She meant to include them both in the order, but she specifically looked at Brent when she said it. "Letitia doesn't know you. If she's really upset, a strange face might upset her more."

"What if I followed you?"

"We don't know where she is. If you came upon her unexpectedly, it might only frighten her more."

Brent nodded.

"Oh, be careful," Jerusha called after her as she made her way up the porch steps. "I'll be listening out here to run for help if you scream."

"Thanks."

Cassie entered the house.

She'd heard of women who had lost their minds after being carried off into captivity by Indians. She'd heard of women who lost their wits after suffering a tremendous shock. What had happened to Letitia?

The downstairs was undisturbed. Cassie supposed marauding Indians were ruled out. Cautiously she went upstairs. Letitia and Robert's bedroom was fairly neat.

She stood in the doorway of her own bedroom, appalled at the utter chaos that seemed to spill from her wardrobe and every drawer. She was shocked at the sight of Letitia, who sat huddled in the midst of it all, rocking back and forth and fiercely clutching the leather bag that had contained Sebastian.

Then Cassie spotted the cause of all the trouble. Sebastian sat on the floor in front of Letitia.

Cassie couldn't see what Sebastian was showing Letitia. All she saw was a cloudy haze filling the entire sphere. Obviously the visions were meant for Letitia and Letitia alone. He'd been showing her something—something so wild or fantastic or horrible—that her mind hadn't been able to cope with it at all.

What had Aunt Flora told her? No one but a female of the direct Bowen line must ever know of Sebastian's existence. Aunt Flora hadn't specified the consequences of anyone else finding Sebastian. Had she even known what they were? Had anyone but a female of the direct Bowen line ever seen Sebastian before? Were the consequences too horrible to contemplate? Looking at Letitia cowering on the floor, Cassie could readily believe that was so.

For a brief moment, Cassie contemplated calling on Brent to help. No. She abruptly changed her mind. This was her family, her problem. Just look what problems had arisen when she'd allowed him into her life before. He'd made it clear enough he was no longer involved with her. She wasn't about to invite him back in. She'd take care of this herself.

Cautiously Cassie approached Letitia. She had to find out what had happened to reduce her sister-in-law to this condition. She had to find out if she had any wits left. She had to see if there was any possible way to help her.

"Letitia," she called softly. "Letitia, it's me. Cassie. Do you recognize me? No one's going to hurt you, Letitia. Do you know who you are? Do you know where you are?"

Letitia turned to her. Her hair was tousled. Her eyes were wide and red-rimmed. Cassie truly feared for the woman's sanity.

Then Letitia blinked. Her gaze sharpened, and she threw Cassie a beaming smile of joyful recognition.

"Oh, hello, Cassie. So nice to see you, dear. You're home early. Is it time for dinner already? I hope so. Mrs. Parker is such a fine cook. Did you have a good time out in your oil field today? I hope Robert enjoyed himself, too. We've been having a lovely time here at home."

"We?"

Cassie blinked in shock. Instead of a dangerous, raving lunatic, Letitia had turned into what seemed, at the moment, to be an extraordinarily pleasant person. That wasn't a surprise. It was a miracle.

Behind the pleasant smile, Cassie could see it all in Letitia's eyes. That's what Jerusha had said. It was all in the eyes. What horrors had Sebastian shown her? The coming war? Her own death? Only Letitia and Sebastian knew. Cassie doubted Sebastian would reveal his secrets to her. She seriously doubted that Letitia would ever be able to recount what she'd seen.

Letitia stared, wide-eyed. She appeared to be afraid to blink, as if blinking would take away what little safety she felt she had left, or as if blinking would show her yet another scene, so horrible her mind couldn't grasp it.

"Letitia, what happened?"

She pointed at the crystal ball. "He showed me pictures." Her expression alternated between smiles and scowls. "Pretty pictures. Scary pictures. Beautiful pictures. Horrible pictures. Shame on you," she addressed Sebastian. "Things I've never seen before. Things . . . I don't ever want to see again!"

She screamed and held her hands up to cover her eyes. She dropped the leather bag. Cassie quickly scooped it up.

Summoning her nerve, Cassie did something she'd never had the courage to do before. She grabbed Sebastian while he was still glowing with images. Both hands surrounding him, she held him close to her face.

"That's enough!" Cassie commanded. "Stop it. Stop it now. My niece and nephew still need a mother to raise them. Robert can't do it on his own. I can't allow you to drive her completely insane."

Sebastian went completely blank.

She heard footsteps running up the stairs. Quickly she put Sebastian back into his case. She shoved him into the bottom of her wardrobe and slammed the door shut.

"Cassie!" Brent, breathless, exclaimed from the doorway. "I heard a scream. Are you all right?"

With long, quick strides, he crossed the room as if no one but the two of them were present. Cassie knew, from the way he held his arms, he was about to embrace her.

Before he could touch her, she'd moved away from the wardrobe, toward Letitia. In addition to all the excitement and commotion, she couldn't bear to have him touch her again, to add to her pain and confusion.

"It wasn't me. I'm fine," she told him. "I don't know what's wrong with Letitia."

Jerusha had arrived, and stood there, looking down on the woman who was rocking back and forth on the floor with her hands covering her face. Suddenly Letitia dropped her hands, looked up at Jerusha and smiled.

"Hello, Jerusha. Did I ever thank you for keeping my bedroom so tidy, and for the lovely meals you've served us?"

Jerusha stared at her, unsmiling, unblinking, speechless, for a moment. Then she looked at Cassie. "Whatever happened to her, can we see if we can get it to happen to Mrs. Andrews?"

Brent chuckled. "Why don't we try to get her into bed and keep her quiet and comfortable until we can get Doc Carver to come out and take a look at her?"

"I'll send Olivier for him," Jerusha offered.

Robert, red-faced and puffing, appeared in the doorway. "Oh, you wouldn't wait for me."

"I'm sorry, Robert," Cassie said. "I certainly would have waited—if I had known you were there."

"Oh, well, um . . . I was sort of off to the side—"

"With August Harvey," Brent grumbled.

"Well, yes, we were sort of watching," Robert admitted.

"Like you always do."

Letitia turned and smiled at her husband. "Why, hello, Robert dear."

"Letitia?"

"Yes, dear?"

"What happened to you?"

"Oh, he showed me pictures."

"He? Who is he?" Robert demanded.

"Oh, botheration. He was so fascinating, I'm afraid I neglected to get his name."

Letitia pointed to the empty spot Sebastian had recently occupied. Cassie breathed a sigh of relief that she'd been able to sequester him before anyone else had seen him. The last thing she needed was for Sebastian to drive them all crazy.

"He . . . well, my goodness." She glanced wildly around the room and peeked under the bed. "He was right there a minute ago."

"Who?"

"A little round, bald fellow who showed me pictures. Why,

t was wonderful. So interesting. Almost as good as televi-ion."

"Tele—? What in blazes are you talking about, Letitia?" Robert demanded.

"We'll have to see if we can't get one of them, Robert."

"One of what? I still don't know what you're talking about."

Brent grabbed his arm and whispered, "Hush, Robert. We don't want to set her off again, do we?"

"I . . . I guess not."

"I hope you had a nice day at the oil field with Mr. Harvey, Robert," Letitia said.

"Yes."

"That's good, because I'm afraid we must leave here to-morrow."

"We must? Tomorrow?"

Ever since they were children, when Robert was puzzled, he not only stared at what was puzzling him. He had a tendency to leave his mouth hanging open. His mouth was hanging open now, and Cassie didn't blame him in the least. Letitia's announcement had taken her by surprise, too. She'd never expected benign compliance. She'd actually expected to have to drag Letitia to the train station, screaming and kicking.

"Oh, yes," Letitia said. "Absolutely."

"I thought you said we were going to fight this out to the last."

"Oh, no. I was quite mistaken, dear. I'm sorry if I caused you any trouble. Thank you for your gracious hospitality, Cassie. I'm sorry if we caused you any inconvenience."

"But the inheritance, you know . . ." Robert's voice trailed off, as if he were afraid of giving away too much of a plan that was already pretty obvious to Cassie. "Mr. Harvey. Cassie being . . . you know." He twirled his finger at the side of his head.

"Don't be silly, Robert dear. Cassie's not crazy. And I just can't bear to be parted another moment from my dear children."

"The children? Oh, botheration!" Robert declared. Then he

turned to Cassie and whispered, "What happened to her?"

"I don't know." Technically, she wasn't lying. She really didn't know for certain what Sebastian had shown Letitia.

"Well, whatever it was, I think I'm going to like the change."

Letitia went peacefully to her bedroom. She gratefully accepted the bowl of chicken broth and the warm milk and honey Jerusha brought her to help her sleep.

"Well, it looks as if all the excitement here is over—for the time being," Brent told Cassie. "I hope this doesn't happen again."

"I doubt it."

He turned and headed down the stairs.

"Mr. Conway," Cassie called after him.

He continued on his way.

"Mr. Conway. Brent."

He stopped.

Cassie stood on the step above him. Now she could look directly into his eyes. Jerusha had told her it was always in the eyes. All she saw in Brent's eyes was caution, and a deep, troubling sadness.

"I'd like to thank you for your help. I know I was rude and unkind to you at first. The only excuse I can offer is that I was very distraught over the uncertain condition of my sister-in-law."

"I'm glad she'll be all right."

"Oh, more than all right. It's quite . . . an improvement."

Brent nodded, then turned and continued down the steps.

Cassie hurried after him. This was the perfect opportunity to stop Sebastian's latest, horrifying vision.

"Robert and Letitia will be leaving tomorrow."

"I heard."

"They've decided not to continue their attempts to have me declared incompetent."

"I'm happy for you."

"So, you see, there's really no reason for them to be a problem anymore. Or for Mr. Harvey to be a problem, either."

"That's good for you."

"So, whatever animosity you might have had against him . . . well . . ." Her voice trailed off. How could she tell him he really didn't have any reason to kill Mr. Harvey in cold blood?

"Any animosity I have against him has nothing to do with you. So just set your mind at ease about that."

"But—"

"If you must know, August Harvey was the bane of my childhood. Wherever there was a group of kids ready to tease me about my clothing, about my home or my family, about my lunch or the lack thereof, there was August, leading the pack. There. Has that satisfied your insatiable curiosity?"

"You two don't . . . still go hunting together or anything, do you?" Cassie asked instead. It wasn't the past that worried her. It was the future.

"No."

"Good. You two don't . . . clean your guns together or . . . anything like that, do you?"

"Cassie, is this turning into one of those silly things like with Abel?"

"Abel?"

"Abel at the Fish Fry. You watched him and watched him until he swallowed that piece of fish wrong."

"I did not cause that. I can't help it if he eats clumsily. I can't help it if I *know* certain things. I know you won't believe me, but—"

"So now you're going to badger me about August and guns until I shoot him. Is that it?"

"No! Never!" She reached out and clutched the sleeve of his jacket, as if that could hold him there and hold off the future. "Please listen to me, Brent. Please believe me for once. Stay away from him and guns. Please."

"Don't worry about it. I don't even own a gun."

"Does Mr. Harvey?"

Brent sighed with exasperation. "You just won't leave it alone, will you?"

"No. Never."

"Why?"

"Because . . . I still love you, Brent."

She never thought she'd say it to him again. She thought she'd hate him for the rest of her life for the way he'd lied to her and played her along. She hadn't really thought she could still love him until she looked up at him.

"I love you, Brent," she repeated.

"I thought you were angry with me."

"I was. I still am. But that doesn't mean my love for you stops. I told you I'd love you forever. You asked me if I'd wait for you forever. I will. I always will. That hasn't changed, either."

She folded her hands in front of her. He'd probably think it was to indicate that she'd said her piece and was finished, and now he could leave. He wouldn't know she held her hands together tightly in front of her so she wouldn't reach out to embrace him, to surround him with her love, at least for the little while longer that she could hold him.

She expected him to leave.

Brent stood silently at the bottom of the steps. He looked at her without saying anything for a long time.

Had she said too much? she worried. What kind of woman told a man who was betrothed to another woman that she was still in love with him? Was now the time to tell him about their baby?

Several times he looked as if he might speak, but changed his mind. At last, his gaze dropped to the floor.

"I . . . I have some very important business to take care of right now, Cassie. I'll see you tomorrow." He rushed out the door.

Cassie sat on the bottom step, hung her head in her hands, and cried.

Seventeen

"Evaline," Brent began. He stood in the doorway to the dining room of the McAlisters' mansion. The late-afternoon sunlight bathed the room in a golden and rosy glow.

"Brent, I'm so glad to see you. We have to decide. Do you think we should choose this pattern or this?" Smiling, Evaline alternately held up two china plates.

Moving a little closer to her, he tried again. "Evaline."

"Mother seems to prefer the pink rose pattern. I am more partial to the plainer white with the gold trim. Much more classic and generally useful, don't you think? I mean, suppose we should serve something that doesn't go with pink?"

"Evaline, I don't think we should get either of them."

"Oh, no, we don't have to *buy* them. We just have to choose a pattern we like. My godparents are giving us a complete set of bone china for a wedding gift."

"No, Evaline. That's not what I mean."

"Oh?"

"Evaline, please put them down and come sit here with me."

She placed both dishes on the long, mahogany dining room table.

He took her hand and led her to a sofa in a small alcove.

He still held her hand after they were seated. He wanted to maintain some kind of contact with her, in the hope that she might somehow know that he still cared about her, her future, her happiness, even though he had decided not to be a part of it.

If that didn't work, at least holding one of her hands might keep her from hitting him too hard.

"What I have to say to you, Evaline, is very important and very private. I don't want to risk having your parents walk in on us without some sort of warning. I want you to be able to keep your reaction to what I'm about to say private, too. I have too much respect for you to do otherwise."

"Goodness, Brent. Why so serious? What is the problem?"

Brent pressed his lips together. After all the thought he'd given to this matter during these past few weeks, he'd never really considered how to begin.

He found it difficult to look her in the eyes and say this. He studied her hand, the small fingers, the delicate veins on the back. A little hand like that couldn't hit him too hard, could it?

"Evaline, I told you once I loved you and wanted to marry you."

"Yes."

"But then your parents took you away for a whole year. I didn't see you. I didn't hear from you. My life went on. So now, in all honesty and in all honorableness, I must tell you. In that time, I . . . I met someone else."

"Cassie Bowen."

Brent looked up. "How . . . how do you know?"

"Brent, you never showed any real interest in any of the other girls in town. Cassie's the only new girl. It doesn't take a genius to figure out this one."

"Oh."

"Besides, I've seen the way she looks at you. I've seen the way you don't look at her when I'm around and the way you still watch her when you think I'm not looking."

Brent hung his head. "Sorry."

"Don't be. No woman is ever that stupid, Brent, unless she wants to be."

"Oh." No woman might be, but he sure felt stupid right about now.

"Are you angry with me?" he asked.

"No. Not really."

"That's good. I really didn't mean to hurt you." That also meant he could release her hand without any danger of her hitting him.

"In a way, I'm sort of flattered that you'd still consider marrying me after all this time."

"I'm glad you understand."

She nodded with modest admission.

"I hope you'll release me from our betrothal—"

"Of course, Brent," she responded quickly.

"I'm glad."

"As a matter of fact, I'm glad, too, Brent. You see, I've never wanted to marry you."

"What?" He'd certainly never taken that development into consideration.

"Not that you're not a handsome, witty, educated, intelligent man, Brent. You're a pleasant companion. You dance fairly well for an American male. I'm sure you'll be a good provider, a good husband and father."

"Then why did you go along with this charade? Why was your father—?"

"Because . . ."

Evaline rose and paced back and forth in front of the sofa. Her tiny hands wrung the delicate handkerchief to shreds. He was glad she hadn't hit him.

"Brent, while I was in England, I met someone else. He's very wonderful. I fell in love with him very quickly, and he with me. But he's only the younger son of a younger son. He has no money, no employment, and no hope of ever inheriting anything more."

"But why would your father try to blackmail me into marrying you? Why didn't he just let you marry this fellow or, if he wasn't acceptable because he was too poor, why didn't he try to find—?"

"Because by the time my father found out and refused to let me marry Collin, it was too late."

"Too late? He's dead? Goodness, that's morbid, and I'm very sorry for you."

"No, no. Collin is very much alive, but . . . I'm pregnant with his child."

"You? Now?"

"Of course now. Goodness, Brent, I thought you were intelligent."

"I am. It's just—right now I'm pretty flabbergasted, too."

"My father refused to allow me to marry so impoverished a man. 'Money gets money,' he always says. No one else would have me now. My father insisted we see if you were still . . . interested. I had no choice but to go along. Even if I don't love you, it wasn't as if I don't find you likable."

"That's hardly flattering," Brent grumbled with injured pride.

"No less flattering than you agreeing to marry me for a newspaper."

"I'm sorry. I guess you do have a point there," Brent had to admit.

"If I married you, the baby would have a name," Evaline continued. "We'd be living far away in San Francisco. We could lie to everyone about how many months there were from the wedding to the birth."

"I see." Brent sat there silently for a moment. "I'm sorry I can't help you, Evaline."

"I'm sorry my father tried to trick you and bully you. I'm ashamed I took part in it. I didn't know what else to do."

"What will you do now?"

"I'm going back to England. Collin has sent for me. I've got a little money saved. He gets a small allowance. Not a lot, but we'll make the best we can of it."

"I hope it all works out for you and this fellow, Evaline."

"Papa will have a fit of the apoplexy. Mama will pinch her

face up even more tightly and probably won't speak to me for a few weeks."

"But I hope you'll eventually be happy."

"I will." She reached out and took his hand. "I hope it's not too late for you to be happy, too, Brent."

"I will be," he assured her. "If I can live through the ordeal of telling your father I'm not going to marry you."

The sun had set. The corners of the study were shrouded in darkness. The fire blazed behind McAlister like the roaring flames of Hell, fueled by the man's anger. Brent could almost smell the brimstone.

"You *will* marry Evaline," McAlister repeated the words he'd used the first time Brent had presented him with the possibility that he might not marry his daughter.

"No, I will not," Brent stated. "This is not cowardice or foolishness. This is not a spur-of-the-moment decision. I've thought about this a long time, McAlister. Evaline doesn't want to marry me, and I don't want to marry her."

"You *will* move to San Francisco." The tip of his cigar glowed as fiery as his temper.

"I'm staying here with my own newspaper and the woman I hope to make my wife. Your daughter—your only daughter—is moving to England to marry the man she loves."

"You *will* give my grandchild a name."

"He already has a name—a fine name and heritage—waiting for him over there in England."

"You *will* run my newspapers."

"Have you been listening to a word I've said, you selfish, pigheaded old goat?" Brent shouted. "Have you ever listened to Evaline and what she wants? Do you ever think of anything besides yourself and your money?"

"I'll ruin you," McAlister threatened, hammering his fist on his mahogany desk. "I'll have my newspaper up and running before the month is out. By December, you'll be so ruined, you won't be able to afford a Christmas goose."

Brent stood nose to nose with McAlister and declared, "Now

I've got some news for you. I'll still be here, printing the *Argus* to the very end, however long it manages to survive anything you try to do to us."

"I said I'd ruin you. I meant it."

"I don't care."

"What? Of course you care."

"I care about a lot of things. But I don't care what you do. Go ahead. You can try to do your worst. I won't change my mind."

"Your father worked hard all his life for that newspaper. That's a fine tribute to his legacy."

"But it's *my* newspaper now. My father was a fine man, and the *Argus* was a damn fine newspaper when my father ran it. If it goes out of business now, well then, that's my affair. It has nothing to do with my father—or his memory."

"You worked your way up from almost nothing for what you have today, just to lose it all."

"I'll do it again, too," Brent declared confidently. "And this time I'll do it even better because I know where the pitfalls are."

"Not in this town you won't."

Brent threw his arm out. "There's a whole country out there, McAlister. Vast expanses where nobody lives—yet. But they will. And they'll all need a good newspaper. I'll give it to them. I'll find someplace else."

"Not without any money you won't."

Brent laughed as loud and as hard as he could, just so McAlister could get a hint of how little he regarded this particular threat.

"Starting out with no money puts me ahead already. When I inherited the *Argus*, we were so far in debt we didn't know what black ink looked like."

"You can't do this, Conway."

Had McAlister given up his threats?

"I can and I will."

"Not to me, not to my daughter."

"I'm not doing this to hurt Evaline. I'm doing this for her

happiness. If you've got any sense, you'll write me off as a bad venture. Concentrate on making your daughter and your grandchild happy and getting to know your son-in-law before you lose them, too."

"Look what you're giving up, Conway!" McAlister shouted. "Everything you've worked for, hoped for, dreamed about."

"What do you know about hopes and dreams?" Brent shook his head. "You just don't understand, do you? I'm not turning down your dubious offer to get anything. I'm turning you down because you can't give me what I realize now I want most in this world."

"Your newspaper? Money? Social position?"

"Nothing means anything to me without the woman I love. I love Cassie Bowen."

"Who?"

"Never mind. You won't be invited to the wedding anyway."

"Bowen. That's the crazy woman who built that drill outside of town." McAlister tapped his cigar. "She's got money. Not as much as me, but—"

"It's not the money. She's bound to lose most of it on that crazy scheme anyway. It's her. Without her, nothing else means anything. Even if I had everything you offered me, I can't live without her. I don't want to live without her. I *won't* spend my life without her. And I'm going to go tell her so."

Brent stepped over to McAlister's desk and flipped open the lid of his humidor. He pulled out a long cigar and lit it. Sending up billows of smoke, he strode out of McAlister's office, out of his home, and out into the cool night breeze.

For the first time in weeks, he really felt good about himself.

Brent had taken his time walking down the mountain back into town. It wasn't easy navigating that path in the pitch-black night. He'd also had a lot to consider. He'd taken some time to calm his anger at McAlister's selfishness. He'd taken a little time to gloat over his victory, too. He wished Evaline and her Englishman all the luck in the world. Most of all, he prayed that Cassie still loved him enough to forgive his foolish stubbornness and marry him after all.

Abel was just opening the store for the morning's business when Brent strolled by.

"Brent," Abel called cheerily. He waved with one hand while the other rested on the broom handle. "I haven't seen you keeping these kinds of hours since we were both young and fancy-free."

"I've been talking with Evaline."

Abel chuckled as he swept the front sidewalk. "Goodness, Brent. I didn't think that lady would keep these kinds of hours with a gentleman, even her betrothed."

"She doesn't. We ended our discussion long ago."

"I couldn't help notice you came from the direction of her house. If you don't mind my asking, where have you been and what in the world have you been doing the rest of that time?"

"I had a little disagreement with her father."

Abel looked him over. "And you're still in one piece? If you don't mind my asking, what did you argue about?"

"It seems neither Evaline nor I want to marry each other."

"It's about time you figured that out."

"McAlister wouldn't take no for an answer."

"Typical."

"She's in love with a man she met in England. She's going back there to marry him."

"And you?"

"I want to marry Cassie—if she'll still have me after I manage to explain this fiasco with Evaline. I figure, if I can forgive her foolishness with this petroleum drill, she ought to be able to forgive a little temptation I had in the form of a big-town newspaper."

Abel chuckled. Then he stopped and frowned as if concentrating very hard on putting a puzzle together. He reached up and rubbed the back of his head.

"You know, Brent, I've got something in here you just might want to take a look at."

He motioned for Brent to follow him into the store. He took

his usual place behind the grillwork and sorted through several pieces of mail.

"Now, mind you, I just deliver it and send it out again. Ordinarily I wouldn't go poking through other people's mail."

"Not you, Abel."

Abel held out a long envelope. "But this letter just came for Mr. Harvey."

Brent held out his hand. Abel pulled the letter back.

"Now, I can't go giving it to you, Brent. I can't give this to anyone but the person it's addressed to."

"Abel, what—?"

"And I can't let you go opening it."

"Of course not."

"But if I just happened to lay it down here for a minute while I had to go off and do something else, well, I can't help it if you're so dang nosy you'd look at another person's mail by holding it up to the light."

Abel set the letter on the counter and slid it toward Brent. Then he went off in search of something extremely elusive that would probably take him approximately as long to find as it would take Brent to read the letter.

Brent held the envelope up to the light from the window.

"To August Harvey. From Titusville." Brent looked up from the letter. "Say, Abel, isn't that where August said they were drilling for rock oil, too?"

"Yep."

"Would you say this paper looked like a share in the Seneca Oil Company?"

"Never having seen one before, I'd say it was hard to make a judgment. Having seen other stocks, however, and being able to make out 'Seneca Oil' on that paper amid all the curlicues and engravings, I'd say you had a pretty good chance of being correct."

"If August has been investing in this other company and Cassie's well comes in first—"

"I'd say the value of his stock would diminish somewhat."

"That's what I thought." Brent tapped the edge of the letter rhythmically against the counter. "So it would certainly be to his benefit if Cassie were declared incompetent and all her assets transferred to the custody of her brother, who could then close down her operation."

"Sounds plausible to me."

"And now that Robert and Letitia have decided to give up their greedy pursuit, and go home instead—"

"What would August do to prevent Cassie's well from coming in?"

"How desperate is he?"

"Does he have to be desperate to do underhanded things? He's a lawyer, isn't he?"

Brent shook his head. "It all sounds so diabolically planned."

"Come on, Brent. You, of all people, know August has been a first-rate bastard since the day he was born."

"We know Cassie's well is just a crazy idea. It won't really produce anything."

"But August doesn't know that," Abel said. "He can't take the chance that it might."

"Why should it bother August so much that he'd plan something mean and vile?"

"He doesn't necessarily have to plan anything. All he has to do is take advantage of the first opportunity that presents itself."

"I've got to find her. Thanks, Abel," Brent said, tossing the letter back onto the counter. "I've got to get her to marry me. I've got to make sure August doesn't do anything stupid."

"August will always do something stupid," Abel told him. "Just make sure he doesn't do anything deadly."

"Cassie!" Brent called as he took her front porch steps two at a time. "Cassie!"

He hammered on the front door. No answer.

Was she still so angry with him that she even refused to open the door, much less let him in? She wouldn't be once he told her he loved her—too much to marry Evaline on some paltry pretense of a bigger newspaper business deal. She wouldn't be angry once he asked her to marry him.

Would she still accept him? She had to! His whole world meant nothing to him without her.

He knocked on the door. "Cassie!"

Still no answer.

Robert and Letitia had probably already left earlier this morning to catch the tram back to Philadelphia. Olivier had probably driven them in the wagon. Jerusha and Mrs. Parker were probably still at home. But where was Cassie? He seriously doubted she'd accompanied her brother and his wife all the way to Pittsburgh just to bid them a fond farewell.

Suppose something had happened to her? He didn't trust August, not as far as he could throw him. Especially since August knew how very much Cassie meant to him.

He tried the doorknob. It turned easily in his hand.

"Cassie?" he called as he entered the house.

Only the slow *tick, tick, tick* of the clock on the mantel in the parlor echoed through the house. No clattering dishes from the kitchen. No pleasant chatter from the parlor.

Was Cassie upstairs?

Nobody had yet figured out what had made Letitia so strange. Suppose the same thing happened to Cassie?

"Cassie?" he called as he hurried up the stairs.

Her bedroom was clean and tidy, no clothes laying scattered about this time. Not from Letitia's mad spree. Not even from their own lovemaking, he thought with a pang of regret.

Soon, he told himself. Soon, and for the rest of their lives.

He glanced around the room one more time. What in the world was that on Cassie's night table? Well, son of a gun.

He'd always known Miss Flora had a bizarre and varied collection of unusual objects. He'd heard about these things in carnivals, traveling circuses, and gypsy caravans, but he'd never actually seen a crystal ball. Not up close and in person.

Grinning, he slowly approached it. Cassie must certainly like it, to keep it out on her night table. He wouldn't want her to catch him here and accuse him of prowling through her house uninvited. He just had to have a closer look at this thing.

He smiled. He didn't blame Cassie or Miss Flora for liking it. It was perfectly clear, and very beautiful the way it caught the sunlight.

Suddenly he grew more serious, and the smile dropped from his face. Was that light actually shining from *inside* the crystal ball?

He stepped closer.

It was more than a light. It was an actual picture forming inside.

Was this what Letitia had been babbling about? The little round bald fellow who had shown her pictures that drove her insane. What had this thing been doing to Cassie? What was this thing going to do to him? Cautiously he watched and waited.

The images weren't like a painting on the outside or even the inside of the glass. They didn't have the translucent quality of an ambrotype. Little figures formed and moved inside the solid ball.

Brent drew back with a start. It was an image of himself, naked. Well, son of a gun, he'd always known he was a good-looking man.

There was an image of Cassie, too. His heart lurched. Oh, Cassie—beautiful, soft, tender, naked in his arms, her long auburn hair flowing down her back, over her shoulders and across her breasts. How he longed to hold her again.

If this was the sort of thing that was intended to drive him crazy, he'd pay for a front row seat.

By golly! Where could he get himself one of these?

Fascinated, mesmerized by the tantalizing images of himself and Cassie, Brent watched the images turn in a passionate embrace. He watched himself move away from her for a moment.

Brent blinked and stared at the image. Cassie was great with child.

"She's pregnant?" he murmured. He stretched his hand out

toward the ball. His fingertips touched the cold crystal. "My child? My child."

A chill ran up his arms. He felt his face widening in a grin. Now he understood why Abel had always been so darn happy. He had to find Cassie, wrap her in his arms, and marry her as soon as he could find Reverend Markham. First he had to find Cassie. Where was she?

He managed to pull himself away from his close inspection of the ball. He was about to turn away when the picture suddenly changed.

The morning sun rose behind the tall tower, sending long slanting rays over the oil field.

"That darn thing!" Brent protested. "When will she get that out of her stubborn mind so I can get it out of my life?"

But there were no workmen around the tower at this early hour. Cassie, pregnant with his child, walked alone.

Not quite alone. What was August doing lurking around the equipment?

The tower slanted, teetered, collapsed on Cassie, crushing her to death with all that ridiculous equipment.

If the crystal ball showed the future, the way he'd heard all other crystal balls did, Brent knew he had to find Cassie right away.

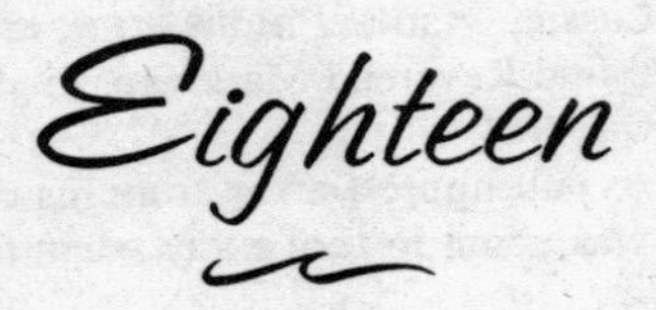

Eighteen

"Cassie! Cassie!" Brent called as soon as he spotted her. He was still running across the field. She stood, looking so beautiful and desirable in the rosy light of dawn, directly under the very dangerous tower he had seen collapse.

"Cassie, I've got to talk to you."

Even from this distance, he could see her face light up at the sight of him.

She was too close to the tower. He had to get close to her to talk to her, to convince her to leave. That meant approaching the tower himself, and that could mean it would collapse on him, too. How could he save her if he was dead? How could he live if she should die? Their baby, too. He rushed to her side.

"Cassie, you've got to stop. You've got to leave here, now."

The smile fled from her face. As he caught up to her, her eyes, sad and weary, studied him.

"Why do you keep telling me that?" she complained. "Why can't you believe me just once? Why can't you trust me to do the right thing on my own?"

"I trust you completely. I don't trust August."

"August, August, August." She did everything but stamp her

foot on the oily ground in irritation. "I'm sick to death of hearing about August and all your troubles with him."

"It's not just my troubles. It's yours, too."

She shook her head. "My troubles with him are over. They ended the minute Woody drove Robert and Letitia out of Lyman's Gap."

"No, they didn't."

"What are you talking about?" she demanded.

"Move away from the tower, and I'll explain it all to you if I can."

"No. I'm tired of you telling me what to do. I'm tired of you trying to run my life."

"All right, then, damn it! I'll show you and endanger both our lives."

"What are you talking about?"

Brent grabbed her by the wrist and pulled her to the base of the tower.

She tried to resist, but he was too angry to let her go. She'd been so stubborn, and he'd gone along, trying to humor the crazy lady. The time had come to show her the truth, whether she liked it or not.

He pointed down. Sawdust lay scattered in little piles in the grass.

"See that?"

Cassie bent down to see the boards closest to the ground. "They're split . . . and broken. This is shoddy workmanship."

"No. These boards have been deliberately split. Not so much that it would be noticeable to any of the workmen during the day. Not so much that anything would happen right away. That would arouse too many suspicions. But after a while, the least strain will bring this tower crashing down, ruining the equipment and—"

"Killing anyone who might be working here at the time." Cassie turned worried eyes to him. She stood up and slowly backed away from the tower, as if even the slightest movement would send it toppling.

"Or anyone who might be here observing," he added.

Brent saw the trouble in her eyes deepen.

"I'm the only one I allow beyond the fence—"

"It would kill you, too."

"How did you know about this? Who would do such a thing?"

"I've been trying to tell you. August Harvey."

She placed her hands on her hips and glared at him. "You really don't like him, do you? You like blaming him for this sort of thing. Why would you think he'd do this?"

"Because he couldn't talk you out of this logically. He couldn't bully you out of it. He's failed at having you declared incompetent and getting your brother to take over the finances and cancel this venture."

"Why would this matter to him, anyway? Oh, I know he made a big fuss about me not spending so much—but it's my money. Whether this thing made a profit or not, he'd still have gotten paid, if he hadn't made me so angry with his condescending attitude that I fired him. What does he have to lose if I succeed?"

"A lot of his own money."

"No." Cassie shook her head. "It couldn't be him."

The hardheaded woman was still refusing to believe him. At last he knew how she felt when no one believed a word she said. On the other hand, his accusations made a lot more sense and were supported by a lot more evidence than her wild predictions.

"Did you know August was investing in the Seneca Oil Company?"

"He can invest where he wants."

"But that's the company that's drilling for petroleum farther north."

"That's not important. If my well comes in, he'll still make a lot of money."

"Probably. But he'll make more if theirs is the only well."

"How do you know all this? Why should I trust you, anyway? You don't like August. You played with my affections to get me to sell you this property when you know you're going to marry Evaline. You told me you'd given Abel the bank draft when you hadn't. That's twice you betrayed me, Brent. I'm not going to trust you a third time when you've given me every reason *not* to—Oh, my!"

Cassie couldn't help but stare into thin air as she let waves of highly illogical logic roll over her.

"What's wrong, Cassie?" He took her by both arms and gave her a little shake. It failed to rouse her. "What happened to Letitia isn't happening to you, is it? Not here. Not now. Cassie!"

"I . . . No, no." Her eyes were beginning to focus better. She'd begun moving normally again. "It's all coming together now."

"What?"

"I have lost something I couldn't afford to lose. I have loved a man with no hope of him ever loving me in return." She studied his face in the morning light. "All the while I thought you loved Evaline, and knew you were going to marry her, I may have hated what you did, but I never stopped loving you, Brent. Never."

"That's good to hear." He pulled her against his chest. She didn't struggle for him to release her. It felt so good to hold her again.

"But I never trusted you when I had no reason to trust you, Brent."

"Everyone—even your own aunt—told you what a scoundrel I was."

"I don't base my judgement on someone else's gossip, not even my own aunt's. You'd never betrayed me personally—before."

She pulled away slightly, just enough to be able to look into his eyes, as if searching for a reason to trust him now.

"I still have no reason to trust you."

Apparently she didn't find what she'd been looking for.

"Why should I take your word that August did this? I haven't allowed anyone else around the tower. How could you know about that damage?"

"Well," he began slowly. Out of everything, this might just be the hardest thing to explain. "I went to your house, looking for you. When I couldn't find you, I went inside."

"Uninvited. What brass!"

Brent was glad to see the hint of amusement playing in her eyes. It had been so long since they'd bantered with each other. He'd missed it.

"I went upstairs, into your bedroom."

Cassie's hand flew to cover her mouth. "Oh, my goodness. I forgot."

"I guess so." He grinned at her.

"In all the excitement, I forgot to put Sebastian away."

"Sebastian? It has a name?"

"Of course he does. But you're not supposed to know about him." She sighed with resignation. "So, you've seen him."

"Is that why Letitia went a little mad?"

"She found him while searching for my jewels. I figured she would sooner or later, so I hid all the best pieces in my shoes. I guess what he did to Letitia was Sebastian's way of protecting me."

"That's some pretty strong protection. Better than a mastiff." He laughed.

Cassie looked up at Brent, puzzled. "But if you saw him, too, why are you here? Why aren't you babbling and drooling all over yourself on the bedroom floor?"

Brent shrugged. "I guess he showed me something different."

"He showed you pictures? You actually saw images in him, too?"

Brent pulled her closer again.

"He showed me you . . . and me. Together again. I liked what I saw, Cassie."

She closed her eyes and turned her face away from him. He watched her cheeks flush pink. "I'll bet you did."

He held her chin and turned her face back to him.

"Cassie, he showed me something else, too. Something very important to me."

Cassie knew immediately what that traitorous Sebastian had shown him. That was *her* secret! Jerusha hadn't tattled on her, but she couldn't trust her own crystal ball!

"What did he show you?" she asked anyway.

"He showed me our baby, Cassie. Yours and mine. Why didn't you tell me?"

She glared at him in disbelief. "You oaf! What was I supposed to do? Ruin your life, your plans for the future? Force you to marry me when you're betrothed to Evaline?"

"I'm not. Not anymore."

"What?"

Brent's hand slipped down from her shoulder to take her by the hand. Gently he began to tug her away from the tower.

"Last night, after I left your house, I went to see Evaline, to try to explain to her. I broke our engagement, and she agreed. I told her I couldn't marry her when I was in love with you."

Cassie didn't say a word. She just held him as tightly as she could. It had been so long since she'd enjoyed the warm masculinity of him. Her body ached to welcome him again.

She'd go home with him. They'd marry. She'd have their baby. She'd never have to be alone again. She'd never have to watch Sebastian's horrible visions again.

"Well, well, well. Isn't this a touching scene?" August emerged from behind the long, low work building.

Brent pulled away from Cassie, placing himself between her and August. "How long have you been hanging around here, eavesdropping like a snake in the grass?"

"Longer than you have," August said as he came closer to them.

Cassie could see the gun in his hand.

"I'm surprised. I never figured you'd be smart enough to figure out what I've been up to, Brent. But that was what made my plan so workable. Its simplicity. Even Robert and Letitia could go along with it and be perfectly convincing. Although I'll never know how you managed to get Letitia to change her mind."

"I had a little help from a friend," Cassie told him.

"Well, you've got no help now."

"Why do we need help, August?" Brent demanded.

Instead of answering him, August turned and examined the tower.

"You know, Woody was right for once about something besides pigs. This tower isn't that well built. It'll probably fall down soon. Even if it doesn't, everyone knows how easily petroleum catches fire. And if, in the ashes, they happen to find the bodies of the owner and her neighbor who came out just to take a look and were killed in the accidental explosion—well, what a shame."

"You don't have to kill me to make money, August," Cassie said.

"But I need to make a lot of money. I've always hated poor people. That's why I've never been fond of you, Brent."

"The feeling is mutual, August, although for slightly different reasons."

"While I always had you to feel superior to, I hated feeling inferior to Miss Flora, and those damned arrogant McAlisters. Then when you actually began making money from that newspaper, and built that ostentatious house, Brent—well, that really galled me. I need a lot of money."

August shrugged and turned to Cassie.

"Miss Bowen, it was nice working with you until you got too uppity. Brent, it's been a pleasure tormenting you all your life. Sorry I can't accommodate you any longer."

Cassie heard the hammer of August's gun pull back.

Before August could fire, a rustling in the bushes distracted him. He glanced toward the sound.

Brent seized Cassie's hand and dragged her along behind him, toward the shelter of the stack of barrels.

August fired wildly. The bullet ricocheted off one of the stacked barrels, sending the pile tumbling down, barely missing Cassie, but pinning Brent beneath two of them.

"Oh, you're stuck. What a shame." August stood, gloating. He watched what was left of the barrels that still balanced precariously above them, and the tower that had begun to totter, apparently waiting until it was safer to draw nearer and finish them off, or waiting for the tower and the barrels to do it for him. "I do hate shooting fish in a barrel." He laughed hard at his horrible pun.

"Just shoot me and get it over with, August," Brent growled. "Don't kill us with your bad jokes."

August just laughed again, this time with less humor and more malice.

"Run, Cassie," Brent commanded. He groaned under the weight of the barrels. "Save yourself and the baby."

"I have no life without you, Brent." She knelt beside him, holding his hand.

"Think of our baby."

"Something will happen. Something's *got* to happen. The curse isn't ended yet."

"Curse?"

"I'll explain later. It can't be broken. I saw you shoot and kill August. Sebastian always shows me the truth. Something else must happen."

"What? And you better figure it out fast." Brent groaned with pain.

"Because . . ." she said slowly as she recalled the last condition, "no one has ever believed a word I've said."

"I believe you," he declared. "Now, get out of here."

"You think you folks might be needing this?" Olivier asked, holding out a shotgun to Brent.

"Where did you come from?" Cassie demanded.

Olivier stretched out his long arm. "Over round the edge of the clearing."

"Was that the noise that distracted August?"

"I suppose so. Here." He held out the gun to Brent.

"I love stalking my prey," August called to them as he slowly approached across the field. "I hate when they're trapped like this, but it'll only make my story of the fire more plausible, in that you were trapped and couldn't escape. Such a pity."

"Take the gun and shoot him, Mr. Conway, before he kills us."

"I can't take it," Brent told him. "My arm's caught. I'll never be able to aim and fire. You've got to do it, Olivier."

Olivier laughed. "I ain't no fool, Mr. Conway. I ain't going to shoot a white man. You know what would happen to me."

Cassie heard the click of August's gun, his footsteps drawing closer.

"Oh, give me that!"

She grabbed the gun and swung it across. Both barrels discharged wildly, and missed August completely. Both barrels emptied into the side of the tower. The wood splintered, the boards creaked, the moorings groaned. The tower shuddered and tumbled over, crashing down on August.

"Well, I'll be!" Olivier exclaimed.

Cassie set the gun in her lap and stared with tears in her eyes, at the remains of her tower and the man who had tried to murder her and the man she loved.

"I guess we ought to go get Doc Carver," Brent said as Olivier rolled the barrels off him.

"Appears to me as if Mr. Harvey's going to have more need of Mortimer Farris for a coffin," Olivier commented.

Brent shook his head. Free at last, he rose, rubbing his scraped and bruised limbs. He looked at August's limp arm and hand, still clutching the gun sticking out from the pile of rubble.

"I spent so much time hating him. I never realized how much time he'd spent hating me. Now I just feel sorry for him."

"I'll go fetch the doc and Mr. Farris," Olivier volunteered. "Why don't you take Miss Cassie back to the house so she can rest?"

"Good idea, Olivier. I owe you more than my thanks."

The tower lay in ruins. The drills were bent and twisted beyond repair. The steam engine was completely destroyed.

"It's all gone," Cassie said sadly. "It'll take months to rebuild it all, order new materials, make new drills. By the time

I can rebuild, they probably will have drilled through to the petroleum in Titusville. If only August had been more patient."

"But you *will* rebuild, won't you?" Brent asked.

"Why bother?" Cassie asked.

"Because I know you. You'll drill here again."

"Do you believe me, then, that we really will find petroleum here?"

"No."

"Oh, then why did you even bother to come here?" she wailed.

"I'm sorry, Cassie. I don't believe your crazy predictions. I never have. But I believe in you because I love you."

Cassie shrugged. "I guess I can settle for that."

Brent extended a hand to help Cassie rise. "Well, will you look at that?" he exclaimed.

Cassie looked to her side, expecting to see a rattler or a cottonmouth slithering toward her. Instead, she saw a slick trail of petroleum oozing downhill through the grass.

"Well, I'll be danged."

"Petroleum," Cassie whispered. "Aunt Flora was right. I was right." She sprang to her feet. Tilting back her head, she looked at the shattered remains of where the tower had once stood. "Tomorrow morning, we'll start rebuilding this."

Brent heaved a sigh of resignation. "By the way, where'd you get the gun, Olivier? Why'd you bring it out here, anyway?"

"It's my old hunting gun. Jerusha made me bring it." He shook his head. "I swear, that woman pestered the living daylights out of me until I finally did what she wanted. She said she knows you don't have one. She said you couldn't kill Mr. Harvey without it."

"She believed what I told her? She believed me?" Cassie murmured aloud to herself. She could hardly believe it now. "Someone actually believed what I predicted. Practical Jerusha, of all people."

Olivier snickered. "She believes all sorts of that stuff. You didn't know her mama in New Orleans."

Cassie smiled. "Then the curse truly is broken at last."

• • •

"Stop! Stop! You'll hurt yourself," Cassie squealed as Brent lifted her in his arms and carried her through the doorway of her house. "I need you for better things."

"I'm fine, my love. I never felt better." He tugged her close and kissed her neck. "I assure you, I'm undeniably prepared for much better things."

"Laying under barrels makes you feel better?" She clasped her arms around his neck so she wouldn't fall.

"Lying on top of you makes me feel even better. I'm alive. I'm holding the woman I love in my arms. I never felt better in my life. For now."

With bounding strides, Brent carried Cassie up the stairs and into her bedroom. Sebastian sat where she'd left him on the night table.

Gently Brent laid her on the bed.

"It's been too long," he told her.

"I hated every minute I was away from you."

"I'll never leave you again, my love."

"Yes, you will. The war—"

"Don't tell me about the war!" he scolded.

"You'll come back."

"If I were a thousand miles away, I'd always come back to you."

"I'll always be waiting."

She reached up to pull him down to her. She kissed his tender lips, his beard-roughened cheeks and chin. His whiskers prickled her sensitive lips, making her long for more of his kisses. She trailed kisses down his throat until she came to his collar.

He toyed with the buttons of her dress, slowly unfastening them, one by one. She matched him button for button, until her short bodice had at last run out of them, and his long shirt remained fastened with several more.

"No fair, no fair!" she cried, "making me wait for more of you."

"The longer I make you wait, the more you'll want me."

"It's been too long. I've missed you, your touch, your love. I couldn't possibly want you any more than I do now."

"Just wait."

His lips caressed her neck and breast. As he unfastened her corset, his tongue trailed a cooling moist track between her warming breasts, and alternated a fevered path between each nipple.

His tongue flickered the rosy erectness until sparks of lightning coursed through her veins and shot down into the pit of her stomach. She twitched and ached for him.

"Now, my love?" she asked.

His hot, callused hands smoothed across her stomach and over her hips, kneading her thighs until she felt the muscles between her legs tighten in anticipation of him.

"Now, my love," she pleaded.

She twitched again as she felt his searing hot manhood resting on her thigh, taunting, teasing without entering while she felt her own moistness preparing for him.

She wrapped her arms around his neck and her legs about his waist.

"I must have you or I shall die with wanting."

"Now, my love," he answered her.

Gently, insistently, he delved inside, plunging and rocking.

She felt complete at last. Safe in his love. Secure in his embrace. Blissful in the magic of their union. Enchanted with the waves of pleasure he brought over her, and the shuddering joy she knew he, too, felt.

He lay beside her, cradling her head against his chest. The hairs of his chest tickled her cheek and nose. She smiled.

"We'll talk to Reverend Markham tomorrow," he told her. He ran his fingertips up and down her arm.

"Yes."

"We'll arrange the wedding as soon as possible."

"Of course."

"We'll convert Miss Flora's old bedroom into a nursery."

"Of course."

"Would you like to take a wedding trip back to Philadelphia?"

"Of course not. I'd like my marriage to start out happy and stay that way."

"Don't you know it will be, Cassie? It will be because I'll do my best to make you happy."

"I will, too."

"What about Sebastian?" He nodded toward the perfectly clear, blank crystal ball sitting on the night table. "What sort of predictions did Sebastian make for our future happiness? Not that I'm going to believe any of it, of course, but . . ."

Cassie looked to Sebastian, but there were no pictures lighting up the inside.

"It doesn't matter. The curse is ended," Cassie said. "There won't be any more predictions. But I think that's all right."

All she could see in Sebastian was the reflection of Brent and herself, cradled in each other's arms.

"I must admit, in spite of all the problems he's caused, I'm going to miss him."

"Oh, I think if you describe them to me in very minute and accurate detail, we might be able to duplicate whatever scenes he may have shown you. Maybe even invent a few of our own."

Brent chuckled and tugged her more tightly to him. She snuggled more closely into his embrace.

"Just so we can be certain of that, do you remember the last things Sebastian showed you?"

"They're not what you think," she warned.

"Try me. I'm a very adventurous sort of guy."

She pulled back from him just a bit and looked him directly in the eye. Very seriously, she pronounced, "Buy windows, apples, and Z-rocks."

Brent shook his head, as if trying to sort things out in there. "What kind of prediction is that?"

"I'm only telling you what I saw."

"I can see why he nearly drove you crazy. Windows I can understand. Everybody needs windows in their houses, shops, factories. With the country growing the way it is, people will be building more and needing new windows. That makes sense."

"Not just any windows," she elaborated. "Tiny soft windows."

"Why would people want small windows when they could have big ones?"

"I don't know. How can windows of hard, brittle glass be soft?"

"I'm not sure I understand about the apples, either."

"I'm only telling you what I saw. People need to eat, certainly, but I don't see how anyone would be able to make a fortune selling plain red apples."

"And that last one. 'Buy Z-rocks'," he repeated aloud to himself. "First it was rock oil. Now it's Z-rocks. What are Z-rocks? Some kind of new ore underground that you intend to dig for?" he teased.

"I don't know. All I know is that it's important to tell our children to tell their children to tell their children to buy windows, apples, and Z-rocks."

DO YOU BELIEVE IN MAGIC?

MAGICAL LOVE

The enchanting series from Jove will make you a believer!

With a sprinkling of faerie dust and the wave of a wand, magical things can happen—but nothing is more magical than the power of love.

❑ ***SEA SPELL*** by Tess Farraday 0-515-12289-0/$5.99
A mysterious man from the sea haunts a woman's dreams—and desires...

❑ ***ONCE UPON A KISS*** by Claire Cross 0-515-12300-5/$5.99
A businessman learns there's only one way to awaken a slumbering beauty...

❑ ***A FAERIE TALE*** by Ginny Reyes 0-515-12338-2/$5.99
A faerie and a leprechaun play matchmaker—to a mismatched pair of mortals...

❑ ***ONE WISH*** by C.J. Card 0-515-12354-4/$5.99
For years a beautiful bottle lay concealed in a forgotten trunk—holding a powerful spirit, waiting for someone to come along and make one wish...

VISIT PENGUIN PUTNAM ONLINE ON THE INTERNET:
http://www.penguinputnam.com

Prices slightly higher in Canada

Payable by Visa, MC or AMEX only ($10.00 min.), No cash, checks or COD Shipping & handling: US/Can. $2.75 for one book, $1.00 for each add'l book; Int'l $5 00 for one book, $1.00 for each add'l. Call (800) 788-6262 or (201) 933-9292, fax (201) 896-8569 or mail your orders to:

Penguin Putnam Inc.
P.O. Box 12289, Dept. B
Newark, NJ 07101-5289
Please allow 4-6 weeks for delivery
Foreign and Canadian delivery 6-8 weeks

Bill my: ❑ Visa ❑ MasterCard ❑ Amex ________________(expires)
Card# ________________
Signature ________________

Bill to:
Name ________________
Address ________________ City ________________
State/ZIP ________________ Daytime Phone # ________________

Ship to:
Name ________________ Book Total $ ________________
Address ________________ Applicable Sales Tax $ ________________
City ________________ Postage & Handling $ ________________
State/ZIP ________________ Total Amount Due $ ________________

This offer subject to change without notice. **Ad # 789 (3/00)**

Nothing is more powerful than the magic of love...

The breathtaking

MAGICAL LOVE

series from Jove

❑ ***MAGIC BY DAYLIGHT*** by Lynn Bailey
0-515-12701-9/$5.99

He's the only one who can put an end to the strife that's destroying the faery kingdom—but his mission involves a mortal woman with boundless passion...

❑ ***MY LOVING FAMILIAR*** by C. J. Card
0-515-12728-0/$5.99

When a handsome druggist falls under the spell of a talented herbalist, she uncovers the magic in his skeptic heart...

❑ ***IT TAKES TWO*** by Adrienne Burns 0-515-12751-5/$5.99

A warlock and his witchy wife have been sentenced to a life behind bars—in a pet shop birdcage, that is...

❑ ***BEDAZZLED*** by Christine Holden 0-515-12774-4/$5.99

Despite all her material possessions, a wealthy woman cannot buy the one thing her heart truly desires—the love of Jordan Bennett...

Prices slightly higher in Canada

Payable by Visa, MC or AMEX only ($10.00 min.), No cash, checks or COD. Shipping & handling: US/Can $2.75 for one book, $1.00 for each add'l book; Int'l $5.00 for one book, $1.00 for each add'l. Call (800) 788-6262 or (201) 933-9292, fax (201) 896-8569 or mail your orders to:

Penguin Putnam Inc.
P.O. Box 12289, Dept. B
Newark, NJ 07101-5289
Please allow 4-6 weeks for delivery
Foreign and Canadian delivery 6-8 weeks

Bill my: ❑ Visa ❑ MasterCard ❑ Amex ______________(expires)
Card# ______________
Signature ______________

Bill to:
Name ______________
Address ______________ City ______________
State/ZIP ______________ Daytime Phone # ______________

Ship to:
Name ______________ Book Total $ ______________
Address ______________ Applicable Sales Tax $ ______________
City ______________ Postage & Handling $ ______________
State/ZIP ______________ Total Amount Due $ ______________

This offer subject to change without notice. **Ad # 877 (3/00)**